EDEN REBORN

GARRIAN WADE

GARRIAN WADE

Eden Reborn

"Grief is the price we pay for love"

Contents

1

Happy Birthday

The heat was unimaginable, pressing against him like a living thing. It felt almost conscious — like the sun itself had leaned close to whisper in his ear.

But the fiery orb spoke no words, only blinding light and smothering heat. Chris strained to make sense of it, desperate for meaning — but all he found was silence and fear.

The world around him blurred, folding into itself. He sank deeper, weightless, drowning in the overwhelming blaze. Somewhere in the haze, a faint voice stirred — not with words, but with the raw force of something vast and ancient reaching out to him.

And then —

A single cold droplet hit his skin.

Chris jolted awake, gasping, as the rain poured down around him.

He sat up slowly, blinking against the downpour, heart hammering in his chest. The shattered remains of the city rose up around him like broken teeth, silhouetted against the black sky.

"Where am I?" he thought, disoriented. The dream clung to him like smoke, its edges already fraying in the waking world.

Then it hit him, cold and sharp:

"I need to get home before midnight."

He glanced at his watch, squinting through the maze of cracks on its shattered face to make out the time—11:11. With a heavy sigh, he began the lonely trek back to his house. The buildings he passed were crumbling, their structures barely holding together, each one a testament to a world ravaged by some unspeakable catastrophe. The streets were silent, save for the faint echo of his footsteps.

At last, he arrived at the house where he had spent his entire life growing up. Time and tragedy had not been kind to it. The once-warm home now stood as a burnt and broken shell, its charred walls whispering of memories long past. As he approached, a wave of sadness washed over him, tinged with a bittersweet nostalgia that lingered in the ashes of what used to be.

The house was a blackened husk, barely recognizable. He could almost hear Sophie's laughter echoing in the halls; feel the winter fire warming his skin. As he stood there, he couldn't help but compare the vibrant past to the bleakness of his present.

He walked into the family room—now repurposed as the dining room—and froze. His mother sat at the table, a pot of stew steaming beside four bottles of red wine and a loaf of bread. In the center of it all was a single candle, its flickering flame casting uneven shadows across the room. The sight of it sent a shiver down his spine, a chill that rooted him in place.

Taking a deep breath to steady himself, he was about to speak when his mother's voice broke the silence, startlingly energetic, cutting through the heavy air like a sharp blade.

"Happy 16th birthday, Chris!" his mom exclaimed, her voice trembling with a mix of excitement and emotion.

Chris's eyes darted to the table. The modest spread before him was more food than he had seen all week. His stomach growled faintly, but the weight of the moment held him still. His mom's face was glowing, her eyes shimmering with tears that she tried, and failed, to keep from spilling over.

"It's not much," she said, her voice cracking.

Chris shifted awkwardly, unsure whether to look at her or at the flickering candle on the table.

Through her tears, she found her voice again, each word laden with love and pride. "But through everything we've been through…" Her voice faltered, and for a moment, she paused, wiping her cheeks as if to compose herself. When she spoke again, her tone was steadier but no less emotional. "I'm just so proud of you, Chris. You've stuck with your job at the restaurant, growing a little more every single day. You're turning into such a strong young man."

She paused, her expression softening, and a tender, wistful smile lit up her face. Her gaze lingered on him, as though seeing both the boy he had been and the man he was becoming. "But you'll always be my baby," she said, her voice breaking slightly. "I love you, Chris."

The words hung in the air, warm and fragile, a reminder of the bond they shared.

The room seemed to hold its breath, the soft flicker of the candle casting fleeting shadows between them. Chris swallowed hard, his throat tight, the weight of unspoken words pressing down on him. He didn't need to say anything; the look in his mother's eyes conveyed everything—love, pride, and an unwavering belief in him.

Chris held his mother tightly, burying his face in her shoulder. *Don't let go. Not yet.* He squeezed his eyes shut, as if that could stop the truth from clawing its way to the surface.

"I love you too, Mommy," he whispered, then leaned forward and blew out the candle. Darkness swallowed the tiny flickering light, leaving only the warmth of her embrace.

Behind the hug, shame burned in his chest—the lies, the failures, the truth he couldn't bear to tell.

"Are you sure everything's okay?" Her voice was gentle, but it cut through him like a blade.

Chris forced a chuckle, pulling back just enough to nod. "Yeah. Just tired." A lie. Another one to add to the pile.

A month ago, he had a job. Stability. A routine. But that was before—before his boss's son ran his mouth about Dad, before Chris's patience finally snapped. He could still feel the weight of that punch, still hear the stunned gasps that followed. The moment his fist connected, he knew—his job, his future, everything was gone.

And the worst part? He wasn't even sorry for it.

He used to tell himself he could endure the whispers, the sideways glances. That he didn't need to defend a dead man's name. But some things—some people—weren't worth forgiving.

His mother's hand found his cheek, her thumb brushing lightly over his skin. "You know you can tell me anything, right?"

His stomach twisted. He wished that were true.

If she knew how bad things had gotten, it would break her. The lost job, the stolen meals, the nights spent with nothing but an empty stomach and an even emptier future. She thought he was still working, still holding on. She still believed in him.

He couldn't take that away from her.

Chris forces a smile, pressing a quick kiss to her forehead. "Of course, Mom," he says as he pulls away.

They spent the next hour eating together, sharing a meal that tastes better than he expected. His mother opened a bottle of wine, insisting they share a glass—or two. The warmth of the drink loosened her up, making her smile more, talk more, reminisce more. For a while, it almost felt normal. Almost.

But as the night wears on, the weight on Chris's chest never fully lifts. He swirls the last bit of wine in his glass, staring at the deep red before finally setting it down with a quiet sigh. "I should get some sleep."

She nods, but there's hesitation in her eyes. "Well, alright. Get some rest. Good night, Chris. I love you. Your father would be so proud of you," she calls after him, her words slurring slightly as she smiles, tipsy but sincere.

"Good night," Chris says as he walks to his room, closing the door behind him.

Chris laid in bed, staring blankly at the cracked ceiling as rain hammered against the windows. His mother's words still echoed in his mind — *"Your father would be so proud of you."*

He turned his head away, blinking back the sting in his eyes. *Proud?* Of what? Of a son who couldn't even hold onto a job?

A son who spent his days lying to his mother, scraping by on loose change and stolen meals?

The shame festered underneath, gnawing at him. Shame had a way of unearthing old ghosts — and tonight, they clawed their way free. The ache in his chest deepened, dragging him backward through the years, back to the last time his world had crumbled.

Back to the day the fire came.

The shrill sound of his alarm jolted Chris awake. It was the first day of the new school year, and he couldn't contain his excitement. He couldn't wait to see his friends, especially Sophie. Grinning, he jumped out of bed and hurried to get ready.

The start of the school year filled him with anticipation. He was eager to see his friends and showcase the brilliance he had nurtured over the summer. His father's lessons had been intense but enlightening, and Chris felt ready to shine.

But as he walked into the classroom, his excitement waned. The familiar space felt strange, almost alien. School began with the usual prayer and pledge to the Church, but everything that followed threw him off balance. Each lesson being taught—history, science, philosophy—felt completely at odds with the truths his father had instilled in him over the summer.

As the day wore on, Chris's confusion deepened. The Church's teachings seemed to rewrite fundamental concepts, pushing ideas that directly contradicted the lessons his father had so carefully taught him. It was as if he had stepped into a world where everything he believed was wrong.

Chris tried to speak up, voicing his concerns during class. Each time, his teachers shut him down, their dismissive tones making him feel small and out of place. Doubt crept in, gnawing at him. His father worked for the Church. His research was for them. So why did the curriculum conflict so sharply with what his father had taught him?

As the day dragged on, the excitement Chris had felt that morning was replaced with an overwhelming sense of conflict and disillusionment. The world he thought he knew seemed to tilt further off balance with every lesson, every unanswered question. By the time the final bell rang, the anticipation for the school year had soured into a heavy mix of dread and confusion. He felt adrift, lost in a sea of uncertainty, struggling to reconcile the life he knew at home with the reality he now faced.

Chris trudged home from school, the weight of his thoughts heavy on his shoulders. He needed to talk to his father, and the conversation felt too important to delay. As he stepped through the door, his mother greeted him with her usual warmth, her smile brightening the room.

"Happy birthday!" she exclaimed, pulling him into a hug. "We have a very exciting evening planned for you, but before I spoil the surprise… How was school today, sweetie? Did you see Sophie?" Her voice carried that familiar sly tone, her not-so-subtle hopes for Chris and Sophie to become more than just friends shining through.

Chris managed a small smile at her teasing, but shook his head. "I saw her, but she wasn't in any of my classes," he replied, his tone deflated. Quickly, he redirected the conversation. "But never mind that. Where's Dad? I really need to talk to him."

His mother tilted her head, concern flickering in her eyes. "He's on his way back from work. He should be here soon. What's going on? You know you can talk to me about anything."

Chris hesitated, his gaze dropping to the floor for a moment before he looked back at her. "I know. But this is something I need to talk to him about," he said firmly, his resolve unshaken.

She sighed softly, a playful smile tugging at her lips as she ruffled his hair. "Now, your father may be very smart, but don't forget—I'm the one who takes care of both of you, so that makes me a genius."

Chris couldn't help but chuckle faintly at her words. For a moment, the weight on his shoulders felt lighter. But as he glanced toward the door, his thoughts drifted back to the conversation he knew was coming.

Chris whispered softly, "I know," his voice barely audible. His mother's expression shifted, her worry deepening. She opened her mouth to ask what was troubling him, but before the words could leave her lips, the front door swung open with a bang.

Chris's father, Giuseppe, strode in with a look of unshakable determination etched on his face—a look Chris had seen before, one his father wore whenever he was up against something monumental. Giuseppe didn't stop to greet them or explain. He moved straight to the other room, his movements hurried and precise, and began shoving papers into the fireplace.

"Giuseppe!" Chris's mother, Mariah, called out, her voice laced with panic. She hurried after him, watching as the flames consumed the documents. "What's happening?" she demanded, her hands trembling at her sides.

But Giuseppe didn't answer. Instead, his voice rang out, sharp and commanding, as he continued destroying the papers. "Mariah, get Chris and the emergency bag. Now! Take him and go to your mother's house!"

The urgency in his tone struck like a bolt of lightning, sending a shiver down Chris's spine. He looked at his father, then his mother, confusion and fear swirling in his chest. Something was very, very wrong.

Mariah was stunned, but she knew better than to question her husband when he was in this state. She quickly gathered Chris and the emergency bag. As Chris and his mother headed for the back door, two towering figures abruptly blocked their path. The men were both six feet tall and clad in long white robes, donning bird-shaped masks reminiscent of doctors from the Black Plague.

Their robes were as white as freshly driven snow, a brilliant contrast that seemed to shimmer in the light. Pitted against the jet black of the bird masks, the combination was haunting enough to send shivers down their spines. The intimidating figures forced Chris and his mother back into the family room.

As they turned around, their eyes widened in alarm as they saw two more men entering through the front door and another through each of the windows. In a matter of seconds, eight of the eerie beings encircled the room, trapping them like prey. Chris's mind raced, struggling to make sense of the chaos unfolding around him.

Draped in ghostly white robes that seemed to ripple like smoke, the men stood silent and imposing. Each robe bore the same ominous symbol—a Red Cross inscribed within a circle. The mark seemed to pulse faintly, as though alive with a sinister energy.

The moment Chris's eyes locked onto those crosses, an icy dread washed over him. He didn't need to ask who they were. He already knew. These were men of the Holy Church. Just as Chris was trying to make sense of the scene, another figure appeared out of the other room. This man was slightly taller than the rest, and he dragged behind him his bloodied father by the collar. His own robe was a deep, blood-red color, and on it was a white cross inscribed within a Circle. The sight of the new arrival was as chilling as an icy wind on a winter's day. With no mask, his silver hair glinted in the light like the edge of a freshly sharpened blade.

The man shoved Giuseppe into the center of the circle, the robed figures closing ranks around them. Chris and his mother stood frozen, their hearts pounding as the tension in the air became suffocating.

"Well," the man said, his tone calm but with an edge of cold authority. "Looks like we've got the whole family together. I would have preferred to avoid this little spectacle, but Giuseppe, you really left me no choice."

Giuseppe staggered to his feet, his expression a mix of shock and fury. "Vincent, there's no need for this! What information are you acting on?" he shouted, his voice trembling with a combination of anger and desperation.

Vincent's expression hardened, his eyes narrowing as he stepped closer to Giuseppe. The calm facade melted away, replaced by something far colder. Leaning in, he spoke in a voice so low and menacing it made Chris's skin crawl. "Now, now, Giuseppe," he said with a sinister smile. "No need to play dumb."

He straightened, his tone sharpening as he continued, "Let

me make this simple for you. I'm going to ask you one question. If you refuse to answer, I'll kill your wife." He paused, letting the threat hang in the air before delivering the next blow. "If you answer, and I decide you're lying, I'll kill your wife. And then, Giuseppe," he said, his voice dripping with mockery, "You're a smart man. I'm sure you can see where this is going."

Vincent leaned forward, his cold eyes boring into Giuseppe's. "Now, where is the file?" he asked, his voice calm yet laced with menace.

Giuseppe hesitated, his jaw tightening before he finally spoke. His voice was steady, but low, measured. "It's not here. I'll tell you where it is—but only if you leave my family out of this."

Vincent's lips curled into a humorless smile, his tone sharp as a blade. "I thought you were smarter than this, Giuseppe. Negotiating only works when you have leverage."

Giuseppe's gaze didn't waver, though Chris could see the tension in his father's face. After a moment, Giuseppe nodded, his voice calm but firm. "That's an accurate statement," he said. "But you see, I *do* have leverage. You need the file, but I'm the only one who can unlock the encryption. Without me, it's worthless. Without me, you lose everything."

Chris watched the exchange, his heart pounding in his chest. His father's words felt like a lifeline in the chaos, but the tension in the room was unbearable. Chris wanted to move, to speak, to do *something,* but his body refused to obey. He stood frozen, paralyzed by fear, the scene playing out like a nightmare he couldn't wake up from.

Vincent's glare shifted briefly to Chris and his mother, his cold eyes narrowing before turning back to Giuseppe. His voice dropped to a low, dangerous tone, each word deliberate. "Normally, I wouldn't be this agreeable," he said, the menace in his voice unmistakable. "But today, I'm feeling generous."

He took a step closer, his towering presence casting a shadow over the family. His gaze lingered on Giuseppe, calculating and unyielding. "I give you my word," he continued, "I will not harm your family… in exchange for the location of the file."

Turning to the robed figures surrounding them, Vincent issued a curt command. "Gentlemen, leave us. I require some privacy."

The eight robed men shuffled silently out of the room, their ghostly forms vanishing into the dim light. Vincent turned back to Giuseppe, leaning in until their faces were only inches apart. His voice dropped to a whisper, icy and relentless. "Now… the location."

Giuseppe hesitated, his jaw tightening as he weighed his options. The tension in the room was suffocating. Finally, he exhaled and spoke, his voice firm but resigned. "The file is at the capital," he said. "Third quadrant. Level five."

Vincent straightened, a satisfied smirk curling at the corners of his lips. "Very good," he said smoothly, his tone dripping with smug triumph. He raised a hand to his earpiece, his voice sharp and commanding as he relayed his orders.

"It's in the capital," Vincent said. "Third quadrant. Level five. Tear the area apart if necessary. I want confirmation as soon as the file is located."

As Vincent finished, his eyes flicked back to Giuseppe, his expression one of cold amusement. The room hung heavy with silence, the air thick with unspoken threats. Chris could only watch, his heart hammering in his chest, as his father stood firm under the weight of Vincent's chilling gaze.

Giuseppe placed a firm, yet gentle hand on Chris's shoulder, his grip steady despite the surrounding chaos. He could see the fear in his son's wide eyes, the uncertainty written across his face. Giuseppe's voice softened, though it carried the weight of urgency. "Son, listen to me very carefully. I love you. No matter what happens, you must take care of your mother. I have to go away for a while."

Chris's heart clenched, panic rising as he processed his father's words. "Dad, what is this guy after?!" he blurted, his voice trembling. He stared up at Giuseppe, searching for answers, for something to cling to amidst the storm of emotions swirling inside him.

Giuseppe's expression was unyielding, more serious than Chris had ever seen. The tension in the room was suffocating, like the charged air before a violent storm. Chris's voice dropped to a whisper, barely audible. "What are we going to do, Dad?"

Giuseppe knelt slightly, bringing himself to Chris's level as he looked his son squarely in the eye. His voice was calm but resolute. "We're going to get through this, Chris. But we have to be careful. We can't trust the Church. Not anymore." He paused, his gaze steady and full of conviction. "I can't tell you all the details yet. But I have a plan."

The words hung in the air like a fragile promise, offering a glimmer of hope in the face of the unknown. Chris nodded slowly, the weight of responsibility settling on his young shoulders as he tried to match his father's resolve.

Chris nodded, but was still afraid. He had a thousand questions running through his mind, but he knew his dad couldn't answer them now. Giuseppe had always taught him to trust his instincts, but right now, his instincts were telling him to run as far away from this situation as possible. But he couldn't. He had to stay strong. For his dad, for his mom, and for himself. He couldn't let the fear consume him.

"Great news," Vincent announced, his tone unnervingly calm. "We've found the file."

Before anyone could react, Vincent drew his sword in a single fluid motion. The cold steel glinted ominously in the dim light, making Chris and Mariah gasp in horror. But before they could plead or protest, Vincent swung the blade with chilling precision, slicing through Giuseppe's legs.

Chris and Mariah's screams ripped through the air, raw and heart-wrenching. "No!" they cried in unison, their voices echoing off the walls.

Giuseppe collapsed to the ground, clutching at the stumps where his legs had been, his face twisted in agony and disbelief. Blood pooled rapidly beneath him, staining the floor a dark crimson. Through his pain, he looked up at Vincent with desperate eyes. "Vincent, what are you doing?" he pleaded, his voice shaking. "I told you what you wanted! You need me for the encryption!"

Vincent chuckled, his expression void of empathy. "How bold of you," he said, his voice mocking and cold, "to presume you're the only one capable of breaking the encryption. Do you truly believe you're special?"

"You idiot!" Giuseppe spat, his voice raw with fury despite the agony wracking his body. "I'm the only one! I created it!"

Vincent's smirk widened as he casually shrugged. "Perhaps," he replied, his tone dripping with disdain, "but you didn't accomplish that alone, did you? I've assembled a team, your team. Cracking your encryption will be child's play. You've overestimated your importance."

Giuseppe's voice cracked with desperation and frustration. "You don't understand what you're meddling with! This power you're seeking—it's too dangerous for anyone to control!"

Vincent leaned closer, his voice brimming with arrogance. "Ah, but I am no ordinary man," he said with chilling conviction. "I am a man of God, a man of the Church. If anyone on this wretched planet is worthy of wielding such power, it is me. Who better to claim it than someone who serves a higher purpose?"

As the words left Vincent's lips, Chris, his heart pounding with a mix of fear and rage, pushed himself to his feet. He clenched his fists and stepped toward Vincent, his legs trembling but determined. "Stop this!" Chris yelled, his voice shaking with both anger and desperation.

Vincent turned to him slowly, his icy gaze locking on Chris. With deliberate ease, he raised his sword, pointing it directly at the boy. The sharp tip hovered inches from Chris's chest. "Come on," Vincent said, his voice low and menacing, "you're smarter than that."

Chris froze, the cold steel so close he could feel the chill radiating from it. His breath caught in his throat, and for a moment, his resolve wavered. Slowly, reluctantly, he backed down, returning to the floor beside his sobbing mother. Vincent watched him with a smug grin, satisfied with the boy's submission.

The tension in the room was suffocating, the air thick with dread and despair. Chris knelt by his mother, clutching her trembling hand as they both stared helplessly at Giuseppe, who lay bleeding and broken before them. The storm brewing in Chris's heart was undeniable, but for now, all he could do was endure.

Giuseppe could feel the hostility emanating from Vincent, and his heart sank. "I've known you for a long time," Giuseppe said, his voice trembling. "We've been competitors, colleagues, even friends."

Vincent's eyes narrowed, his grip tightening around the hilt of his sword. His voice was venomous, each word dripping with bitterness. "When you picture our relationship, you see it as a friendly rivalry laced with respect," he spat. "But with every triumph, every victory, every breakthrough, I grew to hate you. Living in your shadow—always second to you—I'm done with it."

The words struck Giuseppe like a physical blow. He stared at Vincent, stunned, trying to process the depth of the resentment he had never suspected. "Vincent," he said, his voice steady but pleading, "you've let jealousy and greed poison you. It's infected your soul. It's broken your heart."

Vincent's expression twisted into a cruel smirk. "Well, if mine is broken, allow me to break yours as well," he snarled.

Before Giuseppe could respond, Vincent swung his sword with ruthless precision. The blade pierced Giuseppe's chest with a single, devastating thrust. He crumpled to the floor, blood pooling beneath him as his breath came in ragged gasps.

"No!" Chris's voice broke as he and his mother screamed in unison, their cries filled with anguish and horror.

Vincent leaned over Giuseppe, his tone calm, almost solemn, as he addressed the dying man. "Giuseppe, do not fear. I am a man of my word, and I promised that in exchange for the location of the file, I would not harm your family. And I won't." He paused, a cruel glint in his eye. "However, I can not guarantee the flames will honor our deal."

With that, Vincent straightened, his gaze cold and unwavering as he turned to his men. "Burn this house," he ordered, his voice carrying the weight of finality. "And every standing structure within a three-kilometer radius. We're done here."

He paused, his eyes sweeping over the ruined scene one last time. Then, in a voice devoid of hesitation, he added, "Let the flames send a message—this is the fate of anyone who dares to defy the Church."

"Yes, Cardinal!" the men replied in unison, their robed forms moving swiftly to carry out his command.

Chris clung to his mother as the world around them erupted into chaos, their screams drowned out by the sound of roaring flames and the echo of Vincent's footsteps fading into the night.

The crackle of flames roared around Chris and Mariah as they huddled close to Giuseppe's broken body. The suffocating heat pressed in on them, but their tears flowed freely, unstoppable as torrential rain. Every sob carried the weight of their grief, every tear falling heavy with despair. Giuseppe's breaths came in shallow, ragged gasps, the blood filling his lungs, making each one a struggle.

With trembling hands, Giuseppe reached for them, pulling his wife and son closer. His voice was barely audible, but the raw emotion in his words cut through the chaos. "I love you, Mariah," he whispered, his gaze locking onto hers. "My beautiful wife. I love you, Chris," he continued, turning to his son. "My wonderful boy."

His eyes fluttered shut for a moment, then reopened, glistening with a mixture of love and regret. "I'm sorry," he breathed, his voice cracking under the weight of his remorse.

Giuseppe's chest rose one last time as he whispered again, "I'm sorry." Then, his body went still, leaving Chris and Mariah in stunned silence, clutching the man they had loved so deeply, now gone forever.

The flames continued their relentless march, eating away at the walls and filling the air with smoke. Chris sat frozen beside his father's lifeless body, the weight of the moment numbing his mind and body. The roar of the fire became a dull hum, drowning out everything around him, leaving him in a deafening silence. His tear-filled eyes remained fixed on Giuseppe, unable to look away.

Through the haze, his mother's voice broke through, desperate and trembling with panic. "Chris! We have to move!" she cried, her calls growing more frantic as the fire closed in. But Chris didn't respond. He couldn't. His gaze remained locked on his father's still form, the rest of the world fading into irrelevance.

Only when Mariah, summoning all her remaining strength, hoisted Chris onto her shoulders and stumbled through the smoke and flames did she bring him back to reality. The searing heat clawed at their skin as they navigated through the inferno, the house collapsing behind them.

When they finally burst through the door into the open air, the world outside offered no relief. Flames engulfed every house, shop, and structure around them, a hellish prison of fire. Mariah, exhausted and coughing violently, collapsed onto the ground. Chris stood numbly beside her, his vacant eyes staring back at the burning house, still seeing his father's lifeless body in his mind.

The heat intensified, evaporating the tears that had streaked his face. But with the tears gone, Chris felt only emptiness. The grief was a hollow weight in his chest, and the despair of everything they had lost pressed down on him like an unyielding force.

The world around him was burning, and there was nothing he could do but stand there, helpless and alone, watching as the flames consumed everything he had ever known.

The memory of that night burned in Chris's mind as vividly as the flames that had devoured his home. His father's last words echoed again and again in the hollow spaces of his chest — *I'm sorry.*

Chris exhaled slowly, blinking back the sting in his eyes. The darkness of his room pressed down around him, heavy and still. Only the faint ticking of the battered clock on the nightstand marked the passing of time.

He was no longer that terrified boy clinging to his mother's side. But some nights — nights like this — he still felt twelve years old, still felt the smoke choking him, still felt the crushing weight of everything he'd lost.

Swallowing hard, Chris sat up, his gaze falling to the stack of his father's scorched research papers beside the bed. The real world offered no comfort. Only more questions. Only more things to lose.

Something has to change, he thought again, the words carving themselves deeper into his bones.

Chris wiped the back of his hand across his eyes, shoved down the grief like he always did, and pulled the first notebook into his lap.

The advanced math equations and theories that littered the pages of the documents reminded Chris of the countless hours he had spent sitting at his father's feet, trying desperately to soak up his knowledge and wisdom like a sponge.

Chris flipped through the charred pages, the faint smell of smoke still clinging to them, as memories of his father surfaced unbidden. He could almost see his father leaning over his shoulder, the glimmer of pride in his eyes, when Chris grasped a tough concept. The way he'd patiently guide him through mistakes, his voice warm and steady, played like an echo in

Chris's mind.

The notes and diagrams on the pages were a testament to his father's relentless curiosity. Chris could picture him gesturing animatedly, his fascination with the mysteries of the universe lighting up their small study. Even the smallest details—his father's obsession with gelato, the soft chuckle that followed his favorite sayings—hovered in Chris's mind like ghosts of a life that once felt boundless.

Chris's fingers brushed over the edges of a particularly charred page. The words were faint but still readable, and as he studied the text, something emerged—a peculiar pattern hidden within the scrawls and calculations. His brow furrowed as he leaned in closer, the room falling silent except for the rustle of paper.

The further he read, the more his heart raced, the pieces clicking together like a puzzle just beginning to take shape.

Chris had pored over his father's work so many times that every book, scrap of paper, and hastily scribbled note felt etched into his very being. He could almost hear his father's voice in the margins, see his handwriting come alive as if guiding him through the dense maze of thought. Every word, every number held meaning—or so Chris believed.

Examining his father's research notes, Chris discovered a pattern in the numbers: he spelled out certain numbers, but used numerals for all others. Chris frowned, flipping through pages, double-checking his observation, Chris felt his pulse quicken. It was deliberate. It had to be.

He tore through his father's research, flipping through pages filled with precise calculations, theories, and diagrams. At first, everything seemed methodical, structured—until he noticed something strange. Certain letters were capitalized without any grammatical reason, standing out against the otherwise meticulous lowercase text.

Chris leaned in, scanning page after page, his mind racing. The pattern wasn't random. Only specific pages contained these inconsistencies. The page numbers were the numbers that were always spelled out. His fingers trembled as he grabbed a pen, carefully jotting down each capitalized letter alongside the page numbers where they appeared.

Letter by letter, number by number, the pieces started to fall into place. A message was hidden here. He just had to piece it together.

When he finished, Chris stared at the list of letters and numbers before him. They seemed random, a meaningless jumble mocking his efforts. He squinted, tilting his head as if a different angle might coax a hidden message from them. His mind raced, chasing patterns and connections. Nothing fit. The letters refused to align, stubbornly guarding their secret.

Chris sighed, leaning back in his chair, his frustration mounting. The page blurred as his tired eyes closed briefly. The letters and numbers swirled in his mind, but they led nowhere. "What am I missing?" he whispered to himself.

Then:

"Trust the patterns," his father had once said. *"Look closer."*

Chris squinted at the notes.

Letters. Numbers.

Chess.

"Chess?" he whispered, his fingers trembling as he flipped through the notes.

e4 Nc6, Nf3 Nf6, Bb5 a6, Ba4 e5, O-O Be7, Re1 b5, Bb3 d6

Chris dug through his room, heart pounding, until his fingers closed around the worn edges of an old chessboard. He set it on his desk, carefully placing each piece in accordance with the sequence. Move by move, the game unfolded.

c3 O-O, h3 Na5, Bc2 c5, d4 Qc7, Nbd2 Re8

His father's strategy became clear—not just a game, but a lesson. A puzzle. A hidden truth waiting to be revealed.

Nf1 g6, Ne3 Bf8, dxe5 dxe5, Nd5 Nxd5, exd5 Nc4

Chris's breath quickened. Why these moves? What was his father trying to say? The sequence continued, each placement more intentional than the last.

b3 Nb6, c4 Bg7, Bb2 f6, Nd2 f5, a4 b4

He placed the final piece.

a5 Nd7, Nf3 e4, Bxg7 Kxg7, Ng5 Nf6.

A soft *click* echoed from the board. Chris froze. The center shifted slightly, revealing a hidden compartment. Inside, nestled in the shadows, lay a small computer chip.

His father hadn't just left behind a game.

He had left behind a secret.

2

Infiltrate

Chris turned the chip over between his fingers, staring at it like it might whisper the truth if he waited long enough.

"What were you hiding, Dad?" he murmured.

Snapping out of it, he jammed the chip into the battered laptop he had scavenged the week before. The screen flickered, and a password prompt appeared. Chris's pulse jumped.

He typed his own birthday. No luck.

Frowning, he leaned back, staring at the blinking cursor like it was taunting him. His father had been deliberate with everything he did. This wouldn't be random.

Family.

Chris punched in his mother's birthday.

The screen flickered, and the prompt vanished. Files exploded across the display — folders filled with strange titles: **Quantum Tunneling. Soul Essence. Purgatory Transfer Protocol.**

Chris's chest tightened. He scrolled feverishly, heart hammering.

One file stood apart.

Chris.

He clicked it.

His father's voice came alive—not in sound, but in words:

"Chris, if you're seeing this, I'm gone. I'm sorry. I hoped you'd never need this."

Chris's breath caught. He blinked hard, forcing himself to keep reading.

"The Church you know is a lie. I helped build it, not realizing what it would become. Fear. Control. Death masked as salvation. I tried to stop them—but it wasn't enough."

"Everything they've done—all the experiments, the murders—it's here. In these files. The truth is now yours, son. I believe in you. Never let fear decide who you are."

The words blurred as Chris wiped his sleeve across his eyes. His hands shook. His father's burden now rested squarely on his shoulders.

For a moment, Chris just sat there, letting the silence press in. His first instinct was to tell his mother. But no—his father had hidden this for a reason.

This wasn't something he could share.

Not yet.

Taking a shaky breath, Chris dove into the folders. He studied the research notes, blueprints, & formulas. He discovered horrifying experiments using innocent people, all in the pursuit of a project. A gateway. A **portal**. Something that was meant to pierce the veil between soul and body, between life and something beyond. A portal to travel through time itself.

And the Church had twisted it all into a weapon.

Chris stared at the schematics, heart pounding. His father had tried to stop it. Had died for it.

He clenched his fists.

Was he going to expose them? Does he want me to expose them?
Maybe... maybe I could do more than just expose them.

A reckless thought struck him, wild and desperate.

He could use the portal.

Not for power.

For **him**.

I can warn him. I can save him. I can stop all of this before it even starts.

The plan was insane. It would probably kill him.

But standing still would kill him faster.

Chris slammed the laptop shut, breathing hard. His decision made.

Chris packed the chip carefully into his jacket and pulled his hood over his head.

If the Church had stolen the future once, they wouldn't get the chance to do it again. Not this time.

Chris pulled his hood tighter as he stepped out into the cold, damp air. The city loomed around him, a maze of crumbling stone and rusted steel. Towering structures leaned precariously, their windows shattered and facades blackened from age and neglect. Smoke curled from makeshift fires in alleyways where the hungry huddled for warmth, their faces gaunt and hollow. The scent of burning trash mixed with the stench of stagnant water, a reminder that the sewers beneath the city overflowed more often than they drained.

But above it all, untouched by ruin, was the Church.

Its marble-clad dome rose like a crown above the city, each sculpted detail untouched by the crumbling streets below. Intricate stained glass windows caught the morning light, scattering color across flawless stone walls that looked carved by divine hands. When the bells rang out, their sound rolled through every alley and ruin—a solemn hymn to enduring power.

The Church of Kings in Christ controlled everything. Every business, every trade, every scrap of bread passed through their hands. Shops paid tithes just to keep their doors open. Those who couldn't afford it were left to rot in the streets—or disappear entirely. Faith wasn't just belief here. It was currency. And power.

Chris knew the risks. But there was no other choice.

"If I can separate my soul essence from my body, It can work. It has to work. Once I do this, there's no turning back. I need to use the portal."

The plan was simple—steal what he needed and get out. No unnecessary risks. But as he moved through the crowded market square, the hunger and desperation etched into every face reminded him why this mattered. Families wrapped in patched blankets whispered prayers at the base of the church steps, begging for mercy. A merchant bartered with a robed official, lowering his head as the man sneered and collected payment from a trembling hand.

Chris focused. He spotted his mark.

A church official in his ornate white robes, the red cross embroidered over his chest, emerged from the main gates. The badge clipped to his waist gleamed under the pale light. Chris fell in step behind him, keeping his distance. The man's robes were spotless, unlike the people he brushed past without a glance.

The official turned off the main street, weaving deeper into the shadows of the city. Chris knew this route—it led to the brothel district. The perfect place for someone powerful to disappear from prying eyes.

The red lanterns cast flickering light on the damp cobblestones as the official disappeared inside. Chris lingered near the entrance, blending in with the crowd as patrons stumbled in and out. He counted the seconds, then slipped in unnoticed.

The scent of cheap perfume and stale alcohol clung to the air. Dim candle light flickered along the walls, dancing shadows masking faces. The official was already at the bar, his back turned, distracted as he exchanged a handful of church-issued tokens for a drink.

Chris moved without hesitation. He brushed past the man, his fingers slipping beneath the folds of the robe. The cold metal of the badge met his palm. A perfect lift.

He didn't stop to admire his work. By the time the official had finished his drink, Chris was already back on the street, the stolen badge tucked safely beneath his cloak.

The Holy Capital stood like a fortress, its stone walls reinforced by rows of watchful sentries. Massive flood lights illuminated the perimeter, and the gates loomed in front of him.

Large mechanical gears drummed softly beneath the stone as Chris approached with purpose, the badge pressed tightly in his fist. Two guards flanked the entrance, their faces masked beneath polished helmets. He said nothing as he presented the badge, hoping the layers of dirt and grime coating his cloak made him appear like just another courier on church business.

A sharp beep echoed as the scanner read the badge. One guard squinted at Chris but, after a moment, nodded him through. The gates parted with a low groan.

Too easy.

Inside, the silence was heavier, the air colder. Ornate corridors stretched endlessly, the marble floors so polished they reflected the light from the chandeliers above. But beneath the elegance was tension—the kind that settled deep, where secrets festered.

Chris moved swiftly, recalling the blueprints he'd memorized. He discarded the grimy clothes and moved through the compound. The cooling unit was in the lower levels, the most secure part of the compound. His stolen badge got him through the first checkpoint, and then onto the second. The second guard lingered longer, squinting at Chris's badge. Chris forced himself to meet the man's eyes, heart hammering. For a sickening second, he thought the guard might call him out — but with a grunt, the man waved him through.

Chris continued moving through the compound. Cautiously, he pried open a maintenance hatch tucked behind a pillar and crawled inside the ventilation shaft. The metal groaned softly beneath his weight as he inched forward, following the narrow passage toward the core.

His pulse hammered in his ears.

Sliding out into a deserted corridor, Chris took a steadying breath. He was close. The central elevator was just ahead, the only direct path into the restricted vaults. Kneeling, he withdrew a set of worn tools and began working on the security panel beside the doors, bypassing the scanner with careful precision. Sparks danced as he cut through the circuits, his breath measured.

The system blinked. Disabled.

Chris smirked. *Far too smooth.*

"Hey!"

Chris froze, tools still in hand as three guards rounded the corner, blocking the elevator.

"Restricted area," one barked. "Security pass. Now."

Chris straightened, shoving his tools into his cloak. "Apprentice of Cardinal Vincent," he snapped. "Urgent repairs. You want to explain to him why you're wasting my time?"

The guards shifted, uncertain. One muttered into his comm, the others eyeing Chris with suspicion.

"Vincent sent you?" the lead one said, voice tight.

Chris let frustration bleed into his voice. "You want to call him and wake him up? Be my guest. Or you can let me finish before this place goes dark."

A beat of hesitation. Then the guards backed off—just a step—but it was enough.

Chris turned back to the panel, fingers flying.

Chris felt the tension in his chest ease slightly. *Not perfect, but it'll hold... for now.*

Wasting no more time, he turned back to the elevator panel, fingers working quickly as he finished disabling the lock system. A final spark. The lights blinked. System down.

The elevator doors hissed open with a low hum. Chris slipped inside and pressed the command for the lowest level, the doors closing just as the guards turned back toward him.

Too late.

The descent began. Chris clenched his fists, exhaling slowly as the air grew colder, the elevator sinking deeper into the heart of the Capital. He was in. But the hardest part was still ahead.

Chris's breath came in short bursts as the elevator descended into the heart of the Holy Capital. The hum of machinery pressed against his ears, but his mind was racing ahead. *The notes said the lower labs should be empty. Radiation risks. Tight schedules. No one should be down here.*

The elevator jolted to a halt. The doors slid open with a mechanical hiss, revealing a dimly lit laboratory. Pale, flickering lights cast long shadows across steel walls, the scent of burnt metal and chemical sterilizers lingering in the stale air. Chris took a cautious step forward.

Cold steel pressed against the back of his head.

He froze, every muscle tensing.

"Don't move!" a voice trembled behind him. The barrel dug deeper against his skull.

Chris held his breath, pulse pounding so hard he thought his ribs might crack under the pressure. No alarms. No gunshot. Just the stammering, nervous voice of a man barely holding it together.

"Stay—stay where you are!"

Not a guard. Chris raised his hands slowly, his voice calm but strained. "Easy… I'm not here to hurt anyone."

The voice quavered again. "Who sent you? Was it Vincent?!"

Chris turned his head just enough to see him. A tall, thin scientist with a stained lab coat and a rifle trembling in his hands. His wild, bushy mustache twitched with every ragged breath, his face pale and sweat-slicked as he stared Chris down like a trapped animal.

"I'm not with Vincent. I'm not with the Church," Chris said carefully, hands still raised.

"Liar!" the man shouted, voice cracking as the rifle shook harder. "You people took everything from me—my wife, Julia… my daughter, Eliza. My home. And now you're here to finish the job. For *that* machine!" His voice broke, grief clawing its way into his words.

Chris saw the cracks forming—the anguish, the pain. And a hesitation. He could use that.

His stomach twisted. *Do it. Say what you have to say.*

"I know what they've done," Chris whispered. "I'm not here for the portal. I'm here to stop them from ever using it again. The Church has lied to all of us. But we can expose them. Together."

The man's grip wavered, his lips parted as if to speak, but fear still anchored him. "You… you're lying. The portal has done nothing but kill. I won't help you activate it. Not again."

Chris clenched his jaw, stepping closer with measured calm. *Not a lie. Just not the whole truth.*

"We don't have to use it," a jagged edge of guilt twisted in his gut. Dad would have hated this—using someone's pain. "but we *can* use the equipment here—this tech, the data stored in it. We can broadcast the truth. Show the world everything the Church has done. If people see it for themselves, they won't be able to hide anymore."

John's expression wavered, his eyes glassy with grief. "You… you think they'll listen?"

Chris nodded, the weight of his father's last words echoing in his mind. "They will. And if they don't—then we fight. But at least they'll *know*. No more secrets."

Silence stretched. Then, finally, the rifle lowered. John's hands trembled. His finger twitched over the trigger. His mouth opened and closed, trapped between rage and hopelessness.

"They lied before," he whispered hoarsely. "Said it was for peace. Said the portal would save lives."

Chris didn't move, didn't breathe.

Slowly, with a broken sob he tried to smother, John lowered the rifle—only a few inches.

"My name is John," the man whispered, his voice hollow.

"My name is Chris," Chris said. "Will you help me?"

John nodded hesitantly. "What do we do?"

The hum of machinery echoed louder as they worked side by side, reconnecting circuits, rerouting power through corroded panels. Sparks danced as the portal core warmed, the faint glow of energy pulsing behind thick glass.

Chris's hands worked quickly, slipping in the last components— the ones John didn't know about. He could feel the weight of the lie, pressing heavier with every wire he connected. *This is the only way. I'm sorry, John.*

Above, the guards who had confronted Chris earlier stood uneasily before the council chamber, their discomfort growing as they faced the seven robed figures of the Church's highest authority. The scent of incense was thick, mingling with the oppressive silence.

Council Member Margaret's sharp voice broke the tension. "What is the meaning of this interruption?"

One guard, his voice hesitant, stepped forward. "Councilors, we believe there has been a breach. A man claiming to be a student of Cardinal Vincent was caught tampering with the central elevator. He had clearance but... something felt off."

Outrage rippled through the room.

"Impossible!" snapped Council Member Hugh. "Vincent would never allow unauthorized personnel in restricted areas!"

Vincent remained calm throughout the discussion, observing his fellow council members carefully. "I understand your concerns," he spoke up. "However, there's a simple solution. We simply investigate this so-called intruder and if these guards are correct about the matter, we shall kill all four of them."

"Wait, wait. We're the ones who told you about them", the guards pleaded.

"Yes, but you are also responsible for allowing such a blatant lie to stop you from performing your duties." Vincent retorted. "Now sound the alarm and have all available personnel directed to the central elevator, we shall see who this intruder is."

The wail of alarms filled the lab like a living thing. Red emergency lights bathed the walls, the once-sterile room now cast in violent crimson.

"They know we're here," John whispered, his voice tight with fear. "We're out of time."

Chris kept working, fingers flying over the controls, heart pounding. The portal's energy surged, pulsing brighter, swirling with unstable energy just beyond the containment glass. The elevator shaft groaned. *Vincent was coming.*

"Almost there, now to set it back—five years ago." Chris muttered under his breath.

The final circuit locked into place. The portal flared to life, its swirling core rippling with vibrant hues of purple and white. Raw power thrummed through the air.

John's eyes widened—not in relief, but in betrayal. He staggered back, his face twisted with disbelief. "You lied to me. You—you're *activating* it!"

Chris didn't deny it. He couldn't. "I had to, John. I'm sorry."

The elevator doors crashed open.

Vincent entered, flanked by armored guards. His voice thundered through the chaos. "STOP THEM!"

Gunfire erupted. Bullets tore through the control panels in a storm of sparks, arcs of wild electricity dancing across the machines. Chris barely had time to react—he dove, the searing heat of a round grazing his shoulder as he hit the floor hard. Pain flared, hot and sharp, as blood splattered against the cold tile.

His leg. His arm.

Wounds deep and unforgiving.

The portal loomed behind him, unstable, the swirling energy wild and violent—panels blinking erratically, the core flaring in unstable pulses of blue and white light

"This is all your fault!" John's voice broke through the chaos, raw with fear and betrayal. He pressed himself against the wall, eyes wide as the gunfire raged.

Chris struggled to rise, his body screaming in protest, but he forced himself to his feet. Blood soaked his clothes, warm and relentless, staining the ground beneath him.

He locked eyes with John, chest heaving.

"I'm sorry," Chris gasped, voice ragged. "But I *have* to finish this!"

Bullets tore into Chris's side and leg, red-hot pain lancing through him. His body screamed for him to fall. To stop.

But the portal roared ahead, unstable and wild — a cyclone of light and shattered sound.

Vincent's voice cut through the chaos:

"Kill him!"

Another shot cracked the air. Chris stumbled, but he forced

himself forward.

The portal's energy lashed out, the air rippling with heat and distortion. Sparks rained down. The ground shook under his feet.

He heard his father's voice in the back of his mind, steady and sure:

Never let fear decide who you are.

Chris gritted his teeth.

For Dad. For Mom. For everyone.

A final gunshot split the air.

Chris dove.

Light swallowed him whole.

Time shattered.

Pain vanished.

The world fell away into a blinding void.

For a moment, there was nothing but endless white, stretching into forever.

Then—

Chris gasped for air, his lungs burning as he clawed at the grass beneath him.

I'm alive, he realized, the thought raw and disbelieving.

Chris blinked, the blinding light fading—until he saw it.

A world untouched by ruin.

A vibrant, untouched world. Alive!

And nothing like home.

3

Eden

A soft breeze caressed Chris's face as he stirred, disoriented.
The scent of fresh flowers filled the air, mingling with the
rustling whisper of leaves swaying gently above. When he

opened his eyes, the sight stole his breath. Towering emerald trees stretched toward a sky of perfect blue, the sun blazing high above, its warmth wrapping him in a gentle embrace. Vibrant flowers of every hue blanketed the ground in a dazzling tapestry, more vivid than anything he had ever seen.

It was paradise.

Exotic animals roamed freely in the distance—creatures both familiar and strange, coexisting in a harmony so pure it felt unreal. No decay. No ruin. No suffering.

But no people either.

Chris spun in place, trying to process the overwhelming beauty of this strange world. Yet as he moved, something felt... wrong. His balance was off and his movements were unnatural. His heart pounded as he looked down at himself—smooth, pale limbs that weren't his own.

What the hell?

His voice echoed differently, hollow, distant. He stumbled toward the nearby stream, drawn by the need for confirmation.

The reflection staring back sent a cold jolt through his chest.

It wasn't his face.

An all-white, featureless form stared back from the water, humanoid yet stripped of identity. No hair, no skin, just a blank canvas of pale ivory. The only detail were his eyes—void-like, infinite pools of obsidian black. And within them, swirling faintly, were stars. Nebulae. Entire galaxies suspended in their depths.

Chris staggered back from the water's edge, panic rising like a vice around his chest. *What happened to me? Where's my body?* He flexed his fingers, watching the unnatural movements of this strange vessel. *Am I... dead?*

Suddenly, a voice called out from a hilltop.

"Hey! How ya doing?"

Chris's head snapped toward the sound.

A woman stood atop the hill, clutching a bundle of papers close to her chest. From this distance, he couldn't make out her features, but she seemed… calm. Friendly, even.

Instinct flared—*Hide.*

Don't let her see you like this. You'll terrify her.

Chris tried to run, but his unsteady legs betrayed him. He stumbled and collapsed onto the soft grass. Cursing under his breath, he scrambled to his feet, but it was too late. The woman had already begun her descent, her steps light and unhurried.

"Hey," she called again, voice gentle but curious. "You… can understand me, right?"

Chris braced for fear, for screaming, but none came. She wasn't afraid.

In fact, as she approached, her gaze softened with fascination.

"Wow…" she whispered, stopping just a few feet away. "Your eyes… they're beautiful."

Chris blinked, his chest tightening with confusion. *She's not afraid?*

The woman tilted her head, staring deeper, captivated. "It's like… I can see entire worlds inside them."

Chris wanted to speak, to explain, but the words caught in his throat as he finally took in her appearance.

She was stunning.

Her dark skin radiated warmth under the sunlight, her vibrant ruby-red hair cascading in soft waves over her shoulders. A flowing white dress draped over her figure, pristine yet simple, blending seamlessly with the serene landscape. But it wasn't just her appearance that held him.

It was her presence—serene, inviting, as if she belonged to

this perfect place.

"What's your name, new friend?" she asked, smiling, her voice melodic, filled with genuine kindness.

"I… I'm Chris," he replied, the sound of his own voice foreign in his ears.

The woman's smile deepened, radiant and warm.

"I'm Lilith," she replied with a soft smile, her ruby-red hair catching the sunlight. "It's nice to meet you, Chris. It's been a while since I've had someone to talk to. The animals are lovely company, but they're not exactly skilled conversationalists."

Chris nodded, his mind still spinning. Her presence was so calm, so welcoming—it almost made him forget his strange form. But curiosity gnawed at him.

"Are you… the only person here?" His words hung awkwardly in the air.

Lilith's smile brightened, her eyes glimmering with something playful. "Oh no, I live here with my husband."

Chris felt a strange twinge, a sinking disappointment he couldn't quite place. *Of course, she has a husband.*

"You… have a husband?" he asked, trying to keep his voice neutral.

Lilith nodded, a teasing spark in her eyes. "Yes, I do. And he can be quite protective when he feels like it."

Chris hesitated, trying to push aside the strange feelings. He shook his head, refocusing. "Lilith… can I ask you something?"

She tilted her head, grinning. "Of course! Although, technically, you just did. And now I've answered. That's how conversations work, right? Question, answer. Back and forth?"

Chris exhaled a short laugh despite himself. "Yeah, I guess so. You said you *live* here. Where exactly is—"

"Li-lith!!"

A deep voice echoed from beyond the trees, cutting Chris off.

Lilith turned, cupping her hands around her mouth. "I'm over here, darling! I made a new friend!" Her voice was as cheerful as ever.

The voice called back, louder this time, laced with irritation. "How many times have I told you not to wander off alone?"

Through the trees, a figure emerged. He was tall, broad-shouldered, and moved with the confidence of someone used to being in control. His dark, sun-bronzed skin contrasted with his tousled black hair, and the lingering look of concern softened only slightly his sharp features on his face.

He jogged over, stopping just short of Chris, eyeing him carefully before his face smoothed into a polite, though slightly guarded, smile.

"Chris," Lilith said brightly, gesturing between them. "I'd like you to meet my husband. Go on, honey, introduce yourself."

The man straightened, forcing a smile that didn't quite reach his eyes. "I'm Adam," he said, his voice calm but measured. "And I see you've already met Lilith."

Chris nodded, unsure of what to make of Adam's lingering gaze—or the tension beneath his carefully polite exterior.

"Hey, Chris," Lilith said, her voice light with excitement. "Weren't you asking about directions earlier? Perfect timing! I've been mapping the area."

She unfolded a collection of hand-drawn papers, revealing a beautifully crafted map filled with tiny sketches of trees, birds, rivers, and hills. Each detail felt alive, every line meticulously drawn.

"It's still a work in progress," she continued, brushing a stray curl from her face. "But I'm hoping to map the entire world someday."

Chris blinked, surprised. What she called *not much* was already a stunningly detailed representation of the vast, vibrant landscape surrounding them.

"So… where were you hoping to go?" she asked, tilting her head.

Chris hesitated, glancing around at the endless stretch of untouched beauty. Towering trees, golden meadows, and crystal-clear streams painted a paradise unlike anything he'd seen before. It was overwhelming—the sheer perfection of it all. *This can't be Earth...*

"I don't want directions," he said finally. "I need to know… where am I? What *is* this place?"

Lilith's expression softened. She gestured around them, as if the answer was self-evident. "This world is called Earth. And this… this place is Eden."

The word lingered in the air, heavy with meaning.

Eden.

The name sent a chill through Chris, a flurry of wonder and disbelief washing over him. *Eden?* The one from stories? From the Bible?

His gaze drifted back to the landscape—the perfect harmony of life, the vibrant green untouched by decay. For a moment, he was speechless, struggling to process the magnitude of what she was saying.

It was too perfect.

"But… this *isn't* my Earth," he whispered. "I'm… I'm from Earth too. Or another version of it, I guess. Are there… other worlds?"

Lilith nodded thoughtfully, tucking the map back into her bundle. "Well, my creator says there are eight others, but never told me much about them."

Chris's mind spun with questions—*Who was her creator? How had he gotten here? Was there a way back?* He felt untethered, adrift in a place where the rules felt different, yet achingly familiar.

"Anyway," Adam interjected, glancing at the horizon where the sun hung low, painting the sky in warm hues. "It's getting late. We should head home."

Lilith nodded before turning back to Chris. "Do you have somewhere to stay? A place to rest?"

Chris shook his head, feeling the weight of uncertainty pressing down again. "I… honestly have no idea where I am or what to do next."

"Perfect," Lilith said brightly. "Come with us! You can stay at our home. We'll have dinner too—are you hungry?"

Chris hesitated, but nodded. He wasn't sure if he could even *feel* hunger in this strange new form, but the kindness in her voice eased his tension.

"Yeah. Thank you. That sounds… good."

They began their walk, following a narrow dirt path winding through the idyllic landscape. The beauty was overwhelming—fields of wildflowers swayed gently in the breeze, their colors more vibrant than anything Chris had ever seen. The scent of jasmine and lavender lingered in the air, mingling with the damp earth beneath their feet. Birds sang from the canopy above, melodies so sweet they felt orchestrated.

Chris couldn't help himself. "How long have you lived here?" he asked, his curiosity bubbling despite Adam's brooding silence.

Lilith smiled, happy to answer. "Oh, forever, I think. I explore mostly, map out the world. Adam tends to the orchard and makes sure everything stays peaceful."

Chris nodded, absorbing every word. But as he continued asking questions—what they did, how this place worked, who their creator really was—Adam's jaw tightened. His responses grew shorter. Annoyance simmered just beneath his carefully polite mask.

Chris noticed. And slowly, he fell quiet.

Something felt… off.

But for now, he followed. Because he had nowhere else to go.

The journey continued in silence, the sounds of rustling leaves and birdsong filling the air—until Adam finally broke it.

"Have you noticed how the animals here behave, Chris?" he asked, his voice calm but with a trace of something heavier. "It's almost like they understand one another… as if they communicate without words."

Chris nodded, glancing around at the harmonious scene— the deer grazing peacefully beside wolves, birds perched comfortably near prowling wildcats. No fear. No struggle. Only balance.

"Yeah," Chris said, his voice filled with quiet awe. "It's… like they're connected. Part of something bigger. A bond, maybe?"

Adam's expression shifted, the corner of his mouth tightening as he straightened. "That's because they are ours." His voice took on a strange weight, a quiet thunder beneath the words. "The fish of the sea, the birds of the air, the cattle on land. All of it. Dominion was given to us over every living thing. They exist under our rule."

Chris blinked, the statement jarring against the gentle peace that surrounded them. He said nothing, but the way Adam spoke lingered—a certainty in his voice, as if the harmony wasn't natural but enforced. It didn't sit right.

Lilith, however, seemed unfazed, humming softly to herself

as she led the way forward.

When they arrived at the house, Chris's breath caught. He hadn't expected anything like this.

The home seemed to rise from the earth itself, as though it had always belonged there. Warm, honeyed wood framed the structure, with vines curling along the edges of a sloping roof. Flowers bloomed wildly along the porch, their colors spilling over like nature had claimed the place but chose to adorn it instead of consume it.

It was both elegant and simple, not primitive but untouched by excess. A well sat nearby, and Chris noticed the faint trail of smoke from the hearth, the scent of firewood lingering in the air. No signs of advanced tools or machines—just the essentials crafted with care.

How could a place like this even exist?

"This is our home," Lilith said, turning back to him with a smile. "Come, I'll show you where you can rest."

She took his hand gently, leading him up the wooden steps. The creak of the floor beneath them was the only sound as they ascended to the second level. The room she guided him into was modest, yet inviting. A small bed with a woven blanket rested against the wall. Sunlight filtered in through a simple window, painting soft patterns across the bare wooden floor.

A full-length mirror stood in the corner, its surface slightly rippled, and a small desk held parchment with three carefully placed ink pens—one red, one blue, and one black. It felt both sparse and personal, as if waiting for something to be written.

"Make yourself comfortable," Lilith said warmly. "I'll call you when dinner's ready."

The door closed gently behind her.

Chris sat on the edge of the bed, his gaze drifting from the mirror to the parchment before finally settling on the window. The beauty outside felt unreal, but it did nothing to quiet the storm inside him. His thoughts circled endlessly—*How did I get here? How do I get back? Are they even looking for me? Do they know I'm alive?*

Am I?

His pale, featureless hands flexed, that same strange vessel he had awoken in. A body that wasn't his. Would he even recognize himself if he ever made it home?

The ache in his chest deepened, and he sank further into his thoughts. Until—

"Chris!"

Lilith's voice, warm and melodic, drifted up the stairs. "Dinner's ready!"

He stood slowly, shaking off the spiral of uncertainty, and made his way back down.

The dining room was as simple and warm as the rest of the house. The long wooden table was set with woven plates, and the food waiting for him was… simple. Fruits of all shapes and colors, bowls of berries, leafy greens, sliced vegetables arranged with care.

No bread. No meat.

Chris hesitated as he sat, curious how this body would even process food—if it could.

Adam and Lilith sat at the table, both waiting with quiet smiles. Lilith's expression was soft and welcoming. Adam's… measured, watchful.

Chris picked up a slice of fruit, feeling its texture between his fingers before taking a cautious bite. The sweetness burst on his tongue. Real. Grounding.

For the first time since arriving in Eden, he felt something familiar—something human.

And yet, as he glanced across the table at Adam's steady, lingering gaze, he couldn't shake the sense that something was being left unsaid.

"I really appreciate you both taking me in," Chris said, his voice careful, measured. His eyes dropped to his pale, featureless hands resting in his lap. "Especially considering… well, how I look."

Adam, who had been tearing into a handful of fruit, paused mid-bite. He studied Chris with an expression just shy of polite curiosity, though something colder simmered beneath the surface.

"Yes, I've been meaning to ask about that," Adam said, his tone shifting. "I've named every living thing in Eden, and I've never seen a creature quite like you. Some kind of… sub-human, perhaps?"

Chris's grip tightened around the edge of his plate. He glanced toward Lilith, searching for some reaction—some reassurance— but she hadn't touched her food. Her gaze stayed on her plate, face unreadable.

"I'm human," Chris said quietly, forcing the words out. "At least, I think I am. Something happened to my body, but I… don't know how or why."

A hollow silence followed.

Adam resumed eating with little thought, drinking deeply from a clay cup as if nothing were amiss. But Chris felt it.

Lilith, once so bright and welcoming, had dimmed. Her usual warmth had faded, her presence quiet and withdrawn. When Chris asked her anything, she replied with short, half-hearted answers, her smile absent.

The stark difference from earlier left him uneasy.

"I think I've had enough for tonight," Lilith said suddenly, her voice soft but distant. She pushed her plate aside, still untouched.

Adam didn't seem concerned. He offered her a pleasant smile as he wiped his hands. "Of course, dear. Sleep well. I'll see you in the morning."

Chris watched as she rose from the table, her movements slow, almost reluctant. She disappeared up the stairs without another word.

The energy in the room felt... wrong.

Adam remained calm, even cheerful, as if nothing had changed. But Chris could feel it—an imbalance, a tension pressing heavier with every passing moment. He couldn't quite name it, but it sat in his chest like a weight he couldn't shake.

He excused himself shortly after, retreating to his room.

Lying on the small bed, Chris stared at the wooden ceiling, the events of the evening looping in his mind. Something had shifted. Lilith's behavior. Adam's odd composure. The way she'd barely spoken.

What changed? What am I missing?

A creak from below snapped him out of his thoughts.

The sound of a door.

Chris sat up, heart racing, and crossed the room to the window.

Lilith.

She was tiptoeing through the garden, slipping into the trees beyond the house. Alone.

Chris didn't think—he moved.

Descending the stairs as silently as he could, he stepped out into the cool night air. The scent of damp earth filled his lungs, the moonlight painting the forest in pale silver hues.

Lilith was ahead, moving deeper into the woods.

Chris followed, careful to stay hidden among the trees, his breath shallow. Every step she took seemed… purposeful. Focused.

Something wasn't right, and he had to know why.

His heart pounded with apprehension as he ventured further into the dense thicket of towering trees. Chris took care to remain hidden, mimicking the movements of a skilled tracker. He avoided branches, leaves, and anything else that would make a sound. He didn't want to alert her before he found out what she was doing. As they ventured deeper into the woods, Chris couldn't help but speculate on Lilith's motivations.

Was she meeting some other person? Engaging in some nefarious activity? Or was she simply seeking solace in nature's embrace? His mind raced with possibilities, each one more tantalizing than the last. Minutes turned into hours as he continued his pursuit.

Finally, they reached a small clearing bathed in a magical glow, where Lilith stood by a single tree.

The forest twisted unnaturally, the very air heavy with something ancient and wrong.

The shadows weren't natural. They stretched too far, curling and writhing beneath the pale moonlight as if reaching for something. They clung to the branches. Crawled along the earth. And they pulsed—like a heartbeat—thick and alive around *her*.

Lilith knelt at the base of the pale tree.

The bark was smooth as bone, almost luminous under the moon, but its branches bore something unnatural—large, swollen orbs of blood, hanging heavy like they could burst at any moment. Their deep crimson skins seemed to pulse in rhythm with the shadows pooling at her feet.

The darkness clung to her too, wrapping around her limbs in delicate coils, feeding on her presence.

Chris felt it now.

Something is feeding on her.

"Lilith?" His voice was quiet, careful, as he stepped from the cover of the trees.

She didn't move.

The shadows rippled in response, tightening around her wrists like invisible chains.

"I—" Chris hesitated, swallowing the lump in his throat. "I didn't mean to follow you… I just—I was worried. You haven't been yourself since—"

She stood.

The movement was too sharp. Too sudden.

When she turned, his heart seized.

Her eyes.

Blood-red.

The warm amber light he'd seen before was gone, replaced by a searing, unnatural glow.

The shadows flared around her.

Chris felt the pull of something primal—wrong—deep in his chest.

"Lilith?" His voice shook.

And then she *moved*.

A blur of pale white.

Chris didn't even see the punch until her fist collided with his chest.

The impact was catastrophic.

The world shattered around him as he flew backward. Trees cracked, splintering like dry kindling as his body tore through them. Bark and dirt exploded in his wake, the wind howling past his ears as he crashed into the earth with bone-rattling force.

Silence.

Chris lay sprawled in the dirt, blinking up at the fractured canopy. His body ached, but not like it should have.

He was alive.

His body—this strange vessel—had absorbed the blow. Not unscathed, but *intact*.

But then he felt it.

A slow, thick sensation crawling down his cheek.

Chris raised a shaking hand, brushing it across his face.

The liquid was black.

It oozed thickly from the cracks along his skin, dripping onto the ground beneath him—dark, viscous, unnatural.

My blood.

But it wasn't just his blood that was wrong.

Her.

Lilith.

He staggered upright, clutching his ribs as he stared across the clearing.

She hadn't moved.

She stood beneath the pale tree, the blood-red fruit behind her seeming to pulse even brighter, shadows coiling tighter around her form.

But beneath the void in her eyes, something *shifted*.

Like she was struggling.

She's still in there.

"Lilith!" he shouted, his voice ragged. "I don't know what's happening, but *you have to fight this!* Whatever this thing is— *you're stronger than it!*"

For a moment, her face *twitched*.

A crack in the mask.

And then—

A voice.

It wasn't hers.

It poured from her lips in a low, venomous rasp.

"She is mine now. She will suffer."

Chris felt the words pierce deeper than the pain in his body.

But then—another voice.

Softer. Faint.

"Chris... I can't win this battle. It's up to you now."

Her body *convulsed*.

The shadows writhed violently, clawing up her arms as if trying to consume her entirely.

Chris clenched his fists.

No. I won't let you take her.

"I'm not leaving you, Lilith!" he shouted. "You can *fight* this!"

The voice snarled back.

"You are nothing. She belongs to me."

Chris lunged.

He didn't want to hurt her. But he couldn't let her stay trapped like this.

His fist connected with her shoulder, trying to knock her off balance—*break* whatever invisible hold was on her.

Lilith barely reacted.

She struck back.

Faster this time—her palm colliding with his ribs in a brutal blow that sent him staggering.

Pain flared worse than before.

More of the black liquid seeped from the cracks along his arms, his face.

But she's fighting it. I can see it.

Her face twisted and her body trembled as if she was being pulled apart from within.

"Lilith, *please!*" he cried, voice breaking. "You're not this! I know you can fight it! I know you're still—"

For a heartbeat—

Her eyes shifted.

One red.

The other amber.

And then the tears came.

Pouring down her cheeks.

But they weren't the same.

From her left eye, clear water streamed. Pure. Clean.

From her right eye, thick red *blood* spilled, streaking her face.

The shadows hissed violently, writhing as if the presence inside her was losing control.

"She is mine."

"Chris... help me."

Chris didn't think.

He lunged forward, wrapping his arms around her trembling form, pulling her against his chest.

The shadows lashed out violently, clawing at his skin.

But he didn't let go.

"I'm here," he whispered, his voice raw. "I'm not letting go. You're stronger than this. *Fight.*"

Her tears—water and blood—streamed from her eyes, dripping onto his face.

And then he *felt it.*

A surge.

The tears sank into the cracks along his skin.

And the power *ignited.*

His eyes—those void-like pools—flared to life, no longer empty but burning *white*. Flames roared to life from his fingertips, spreading up his arms, wild and uncontrollable.

"Lilith—stop! I can't—control—"

The pale tree behind her burned.

The blood-red fruit withered, bursting into sickening pops as the flames spread further, the forest itself igniting with unnatural heat.

Chris clutched his chest, feeling the energy twist inside him, searing his vessel from within. The black liquid oozing from his body *boiled* as the power burned hotter.

"I can't hold it!" he screamed.

But Lilith didn't move.

Then he heard her.

"Chris… It's okay. Let go."

The flames detonated.

A white-hot eruption burst from his core—engulfing the entire clearing.

The pale tree disintegrated.

The shadows—obliterated.

And then—

Silence.

Chris's body crumpled to the earth, the flames gone, his vessel cracked and bleeding black.

His vision blurred.

The last thing he saw before unconsciousness claimed him—

Lilith. Collapsing beside him. Her eyes were no longer red. But amber. And full of tears.

4

Eden Preparatory Academy

4

Chris jolted awake, a ragged gasp tearing from his throat as his body surged upright.

His heart pounded like a war drum, echoing in his chest as fragments of fire and shadows clawed at the edges of his mind. The pain. The heat. Lilith's blood-red eyes—her tears streaking down her face.

Lilith.

But it was gone. All of it.

The world around him was… quiet. Still.

And completely unfamiliar.

He blinked, disoriented, struggling to piece together where he was. Pale gold accents, pulsing gently like veins of energy, filled the room; the room was sleek, smooth stone in hues of soft slate and pearl.

Strange symbols traced along the edges of the walls, faint and fluid, almost like they were breathing in sync with the room itself. It felt… alive.

Yet familiar. Chris squinted, his breath still unsteady as he scanned the space. The sensation clung to him like a whisper—déjà vu, just out of reach.

Have I been here before?

A window, more like a panel seamlessly fused into the wall, shifted as he stood, widening to reveal a sprawling city beyond. Towering structures of smooth stone and crystalline panels spiraled upward, reflecting the morning sun. Bridges hovered mid-air, weightless, linking structures that defied gravity.

It felt ancient.

Yet… impossibly advanced.

Where am I?

Chris forced himself to stand, his limbs aching but functional. He felt *whole*. Solid. And yet…

He caught his reflection in a curved mirror set into the wall, though it didn't seem like glass at all—more like a surface made of rippling light.

And the reflection staring back—

It's me.

No cracks. No void-black eyes. No seeping black liquid. Just his face.

His human body.

Chris's breath caught as he ran a trembling hand along his jaw, half-expecting the skin to fracture—to twist back into the empty vessel he'd become.

But it didn't.

I'm back... was it a dream?

The thought barely took shape before confusion surged in like a tide.

How?

The last thing he remembered—the fire. The unbearable heat. Lilith's voice, distant and broken. Shadows swallowing light. That blood-red fruit, pulsing with unnatural power.

Then the explosion.

And now...

"Chris! Come down for breakfast!"

The voice struck like a hammer to his chest.

Soft. Familiar.

Her voice.

His breath caught. His heart twisted.

No. That wasn't possible.

He stared at the door—sleek, seamless, gently humming as if waiting for his command. Even his clothes were unfamiliar: a pale tunic laced with silver lines, stitched like circuitry, no buttons, no seams. The fabric felt impossibly smooth, weightless.

Like the room.

Like… *everything.*

What is this place?

He turned, searching the room for any trace of reality. That's when he saw it—something sitting on the polished desk.

A phone.

Hands trembling, he picked it up. The screen lit up instantly. No password. No lock.

Just a photo.

Him. His mom. His dad. All of them smiling. Whole. Alive.

He swiped.

More photos. Birthday cake. A trip to the mountains. Laughing over dinner. Even the old chessboard he and his father used to battle over—still mid-game.

His knees nearly gave out.

"Chris?" the voice called again, quieter this time, gentler. "Are you coming?"

The scent of breakfast wafted in—eggs, toast, cinnamon. Too real. Too warm.

The door hissed open before he could reach for it.

The hallway glowed softly. Inviting. Deceptive.

His grip tightened around the phone.

Something was wrong.

But he stepped forward anyway, his heart thundering in his chest, pulled by the warmth of her voice—and the cold whisper of something he couldn't remember chasing him from behind.

The walls shifted as he walked—subtle ripples of color following his presence, pale symbols flickering and fading out of existence as he passed.

Everything was too perfect. Too still.

And yet the voice…

It was her.

It had to be.

But with every step, the question echoed louder.

What is this place?

Chris followed the voice, his steps hesitant as he descended the unfamiliar staircase. The golden light along the walls dimmed slightly as he moved, the soft pulse of energy quieting with every step.

The kitchen was no less surreal than the rest of the house.

Sleek surfaces glowed with a subtle warmth, the smooth stone counter tops reflecting the soft light above. The space felt impossibly clean, yet strangely familiar, as though someone had frozen it in a perfect memory.

But it wasn't the room that made his heart lurch.

It was *them.*

His mother. His father.

Sitting together at the table, speaking in soft voices, laughing gently with someone who shouldn't be there.

A little girl.

She couldn't have been older than three, with dark curls and wide, curious eyes that sparkled as she clumsily poked at the food on her plate. Bright and carefree giggles filled the air; fruit smeared her tiny hands.

Chris's stomach twisted.

Who is she?

His mother noticed him standing frozen in the doorway, her face lighting up with that same familiar warmth.

"Chris! There you are! Come sit down, breakfast is getting cold." She gestured to the empty seat beside her, her voice as natural as if everything were completely normal.

It wasn't.

Chris stepped forward, moving on autopilot as he approached

the table. Every muscle felt stiff, his pulse roaring in his ears as he slid into the chair.

He couldn't stop staring at the girl.

The way she looked at him—so innocent, so *familiar*—as if she'd known him her entire life.

But he didn't know her.

Swallowing hard, he finally managed to speak, voice hollow. "Who… who is she?"

His mother blinked, glancing at his father with quiet confusion before offering a soft, patient smile.

"Chris… What do you mean? That's your sister."

The words slammed into him like a hammer to the chest.

Your sister.

No. No, that wasn't possible.

He didn't have a sister. He'd *never* had a sister.

His heart pounded faster, heat rising in his chest as his gaze snapped toward his father—the man he *knew* was dead.

Chris's voice cracked, barely a whisper.

"Dad… you're supposed to be gone."

His father's expression shifted, softening with quiet concern. Slowly, he reached across the table, his hand closing gently around Chris's trembling one.

The warmth of his touch. The calm weight of it.

Real.

"Son," he said, his voice steady and full of love. "I'm right here. I haven't left."

Chris felt like he was being split in two.

The memories of his father's death, the unbearable grief—*it was real.* He *knew* it was real.

And yet, here he was. Whole. Alive. Looking at him the same way he always had.

This can't be real.

It was like standing between two colliding worlds—one where he had mourned, where he had *lost*—and this perfect, impossible scene.

Which one was true?

Which one was a lie?

His parents exchanged hushed whispers, glancing at him with increasing concern.

"Chris," his mother said, her brows furrowing. "Are you feeling alright? "

Chris's chest tightened, words caught somewhere in his throat.

What am I supposed to believe?

But no answer came.

He just sat there, trapped in the impossible.

"Of course!" his dad exclaimed, voice warm and full of encouragement. "Never thought I'd see you nervous about today. No need to worry—you'll be fine."

Chris forced a smile, masking the tension twisting in his chest, and chuckled weakly as he started eating.

Just play along, he told himself, poking at his food. *Maybe everything else was just a dream. This feels so real... maybe it's better not to question it.*

The meal passed in quiet conversation, his parents oblivious to the storm of doubt swirling inside him. Once finished, Chris excused himself and returned to his room, the uneasy weight in his chest pressing heavier with each step.

The door clicked shut behind him, sealing him alone with his thoughts.

The room felt... wrong.

It looked like his. His neatly made bed, the window letting

in soft morning light, and shelves stacked with books and decorations suggested it was his room. But they weren't.

His gaze lingered on the details—the little things that gnawed at him.

The clothes in his closet were too new, too perfect. Shirts, jackets, and pants neatly arranged as if they had always been there. But Chris didn't recognize any of them. He ran his fingers over the fabric, searching for something—*anything*—that sparked a memory.

Nothing.

Moving on, his eyes landed on the trophies crowding the shelves.

Dozens of them. Glistening, untouched. Academic honors, other achievements—awards bearing his name in bold, gleaming letters.

I don't remember any of this.

He felt as if he were walking through a stranger's life, some carefully crafted reality sculpted around him.

How could I forget so much?

Desperate for clarity, his hands trembled as he reached for a photo album tucked on the shelf. He flipped through the pages, each image more bewildering than the last. Birthday parties. School events. Vacations with smiling faces. His face. His family.

Yet they were nothing but fragments. Shadows of a life he couldn't remember living.

Until he saw *her*.

The picture caught his breath in his throat.

It was him and Sophie.

The pose, the expressions—it was almost identical to a photo he *knew* he'd taken before. But the setting was different. Their clothes were different.

But everything else… the way they smiled, the way they stood close… was the same.

Chris stared at the image—his mind screamed even before he understood why.

It was wrong.

The smiles were right. The faces were right. But the world behind them—the setting, the feeling—was wrong.

"Chris?" His father's voice echoed from downstairs, snapping him from the trance.

"Almost time to go! Are you ready?"

Chris swallowed hard, forcing the photo album shut with trembling fingers.

"Yeah," he called back, voice tight. "I'm coming."

But as he left the room, that picture stayed with him—burned into his mind as proof that something here was *wrong.*

Chris stepped outside, heart pounding with a strange mix of anticipation and unease.

The world beyond the door was… perfect. Too perfect.

Vivid colors burst from every corner of the landscape— trees with shimmering leaves swayed gently in the breeze, their hues richer than anything he'd ever seen. The air felt impossibly crisp, every breath invigorating, as though someone had purified it to its essence. A subtle scent of blooming flowers lingered, never overwhelming, as if the entire environment had been designed for harmony.

Everything shimmered with life—too much life. Colors bled richer than nature allowed. Smiles stretched too wide. Laughter floated in the air, too constant, too clean. Chris felt it in his bones: a world polished to perfection, too smooth to trust.

He followed his father toward a sleek car parked in the

driveway, a model he recognized but somehow… different. The car seemed sculpted, seamless, as though someone had polished the metal to perfection. A soft, ethereal glow radiated faintly from the body, not the harsh glare of headlights but something gentler, pulsing in rhythm with the sun above.

Chris ran his fingers along the frame as he climbed inside, noticing how the energy flowed along the dashboard. The displays were unlike anything he'd ever seen—holographic panels showing elegant, fluid data streams: energy efficiency, solar absorption, and environmental balance reports, all shifting in real time.

It runs on sunlight.

He hadn't noticed it before, but as the car pulled out onto the main road, the entire city seemed to hum with the same soft energy. Buildings towered gracefully, smooth and clean, every structure adorned with shimmering solar panels that blended effortlessly into the architecture.

No exhaust. No pollution.

The streets were wide but silent, save for the faint hum of solar-powered vehicles gliding above the ground, suspended in graceful motion.

Chris gazed out the window, mesmerized.

No potholes. No grime. No signs of decay or struggle.

The city felt… alive. Thriving. *Perfect.*

His father was driving, calm as ever, smiling as if nothing about this world was unusual.

Chris stared at the reflection of his face in the window, trying to ground himself. *Was everything else a dream? The pain? The fire? Lilith?*

The car slowed as they approached a massive structure at the city's center.

Eden Preparatory Academy.

Was he still in The Garden of Eden somehow?

The name etched in shimmering letters along the pristine facade made his stomach twist.

The towering building was breathtaking—tall, symmetrical, the walls made from the same pale, glass-like stone that seemed to absorb and reflect the sunlight at once. Nature and technology intertwined seamlessly, vines woven into the architecture, subtle lights dancing along the structure as if the building itself was breathing.

But beneath the beauty, there was something… imposing.

Chris felt it in his chest as the car came to a gentle halt.

His father turned to him with the same warm smile.

"Ready, son?"

Chris forced a nod, but his fingers clenched against his knee, the unanswered questions pressing harder than ever.

I need to figure out what's really going on here.

The building towered above Chris, its presence commanding attention with an almost overwhelming sense of grandeur.

"Eden Preparatory Academy?" he asked, his voice quiet, uncertain. "Where are we going?"

His father blinked, clearly puzzled by the question.

"Here," he answered with a gentle frown. "Chris, I know you're nervous, but you're starting to sound strange." He gave Chris's shoulder a firm, reassuring squeeze. "It's just the first day. You'll do fine. Now come on—the selection process starts soon."

Chris nodded but said nothing, swallowing the confusion twisting inside him.

Don't question it. Just go along with it.

His father was alive. His family was together.

That had to be enough.

Even if nothing else made sense.

Chris followed the signs leading to the auditorium, the steady hum of voices growing louder with every step. When he finally stepped inside, his breath caught. The space was massive—easily packed with over two thousand students. Conversations echoed across the high ceilings, laughter and nervous chatter blending into a constant roar.

Chris scanned the crowd, his pulse quickening. Students filled every corner, standing in groups, chatting in hushed excitement. He felt out of place, the sheer size of the crowd pressing in on him as he slipped quietly into a seat near the center.

Just blend in. Play along.

A minute passed. Then two.

Suddenly, a voice cut through the noise, calling his name.

He ignored it at first. *Must be another Chris.*

But then a hand clamped firmly on his shoulder.

"Chris?"

A hand landed lightly on his shoulder.

Chris turned—face to face with a boy who looked strangely familiar.

Recognition flickered—the photo album.

The boy smiled, a little awkward, clearly trying to hide nerves. "Man, can you believe this? They cut the spots again this year. Only fifty are getting in."

He pulled at a strip of jerky absently, chewing like it gave him something to do with his hands.

Chris blinked, keeping his face neutral even as panic curled in his chest. *Fifty students? Getting into what?*

Before he could think of a response, another voice rang out

from behind him.

"*Eli!* Don't lie to him, I said they *cut* the spots by fifty, not that they're *only* taking fifty. Learn how to *listen* for once!"

Chris turned, and his breath caught.

Sophie.

Her smile was warm, her hair catching the sunlight from the windows, and for a heartbeat, everything else disappeared.

She was *here*.

Relief hit him so hard he acted without thinking—closing the distance and wrapping her in a tight hug, his arms holding on for just a second too long.

"Well, *hi* to you too, Chris," she laughed, a cheerful lilt in her voice as she pulled back slightly. "You okay?"

Chris quickly let go, wiping his hands on his jeans, trying to compose himself.

"Yeah. Yeah, I'm fine," he said, forcing a breath. "It's just… it's been a long morning."

She studied him for a second, head tilting with quiet concern, but didn't press.

"*Anyway,*" Sophie said, turning back to Eli with mock exasperation, "you're seriously the worst at explaining things. How do you *always* manage to twist everything I say?"

Eli held up his hands, still clutching the jerky. "Hey, hey—I just misunderstood, okay? No big deal."

Chris chuckled, some of his tension breaking as Sophie shot him a knowing look, clearly used to Eli's antics.

"*No big deal?*" she repeated mockingly. "You just told him we're practically guaranteed to fail, *Eli.*"

Eli grinned, completely unfazed. "Details! It's still pretty bad odds, but that's fine because we're making it in, no question. We *trained* for this. Our soul essence is strong enough. It's just time to prove it. Right, Chris?"

Chris blinked. *Soul essence.*

His mind raced. They know about that too?

But Sophie was already rolling her eyes. "Now you're getting way ahead of yourself, Eli. You *know* nothing's guaranteed."

Eli waved her off with a grin. "Nope. Positive thinking only, Soph. We *deserve* this. You'll see."

Chris nodded, forcing a smile as they both looked at him. "Yeah… yeah, of course. We've got this."

But inside, his mind was spiraling. *What were they talking about?*

Before he could ask, a commanding voice boomed through the auditorium, silencing the crowd.

"May I have your attention, please?"

The room fell quiet.

Chris turned toward the stage, his stomach knotting tighter.

A figure stood at the front, positioned beneath seven towering banners, each bearing a distinct symbol—a sword, a flame, a tree, a serpent, a shield, a crescent moon, and a sun.

Seated beneath those banners were seven robed figures.

And there—beneath the sun—was his father.

Chris's eyes drifted back to the man speaking. His chest tightened as he took in the sharp, severe face. It was the way his presence seemed to darken the room despite the sunlight streaming in.

The man who killed his father.

Chris felt his blood run cold.

No. No, this can't be real.

The voice echoed again.

"The Selection will now begin."

Chris sat frozen, heart pounding so loud it drowned everything else out.

"My name is Vincent Sinclair, Captain of the House of Michael. It is my duty and honor to address you today as you prepare to face the trials that will determine if you are worthy to join the ranks of the Angel Corps."

His gaze swept the sea of faces, lingering long enough to make each student feel as though he were speaking directly to them.

"Since the days of the ancient Garden of Eden, when Adam and Eve first walked among creation, the forces of darkness have waged war against the will of God. Satan and his fallen angels have sought, for millennia, to corrupt, steal, and destroy all that our Creator has made."

The words echoed, heavy and absolute, rippling through the crowd. Chris felt a strange chill as Vincent continued.

"But God, in His infinite wisdom, did not leave us defenseless. In the wake of this relentless conflict, He called forth seven of His mightiest archangels—Michael, Gabriel, Raphael, Uriel, Sariel, Raguel, and Remiel. They stood as pillars of peace, protection, and prosperity, leading the charge against the darkness. And with their guidance, they gifted humanity a divine power: the ability to harness soul essence—the spiritual energy that binds our very being to the divine will."

Chris felt a shift in the air as Vincent spoke the words. The mention of *soul essence* lingered like a heartbeat, and for a moment, he swore he felt it—something stirring within him.

Vincent's voice deepened, resonant with conviction.

"This power is entrusted to those who will stand against the forces of corruption and chaos. *You* have been called here to determine if you are worthy of wielding it in the service of God's kingdom. But power alone does not make one great. Power without discipline, without understanding, corrupts. Thus, the

Seven Houses were established—bastions of faith, strength, and sacrifice, each carrying the virtues of the archangels themselves. To stand among them is to become a vessel of God's will, a light against the coming darkness."

Chris swallowed hard, his chest tightening under the weight of those words.

"The trials you face," Vincent continued, stepping closer to the edge of the stage, "are not mere tests. They are sacred. They will reveal the truth of who you are. They will challenge your mind, your body, and your spirit—because *all* must be strong."

"The *first* test will measure your intellectual fortitude—your ability to seek truth, discern wisdom, and confront knowledge with humility and courage. For how can one serve the Light without first seeking understanding?"

His gaze lingered for a moment on the students, and Chris noticed many of them sitting straighter, nodding.

"But knowledge alone cannot protect the innocent," Vincent continued, voice rising. "The *second* test will demand physical excellence. Strength, endurance, and agility—these are not for vanity but necessity. You must become a shield for the defenseless, able to stand firm when others would fall."

Chris caught a glance of Eli, who clenched his fists with quiet determination.

"And finally," Vincent said, voice softening but not losing its weight, "the most profound of all—the *soul essence test.* This trial will measure not your strength, nor your mind, but your spirit. It will seek the truth of your heart, the purity of your faith, and the depth of your connection to the divine."

"For without a steadfast spirit—without unwavering faith— you cannot hope to stand against the forces of darkness."

The room felt still, every breath held as Vincent's words

settled over them like a mantle.

"But let me be clear." He drew in a breath, his expression solemn. "There is *no shame* in not making it. Each of you has been brought here for a reason. Some will walk the path of the Seven Houses, called to defend the faith. Others will serve in different ways—through compassion, teaching, or healing. All paths are noble in the eyes of God."

"What matters is that you give everything. That you fight with integrity, courage, and truth. Your worth is not defined by selection—it is defined by how you choose to *stand* in the face of these trials."

A pause. The silence was deafening.

Then, in a measured tone, Vincent concluded.

"The trials begin now. Report to your assigned locations. May your heart be steadfast, and may the light of the Almighty guide your steps. *Go.*"

The moment he finished, the room erupted into movement.

Chairs scraped back. Conversations reignited in hushed tones. Students shuffled toward the exits, some murmuring prayers under their breath, others sharing nervous glances.

Chris sat frozen for a heartbeat longer, Vincent's words echoing inside his mind. *Mind. Body. Soul essence.*

It felt more like a sermon than a school orientation.

Suddenly, a voice broke through the fog.

"Chris! Let's *gooo!*"

Eli, grinning and waving wildly from across the aisle, earned a few irritated stares as he practically danced in place.

Chris forced a shaky smile and stood. "Yeah. Yeah, I'm coming."

5

Trials

The trials began. The examination hall was vast and silent, the only sound was the scratching of pens against parchment.

Beneath towering stained-glass windows—where angels triumphed over darkness—rows of students bent silently over their desks.

Chris sat near the center, the weight of the exam paper heavy beneath his fingertips. The golden seal of Eden Preparatory Academy was pressed at the top, glimmering faintly in the light. He stared at the parchment as the first question swam into focus.

"Describe the formation of the Seven Houses following the First War of Heaven's Veil. Which Archangel's house led the first defense against the Siege of Ashkavon?"

Chris blinked. *What?*

The names meant nothing to him. He scoured the back of his mind for anything—fragments of memory, anything he'd learned—but the words felt foreign. He shifted in his seat, moving on.

"Explain the significance of the Angel Corps' establishment following the fall of the first Gate of Celestia. How did the archangels' intervention safeguard humanity's divine grace?"

Chris's brow furrowed. *Safeguard divine grace?*

The questions dug deeper—wars, ancient battles, victories written in absolutes—*The Battle of Obsidian Rain, The Trial of the Twelve Realms, The Purging of the Nine Abysses.* They spoke of epic conflicts, victories of light over shadow, yet never once did they mention failure or fall.

The more he read, the more the pattern emerged.

There was no mention of exile.

No mention of sin.

"Explain how the protection of Eden has preserved divine grace throughout the centuries and why humanity

remains unblemished under the watchful guidance of the Seven Archangels."

Chris's heart pounded.

They don't know...

There had been no fall here. No exile from the garden. No curse. The questions were so absolute, so unwavering, as if the world had never fractured. Humanity had remained under God's grace, untouched by sin—except where Satan had intervened through direct conflict.

That's why everything seems so perfect. This world never lost paradise.

His fingers gripped the pen tighter. The entire foundation of what they were being taught wasn't just different—it was *reversed*. Here, humanity wasn't broken. Evil was an external threat, not something woven into human nature.

"Detail the Archangel Michael's leadership during the First Incursion. How did his intervention prevent the spiritual corruption of the North?"

Chris's pulse quickened.

Spiritual corruption?

There it was again—evil described as an external invasion, a force to be driven out, never something that arose *from within.*

The Seven Houses weren't meant to save the lost. They were designed to *defend* those already whole.

He scanned the questions again, seeking any indication of redemption, repentance—something reminiscent of teachings from his world. But the only threats described were ancient wars, battles where fallen angels and demonic forces tried to breach this perfect, protected world.

The questions spoke of *defense*, not forgiveness.

His heart raced, but he couldn't stop. He had to focus.

The questions kept pressing into theology and history—**"List the divine domains of the Seven Archangels and their corresponding Houses."**

He scribbled what fragments he could remember.

Michael – Protection, Valor

Gabriel – Inspiration, Revelation

Raphael – Healing, Life

Uriel – Enlightenment, Wisdom

Sariel – Judgment, Truth

Raguel – Harmony, Justice

Remiel – Hope, Guidance

He had no idea if the answers were correct, but he had to keep going.

Another question struck him harder.

"Describe the Seven Corruptions introduced by the Adversary and how they have been purged through divine intervention."

Seven corruptions. The words lingered. He'd heard them mentioned before in his father's research notes..

Hatred. Anger. Greed. Anxiety. Fear. Jealousy. Disgust.

But here, they weren't described as human failings. They were *attacks*.

He could see it now—how every word had been crafted carefully, deliberately. Evil was described not as something within the heart, but as a weapon used by Satan to weaken humanity's divine grace.

He felt a sinking dread in his stomach.

What happens if they see me as corrupt?

What happens if they find out where I'm really from?

Chris swallowed hard. His hand shook slightly as he continued scribbling answers, forcing himself to fill in what he could.

But no matter how much he tried, the questions felt heavier—like they weren't just testing his knowledge.

They were testing his *belief.*

The final question stopped him cold.

"In a moment of darkness, when all strength fails, what will sustain your soul?"

Chris stared at the question, the weight of it pressing heavier than the paper in his hands. Darkness wasn't a theory for him. It had taken everything.

The bell rang.

Chris set his quill down, heart still pounding.

He had no idea if he had passed.

And worse—he was no longer sure if he even *belonged* here.

With the knowledge-based exam behind him, Chris now faced the physical test. He stepped into an arena full of spectators and Captains.

The roar of the crowd had faded, replaced by the rhythmic pounding of Chris's pulse echoing in his ears. The physical trial stood before him like a fortress—a sprawling obstacle course carved from stone and iron, towering walls, endless pits, and twisting mazes stretching far into the distance. It was designed to break not just the body but the spirit, and the captains of the Seven Houses stood along the perimeter, watching every movement with hawk-like precision.

Chris wiped his damp palms against his uniform, the fabric already clinging to his skin from the lingering tension of the written exam. *Alright, one step at a time. Get through this, and maybe I'll finally get some answers.*

A sharp horn blast signaled the beginning.

Chris surged forward with the other students, adrenaline

firing through his veins. The first obstacle rose like a jagged barrier—massive stone walls, smooth and unyielding. He sprinted toward the nearest, his mind racing as the other students split off to find different angles of approach.

Think. Test your body, test your mind. Figure it out.

Planting his foot against the base, he pushed upward, fingers grasping for the top. His grip faltered as his fingertips grazed the edge. He dropped back down, heart pounding, but there was no time for hesitation. Digging his heel into the ground, he launched higher, catching the ledge with a grunt, muscles straining as he hauled himself over.

One down.

Beyond the walls, the course stretched ahead—a maze of relentless challenges.

A pit of shifting sand forced him to tread carefully, his legs burning as he waded through. Rope ladders dangled from towering poles, demanding precision and grip strength. Sweat blurred his vision as he scaled the first rope—only to find an even steeper wall beyond.

Chris's chest heaved with ragged breaths, each movement stealing more of his strength.

From above, the captains watched in complete silence, their expressions unreadable. Vincent stood among them, his gaze cold, calculating. Chris felt it, even from a distance, like a blade at his back.

A stone balance beam stretched before him, slick with moisture. The gap beneath yawned open—a pit filled with fog so dense it seemed to pulse. Chris steadied himself, toes gripping the narrow path, when he heard someone slipping behind him.

A student, panicked and trembling, teetered on the edge of

the beam.

Chris's instincts flared. Without thinking, Chris pivoted, lunging backward to catch the other student by the wrist just as their foot slipped from the beam. The impact jolted his shoulder, but he tightened his grip, straining to keep them both balanced.

"Hold on—I've got you," he gritted out.

The other student, pale with fear, nodded, scrambling back onto the beam with Chris's help.

"Thanks," the boy whispered breathlessly, then took off toward the next challenge.

Chris's muscles burned, but his spirit felt lighter. He pressed forward.

The final stretch loomed—the gauntlet. A series of pendulums swing violently back and forth, steel weights attached to thick iron chains. Beyond them, the finish line.

No stopping now.

Chris sprinted forward, timing the arcs of the pendulums as best he could. The first one whooshed by, barely grazing his side. The second clipped his shoulder, spinning him sideways, but he regained his footing with a grunt.

The third caught his leg. Pain seared up his thigh as he collapsed to one knee. The world blurred, the crowd's muffled gasps echoing faintly.

But failure wasn't an option.

Gritting his teeth, Chris forced himself upright, muscles trembling with the effort. He could see the finish line now—so close.

With a burst of speed, he lunged forward, dodging the final pendulum by inches. His foot hit the stone at the finish, and the sound of a bell echoed through the air.

Silence.

Chris bent over, hands on his knees, chest heaving. His clothes clung to his frame, soaked through with sweat, his body shaking from exhaustion.

Then, applause.

The sound swelled—soft at first, then stronger, rippling through the crowd.

Chris blinked, disoriented, before catching the faintest smirk on Vincent's lips.

Was that approval? Or something else?

It didn't matter. He had made it through, and he was proud of his accomplishment.

Until he looked up.

"A leader board?!"

Chris blinked, his pulse quickening as he craned his neck to see the rankings.

The crowd buzzed with excitement as students gathered around the colossal leader board projected high above the stone courtyard. Names flickered across the glowing screen in shimmering gold, neatly ranked from 1 to 1000.

His eyes scanned the top entries, each name paired with a rank.

Sophie Silvestri – Rank: 23

Eli Thorne – Rank: 37

Chris felt a small swell of pride for his friends, seeing their names listed so high. Sophie was excelling, no surprise there— she always had a way of shining under pressure. And Eli wasn't far behind, even after all his nervous rambling.

But then, Chris's stomach tightened as he kept searching.

Row after row of names scrolled by. 100...150...300...still nothing.

Where am I?

Panic twisted in his chest. He scanned further. 600. 700.

Come on...

No. No way.

Finally, near the very bottom, **Rank 900: Chris Cronetti.**

He blinked, waiting for the number to change, to correct itself. But it stayed, cold and unflinching.

900.

He wasn't just barely good enough. He was almost nothing. The weight of disappointment sank into his chest. *900?* Out of 1000? Had he really performed that poorly?

The physical test had been brutal, but he finished. The written exam, confusing as it was, couldn't have gone that terribly… could it?

His knees felt weak, and before he could stop himself, he slumped onto the stone steps, hands in his lap. The voices of the other students seemed to grow louder, pressing in around him.

"Top 10! I can't believe it—definitely going for House of Michael."

"Raphael would be amazing, the House of Enlightenment… I heard they train the best healers and scholars."

"The House of Raphael is where I belong, too. I *know* it."

Everyone around him seemed to have a plan, confident and eager. Meanwhile, he sat there, questioning everything.

Why am I even here?

His mind spun, dragging him back to the blood-soaked memories of his father. The fight. The portal. The fire.

Suddenly, a voice echoed through the courtyard, amplified by some unseen force.

"Attention all students. The final trial is about to begin.

Report to your assigned gates immediately."

Chris exhaled shakily, forcing himself to stand.

No more self-pity. Finish what you started.

The crowd funneled toward the enormous stone archways lining the far end of the courtyard, each marked with a glowing insignia of one of the Seven Houses. Chris followed silently, the murmurs of the other students blending into a dull hum.

As they stood in line, the air buzzed with excitement.

"I hope I get into Gabriel's house," a girl whispered, clutching a pendant shaped like a flame.

"Yeah, well, I'm aiming for Sariel. They say his warriors are the most disciplined."

Chris clenched his fists, his mind racing with doubts he couldn't shake. The rankings echoed in his mind like a hammer on steel.

900.

He had no idea what the final test would be. But as he stood there, waiting for his turn, he promised himself one thing.

I don't care about my rank. I'm going to earn my spot in this world

Chris barely had a moment to catch his breath when a familiar voice called out from behind him.

"Hey!"

He turned to see the boy he had helped during the physical trials jogging up, his face flushed but smiling. Dirt streaked his uniform, and there was a slight scrape on his knee, but his expression was warm with gratitude.

"Yeah," Chris replied, still feeling the ache in his legs from the obstacle course.

The boy extended his hand. "Hi, I'm William. I just… wanted to say thanks. You didn't have to help me back there on the wall climb. I probably would've been wiped out if you hadn't pulled me up. That was — well, it meant a lot."

Chris shook his hand, giving a nod. "No problem, William. My name is Chris and I'm sure you would've done the same, right?"

William laughed nervously, rubbing the back of his neck. "Honestly? Probably not. I was panicking back there. My dad would've chewed me out for losing my nerve."

Chris tilted his head, curious. "Your dad's in the Angel Corps?"

"Yeah. He used to be in the House of Uriel," William said, his voice dropping slightly as he added, "He said it was the greatest honor of his life… told me I had to try, even when I didn't think I'd make it past the first test."

Chris frowned. "What made you decide to go through with it?"

William shrugged, his gaze drifting toward the glowing leader board on the far wall. "He told me it wasn't about being the strongest… It was about standing for something. Protecting people. Giving everything you have, even when it hurts." He exhaled, then looked up at the board, scanning it closely.

His eyes narrowed, then widened. "Hey! I'm there! Look— 918th." He grinned, clearly relieved despite the low rank. Then, his eyes shifted further down, scanning for Chris's name. "What about you? I didn't catch your last name—"

William stopped. His face twisted in disbelief as he spotted the name near the bottom.

"Chris… Cronetti?" His head snapped back toward Chris. "Wait. Are you related to Captain Giuseppe Cronetti? Of Gabriel's house?"

Chris felt a strange knot twist in his stomach. The words rang in his head—House of Gabriel. Captain. He *had* seen his father standing with the other captains on the stage, but the title hadn't clicked.

"Yeah," Chris whispered. "That's my dad."

William's eyes practically doubled in size. "No way! *That* Cronetti? Your dad's a legend here. He's, like, one of the best captains in the entire Angel Corps. I thought Gabriel's house was invitation only! Man, you must be crazy powerful—"

Before he could continue, a mechanical voice echoed across the hall.

"Final trial candidates, please report to your testing chambers."

"Guess we're up," William said with a nervous laugh. "Good luck, Chris. I'm sure you'll crush it."

"You too," Chris replied, his stomach still twisting with unease as they parted ways.

The testing chamber was massive—an immense, spherical space lined with smooth, metallic walls pulsing faintly with blue light. A single console stood at the center, sleek and futuristic, with a glowing hand print embedded on its surface.

Chris approached cautiously, his footsteps echoing in the cavernous space. The voice returned, calm and neutral.

"Place your hand on the console to begin."

Chris pressed his palm into the glowing mark.

For a moment, nothing happened.

The silence dragged, stretching long enough to make him shift uncomfortably. Then the voice returned.

"You have a soul essence reading of 0.1%. Please exit the testing pod."

Chris blinked, staring at the console.

"Wait… what?" He lifted his hand and pressed it down again.

The same voice repeated, calm but cold.

"You have a soul essence reading of 0.1%. Please exit the testing pod."

Chris clenched his fists, stepping back from the console. **This doesn't make sense.** He had tapped into soul essence before—the portal, the transformation… he *felt* the power that day. This machine—was it broken?

Or was he broken?

No. Focus.

He took a breath, heart pounding. He closed his eyes and forced himself to think back. The portal. The heat. The pain. He had felt his body dissolve—become pure energy. That was the soul essence. He knew it was there.

Pressing his hand back onto the console, Chris focused. Harder this time.

The air shifted.

Heat radiated from his palm as the light beneath his hand intensified.

"You have a soul essence reading of 11%…25%…37%…56%… "

Chris pressed harder. Heat surged through his veins. The console's numbers spiked—70%, 90%—and the world fractured

BOOM.

The console exploded. A shock wave of fire and heat knocked Chris off his feet, hurling him backward into the wall. Smoke filled the chamber, alarms blaring.

The doors burst open.

Giuseppe was the first inside, his presence commanding as he stormed into the smoke-filled chamber. Two captains flanked him—one raised a hand, summoning a gust of wind to clear the smoke. The other formed a protective barrier of golden light around Chris.

Chris barely registered the blaring alarms echoing in the chamber, the searing heat pressing against his skin, or the flames licking hungrily at the walls. Smoke coiled through the air, thick and suffocating. His body felt heavy, the surge of energy that had overtaken him moments ago now fully drained.

Suddenly, a blast of icy wind cut through the smoke. Frost spread across the floor in delicate fractals, racing up the walls and consuming the fire in a crackling web of ice. The flames hissed out, steam rising as the last embers died.

From the mist stepped Vincent. His expression was as cold as the frost still lingering in the air. He raised a single gloved hand, and shards of ice drifted from his fingertips, glittering in the dim light as the fire died completely.

Chris coughed, blinking rapidly as his vision blurred. He could barely make out his father, Giuseppe, rushing into the room as the last tendrils of smoke cleared.

Giuseppe dropped to his knees, hands gripping Chris's shoulders. "Chris! Look at me—are you alright? Say something!"

Chris's head lolled weakly, his body too exhausted to respond. His lips parted as if to speak, but the effort failed him.

"What happened here?" Vincent's voice was sharp, cutting through the haze like a blade. His pale gaze flicked from Chris to the shattered console, the frost still spider-webbed across the floor.

Giuseppe shot him a glare. "Now is not the time, Vincent. He needs medical attention."

Vincent folded his arms, unimpressed. "The console didn't simply explode on its own. What did he do?"

Chris's vision blurred again. His head swam, the world tilting sideways. He felt himself being lifted, his father's strong arms supporting him.

"We'll figure that out later," Giuseppe growled, his voice tight with barely contained anger.

Vincent's icy stare lingered on Chris's unconscious form.

"Transfer the remaining candidates to Testing Pod Three," he ordered coolly. "This one… he comes with us."

The last thing Chris felt before darkness overtook him was the reassuring grip of his father holding him close as the world faded into nothing.

6

Memories

Chris drifted back into consciousness, his body heavy and sore. The first thing he registered was the indistinct murmur of voices echoing around him. His eyes blinked open to see a circular chamber with seven towering chairs arranged in a semicircle, each adorned with a distinct flag—just like the ones he had seen on stage during the trials. The air felt tense, thick with authority.

The captains were all there, watching him.

A woman with sharp, perceptive eyes broke the silence first, turning toward Giuseppe. "He's your son. Do you know how he caused the fire?"

His tight jaw and drawn face revealed his stress. He shook his head. "I'm trying to figure it out myself," he admitted, though his voice lacked conviction.

Vincent, standing at the far end of the chamber with his arms folded, spoke next, his voice cold and sharp. "Surely you must have *some* idea, Cronetti. A malfunction like that? Flames don't just burst from a testing pod without reason."

Before Giuseppe could respond, Chris stirred, groaning softly as he sat up on the stone platform in the center of the chamber.

"Finally. Maybe we'll get some answers," another captain muttered, her gaze fixed on Chris with quiet intensity.

Chris rubbed his head, disoriented. "Where... where am I?" His voice cracked slightly as he took in the room.

Vincent stepped forward, his presence looming. "You're in the Captain's Chamber. That's the only question you'll get answered right now. What we need to know is how you nearly destroyed a testing pod designed by *Gabriel* himself." His eyes narrowed. "Start talking."

Giuseppe shot Vincent a glare. "Vincent, relax. It was clearly an accident." He turned back to Chris, his tone softer. "Son, just tell us what happened."

Chris swallowed hard, feeling every pair of eyes boring into him. He hesitated, trying to gather his thoughts. "I… I put my hand on the console like I was told. It said I had a soul essence of 0.1%. That didn't make any sense, so I tried again and the numbers—"

Vincent cut him off with a sharp wave of his hand. *"What do you mean, tried again?* There *is* no trying again! The testing pods are calibrated to perfection. They were *designed* to measure essence without error. The number wouldn't change just because you *felt* it should."

Chris opened his mouth to protest, but another voice interrupted. A man with silver hair and a calm demeanor, seated under the flag of Remiel, spoke up.

"The boy's not lying, Vincent. Look at him—he's clearly shaken. There's no need to interrogate him like this."

Vincent's expression didn't soften, but he took a step back, watching Chris with suspicion.

The woman seated under the flag of Raphael, the same one who had spoken earlier, nodded in agreement with a gentle smile. "The tests for today are complete. All candidates' results will be reviewed, and the final selections will begin tomorrow. We'll make sure all the necessary data is forwarded to each house for review."

Giuseppe exhaled, his shoulders relaxing slightly. "Thank you, Maria." He placed a protective hand on Chris's shoulder. "I'll take him home for now. We'll talk again tomorrow."

Vincent's gaze lingered on Chris, his expression unreadable as he finally gave a stiff nod. "Fine. But we *will* have answers. Soon."

Chris stayed silent as his father guided him out of the chamber, his mind racing. What had just happened? Why had the numbers surged out of control like that? And why did he get the feeling there was far more to this than anyone was saying?

As the heavy doors shut behind them, Chris glanced back once more at the circle of captains, Vincent's icy stare the last thing he saw before the doors sealed completely.

The night air felt heavier than it should have, cool against Chris's skin as he and his father stepped out onto the quiet school grounds. The stars hung low, their pale light barely illuminating the stone pathways beneath his feet. Everything felt…off. Too calm. Too perfect.

Chris looked up, frowning. "It's already night? How long was I out?"

Giuseppe's hand rested lightly on his shoulder, protective but gentle. "A couple of hours," he replied, his voice tinged with concern. "How do you feel?"

Chris hesitated. His body felt fine—whole, real—but his mind was in knots. Flashes of memories swirled together: fire and smoke, the testing chamber, *that other world*. His mother smiling at breakfast. The burning portal. The garden with Lilith. The birth of his sister.

What was real?

He could stay quiet. Let his father believe it was just stress, some kind of fluke. But the weight pressing on his chest wouldn't let him. He needed answers. He needed to *know*.

"Dad…" Chris's voice was tight. He forced himself to speak through the knot in his throat. "I need you to believe me. What I'm about to say—it's going to sound crazy."

Giuseppe's brow furrowed, but his hand remained steady on Chris's shoulder. "Go on. I'm listening."

Chris opened his mouth, but the words felt foreign. He almost backed out. Almost let it slip away.

"I think… I think I'm from a different time."

A heavy silence hung between them. Giuseppe's expression didn't change at first, but Chris caught the slight tension in his jaw.

"You're saying…you're a time traveler?"

Chris shook his head. "No, it's not like that. Or maybe it *is*? I don't know." He exhaled shakily, trying to gather the fractured pieces in his mind. "I have memories, Dad—memories that don't belong here. They're… bad. Painful. A world where you're gone. Where the church…" His voice trailed off, the words catching in his throat.

Giuseppe narrowed his eyes, searching Chris's face carefully. "Chris, I've *been* here. Since the day you were born. How could you remember something like that?"

Chris's chest tightened. He didn't have the answers. He barely understood it himself.

"I—I don't know! I remember this life too—sort of. I have pieces of memories coming back, growing up here, our house, everything. But it feels…overwritten somehow. Like both timelines are running at the same time. Both feel *real*, but they can't be." His voice dropped to a whisper. "I feel like I'm losing my mind."

Giuseppe's face softened, his protective nature overtaking his skepticism. He crouched slightly, meeting Chris's eyes. "Listen to me. You're not losing your mind, alright? We'll figure this out."

Chris shook his head, exasperated. "But how? I can't make sense of it. I can't even tell what's *real* anymore."

Giuseppe's expression shifted, thoughtful now. His hand tightened slightly on Chris's shoulder. "Then we need to *parse* your memories. Break them down, piece by piece, and separate fact from fiction. If both sets of memories are in your head, we'll find a way to untangle them."

Chris blinked. "Parse my memories…? How? It's not like I can just pull them apart on command."

"You don't have to," Giuseppe said with quiet certainty. He straightened and gestured toward the car parked nearby. "Come on. I'll show you."

Chris hesitated for just a moment longer, searching his father's face for any sign of doubt. But there was none. Just calm reassurance.

With a shaky breath, he nodded and followed. Whatever was happening, he wouldn't have to face it alone. Not yet.

They left the school in silence. the weight of the day's events hanging heavily between them. The ride home was quiet, filled only with the soft hum of the engine and the occasional glance from Giuseppe, as if he was searching for the right words but couldn't find them.

When they arrived, Chris followed his father through the front door without a word. Instead of heading upstairs, Giuseppe led him straight to the basement. The familiar scent of metal and old books greeted Chris as they descended the steps, the soft glow of machinery casting long shadows along the walls.

Giuseppe paused, gesturing toward the workbench where strange devices and tools lay scattered among worn journals and loose diagrams.

"Alright," he said, his voice calm but firm. "Let's figure this out."

The basement felt cooler than the rest of the house; the air tinged with the scent of old paper and metal. Soft, ambient hums echoed from the machinery crowding the shelves, casting faint, blinking lights across the walls. Strange gadgets and intricate tools covered nearly every surface—half-built devices, glowing screens, and papers scribbled with diagrams. It looked more like a laboratory than a family home.

Chris lingered near the doorway, his gaze drifting over the controlled chaos. Something stirred deep in his mind, a whisper of recognition just beyond his grasp. He squinted, searching the room for clarity amidst the clutter.

"I… remember this," he murmured, voice uncertain. "It's hazy, but… there's something familiar about all of this."

Giuseppe, already moving through the maze of equipment with practiced ease, turned with a small smile. "I'd hope so. We've spent countless hours down here." His voice was softer than usual, tinged with a nostalgia Chris couldn't quite place.

He watched as his father picked up a polished helmet from the workbench, its surface smooth and gleaming under the dim light. Giuseppe held it out carefully, his eyes narrowing with focus.

Chris hesitated, eyeing the strange device. "What…is this?"

Giuseppe adjusted the helmet slightly, turning it so Chris could see the subtle wiring along its surface. "It's a memory retrieval device. It's designed to reverse the chronology of your memories, making them as clear and accessible as possible."

Chris raised a brow, already skeptical. "Wait—you built a helmet that can…replay memories?"

"Something like that," Giuseppe replied. "It connects our memories directly. If it works, you'll see them clearly—and so will I. We'll be observers, like watching a recording of the past."

Chris stared at the device, heart pounding faster. The implications hit him hard. His father was brilliant—he'd always known that—but this felt like something out of science fiction.

"But…why would you build something like this?" he asked, half in awe.

Giuseppe's expression darkened for just a moment. "I was researching the concept of soul essence and memory retention. There were theories about how the mind stores not just experiences, but fragments of the soul itself. It was the first step in unlocking greater truths. Some speculated it could suppress unwanted memories, but I never wanted that to be the focus." He waved the thought away, pressing on. "But tonight, it's about you. If what you're saying is true, this might help us make sense of it. Or at least separate fact from… whatever else you're experiencing."

Chris's breath caught. Time travel. Soul essence. All of it connected—pieces of the chaos swirling inside his head.

Giuseppe stepped closer, his expression serious but calm. "I need you to relax, Chris. Just focus. Your memories will fill in the gaps naturally. I'll guide you, but you need to trust the process. Are you ready?"

Chris swallowed hard, nodding. His heartbeat felt loud in his ears.

"What do I need to do?"

Giuseppe gently placed the helmet over his son's head, the cool metal brushing against his temples. "Just breathe. Stay open. Let your mind drift. And whatever you see…don't fight it."

Chris exhaled slowly, closing his eyes as the device powered on with a soft hum. Light pulsed at the edges of his vision, the darkness behind his eyelids swirling. Then, slowly, his mind began to unravel. And the memories came rushing in.

"Okay, let's begin," Giuseppe said softly, flipping the switch on the machine. A low hum filled the basement, steady and rhythmic, like the pulse of a heartbeat. Chris shut his eyes as the sensation of warmth bloomed behind his eyelids, a gentle tug as though his mind was being unraveled thread by thread.

"Family," his father's voice echoed through the void.

The darkness lifted.

Chris blinked, disoriented. The world around him shimmered into view—a stretch of pale pink sand, smooth beneath his feet, meeting a turquoise ocean so clear it seemed unreal. The sunlight danced on the waves, a golden shimmer reflecting across the gently rolling tide. The air was warm, carrying the faint scent of salt and wildflowers.

Chris turned slowly, scanning the idyllic scene. Everything felt… distant. Familiar, yet unreachable, like a dream slipping away just before waking.

"Is this really my memory?" he asked, his voice barely above a whisper.

Giuseppe placed a steadying hand on his shoulder and nodded toward the shoreline. "Look closer."

Further down the beach, a younger version of Chris came into view kneeling in the sand. Beside him was a small girl, her brown curls catching the sunlight as she clumsily packed handfuls of wet sand. Their laughter echoed, pure and carefree, mixing with the sound of the waves.

"Is that…?" Chris started, the edges of recognition softening the tension in his chest.

"You. And your sister, Genevieve," Giuseppe answered gently, his voice tinged with emotion. "We come here every summer."

Chris watched, captivated, as the scene unfolded. His younger self was grinning, playfully swatting at his sister's clumsy attempts to build a sandcastle.

"No, no, you're doing it all wrong!" young Chris teased, hands sculpting a perfect tower of sand. "See? You have to pack it tighter!"

Genevieve pouted, her tiny fists flinging a handful of sand in protest.

A genuine laugh bubbled from the younger Chris, full of warmth. "Here, watch me again. I'll help you."

The sun dipped lower in the sky, staining the clouds in soft hues of orange and lavender. The breeze tousled their hair. Joy. Simplicity. Chris could almost feel the sand between his fingers, hearing the whisper of the waves just as he remembered.

"It feels so real," he whispered, voice thick with emotion. "Like I'm *there* again."

Giuseppe nodded, watching his son with a gentle expression. "It's because you are. These are your memories—unchanged. This is what you think of when you hear the word *family*. Beautiful, isn't it?"

Chris opened his mouth to respond, but the words caught.

The sun flickered.

A shadow stretched unnaturally across the beach, coiling into the waves. The vibrant colors drained as the sky darkened, clouds thickening overhead. The scent of salt grew sharp and bitter.

Giuseppe's brow furrowed. "*This…* this isn't how it happened." His voice shifted, tense now, protective. "It didn't rain that day."

The warmth was gone. The sea turned gray.

Chris's heart pounded as the beach dissolved into ash. The children were gone. The pink sands collapsed into scorched earth. Smoke replaced the scent of the ocean—thick, suffocating smoke, heavy with loss.

Where the sun once bathed the beach in gold, now loomed

the charred remains of a house. Their house. Walls blackened and skeletal. Windows shattered. The air was silent, save for the faint crackling of dying embers.

Chris could feel the ache pressing into his chest. His throat tightened.

"I knew it," he whispered, voice trembling. "I knew this was real."

From the ruins, two figures came into view—himself, much younger, clutching his mother's hand. She knelt beside him; her face pale, lips trembling as they stared into what remained of their home. The tears were silent, too painful for words.

Giuseppe took a step forward, his face ashen. "Chris... I don't understand. This never—"

The weight of the memory bore down on Chris like an unbearable force, pressing against his chest, squeezing the breath from his lungs. The charred ruins of the house loomed ahead, skeletal remains rising from the ashes, blackened and broken. Smoke curled lazily in the air, the scent bitter, a scent he would never forget.

Chris's pulse thundered in his ears. His eyes locked on the wreckage as the flickering embers reflected in his dark eyes. The heat, even in this memory, felt too close—too real. His breath grew shallow as he took an unconscious step back, an old fear clawing its way up from the depths of his mind.

The flames had taken so much.

Beside him, Giuseppe took in the scene with wide, searching eyes. He whispered, voice tight with disbelief, "It's like a nightmare. I—I died in a fire?"

Chris's stomach twisted. He shook his head sharply, his voice cracking. "No... no, you didn't. It wasn't the fire." His breathing hitched as his gaze fixed on the charred ruins once more, the sight sparking a deeper, unbearable memory. His fists clenched at his sides, shaking harder. "It was *Vincent.* He killed you. He *murdered* you and burned everything to the ground! The house—our life—you—he—"

The words faltered, tangled in a storm of pain as the surrounding ground erupted.

Fire.

It burst from the scorched earth, a sudden, furious inferno crackling to life, swallowing the space between them. The heat lashed at Chris's skin; the flames reflecting in his eyes like a living nightmare come to life. He staggered back, gasping as the flames roared higher, surrounding the ruins.

The fire seemed alive. It twisted unnaturally, coiling like serpents, hungry and suffocating. The air thickened with heat, pressing in like invisible hands closing around his throat.

Giuseppe took a step forward through the flames. "Chris— look at me!"

But Chris couldn't hear him. His vision blurred as the fire grew brighter, the memory twisting into something far worse. The shadows in the blaze seemed to shift, dancing with sinister shapes—mocking him, pressing closer. His legs refused to move, frozen as the heat grew unbearable.

The fire wasn't just a memory anymore.

It was *fear.*

"Chris!"

Giuseppe's voice cut through the haze as he forced his way closer, the flames licking dangerously at his sleeves. His face was tight with determination, pain etched into his features as he reached out through the inferno.

"*Chris!*"

The sound of his father's voice broke through the panic like a crack of lightning. Chris gasped, blinking, finally meeting his father's eyes through the haze.

"I'm here," Giuseppe said, his voice steady despite the heat. "I'm *right here.*"

The flames didn't vanish all at once. They sputtered and hissed, retreating slowly like a tide pulling back, but Chris could still feel the scorch lingering on his skin. The air cooled, and the smoke thinned as Giuseppe closed the distance, pulling Chris into a fierce, protective embrace.

"You're safe," Giuseppe whispered, voice softer now. "It's okay, son. I'm here."

Chris clung to him, his heart hammering, body still trembling. And then—everything shifted.

The burned remains flickered, dissolved into nothingness.

Darkness consumed the scene.

Chris jolted, his breath ragged, as the real world surged back into focus. The low hum of the memory retrieval machine echoed softly, the soft glow of the basement lights pressing in around them. The sudden absence of heat left him cold, his damp clothes clinging to his skin.

Giuseppe was already at the console, eyes narrowed as streams of erratic data filled the screen. The waveform patterns twisted violently, flickering with strange pulses of light that seemed to ripple like echoes of the flames.

"These readings... they're completely unstable," Giuseppe muttered, voice tense as he scanned the data.

Chris sat in the chair, still catching his breath. His hands instinctively rubbed his arms, trying to shake the phantom heat that clung to his skin.

"Dad... what *was* that?" he whispered hoarsely. "It felt *real.* I could feel the heat—smell the smoke. The fire... I—"

Giuseppe turned, his expression grave yet gentle as he spoke.

"It *was* real—at least, in a way. But not how you think." He tapped the screen. "The device reads memory impulses from the hippocampus. It reconstructs events from the patterns stored in your brain. But these… These signals are different."

Chris blinked, still trying to process the lingering fear in his chest. "Different how?"

Giuseppe hesitated for a moment, as if measuring his words carefully.

"I've theorized something for years. Something…beyond biology. The idea that memory can be tied to more than just the brain—something deeper. Something spiritual."

Chris's brow furrowed. "Spiritual? You mean like a…ghost or something?"

"Not exactly." Giuseppe shook his head. "It's what I call *spirit memory.* Think of it like… impressions left behind by the soul itself. Normally, memories stay locked in the mind, but there are cases where they linger—when the soul itself remembers pain or trauma beyond what the brain can hold."

Chris stared at the screen, watching the erratic light pulse like a heartbeat.

"But that felt too real… it didn't feel like a *memory.*"

Giuseppe nodded, voice softer. "Because it wasn't just yours. It's like—" he paused, searching for the words, "—like two sets of memories layered over each other. Two lives converging."

Chris swallowed hard.

"So, what does that make me?"

Giuseppe's face was unreadable as he finally answered, "It makes you something we've never seen before."

Chris stared at the floor, his mind tangled in the weight of everything he had just relived. The memories, the fire, the impossible truths pressing against his chest. He spoke carefully, his voice measured but fragile.

"I see," he murmured, the words barely louder than a breath.

Giuseppe studied his son, his expression torn between confusion and concern. "If you're truly from… somewhere else. A different world. A different time—" He paused, leaning closer. "How did you get here?"

Chris met his father's gaze, the truth pressing heavy in his throat. "After you died… Mom and I—" He swallowed hard. "We were lost for a long time. It felt like everything fell apart. But then… you left me something. A clue, a way to fix everything."

Giuseppe's brow furrowed. "A clue?"

Chris nodded. "A machine. It let me send my soul back in time."

Silence thickened between them, the weight of those words hanging heavy in the dimly lit lab. The hum of the memory device was the only sound, faint and rhythmic, like a heartbeat.

"You built it," Chris continued, his voice steadying. "But something went wrong. The machine—there was gunfire. It was damaged. And instead of… fixing things, I ended up somewhere else." He hesitated, then forced the words out. "I ended up in the Garden of Eden."

Giuseppe's face paled. He leaned back slightly, blinking as though he had misheard.

"The Garden of Eden?"

Chris nodded slowly. "I know it sounds impossible. But I was there. I met Adam… and Lilith."

"Lilith?" Giuseppe's expression shifted, disbelief hardening the lines of his face. "No, Chris. There was only Adam and Eve in the Garden. God protected them from Satan's temptations. That's how it was written. His divine grace shielded them."

"That's… what's different," he said. "In my world, Adam and Eve were cast out of the garden after eating from the forbidden fruit. But here…" He trailed off, his voice growing quieter. "Here, that never happened. God never stopped protecting them."

Giuseppe's eyes widened, trying to process the concept. "What you're saying… is that in your original world. Humanity was abandoned by God?"

Chris nodded. "Not abandoned, but humanity was left to deal with sin."

Giuseppe was silent, his gaze distant as he searched for answers that eluded him. "But… what about Lilith?" he asked, voice low and cautious. "There was never any mention of her. If you're right… if history was changed, was she always supposed to be there? What happened to her?"

Chris's stomach twisted. He remembered the pain in her eyes, the unnatural shadows that had consumed her. The blood and water mixing in her tears.

"I—I don't know," he admitted, shaking his head. "But she—something was wrong with her. It was like she was being controlled. And the tree—there was this fruit. It was—" He stopped, the pieces falling into place with a cold certainty.

"What fruit?" Giuseppe asked?

"The tree was destroyed." Chris said as he realized the weight of this new reality.

His voice dropped, softer now. "—Dad…in this world… you're alive. Mom's happy. I even have a sister. And there's no war. No corruption." He took a shaky breath, his voice thick with longing. "This…this has to be better. Right?"

His gaze searched his father's face, desperate for reassurance— for hope.

Giuseppe didn't answer right away. His eyes softened, but behind them, conflict brewed. Finally, he exhaled.

"I suppose so," he said, though the words felt thin.

And in that quiet, a shadow of doubt lingered.

Chris leaned back in his chair, still trying to process everything. The dim glow of the lab's instruments cast soft reflections on the walls, giving the room a calm yet charged energy. He turned to his father, his voice breaking the silence.

"So… what exactly is this school? And why all these trials? What are we really training for?"

Giuseppe set down the data pad he'd been reviewing and folded his arms, studying Chris carefully. "I'm surprised you don't remember more. But, considering your situation, I guess it's understandable. Maybe it'll all come back with time, but I'll explain it again."

He took a step closer, his voice steady but serious. "Eden Preparatory Academy isn't just the best school in the world— it's the heart of the Angel Corps. There are other schools, sure, but none like EPA. This is where the next generation of protectors are forged. And the seven houses of the Angel Corps… they're the elite, trained to face threats no ordinary soldier could withstand."

Chris frowned. "The Angel Corps? Like some kind of… army?"

Giuseppe nodded, the faintest smile touching his lips. "An army, yes—but more than that. Each of the seven houses is named after an archangel. They're not just warriors. They're scholars, protectors, and symbols of divine justice. Each captain leads a house, and I—"

"—You're the captain of Gabriel's squad," Chris finished, the pieces clicking together.

Giuseppe's smile grew. "Right. Gabriel's house values inspiration, revelation, and clarity of purpose. Each house draws strength from its patron archangel's virtues. But it's not just leadership that defines us. The Angel Corps is unique because of something even more important—soul essence."

Chris's brow furrowed. "That's the energy you all use, right? The way they… stopped the fire during my test."

Giuseppe raised his hand. With a flick of his wrist, a spark ignited at his fingertips, crackling to life like dancing threads of silver lightning. They coiled and twisted, then flowed into the nearby circuits along the workbench, causing the machinery to hum as power surged through the room. The dim glow brightened, and the air felt charged with energy.

Chris stared, wide-eyed. "That's… incredible."

Giuseppe let the sparks fade with a slight gesture. "Soul essence is the spiritual energy that exists within all living things. The trials are designed to measure not just physical and intellectual ability, but your connection to that power. The stronger your soul essence, the more capable you are of channeling it into abilities like this."

Chris nodded, still processing. "And the trials… they decide who gets into the Angel Corps?"

"Exactly. The top 1,000 move on. Only the top 100 are chosen for the Angel Corps. The rest serve in support roles—but the Houses, son, are for the best of the best."

Chris hesitated. "And… I made it in?"

Giuseppe reached for the tablet, his smile returning. "Barely. Your soul essence reading was extraordinary—thirty-seven percent, Chris. That's unheard of for a first-year student. But the other tests? Let's just say you need work."

Chris winced. "So… what rank did I get?"

Giuseppe chuckled. "900th. Last batch in."

Chris sighed, but a small grin formed despite himself. "I guess I'll take it. But… I don't think the machine actually broke. I think… I overloaded it somehow."

Giuseppe's expression shifted, a thoughtful frown replacing his amusement. "It's possible. Soul essence can surge under stress, but we'll need to keep an eye on it. If it was enough to break the machine, it's not just powerful—it's dangerous. You'll have to learn how to control it."

Before Chris could respond, soft footsteps echoed down the stairs. He turned to see his mother, Mariah, leaning sleepily against the doorway.

"What are you two still doing down here?" she murmured, rubbing her eyes. "You both have to be up for school in six hours. Whatever you're working on… it can wait. And you two missed dinner."

Giuseppe raised his hands in surrender. "You're right. We're done for tonight."

As Mariah headed back up the stairs, Giuseppe waited until she was out of earshot before leaning closer to Chris, his expression deadly serious.

"What we discovered tonight—your soul essence, the memory data—it stays between us for now. Don't tell your mother. Don't tell anyone. Not until we understand the full scope of what's really happening."

Chris met his father's gaze, feeling the weight of those words. "I won't."

The two of them ascended the stairs, the lab's hum fading behind them. Chris lingered at his bedroom door, hearing his parents whispering goodnight down the hall.

As he lay in bed, staring at the ceiling, his mind refused to

settle. The Angel Corps. Seven houses. Demons. Soul essence.
And somewhere in the back of his mind, the memory of the fire… of Eden… of Lilith.

7

First Day

Despite the late night, Chris and Giuseppe were up on time, moving through the morning in quiet efficiency. Breakfast was brief—shared glances and unspoken thoughts exchanged between bites. The memory of the night before lingered, unspoken but heavy between them.

By the time they arrived at Eden Preparatory Academy, the sun had climbed, casting a golden light across the school's grand facade. The towering structure seemed even more imposing under the morning sun, its stone walls and intricate banners catching the light as students streamed toward its entrance.

Chris followed the flow of students into the expansive

assembly hall, the sheer size of the crowd making his chest tighten. His father had already broken off, moving toward the group of captains standing in quiet authority along the sides of the room. Giuseppe caught his eye briefly, offering a subtle nod—calm, reassuring.

The hall buzzed with restless energy. Rows of neatly arranged chairs stretched toward a grand stage where seven distinct flags hung behind a long table, each marked with the facade of an archangel. Chris found his seat—his name printed clearly on a card resting atop the chair, just like every other student's.

A hush fell over the crowd as a figure stepped onto the stage. Maria, the Captain of Raphael's Squad, approached the microphone, her radiant smile effortlessly softening the tension in the room. She projected warmth, a natural calmness that settled over the sea of students like a gentle breeze.

"Good morning, Eden Prep!" Her voice echoed throughout the hall, filling the space with a vibrant energy.

The students' chatter quieted, all eyes fixed on her as she continued.

"Welcome to your first day at Eden Preparatory Academy. I'm Captain Maria, head counselor and leader of Raphael's squad. I know this might feel overwhelming—fresh faces, new spaces, a lot to take in all at once—but I want you to know that you're not alone. This is where your journey begins."

She paused, her gaze sweeping the crowd with practiced ease, as though she were speaking directly to each student individually.

"You're part of something extraordinary now. This place isn't just a school—it's where you'll grow not only in knowledge but in spirit. We will challenge you and push you beyond what you think you are capable of. But you'll also discover strength you never knew you had. And you won't be doing it alone. We're here with you every step of the way. I've got a team of incredible counselors and mentors who are ready to support you—no matter what you need."

She leaned in slightly, lowering her voice just enough to make the next words feel personal. "Now, I know what you're thinking… 'Where's my handbook?'"

A soft ripple of chuckles spread across the crowd.

"Well," Maria continued with a playful grin, "why don't you take a look under your seats?"

The room filled with the rustling sound of hundreds of students reaching under their chairs. One by one, they pulled out thick, leather-bound handbooks embossed with the words *Eden Preparatory Academy* in elegant gold lettering.

Maria nodded approvingly as the students examined their books.

"Inside these handbooks, you'll find everything you need—school rules, the code of conduct, class expectations… and yes, even a sneak peek at the cafeteria menu. I know priorities," she added with a wink, drawing a few genuine laughs from the crowd.

Her voice grew a shade more serious as she continued.

"But this handbook is more than just a guide. It holds your class schedule and, most importantly, it's tied to your progress. Guard it carefully—it's been specifically assigned to you. In four weeks, we'll reconvene for the final stage of testing. That's when we'll determine which of you will be among the final 100 students selected for one of the seven squads."

A murmur rippled through the hall, a mix of excitement and nervous energy. Chris felt his stomach tighten. Four weeks to prove himself.

Maria clasped her hands together, her smile returning as she wrapped up her speech.

"This journey won't be easy, but greatness never is. Remember: be kind. Be curious. Lean on one another. And most of all—believe in yourselves. We chose you for a reason. You've got this. And we've got you."

The room erupted in polite applause as Maria gave a final nod and stepped back from the podium. Chris clutched his handbook tighter, the weight of it feeling heavier than just the pages inside. Four weeks. One hundred spots.

He swallowed hard and reminded himself—*I made it this far. I'm not stopping now.*

The students clutched their handbooks, excitement buzzing in the air as they traced their way along the maps printed inside, searching for their first classes. Chris walked with the flow of the crowd, flipping through the crisp pages, still adjusting to the overwhelming sense of newness that seemed to cling to everything in this life.

It's real. I'm here now. Just keep going, he reminded himself, scanning his schedule. Soul Essence Strengthening first—whatever that was.

"Hey!"

Chris stopped as Sophie appeared in front of him, her familiar smile disarming yet questioning.

"What happened to you yesterday?" she asked, folding her arms.

Chris froze. His mind raced. Should he tell her the truth? No—he told his dad wouldn't share what happened. He forced a half-smile and shrugged.

"Oh, you know… Dad took me home right after everything. Wanted to work on some soul training stuff," he replied, hoping it sounded casual enough.

Sophie squinted, clearly unconvinced.

"Hmmm." She held his gaze for a beat longer before her eyes narrowed playfully. "Well, I *guess* that makes sense… considering you placed 900th. Seriously, Chris? All that training and *that's* where you ended up?"

Chris winced, even though her teasing was light.

"Hey, it was a long day," he muttered, but he couldn't help cracking a grin.

"And you know," she continued with mock dramatic flair, "Eli even scored higher than you on the written test. *Eli*, Chris! You okay? Do you need tutoring or something?"

Chris shook his head, laughing despite himself. "Alright, alright, I get it. I'll bounce back. So what's your schedule looking like?"

Sophie flipped open her handbook, scanning the neatly written list. "Soul Essence Strengthening first. Then Spiritual Guidance, Gym, and History."

Before Chris could reply, a familiar voice interrupted.

"Hey, hey! You two saving a spot for me, or what?"

Eli bounded toward them, grinning from ear to ear with his signature half-eaten granola bar clutched in one hand. Crumbs dusted the front of his shirt as he threw an arm over both their shoulders.

Chris shook his head. "Man, you always have some food, huh?"

Eli took a dramatic bite of his granola, crumbs scattering as he chewed with exaggerated enthusiasm. "Fuel, my friend. Gotta stay energized if you wanna keep up with this level of genius."

Sophie snorted. "Oh yeah, because that 60% you scored on

the written exam *definitely* makes you a genius."

Eli gasped in mock offense. "Hey! 60% is practically top tier! Plus, it was enough to place me 37th overall. What did you get again?"

Sophie smirked. "23rd. No big deal."

Chris chuckled, shaking his head. It felt... normal. Comfortable. The back-and-forth banter was strangely grounding, easing some of the tension that had followed him since the trials began.

Eli straightened up, attempting a mock-serious expression as he shoved the last bite of his granola bar into his mouth. "Alright, alright. Enough joking around. *Important question time.*" He cleared his throat, pausing for dramatic effect.

Chris and Sophie exchanged a glance, bracing for whatever nonsense was about to come next.

"What lunch did you guys get?" Eli asked, his face deadpan but the mischievous glint in his eyes giving him away.

Chris glanced down at his handbook. "Fourth."

Sophie nodded. "Same here."

"Yes! Me too!" Eli threw his hands up like he'd just won a championship. "I'm telling you, fourth lunch is *the* spot. All the cool people will be there. Us. Obviously."

Sophie rolled her eyes but grinned as Chris muttered, "Sure, Eli. Whatever you say."

"I *do* say," Eli continued, grinning. "And you're both lucky to have me there to keep things interesting."

Chris and Sophie exchanged an amused look just as the teasing eased. Sophie's smile softened, her eyes lingering on Chris for a heartbeat longer.

"I was... actually a little worried about you yesterday," she admitted, voice quieter now.

Chris offered a small, strained smile, but the ache in his chest lingered. He wished he could tell her everything—that it wasn't just exhaustion that had pulled him away, but fear. Deep, gnawing fear.

Sophie quickly caught herself, brushing it off with a laugh as she turned to Eli. "Right? We were *so* worried, weren't we?"

Eli nodded a little too enthusiastically. "Yeah, definitely! You kinda vanished on us, man. Oh—and did I mention I scored higher than you? Because that part's important."

Chris exhaled, tension easing as he let the moment slip back into lighthearted teasing.

"Yeah, yeah, thanks for the reminder," he muttered, shaking his head. He glanced at his schedule again, frowning slightly. "Looks like I don't have any classes with you, Sophie. But I do have two with this guy," he added, jabbing a thumb at Eli.

Eli recoiled dramatically. "*Twice*? I have to suffer your presence *twice a day*? Unbelievable."

Chris grinned. "Just try not to slow me down, alright?"

"Pfft. Just don't copy my work."

Sophie shook her head, smiling as she stepped back. "Good luck keeping him out of trouble, Chris. See you at lunch?"

Chris nodded. "See you then."

As Sophie disappeared into the crowd, Eli clapped his hands together. "Alright, first class… History, right? Let's get this over with."

And just like that, Chris felt like he belonged—at least a little more than the day before.

Chris stepped into his first class of the day—History—Eli trailing beside him as they both scanned the room for empty seats. The classroom was expansive, sunlight streaming in through tall windows, making the polished wooden desks almost gleam.

Chris felt that familiar buzz of first-day curiosity mixed with tension as he chose a seat near the back. Eli, of course, flopped into the chair next to him with his usual carefree energy, slouching back like he already owned the place.

Eli leaned over, voice low. "Think we'll need to take any of this seriously?"

Before Chris could respond, a tall, sharp-eyed man with silver-rimmed glasses strode into the room. His presence immediately commanded attention, and the idle conversations died down.

"Yes, you *absolutely* will," the man said, his voice firm but calm as he set a thick stack of papers on his desk.

Eli straightened a little, glancing at Chris with a sheepish grin.

The professor continued, pacing with deliberate steps as he handed out the syllabus. "It is vital to understand how we arrived here—what events shaped our world, the sacrifices made, the lessons learned—so that we may forge a wiser path forward." His voice carried weight, the kind that demanded respect.

"My name is Professor Whitney, and this is *History 101*," he announced, adjusting his glasses. "By the end of this course, you will not only understand historical events, but how they shaped the very fabric of your soul essence. We will explore the ancient texts, the chronicles of past soul warriors, and how their victories—and failures—resonate even now."

Chris flipped open the syllabus, scanning the contents: *The Origins of the Angel Corps, The Seven Houses and Their Archangels, The Age of Great Wars*. Key dates and figures jumped out at him, sparking vague fragments of memory. It was as if he'd heard these stories before, but the details were just out of reach.

Eli skimmed the pages with exaggerated boredom, leaning

back in his chair. He raised an eyebrow at Chris, who was already scribbling notes in the margins.

"Seriously? *Already* taking notes?" Eli whispered with a playful grin. "It's the first day. Chill out."

Chris shrugged, the pen moving steadily. "You know how this place works. They wouldn't hand us all this if it wasn't going to matter later."

Something about the words on the page tugged at him, as if pieces of his past were trying to break through the fog. The stories of past soul warriors, the battles fought against darkness—it wasn't just history. It *felt* personal, familiar in a way he couldn't explain.

Professor Whitney continued, "You will be tested not just on the knowledge, but on the wisdom you gain from these stories. Remember, history is not just the past—it is a mirror reflecting who you are becoming."

Chris felt the weight of those words. Maybe, just maybe, there were answers here—connections to his own fragmented past he hadn't yet uncovered.

Meanwhile, across campus in the Soul Essence Strengthening classroom, Sophie sat in the front row, posture straight, eyes locked on the instructor. This was the class she'd been looking forward to most—a chance to finally explore the potential she'd felt stirring inside her since childhood. A chance to become stronger, like the soul warriors she'd always admired.

At the front of the room, a striking woman with silver streaks in her raven-black hair paced with calm authority. Her name was Professor Selene Moretti, and her presence was as commanding as her voice—firm but not harsh, powerful yet measured.

"This class is not about raw strength," Professor Moretti

began, her gaze sweeping the room. "It is about mastery. Control. Discipline. A soul warrior's power is measured not by how much energy they wield, but how well they understand it."

Sophie nodded, scribbling rapidly in her notebook. *Soul essence resilience... aura stabilization... spiritual alignment.* Each term felt like a key unlocking something deep inside her. She drew a rough diagram of the aura channels, absorbing every word as Moretti continued.

"The exercises we'll be working on will teach you to draw out your soul energy safely. To feel it, control it. You must not force it—your soul is not a weapon to be swung wildly. It is an extension of you, a light to protect and guide."

As she spoke, Professor Moretti picked up a tablet from her desk. "Before we begin, I'll be going over attendance to familiarize myself with you all. When I call your name, please acknowledge it."

Names echoed around the room—Rowan Diaz, Mira Beckett, Caleb Cho. Finally, "Sophie Silvestri?"

Sophie blinked, her hand pausing mid-sentence. She hesitated for just a moment before raising her hand. "Here."

Professor Moretti paused, glancing up from the tablet with an almost imperceptible shift in expression. "Silvestri? As in Anastasia Silvestri?"

Whispers stirred through the class as heads turned toward Sophie. She felt her face heat up as she nodded slowly. "Yes, ma'am… she is my mother."

A hush fell over the room. Professor Moretti's face softened, her expression shifting from stern professionalism to one of quiet reverence. She set the tablet down and spoke more gently, her voice laced with genuine respect.

"Your mother was a hero," Moretti said, her words measured

but filled with emotion. "A soul warrior of extraordinary skill and heart. Her sacrifice saved countless lives. It is an honor to have you in this class."

Sophie swallowed hard, gripping her pen tighter. "Thank you," she managed, though the words felt too small for the weight they carried.

Professor Moretti nodded, her gaze lingering for a beat longer before moving back to the list. "Big shoes to fill," she added softly, the weight of those words heavier this time.

As Moretti resumed calling names, Sophie stared down at her notes, the once-exciting terms blurring under her gaze. The excitement she'd felt moments earlier now mixed with a tight ache in her chest. *Big shoes to fill.*

She forced herself to focus, setting her jaw with quiet determination. If anything, it only made her more resolved. She wasn't just her mother's daughter. She was here to prove herself—on her own terms.

Back in history class, the atmosphere felt more formal and structured. Professor Whitney, with his precise manner and crisp voice, continued outlining the class expectations. His sharp gaze swept the room as he emphasized punctuality, respect, and attention to detail—traits he made clear were essential for any student hoping to excel.

Chris sat attentively, scribbling down notes in neat bullet points as Whitney described the upcoming projects and the importance of historical context in understanding the present. He appreciated the clarity of the lesson. There was something grounding about learning how past figures had shaped the world—it gave him a sense of control, of order.

Eli, however, was anything but focused. His syllabus was already half-covered in doodles—an exaggerated sketch of

Whitney's stern expression, complete with over sized glasses and a tiny cape. He leaned over, nudging Chris and holding up his masterpiece with a smirk.

"Think he'll give me extra credit for this?" Eli whispered, barely holding back a laugh.

Chris bit the inside of his cheek to keep from laughing, shaking his head. He returned his focus to his notes, determined to take this seriously. He shot Eli a pointed glance, silently urging him to at least jot something down. Eli just shrugged and tossed his pencil onto the desk, clearly unconcerned.

Meanwhile, across campus, the energy in Sophie's Soul Essence Strengthening class was far more electric. The instructor, Professor Selene Moretti, had finished the syllabus overview and was now encouraging each student to share their goals.

Sophie sat in the front row, fingers curling around her notebook as she raised her hand.

"My goal," she said, voice steady but measured, "is to strengthen my core essence so I can protect the people around me. I want to be stronger... to live up to my potential."

Professor Moretti's eyes narrowed thoughtfully, but there was approval in her nod.

"Well said, Miss Silvestri. Strength without purpose is nothing. Remember, the power you cultivate must be rooted in service, not ambition."

Sophie nodded and began furiously scribbling notes, catching phrases like *soul alignment* and *energy flow exercises*. But beneath her calm exterior, something churned.

Stronger.

Live up to my potential.

But whose potential? Hers, or her mother's?

Her pen hesitated briefly as Professor Moretti continued. Sophie had spent her whole life hearing the stories of Anastasia Silvestri—the legendary soul warrior whose name echoed with reverence throughout Eden. But Sophie didn't feel legendary. Not yet.

Back in history, the lesson continued without incident. The bell rang, signaling the end of class. Chris packed up his notes carefully while Eli—predictably—shoved his half-doodled syllabus into his bag with a dramatic groan.

"Ugh, reading on day one? This school is ruthless."

Chris shook his head with a grin. "You'll survive."

Their next class was Soul Essence Strengthening. Chris entered the room with a mix of excitement and nerves, aware that this was the class where genuine progress would happen. Rows of students lined the mats as the instructor demonstrated a basic energy alignment technique, explaining the importance of controlling one's soul energy instead of overpowering it.

Chris watched carefully, soaking in every detail. Eli was slouching beside him, scribbling a few half-hearted notes before giving up entirely.

The instructor called for questions. Without hesitation, Chris raised his hand.

"So, when aligning energy flow, how do we know when we've hit the right balance instead of just… forcing it?"

The instructor offered a small, approving nod. "A good question. The balance should feel effortless. If there's tension, you're still trying to control it instead of guiding it. It takes practice."

Chris felt a small surge of satisfaction. He was determined to take this seriously.

Eli, however, elbowed him and whispered with a teasing grin.

"Oh great, now we're gonna get extra homework because you had to be *that* guy."

Chris chuckled but kept his focus, even as the lesson wrapped up.

By the time lunch rolled around, Chris finally felt like he was settling into this strange new life. The rhythm of the classes, the familiarity of the school—everything was starting to click into place.

Spotting Sophie near the lunch line, he wove through the crowd toward her.

"Hey," he greeted, grabbing a tray as they moved along the line. "How's your day going?"

Sophie offered a smile, but seemed more distant than usual. "Good. It's just… a lot."

"You okay?" Chris asked, his voice gentle as he noticed Sophie's distant expression.

Sophie's face brightened, her posture straightening as she snapped back to the moment. "Yeah, I'm fine," she said, her voice lighter, but not quite convincing. "I mean, I'm learning a lot." Then she narrowed her eyes at him, the spark returning. "I *hope* you've been paying attention, too. You know you need to move up in the rankings by the end of the four weeks if you want a shot at a squad, right?"

Chris nodded, forcing confidence into his voice. "Yeah, I know. Trust me, I'm locked in. I'll make it happen."

Sophie's lips curled into a grin. "Good. Because when we make it into Michael's squad, all of this will be worth it."

Chris blinked. "Wait—you want to join *Michael's* squad?"

Sophie laughed, nudging his arm playfully. "Yes! We've *definitely* talked about this before."

Chris frowned, searching his memory and coming up blank

for a second before a vague recollection surfaced. "Oh… right. I remember now," he said, trying to sound more sure of himself than he felt. "But why Michael's squad? Why not Gabriel's?"

Her expression softened, her gaze drifting upward as though picturing the idea. "I know your dad's squad is incredible, and I *respect* what they do, but Michael's squad? They're the best of the best. They lead every mission, every major operation. They're legends in the Angel Corps."

Chris followed her gaze to the massive ranking board mounted on the far wall of the cafeteria. It displayed the current rankings of every student in bold, glowing letters. Sophie's name stood proudly at **23rd**, while his own felt like a punch to the gut—**900th**, right at the bottom of the qualifying list. The gap was more than just wide—it was massive.

Sophie noticed his stare and smirked, crossing her arms. "You, sir, have *a lot* of ground to make up."

Before Chris could reply, Eli appeared out of nowhere, as usual, grinning with a half-eaten granola bar in hand. "And I, gentlemen and lady, am exactly where I *need* to be," he announced proudly.

Chris raised an eyebrow, smirking. "Oh yeah? And where's that?"

Eli wiggled his eyebrows, gesturing dramatically to the board. "37th. My personal favorite number. You're welcome." He took another exaggerated bite of his snack, crumbs clinging to his sleeve.

Chris shook his head with a laugh. "Good job, *Mr. 37th*. But you two better watch out. I'm on the hunt."

Sophie rolled her eyes but smiled. "I hope so, Chris. You two *better* take this seriously. The squads only take the best, and I'm *not* slowing down for you guys."

Chris's grin lingered as he turned back to the board, but the weight of reality pressed heavier on him this time. The difference between his score and hers wasn't just a gap—it was a chasm.

900th.

But he wasn't going to stay there.

A familiar movement caught his eye. Across the room, near the faculty section, his father, Giuseppe, stood with arms crossed, subtly nodding toward him in a silent request to come over.

Chris exhaled, rolling his shoulders back as his confidence settled. "I'll catch up, Soph. Just watch me."

And with that, he left his friends, heading toward his father, determination burning in his chest.

Giuseppe met Chris with a steady gaze, the same reassuring presence he'd always been. "How's it going so far?" he asked, his voice even.

Chris shrugged, though the tightness in his chest lingered. "It's… fine, I guess. I'm learning a lot, but—I don't know, I have so many questions."

"In time, Chris," Giuseppe said, his voice gentle but firm. "For now, focus on your classes. Keep your head down, stay focused, and don't draw too much attention to yourself."

Chris furrowed his brow. "What do you mean?"

Giuseppe's face darkened, just slightly, a trace of concern flickering in his eyes. "Vincent isn't pleased with how your score factored into the rankings. He doesn't think you should've passed the first round."

Chris felt his stomach knot, the weight of those words hitting harder than he expected. *Vincent.* The same man he'd seen in his other life. The man who had killed his father. Now, he was already watching him—already waiting for him to fail. And Sophie wanted to join *his* squad.

Giuseppe rested a hand briefly on Chris's shoulder. "Don't be alarmed. The other captains don't share his concerns. Just… stay sharp."

Chris swallowed hard and nodded. "Got it."

They exchanged a brief, silent understanding before Giuseppe returned to his place with the captains.

Chris exhaled slowly, forcing the tension in his chest to loosen. He couldn't let it get to him. Not today. Pushing the thoughts aside, he turned back toward the lunch tables, rejoining Sophie and Eli, who were halfway through their meals.

"Everything alright?" Sophie asked, raising an eyebrow as Chris slid back into his seat.

"Yeah," he replied, forcing a small smile. "Dad was just checking in."

Eli smirked, leaning in with his signature grin. "So… are we still on for after school? Up for some *unofficial* soul essence training?"

Chris hesitated. The idea of extra practice—outside of the structured classes—was exactly what he needed to improve his rank. And, if he was being honest, it didn't hurt that it meant more time with Sophie.

"Yeah, I'm in," Chris said, glancing her way. "You coming too?"

Sophie returned his look with a small smile. "Of course. Someone has to keep you two from slacking off."

Eli laughed. "Pfft. Please. I *am* the standard for greatness, thank you very much."

They chatted and joked their way through the rest of lunch, the steady hum of the cafeteria fading into the background. For a little while, things felt normal—like they belonged. But as the bell rang, signaling the next class, Chris felt that lingering tension return.

Vincent's watching me.

He shook it off. He couldn't let that fear control him.

Not today.

Chris stepped into the gym. The high ceilings stretched above him while sunlight streamed through tall windows, casting sharp reflections across the gleaming floor. Rows of training equipment lined the walls—weights, balance beams, and complex obstacle setups. The space felt both expansive and intense, a place where strength and discipline collided.

At the center stood Coach Tate, a lean, energetic man whose commanding presence filled the room. His sharp eyes scanned the students as they filed in, his arms folded across his chest. Once the last student settled, he clapped his hands; the sound echoing like a starter pistol.

"Alright, listen up," he began, pacing the front of the gym with deliberate steps. "Physical training isn't just strength—it's building your body into a vessel for soul energy. The stronger your core, stamina, and reflexes, the greater your reservoir for power. The more essence you can control, the greater your impact on the battlefield."

Chris straightened in his stance, absorbing every word as Coach Tate began outlining the day's regimen: agility drills to sharpen reflexes, core exercises for stability, and endurance circuits designed to test their limits. Each movement had a purpose. Each exercise was crafted to forge both body and spirit into a conduit for the energy they were learning to harness.

Coach Tate demonstrated with precision, moving effortlessly through a series of box jumps, plank holds, and explosive sprints, all while emphasizing proper breathing and control. Chris watched closely, memorizing the techniques and the subtle flow of energy behind each motion.

The workout was grueling but satisfying. By the time the session wrapped, Chris felt the ache in his muscles, a reminder of how far he had to go. Yet, there was a spark of pride too—proof he had taken the first step. He wiped the sweat from his face, rolling his shoulders as the students began dispersing.

Pulling out his phone, he quickly sent a message to his father. **"Going to Eli's house to train after school."**

The reply came almost instantly.

"Be safe. Pacing is as important as power. Remember that."

Chris smiled faintly, pocketing the phone as he headed toward Eli's house. Training with friends felt right. He'd improve. He had to.

The sun hung lower in the sky by the time Chris arrived at Eli's place, a modest two-story home with a wide backyard perfect for practice. Sophie was already there, standing at the door, her hair tucked behind her ear as she glanced up and greeted him with a grin.

"Took you long enough," she teased, her arms crossed.

Chris chuckled. "Had to finish being destroyed in the gym first."

The door swung open with exaggerated flair as Eli made his entrance. "Welcome, my fellow warriors," he announced with a dramatic bow, then waved them in.

Sophie smirked. "Wow. Really embracing the whole 'warrior' thing, huh?"

Chris stepped inside, taking in the cozy living room, memories stirring. He'd been here before—countless late-night study sessions and summer breaks. "Where are your parents?" he asked, glancing around.

"Oh, they're both working late," Eli replied with a mischievous grin. "So, we've got the house—and the yard—to ourselves. If we're gonna be the next generation of soul warriors, we need to put in some *real* work before they get home."

"Good," Sophie added, already rolling her shoulders as they made their way through the back door to the spacious yard. "Let's focus today. We've got four weeks to get you out of the 900s, Chris. No distractions."

Chris nodded, matching her determined gaze. He could feel it too—the need to prove himself, to rise above where he had barely scraped by.

They started with the basics, running through the techniques they'd learned earlier in class. Breath control. Grounding stances. Channeling just enough soul energy to light their hands but not overwhelm themselves. The sun dipped lower as they trained, laughter breaking out when Eli dramatically overcharged a pulse of energy, sending sparks across the grass.

"Easy there, Thunderbolt," Chris teased.

"Hey! It worked, didn't it?" Eli shot back, rubbing his hands together as the crackling energy faded.

They pushed each other—correcting forms, swapping tips, and laughing through clumsy mistakes—as the sun dipped lower in the sky. For the first time since arriving at Eden, Chris felt something rare: belonging. The constant weight of being the outsider, the gnawing need to figure everything out, eased from his shoulders, if only for a little while.

But as the training wore on, Chris slowed, a strange chill threading through the warm evening air. He paused mid-movement, his gaze drifting to the horizon. Something about the quiet—the way the light bent, the stillness in the air—set his nerves on edge.

Before he could make sense of it, a piercing chime split the calm.

Chris's phone buzzed violently in his pocket; across the yard, Eli's and Sophie's devices echoed the same harsh sound.

The laughter vanished. All three of them froze as they yanked out their phones, their screens flashing red with a bold, urgent message.

SECURITY ALERT. EDEN PREPARATORY ACADEMY LOCK DOWN. IMMINENT THREAT DETECTED.

Chris's pulse hammered as he stared at the message. "What… is this?" he murmured, his voice tight.

Sophie's face paled, her fingers trembling as she clutched her phone. "No… It can't be," she whispered, barely audible.

Eli's eyes darted between them, panic creeping in. "What?! What does it say?"

Sophie swallowed hard, her voice almost breaking. "It says… the school's under attack. There hasn't been an attack on Eden in *thirty years.*"

8

Assault

The air rippled with unnatural heat, thick with sulfur and scorched stone. Black smoke curled along the shattered gates of Eden Preparatory Academy, the once-pristine grounds now marred by war. At the threshold stood Giuseppe Cronetti, unmoving—his sword alive with crackling electricity. His sharp eyes scanned the chaos as demons slithered from the gaping rift ahead, its pulsing violet glow widening with every heartbeat.

Too many. And more still to come.

Giuseppe exhaled slowly, gripping the hilt tighter. His voice cut through the storm. "Maria—drop the veil. Vincent, hold position!"

The command echoed through the comms, clipped and firm.

Near the southern wing, Maria moved instantly. Her silver fans shimmered as she swept them outward, spinning in a circular arc. A curtain of radiant energy rippled across the school's perimeter—solidifying into a shimmering dome. The veil locked in the battlefield, sealing both allies and enemies inside.

Giuseppe stepped forward without hesitation.

A horned demon lunged through the rift, snarling. He met it mid-charge, blade flashing in a vicious arc. Lightning erupted from the edge, arcing straight through the beast's core. It disintegrated with a burst of yellow crackle and ash.

Then two more replaced it. Then five.

"Vincent, status?" Giuseppe snapped through the comm, turning to slice down another attacker.

Vincent's voice came through, edged but steady. "Eastern flank's holding for now, but the waves are accelerating. We need to close that rift."

Through the wall of smoke, Giuseppe glimpsed Vincent in motion—his blade encased in a shimmering frost-blue aura, water swirling tightly around it. One clean sweep launched a slicing current that froze a cluster of demons where they stood. His squad followed up—one wielding jets of high-pressure water, another shattering frozen forms with spear-like javelins of ice.

But the rift pulsed brighter, birthing more with every moment.

"Giuseppe!" Maria's voice cut in—tense but focused. "North wing—something's shifting near the library. The energy field's thinning. If they breach that wall—"

"I see it," Giuseppe replied, his eyes narrowing as he tracked the pattern. The flow of creatures wasn't random—they were converging.

Maria's fans whipped around her in a storm of silver. Blades of air spun outward, severing limbs and sending demons stumbling backward in spasms of black ichor. But as her path cleared, the earth trembled beneath their feet.

Something bigger was coming.

A towering shape emerged from the rift—twice the size of the others, its armor slick with obsidian mist, runes burning across its frame. The air dimmed, as if its presence swallowed light. Even from a distance, the weight of it pressed into their chests, heavy and suffocating.

Giuseppe's jaw locked. "Vincent—on me."

The real fight had begun.

The earth trembled beneath Giuseppe's boots as waves of corrupted energy surged from the widening rift. The air stank of sulfur and scorched blood. Lightning danced along the length of his blade, arcs snaking like live wires across steel.

More demons clawed free of the void—dozens, maybe more. Their forms twisted and burning, eyes glowing like coals, blackened claws scraping the stone as they shrieked into the open air. The ground itself groaned under the weight of them.

Giuseppe's voice rang out over comms, low and grim. "We'll hold the line. But if that rift stays open—we're finished."

Another demon lunged from the smoke. He cut it down in a flash, a lightning strike coiled around his swing. The creature burst into ash midair.

But the rift only flared brighter.

"Giuseppe!" Vincent's voice crackled through, clipped and strained. "We're thinning at the south wing. If there's a weakness, now's the time."

A tremor rolled underfoot.

Another wave surged—bigger, more feral.

Vincent responded fast. He drove his blade into the ground. Ice raced outward in jagged lines, climbing into a wall of solid frost that slammed up between the courtyard and the oncoming horde. The demons crashed into it with shrieks and flame, hammering against the barrier. For a breath, it held.

Then cracks appeared.

Giuseppe raised his sword to the sky. Thunder answered. He brought it down hard, unleashing a cascade of electricity that forked through the courtyard—jumping from one demon to the next in a crackling web of destruction. Burnt husks collapsed.

Still they kept coming.

"There's no end to them," Maria's voice came through, winded but steady.

Giuseppe scanned the chaos. The demons weren't lashing out blindly. They were converging—pressing harder in one direction.

He followed their pattern—then froze.

On the far hill, three figures ran hard through the smoke.

Chris. With Sophie and Eli at his side.

A surge of panic slammed into Giuseppe's chest. He crushed it.

"Vincent. Maria," he said, his voice sharp. "Hold the line."

Arcs of lightning danced around his blade, flashes casting stark silhouettes across the stone.

Chris saw his father ahead—standing resolute, a storm of frost and thunder raging around him. But as they neared the edge of battle, a choking wave of dread swept over him.

The battlefield was a nightmare.

Demons moved like crawling fire—faces warped, limbs

stretching unnaturally, some looming as towering beasts of shifting darkness. Their shrieks filled the air. Steel clashed. Fire screamed. Ice cracked. Shadows writhed.

Chris stopped cold.

This was real.

The heat pressed against him. Smoke burned his throat. Every breath felt too loud. The swirling vortex yawned wide behind the horde, its violet tendrils reaching outward like roots through reality.

I'm not ready.

A shape lunged from the haze.

Chris stumbled, heart crashing against his ribs—

But before the creature struck, a cyclone of air cleaved it apart. Maria's fans blurred past in a flash of silver.

"Chris!" Sophie grabbed his arm, her voice steady. "Look at me."

His gaze found hers. The chaos dulled for a heartbeat.

"I'm okay," he whispered. A lie—but enough to keep moving.

They reached Giuseppe as another demon collapsed behind him in a burst of lightning. He turned, eyes flaring with alarm.

"What are you doing here?" he snapped. The fear beneath his anger was clear. "You were supposed to stay home."

Sophie didn't flinch. "We couldn't. You need help."

Giuseppe looked at them—unarmed, untrained, but standing their ground.

The fight wasn't over.

And neither were they.

Another demon lunged from the smoke. Without even turning, Giuseppe slashed through it, lightning trailing behind his blade. The creature dissolved into glowing ash with a crackle.

Then the earth buckled beneath them.

Farther down the courtyard, Vincent drove his blade into the ground. Ice burst outward in jagged lines, erupting into a towering wall that slammed up between the squads and the horde. For a heartbeat, the frost held.

Then the cracks came—thin, snaking webs splintering across its face as shadowed claws pounded from the other side.

Chris found his voice. "How did this even happen?" he asked, eyes locked on the glowing rift at the center of the battlefield.

Giuseppe didn't take his eyes off the swarm. "I don't know," he said, grip tightening around his sword, lightning rippling along the edge. "But we won't survive unless we shut that thing down. Three squads aren't enough. Reinforcements are too far."

A sudden gust of wind tore through the air.

Maria cut through the haze in a blur of white and silver, her fans slicing apart a cluster of demons with pinpoint precision. They shrieked and scattered into black mist—but more took their place, the rift birthing them faster than they could fall.

She met Giuseppe's gaze across the chaos. "We can't keep this up forever!" she called, breath sharp but controlled.

Giuseppe turned to the trio—eyes sharp, voice clipped. "If you're staying, listen closely."

He pointed his sword toward the school. "Go to the library. In the spiritual archives, there's a book—"

"The vault?" Sophie cut in, her voice tight with disbelief.

Giuseppe's focus snapped to her. "Wait… how do you—" He stopped, shaking his head. "Doesn't matter. Do you know which volumes?"

"Yes."

He didn't hesitate. From his belt, he unclipped a small comm device and pressed it into her hand. "The Shadow Key is behind the second gate. That's what we need to seal the rift."

He locked eyes with her. "If you see anything—anything—don't try to fight it. Call us. Understood?"

Sophie nodded, her grip tightening around the device. Giuseppe saw the fear behind her eyes—but also the strength.

He placed a firm hand on her shoulder. "You can do this."

Chris and Eli stood close behind her. They didn't speak, but their faces told him all he needed to know.

Giuseppe stepped back, scanning the battlefield as another wave surged against Vincent's splintering barrier.

"Stick together," he said. "Get that key. We'll hold the line."

Sophie turned and ran, Chris and Eli flanking her. Their footsteps echoed across the stone, fading into the mist and fire.

Giuseppe watched until the smoke swallowed them—then turned back toward the rift.

He lifted his blade.

The lightning answered.

—

Inside Eden, the trio sprinted through ruined halls.

Walls shook under distant impacts. Light flickered. Flames licked the ceiling where battle had breached the upper levels. A screech echoed behind them—then the clash of steel, far too close.

A claw tore past Chris's shoulder, raking sparks from the stone. He ducked low, breath sharp, heart thundering.

He looked at Sophie. "How do you know about this vault? And the books—how do you even know which ones to pull?"

She kept running. "My mom told me," she said between breaths. "Every academy has a vault—hidden relics, weapons from soul warriors of the past. She never trained here, but she made me memorize the sequence for Eden, just in case."

Chris watched her eyes flick toward the shadows as they ran. Her voice was calm—but he could hear it now: the tension. The worry.

"What else is in the vault?" Eli asked, stumbling slightly but managing to keep pace. His voice was tense, a thin veil over the fear rising in his chest.

"I… I don't know," Sophie admitted, casting a glance over her shoulder as they neared the grand, arched doors of the library. "My mom never trained here—just told me the books that unlock it. Each academy has its own sequence."

They burst through the doors—and the chaos outside fell away.

The stillness inside was jarring.

The air was thick and silent, the scent of parchment mixing with distant crackling flame. Shadows danced across the shelves as flickering torchlight painted soft arcs across the high ceiling. It felt like the books themselves were holding their breath.

Chris slowed, his voice dropping to a whisper. "It feels… different here."

"Focus," Sophie said quickly. She scanned the shelves with swift precision until her eyes locked onto a familiar section: Spiritual Artifacts and Historical Relics.

"There," she pointed. "Those three—Echoes of Divine Light, The Watcher's Veil, Wells of Eternity. We pull them together."

Her voice sharpened. "On my count. Ready?"

Chris and Eli both nodded. Chris's fingers found the worn spine of his assigned book, his hand trembling slightly. Eli hesitated, then mirrored the motion.

"Three… two… one—now!"

The books slid from their shelves in unison.

Silence.

Then, the shelf rumbled.

Stone ground against stone as the entire structure split apart. Dust drifted in thin streams as a hidden doorway revealed itself—beyond it, a spiraling staircase descended into darkness. A cold draft drifted up to meet them, thick with the scent of damp stone… and something older.

Chris met Sophie's eyes. Neither of them spoke.

They descended.

—

Outside, the world was fire and storm.

Giuseppe stood firm at the shattered gates, his sword a conduit of crackling arcs that lashed across the battlefield. Demons poured from the rift—shadows wrapped in flame—and he met them with electric fury, every strike a thunderclap.

To his left, Maria was all motion and precision. Her twin fans carved through the darkness with invisible blades of air. Black ichor sprayed across the stone as demon after demon fell to her whirling dance.

On the opposite flank, Vincent moved like a glacier in motion—his blade glowing with blue fire, ice erupting in jagged bursts beneath his feet. Demons shattered against the crystal spikes, fragments scattering as his squad surged forward.

And still, the rift fed them more.

The ground shuddered as another wave surged forth. The void pulsed, tendrils of violet energy writhing like serpents in the sky.

Giuseppe lifted his sword to the heavens. A bolt of lightning split the clouds and roared downward, forking through the horde. Ash rained—but new shadows surged to take their place.

"Everyone—regroup in the courtyard!" Giuseppe's voice crackled over the comms.

Maria, Vincent, and their squads converged, forming a wide perimeter. Blood and sweat streaked their armor, but their stances were solid.

Maria wiped her cheek with the back of her hand. "We can't hold this forever."

Giuseppe's eyes locked on the rift. The pulse. The pattern.

"It's being anchored by unstable spirit energy," he said, voice clipped. "If we channel enough pure essence into the Shadow Key, we can seal the tear."

Vincent's gaze narrowed, frost clinging to his gloves. "That relic hasn't been used in years."

"It's still our best shot."

Giuseppe shifted his stance, jaw tight. "We hold this line. No breaches. Three runners are retrieving the key now—we hold until they return."

More shadows surged from the void.

"Kim! Barrier—now!"

Kim slammed her staff into the ground. Wind erupted in spiraling columns, forming a dome of compressed air around the squads. The cyclone howled, deflecting lunging demons and hurling others back in disarray.

"Matthew, lock them down!"

Veins pulsed beneath Matthew's skin as he extended both hands. A sudden weight dropped over the battlefield—demons staggered mid-sprint, crushed under a surge of gravity that warped the ground beneath them. Dust cratered upward.

"I can't hold this forever!" Matthew shouted, his voice cracking under strain.

"Then just hold it long enough!" Giuseppe roared, cleaving

through a shadow-beast that had broken free. Sparks exploded as its body shattered into smoke.

Vincent launched forward again. With a surge of power, he drove his blade deep into the frozen earth. Spires of jagged ice ripped skyward, impaling half a dozen demons at once. The shards exploded outward, catching more in the blast as his squad charged behind him.

"They're breaching the south gate!" Vincent shouted, breath curling in the cold air. "I'll reinforce it. Maria—Giuseppe—cover the east!"

Maria spun without a word, twin fans already in motion.

Giuseppe raised his blade—and lightning followed.

Maria nodded sharply, her twin fans snapping open with a metallic clink. She became a blur, the air swirling around her as a gale rose at her command. She swept her arms in wide arcs, and blades of compressed wind ripped through the charging demons, cleaving their shadowed forms apart in crisp, surgical slashes. Her movements were poetry—precise, unrelenting—her fans spinning like extensions of her will.

Giuseppe answered with force of his own. His sword surged with light as he raised it high, summoning a chain of lightning that exploded across the battlefield. The bolt danced from demon to demon in a web of burning energy. Black smoke and ash choked the air as their twisted forms disintegrated—yet still, the void pulsed.

Stronger than before.

From the heart of the rift came another surge—a tide of shadows erupting outward. A splinter of the horde broke off, their snarls rising above the chaos as they veered toward the academy's interior.

Giuseppe saw it immediately. "NO!" he barked, eyes narrowing as the breach opened.

Vincent was already moving. "I'll take them!" he shouted. Frost trailed in his wake as he surged forward, ice forming beneath his feet as he raced toward the eastern wing.

—

Far below the storm above, the catacombs were quiet—but no less tense.

Chris, Sophie, and Eli crept through the winding corridors, their footsteps muffled on cold stone. The walls were lined with ancient carvings—scenes of winged figures and burning beasts—barely lit by flickering torches that cast long shadows down the narrow path. The rumble of distant explosions echoed faintly above them, a reminder that time was running short.

Chris's chest rose and fell with steady effort. He couldn't see the battle, but he could feel it—the tremor in the walls, the pressure in the air. They pushed forward, deeper into the school's hidden vaults, hunting the one thing that might end it all: the Shadow Key.

When the corridor opened, the three of them stopped short.

A wide chamber sprawled before them, the walls lined with ancient relics resting on pedestals or sealed behind glowing wards. The light shimmered blue and silver, though some artifacts radiated darker hues—echoes of forgotten power still lingering in the air.

Eli let out a low whistle. "Okay… this is insane." He stepped toward a towering war hammer that pulsed faintly with gold light. "This thing looks like it could level a city block."

"Don't touch anything," Chris warned, keeping his voice firm. "We're not here for souvenirs."

Sophie nodded, her focus already shifting across the

chamber—until her gaze landed on a glass dome at the far end. "Wait… is that the Graviton Maul of Darius?"

Chris and Eli glanced at each other, blank.

"It can bend the weight of anything it strikes," she murmured, awestruck. "And those—" she turned to a nearby shelf "—those are the Resonance Chimes of Danielle. They manipulate soul resonance. I read about these."

Chris tried to ignore the strange pull in his chest, the way some of the artifacts stirred something unspoken in him. "We don't have time. Find the key."

Eli, predictably, had wandered again. He held up a set of green-tinted gauntlets tipped with emerald claws. "Okay, these are cool."

"Put those down!" Sophie hissed. "Those are the Verdant Claws of Geo—soul-class weapons. One wrong move and they'll drain your essence before you can blink."

Eli sighed and returned them to their pedestal. "This place is all business."

Chris pointed to the next archway. "Let's go."

They moved into the next corridor. The carvings here were different—more violent. Winged figures stood locked in battle against twisted shadows, the stone worn with age. At the end stood a door, massive and unmoving.

The three of them pushed together. Stone groaned. Dust spilled from the arch as the door finally gave way, opening into a second, smaller chamber.

At the center, on a simple pedestal, rested the Shadow Key.

It wasn't ornate. No jewels. No flare. Just a smooth, obsidian key sitting in perfect stillness.

And yet, the moment they entered, Chris felt it—like pressure on his chest, low and constant.

"This is it," Sophie whispered, stepping toward it.

Eli squinted. "That's it? After all that?" He gestured back toward the relic hall. "Feels a little underwhelming."

Chris approached slowly, extending his hand. As his fingers touched the key, a faint pulse shot through his arm. Not pain. Not heat. Just… awareness. Like the key was alive, and it had just seen him.

He lifted it.

Nothing happened.

No traps. No alarms.

Only silence.

Sophie exhaled. "We've got it. Let's move—"

A low snarl echoed from behind them.

The shadows moved.

Three demons emerged from the dark corridor—tall, skeletal, cloaked in flickering violet light. Their eyes burned. Their claws gleamed. And they stood between the trio and the exit.

Chris stepped in front of the others, instinct kicking in. "Get behind me!"

The first demon lunged.

But it never reached them.

A sharp flash of ice tore across the chamber as a blinding wave of frost erupted. The temperature dropped instantly.

Vincent stepped into the room like a force of nature, blade glowing with pale blue energy. His sword cut clean through the leaping demon. The creature shattered into frozen shards, mist curling where its body hit the ground.

The second demon charged.

Vincent extended a hand. A wall of jagged ice exploded from the ground, cutting off its path.

"GO!" he barked. His voice was ice and thunder. "Get the key to Giuseppe—NOW!"

Chris didn't hesitate. "Come on!" he shouted, bolting toward the stairs.

Sophie and Eli followed close behind, the sounds of Vincent's sword meeting the third demon echoing through the vault as they ran.

Above ground…

Giuseppe stood firm, his blade alive with crackling arcs of lightning, the hum of its power rising with each breath. Around him, the final squads held their formation—exhausted but unbroken. Beside him, Maria spun through the chaos, her twin fans carving wide arcs through the air in a final defense against the last wave of charging demons.

And then—through the smoke and dust—three figures burst from the front of the academy.

Chris led the way, his clothes scorched, breath ragged, the small black key gripped tight in his trembling hand.

"DAD! WE GOT IT!" he yelled, the sound breaking through the clamor like a flare.

Giuseppe turned. Relief flickered across his face, sharp and visible even beneath the strain of battle. "Maria! On me—NOW!"

Chris reached him, pressing the key into his father's waiting hand. The second Giuseppe took it, he dropped to one knee and thrust it into the carved socket at the base of the rift.

A shock wave pulsed through the ground.

The stone flared with radiant energy the moment the key connected—gold, violet, and blue essence erupting outward in a blinding arc.

"Everyone—now!" Giuseppe bellowed. "Channel your essence into the key!"

Around him, the captains and soul warriors reacted in unison. Hands lifted. Swords crackled. Light bloomed as essence surged from every direction—streams of fire, ice, wind, and lightning colliding into a single pillar of radiant force.

The rift screamed.

It buckled.

Reality shivered as the air popped inward, the swirling vortex shrinking violently on itself before collapsing in a final, deafening CRACK—a burst of pressure exploding outward like thunder.

The demons vanished.

The light faded.

And then… silence.

The courtyard stood still, littered with ash and scorched stone. The sky above was clear again, the corruption gone. For a moment, no one moved.

The battle was over.

9

The Archangels

A heavy silence fell over the courtyard, smoke and scorched air still clinging to the aftermath. Smoke lingered in the air, the scent of ozone and scorched earth mingling with the fading heat of battle. Chris, Sophie, and Eli stumbled back into the courtyard, dust clinging to their skin. They exchanged wordless glances as they dusted themselves off, adrenaline still coursing through their veins.

Maria, her fans tucked at her sides, stepped forward from the circle of warriors, scanning the surrounding faces. Her sharp eyes landed on the trio. "Is everyone okay?" she called, voice gentle but commanding as she tried to account for the aftermath.

Before anyone could answer, Vincent emerged from the school, his ice-coated sword lowered but still clutched tightly in his grip, the frost steaming off its edges. His steps were slower than usual, his uniform singed and torn, his expression hard to read beneath the pale, grim mask of exhaustion.

"Captain Vincent!" Sophie called out, her voice cracking slightly with worry as she took a step forward. "Are you alright?"

Vincent barely acknowledged her, his gaze lingering on Chris, brow furrowing as he finally spoke, his voice low.

"What... what were you doing down there?" he muttered, confusion bleeding into frustration.

Chris opened his mouth to respond, but Sophie spoke first, standing straighter despite the tension in the air. "We went to get the key," she said, voice steady but cautious, as though bracing for his reaction.

Vincent's expression darkened. He shook his head slowly, eyes narrowing as his lips pressed into a hard line. "This isn't a game," he snapped, the sharpness of his voice cutting through the fragile calm. "One wrong move, and none of us would be standing here right now."

Chris stepped forward, his fists clenched at his sides, still breathless but unwilling to back down. "My father sent us," he said firmly, voice carrying over the hushed courtyard. "We got the key. We did what we—"

"Giuseppe." Vincent's voice cut him off, colder now, venom laced in his tone as his head snapped toward Chris's father. His glare was sharp enough to cut. "You *always* think you know best. Sending three untrained kids into the vault—risking *everything.*" Chris's chest tightened. He wanted to shout back, to defend his father, but the tension crackling between the captains froze him in place. Vincent's voice dropped lower, almost a growl as his hands curled into fists. "Even revealing the existence of the vault to them… What were you thinking?"

Giuseppe, who had stayed quiet until now, met Vincent's gaze with a calm, unreadable expression. The static hum of fading electricity still crackled faintly around him, but he didn't flinch under Vincent's scrutiny.

"We did what was necessary," Giuseppe replied evenly. "The rift is closed. The school is safe."

Vincent's glare didn't waver. He seemed to wrestle with words left unsaid, the tension between the two men crackling like the remnants of the battle itself. Finally, he exhaled sharply, turning his head away, as if releasing some invisible weight.

"It's fine," he muttered, voice quieter now, more to himself than anyone else. "The demons are gone. The school… is safe."

But Chris saw it—the way Vincent's hand tightened briefly around his sword before he sheathed it. The way his shoulders remained stiff, as though braced for a blow that never came.

"That's the man you want as your captain?" Chris muttered under his breath, his voice sharp as he glanced toward Sophie.

Before she could respond, Maria exhaled a long, steady breath. The tension in her shoulders melted away as the shimmering veil she had cast around the academy dissolved into the air. The energy that had lingered, crackling and heavy, finally lifted. For the first time since the battle began, a fragile calm settled over the battered courtyard.

The squads, drained from the relentless fight, sank onto the charred grass or leaned against the damaged stone walls, their breaths ragged and heavy. Smoke still curled from the scorched earth, and the remnants of battle lingered like an ache in the air. But the victory felt thin—brittle—like the quiet could break at the slightest disturbance.

Vincent stood apart, his blade sheathed but his expression still hard, intense. His eyes, narrow and sharp, locked onto Giuseppe, who was wiping soot from his hands, visibly worn but composed.

"Giuseppe," Vincent called, his voice cutting through the silence like a blade. "Do you know why the rift appeared?"

Giuseppe looked up, his expression unreadable as he dusted ash from his palms. "No," he replied evenly, though there was an undertone of tension. "I'll need time to investigate."

Vincent's face twisted, disbelief flickering across his features as he took a step forward. "Right. Just like you needed time to investigate your son's little 'incident' with the testing pod." His voice dropped, low but sharp enough to slice through the air. "Tell me, Giuseppe, how does your son nearly burn down academy equipment without so much as a consequence?"

Chris, standing nearby, felt those words pierce deeper than he expected. His face grew hot with anger, fists curling at his sides. Sophie noticed and pressed a gentle hand to his shoulder, grounding him with a firm but silent reassurance.

"First, he nearly destroys an advanced piece of technology," Vincent continued, voice cold and cutting. "And not even a day later—this?" He gestured to the broken walls, the still-smoldering wreckage.

Chris's fists tightened further, but before he could speak, Eli stepped beside him, placing a steadying hand on his other shoulder.

Maria, her usual calm touched with steel, stepped forward then, her gaze sweeping over both men. "Enough." Her voice was sharp but controlled, cutting through the rising tension like a blade. "We investigated the incident thoroughly. There was no evidence of Chris tampering with the machine." She turned toward Vincent, her words measured but unwavering. "Pointing fingers won't bring us answers, Vincent. We're all shaken—but fighting amongst ourselves won't explain why the rift opened. It won't help us protect this school."

Vincent's jaw tightened, the frost still lingering in his breath as his arms crossed firmly over his chest. His glare didn't soften, lingering on Chris like an accusation he refused to release.

Chris felt the weight of it—the silent stares creeping from some of the other warriors, as if they had planted the seeds of doubt. Low murmurs rippled through the exhausted crowd, whispers fed by adrenaline and uncertainty.

The heat rising in Chris's chest threatened to boil over. He opened his mouth to speak—but before he could, a voice boomed from above. A voice so commanding, so powerful, it seemed to shake the very foundation beneath their feet.

"Silence!"

The word shattered the tension like a crack of thunder, echoing through the courtyard with such force that the very air seemed to tremble. Silence fell instantly, every whisper and murmur extinguished as the sound reverberated, pressing down on the gathered warriors with an undeniable weight.

Heads turned skyward. The clouds, once heavy with the aftermath of battle, began to shift and part, revealing a radiant, otherworldly light. It wasn't harsh but pure, a glow so brilliant it painted the wounded sky in hues of gold and white. A presence filled the air—powerful, unyielding, yet calm—its gravity impossible to ignore.

Descending from the heavens, seven figures emerged, cloaked in radiant armor that shimmered like living stars. Their majestic wings unfurled, vast and flawless, catching the light as they descended with grace that defied the storm-ravaged earth below.

The archangels.

At the forefront was Michael, his massive sword crackling with divine energy, every step exuding authority. His gaze, sharp as a blade, swept over the crowd with piercing intensity. At his side was Raphael, his wings nearly translucent, casting a soothing, gentle glow that softened the harsh edges of the battlefield. Gabriel held a gleaming silver horn in his hands, his face calm yet firm, the weight of divine purpose evident in his steady presence.

Uriel followed, eyes glowing like twin galaxies, his expression filled with profound wisdom. Sariel moved with quiet grace, her presence steady and unwavering. Raguel, towering with a palpable sense of justice, watched the crowd as though weighing every soul present. And finally, Remiel, calm yet radiating strength, stood with his arms crossed, his gaze both protective and watchful.

Chris felt his knees weaken. He took a half-step back, breath catching in his throat. The weight of their presence was unbearable yet awe-inspiring, pressing against his very spirit. He felt so small—so mortal.

"They're... they're really here," Eli whispered, his voice almost inaudible.

Chris swallowed hard, eyes wide with disbelief. "Is that...?"

Sophie's hand tightened around his, grounding him as she stared upward, her own wonder mirrored in her eyes. "The archangels... all of them," she whispered, voice trembling with reverence.

The sheer magnitude of the moment pressed down on everyone. The archangels weren't just legends—there they stood, the divine guardians who shaped the very foundation of the academy and the realms beyond. Their presence was overwhelming, both beautiful and terrifying—a reminder of the cosmic forces governing not only their school but existence itself.

Maria bowed her head slightly, her shoulders tense but deferential. Giuseppe straightened, his usual confidence tempered with humility in the face of such divine authority. Even Vincent, who moments earlier had been consumed with barely restrained anger, now seemed subdued, his icy glare melting into something quieter, more uncertain.

As the archangels reached the ground, the heavenly radiance softened, yet the power they exuded did not diminish. They stood before the gathered warriors in perfect formation, unmoving yet undeniably commanding. Michael stepped forward, his armor glinting in the fading light, the electricity still faintly crackling along the edges of his blade.

When he spoke, his voice was as steady as the earth itself, deep and resonant, each word carrying the weight of divine judgment and purpose.

"You have endured," Michael said, his gaze sweeping over the scorched courtyard, the battle-weary warriors, the broken walls. "But this battle has left questions. And questions demand answers."

Chris felt his legs tremble beneath him, like the sound alone had weight. The students and squad leaders of Eden Preparatory Academy leaned in unconsciously, as if drawn toward his voice, compelled by something far greater than mere mortal authority.

Chris, still clutching Sophie's hand, felt the weight of Michael's gaze pass over him. He couldn't tell if it lingered for longer than anyone else, but the sensation made his chest tighten all the same.

A ripple of unease passed through the gathered warriors, the weight of Michael's words pressing heavily on every soul present. No one dared speak. The authority in his voice was not just commanding—it was absolute. The lingering echoes of battle still hung in the air, but the divine presence of the archangels made the chaos feel distant, insignificant compared to what loomed now.

Michael's gaze swept across the courtyard, his stern expression unyielding as he continued, "Though the academy's defenses held, one truth troubles us deeply. This breach—this invasion—should have been impossible."

The tension in his voice was palpable, and as his words settled, a murmur of disbelief rippled through the crowd. Students exchanged nervous glances, warriors shifted uneasily, yet none dared speak aloud. The rifts weren't just an attack; they violated the natural order.

Michael raised his hand—just a simple gesture—and the murmurs ceased instantly, as though the air itself had obeyed him.

"We, the archangels," he continued, voice unwavering, "will personally investigate how this rift was torn open. We will search the realms, interrogate the barriers between worlds, and seek the truth wherever it hides. You must trust that no effort will be spared to ensure this threat is understood… and eliminated."

A heavy silence followed, broken only by the distant crackle of lingering elemental energy in the ruined courtyard. Then, Michael's gaze shifted, softening as it fell upon the younger soul warriors, the students still raw from the ordeal yet standing firm. His voice lost none of its power, but the harshness eased, replaced by a commanding compassion.

"But you—warriors of Eden—your purpose remains unchanged. Your duty is to grow stronger, to sharpen your skills, to prepare yourselves for what lies ahead. The defenses you hold are not only for this academy, not only for yourselves, but for those who cannot stand against this darkness. You are the shield for the innocent, the light against the void."

Chris felt those words settle deep within him, a weight both terrifying and empowering. He gripped Sophie's hand just a little tighter, feeling her pulse steady against his own. Around them, the other students stood straighter, absorbing the gravity of the moment, the responsibility being placed on them.

Michael's gaze shifted once more, this time landing on Giuseppe, Maria, and Vincent, lingering for a heartbeat longer than the others. His expression was both a challenge and a warning, as if urging them not to forget the roles they played— guardians, not just of the students but of the realms themselves.

"Captains," he said, voice cutting through the tension like a blade, "remember the charge you bear. You have been entrusted with far more than the lives under your command. You guard the balance between worlds. Your choices, your leadership, may determine whether that balance holds—or crumbles."

Chris could feel the gravity of those words, but it wasn't just directed at the captains. He saw how the surrounding warriors straightened, the message clear. They were all part of something greater, and the consequences of failure extended far beyond their own lives.

Michael took a single step forward, and the air itself seemed to hum with divine energy. His voice deepened, resonant with both warning and strength.

"Make no mistake—this was only the beginning. The rift was but a test. We cannot yet know the full extent of the danger you face, but we fear another assault is not only possible… but imminent. And should they return, they may come in force greater than you have ever known."

The words settled over the courtyard like a heavy storm. Yet, beneath the fear they evoked, there was something else—resolve. Power. Michael was not just warning them; he was calling them to rise.

"Stay vigilant," Michael concluded, his voice echoing like a solemn oath. "Stand together. Fight as one. And know this—so long as your spirits remain unshaken, as long as you hold to the light, we—the archangels—will stand with you."

The finality in his words seemed to vibrate through the very earth, leaving a profound stillness in its wake. For a moment, no one spoke, no one moved. It felt as though the entire academy had drawn a collective breath, absorbing every word as a sacred commandment.

Chris felt something stir deep within his chest, a weight he hadn't noticed before. But it wasn't fear anymore. It was something heavier. Purpose.

The archangels remained a moment longer, their presence both comforting and immense. Then Michael gave a single nod, turning toward the captains.

"Captains report to the chambers for debriefing. The rest of you—go home. Rest. And return stronger tomorrow."

The gathered warriors dispersed, the divine presence lifting but leaving its mark on everyone who had witnessed it. Chris exhaled a breath he hadn't realized he was holding as his father approached him.

Giuseppe's face was calm, but the tension in his eyes hadn't quite faded. He placed a hand on Chris's shoulder, voice quieter now. "Go Chris. I'll join you soon."

Chris nodded, sharing a brief, meaningful glance with Sophie and Eli before stepping away. The battle was over—but something far greater had just begun.

The academy grounds were quiet as Chris, Sophie, and Eli made their way through the lingering twilight. The air was crisp, carrying the scent of pine from the trees that bordered the school. An unspoken heaviness lingered in the air, a result of the echoes of the battle, the archangels' words, and the sheer weight of what they had just witnessed.

For a few long minutes, they simply walked, each lost in their own thoughts, until Eli finally broke the silence.

"Can you believe we met the archangels on our first day of school?" he said, still sounding awestruck. Reaching into his jacket pocket, he fished out a strip of beef jerky and tore off a bite, chewing thoughtfully.

Chris nodded slowly, still processing it all, but Sophie glanced over with a knowing expression. "You know they weren't really *here*, right?"

Chris raised an eyebrow, glancing between them. "Wait—what do you mean?"

Sophie tucked a strand of hair behind her ear, her voice calm but measured. "That wasn't them physically. It was a projection—a message, basically. The archangels can't appear on Earth unless certain… conditions are met."

"What kind of conditions?" Chris asked, curiosity sharpening as he tried to recall what he'd learned about angelic intervention. His mind felt cluttered, pieces of knowledge just out of reach, yet familiar.

Sophie's expression darkened slightly, her voice softening.

"For an archangel to manifest here, there has to be an upper-level demon present. It's about balance. If darkness becomes too strong in one realm, only then can divine power step in. They can't intervene unless the threat meets that level—otherwise, the balance would shift too far in the other direction."

Chris nodded, the fragments of memory beginning to surface. He had heard that before—or at least, it felt like he had. It was hard to tell anymore.

Eli, however, frowned, his usual grin replaced with a scowl. He kicked a loose pebble across the path and shook his head. "So what? They show up *only* when things get that bad? Seems kinda convenient for them. If they wanted to, they could've wiped out that entire invasion in seconds."

Sophie sighed, but her voice remained calm. "It's not about convenience, Eli. It's about the natural order. Too much light would be just as dangerous as too much darkness. The archangels keep balance—they're not supposed to fight our battles *for* us."

Eli made a skeptical noise, stuffing the rest of his jerky back into his pocket. He stared up at the sky where the last remnants of daylight faded, replaced by a vast stretch of stars twinkling faintly in the deepening dusk. "Still feels like they could've done *a little* more," he muttered. "Balance or not, we were pretty close to getting wiped out back there."

Chris smirked faintly at his friend's grumbling but felt the same lingering discomfort. He didn't voice it, though. There was already enough tension without questioning divine beings out loud.

They finally reached Eli's house, a cozy two-story nestled just off the academy's grounds. The porch light flickered on as they approached.

"Well," Eli said, hands in his pockets. "If the world ends again tomorrow, I call dibs on being the one who naps through it." He flashed them a grin, but it didn't quite reach his eyes. "Goodnight, guys."

"Night, Eli," Chris and Sophie said in unison before turning back down the path together.

The quiet returned as they walked along the dimly lit street, the stars above growing brighter with each step. Chris's mind drifted, trying to untangle the strange sense of familiarity pressing in on him. This place, this moment—it felt like it had happened before, though he couldn't explain why. He looked at Sophie, and a stray memory clicked into place.

She's my neighbor. How did I forget that?

Sophie walked with her arms crossed, her expression distant, like she was turning over the events of the day in her head. But after a few more steps, she glanced his way, clearly noticing his silence.

"Are you okay?" she asked softly.

Chris blinked, shaken from his thoughts. "Oh. Yeah. I'm fine," he said, though even as the words left his mouth, he wasn't sure he believed them.

Sophie didn't press, but the quiet that followed felt heavier now, more awkward than reflective. Chris risked a glance at her, wondering why the silence felt so strange. He never thought it would be uncomfortable being alone with her—so why now?

Clearing his throat, he asked, "What about you? You okay?"

Sophie nodded, though her face tightened for a moment. "Yeah. Just… ready to tell my dad everything that happened today."

They continued walking in silence until Sophie suddenly

stopped, eyes narrowing. She turned toward him, realization dawning as her brow furrowed.

"Wait a second," she said, her voice sharp but playful. "You were the one who set that testing pod on fire yesterday, weren't you? When exactly were you planning to tell me that?"

Chris felt his face heat, and he stammered, "Uh… well—yeah, but it's—it's complicated—"

Sophie crossed her arms, tilting her head with a sly smile. "Oh, we *definitely* have time for complicated. We've got, what, ten minutes left on this walk? Start talking."

Chris sighed, rubbing the back of his neck with a sheepish grin. "Alright, alright… So, you remember the machine malfunctioning, right?"

"Oh, please," Sophie teased. "The entire school heard about *that*. Spill."

Chris hesitated, his mind racing. He couldn't tell her everything—not yet—but he knew Sophie too well to offer a half-truth. She wasn't someone who accepted vague answers, not when her trust was involved. Especially after Vincent's accusations, the last thing Chris wanted was to let suspicion linger between them.

He glanced at her, the way she stood there, waiting with her arms crossed, her expression steady yet concerned. Memories of their childhood surfaced—moments of laughter and playful dares, how she was always the one to look out for him when things got tough. He remembered how, when he had nothing, she'd slipped him spare change without a word, acting like it was no big deal. That unwavering loyalty pressed against the knot in his chest.

Finally, he exhaled. "Sophie… Can I trust you?"

Her eyes widened for a moment before softening, her lips

curving into a small, reassuring smile. "Of course, Chris. Don't get a big head or anything, but you're my best friend." She tilted her head, her voice growing gentler. "If you can't trust me, then I'm clearly failing as a friend."

Chris felt the tension ease slightly, a faint smile tugging at the corner of his lips. He nodded and walked a few steps ahead, pausing beside a weathered wooden bench tucked along the academy's garden path. The lantern lights overhead cast a warm glow, flickering gently in the breeze as he sat down heavily. After a moment of hesitation, Sophie joined him, concern still etched into her features.

She watched him closely, speaking softly. "Chris... I trust you. Whatever it is, just tell me. But you've been acting differently lately. Distant. I'm starting to feel like you're carrying the weight of the world alone. So, please... What's going on? Are you really okay?"

Her words hit harder than Chris expected. He stared down at the ground beneath his feet, struggling to find the right words. He wanted to trust her—he *did* trust her—but the truth felt so heavy, so impossible to explain.

He clenched his fists, jaw tightening. "Promise me—do *not* tell anyone what I'm about to say. Swear it."

Sophie's teasing smile disappeared, her posture straightening as she nodded, deadly serious. "I swear."

Chris took a breath, then began speaking. Slowly at first, but the words soon tumbled out in a flood. He told her everything. About the world he came from, the ruins it had become. About her—*their* friendship from that lost timeline. His father's death at Vincent's hands. The mysterious machine that had sent his soul back in time. He spoke of meeting Adam, the strange encounter with Lilith, and how he had awoken here, in a world where everything was… different. Where his father was alive. Where Sophie was beside him once again.

By the time he finished, the weight in his chest felt both heavier and lighter, as if he'd unburdened himself but left behind raw vulnerability in its place. "My father told me not to tell anyone," he admitted quietly. "But… I *had* to tell you."

Sophie sat silently, absorbing it all, her brow furrowed as she pieced everything together. "Wow," she whispered after a long pause. "Give me a minute… that's a lot."

Chris nodded, heart pounding. He braced himself for disbelief, for questions—anything except the calm, thoughtful expression she gave him next.

"So… the rifts," she said slowly, her mind already working. "You think they're connected to all this?"

Chris blinked, thrown off. "*That's* your first question? Not… 'You're insane, Chris'? Or 'You've lost your mind'? That's what you're stuck on? Not the fact that I pretty much created this whole world?"

She shook her head, a small smirk playing on her lips, but there was understanding behind it. "I'm not saying I get all of it. But you're not the type to make something like this up."

Chris exhaled, relief flooding him, but Sophie wasn't finished.

"Look, I don't know how all this works—timelines, time machines, other worlds… But the fact is, the rift opened. If all of that is true, then the world's already made and we're dealing with real problems here, problems that could destroy it all. That's my priority right now. you being here, all of this… it *has* to be connected. That's what matters. We need to figure this out before someone else gets hurt."

He nodded, his pulse slowing for the first time all night. "I don't know if I caused it, but… I can't let this world end up like the last one."

Sophie placed a hand gently on his shoulder, grounding him. "WE won't let that happen. And you're not facing this alone, Chris. You have me. You have Eli. Your dad. The Angel Corps. We'll figure this out together."

Her words grounded him more than any lesson or battle could have. For the first time since the attack, the chaos inside his mind finally quieted.

Sophie shifted on her feet, her gaze dropping for a moment as she searched for the right words. The cool night air felt heavier in the quiet between them, the distant rustle of leaves the only sound. Finally, she broke the silence, her voice soft but sincere.

"Hey… I'm glad you told me. I mean it."

Chris exhaled, shoulders loosening as some of the tension drained from his chest. He met her eyes, the flicker of uncertainty he'd been carrying since the conversation started finally easing. "Yeah… I'm glad I did too," he replied, voice almost a whisper.

They had stopped in front of their houses now, the warm porch lights casting gentle pools of yellow across the street. For a moment, neither moved. The quiet between them shifted— not uncomfortable, but charged with the weight of everything they'd shared that night.

Then, almost at the same time, they both leaned in for a hug. It was a little clumsy, both unsure of how much to give or take, but there was comfort in the closeness. The kind of quiet support that didn't need words.

When they pulled back, Sophie offered a small, shy smile. Chris mirrored it, his heart still racing for reasons he couldn't quite explain.

"Goodnight, Chris."

"Goodnight, Sophie."

They lingered, just for a second longer, before finally turning toward their homes. The sound of retreating footsteps was soft, but the feeling of that hug lingered—like a quiet promise, unspoken but understood.

The grand chamber was cloaked in solemn light, the presence of the seven archangels radiating both authority and reverence as they stood before the gathered captains. The ethereal glow emanating from their wings bathed the ancient stone walls of Eden Academy's council hall in a soft, divine luminance. The battle was over, but the tension had not lifted.

Michael spoke first, his voice echoing with unwavering command. "You fought valiantly today. The Academy stands because of your courage. However, the threat has not passed. The patterns of the demons' movements suggest they were drawn here—called, not by chance."

The captains exchanged uncertain glances. Giuseppe's brow furrowed, Maria folded her arms with a pensive frown, and Vincent remained stone-faced, his gaze fixed on the archangels.

Raphael stepped forward, his expression gentler but no less serious. "We cannot yet determine what they were seeking. The void energy surrounding the rift makes it difficult to trace the source of their attraction. Yet, their focus on the academy grounds was… deliberate. Whatever called them, it remains unidentified."

Gabriel, standing silently until now, raised his voice, resonant and calm. "You must remain vigilant. This attack was not a random surge. If they were drawn here, they may return. And next time, they may come with greater numbers or stronger intent."

The doors of the chamber opened, and the remaining

captains—Jeffrey, Nyla, Mei, and Omari—entered. Michael acknowledged their arrival with a nod before continuing.

"The demons' patterns of movement imply they were searching for something—or someone—but we cannot confirm what it was. Until we understand, all of you must assume that Eden Preparatory Academy remains a target. Reinforce your wards. Strengthen your defenses. And, above all, be ready for the unknown. We will continue to investigate from the celestial realms, but until answers reveal themselves, you are Earth's first line of defense. Do not let your guard fall."

The captains bowed their heads in silent acknowledgment as the light surrounding the archangels intensified. With a final flash of brilliance, they ascended, disappearing in a cascade of divine light, leaving the captains alone in the chamber.

The heavy silence lingered, broken only by the faint crackle of the extinguished portal's energy fading into nothingness.

Vincent was the first to speak, his voice low and tight. "Thirty years, Giuseppe. You remember what happened back then, don't you?"

Giuseppe exhaled slowly, meeting his gaze. "I remember."

Vincent's fists curled at his sides. "Then you know what this filth is capable of. And yet you're keeping secrets. What are you hiding? What is it you refuse to tell us?"

Maria stepped between them, her expression calm but firm. "Vincent, stop. Pointing fingers solve nothing. We need answers, not accusations."

Jeffrey, arms crossed, added quietly, "Maria's right. This is no time for infighting. We need to work together."

Vincent's glare shifted from Giuseppe to Maria, his voice sharp. "I won't apologize for wanting the truth. You may trust him without question, but I don't. Not anymore. And that boy of his—"

Giuseppe's expression hardened, but before he could speak, Nyla's voice, calm and measured, cut through. "Vincent, enough. Whatever this was, it was beyond any one of us. Speculation isn't going to help us be ready for what's next."

Mei nodded. "We will keep a close eye on Chris and his development to see if there's any credence to your words, Vincent, but for now, we need to remain united."

For a long moment, Vincent held his ground, but then, with a bitter exhale, he turned sharply on his heel. "Fine. But don't think for a second I won't be watching him either."

The chamber door closed behind him with a resounding thud, leaving only Maria, Giuseppe, and the other captains standing in the aftermath. Maria let out a long breath, running a hand through her hair as she cast Giuseppe a weary look.

"You know how he gets," she murmured softly.

Giuseppe nodded, his face lined with the strain of the day. "He has his reasons. But we'll get through this. We always do."

She offered a small, tired smile before nodding. "Get some rest, Giuseppe. We've got a long road ahead."

"You too, Maria. Goodnight."

They parted in silence, the weight of the battle and the unanswered questions pressing heavily on all their hearts as they disappeared into the shadows of the academy, the echoes of the archangels' warnings lingering like a distant drumbeat.

10

Next Four Weeks

The sun had barely risen, casting pale streaks of gold through the tall windows of Eden Preparatory Academy's grand assembly hall. The morning light did little to lift the heaviness that hung in the room—shadows clung to the walls, stubborn and unmoved. Students filtered in slowly, some with arms in slings or bandages wrapped around shoulders, eyes dulled with fatigue. The murmurs were quieter today, tinged with unease. Not just from the attack—but from something else.

The doors shut behind the last arrivals. Silence settled.

At the front of the hall stood Vincent. The light behind him turned his figure into a sharp silhouette, tall and cold. His cloak, normally immaculate, bore signs of wear, its edges faintly dusted in ash. The usual shimmer of frost that clung to his soul essence was gone, replaced with something heavier. Still. The expression on his face was unreadable, but his eyes… something had changed. A distant glint sat there now—cold, fixed, and unreachable.

He raised his hand, and the murmurs dissolved instantly.

"Yesterday," he began, voice low but commanding, "Eden Preparatory Academy—our sanctuary, our home—faced an assault unlike any in the last thirty years. We stood on the brink of ruin. But we did not fall."

His words echoed in the stillness like a slow-moving blade.

"Some will see this attack as a sign of vulnerability," he said, eyes scanning the sea of pale, anxious faces. He lingered on the first-years, many still clutching their handbooks like lifelines. "But we are not weak. We endured. And now, we rise."

Vincent began to pace, slow and deliberate. His boots echoed against the stone floor, each step casting long shadows that reached across the room.

"This breach was not an accident. The demons were drawn here. Their movements were not random—they were searching. For something… or someone. And that means we must be prepared. Stronger. Sharper."

A quiet ripple spread through the rows. Glances exchanged. Some cast eyes toward the empty seats—two in the far left row, one in the back corner—left untouched since the night of the attack.

Vincent stopped. His gaze sharpened.

"We cannot depend on divine intervention forever. The power to defend this academy must come from us. From you."

He let the words sink in.

"Strength is not born from waiting for salvation. Strength is forged in hardship. And sacrifice…" His fingers twitched at his side. "…is sometimes necessary."

No one spoke. Somewhere in the back, a quiet sniffle broke the silence.

"We will rebuild. Piece by piece. And we will not return to what we were. No—we will become more. Unbreakable. Reevaluations will proceed as scheduled. The next generation of soul warriors will rise—and they will be ready."

His voice dropped into a near whisper, yet every student leaned in instinctively.

"You must be ready. All of you. Because next time…" His eyes dimmed. "We won't just survive. We will crush it."

Silence. Deep and solemn.

Vincent exhaled softly, a subtle crack in his cold composure, then returned to stillness. "You are dismissed. Remember: unity is strength. And strength will be what keeps us alive."

Eli found him near the back, breaking through the fog in his head.

"Hey, Chris!" he said, sliding in beside him with a grin. "So… how was your walk with Sophie last night?"

Chris blinked, caught off guard. "What do you mean?" he asked, forcing casualness into his voice.

Eli smirked. "Come on, man. Don't play dumb. I saw you two talking after lights out. Pretty sure the stars weren't the only things glowing."

Chris shook his head, trying not to laugh. "Okay, okay. What exactly do you think you saw?"

Eli leaned in. "I think you've had a thing for Sophie since the first grade. And I think—" he grinned wider, "—she definitely likes you back. So… what's the holdup?"

Chris flushed and waved him off. "We're just friends. She doesn't see me like that."

Eli tilted his head with exaggerated disbelief. "Wow. For someone so smart, you're incredibly dense."

Chris gave him a look. "And how exactly are you planning to 'help' me?"

"Oh, it's simple. I set you up. You fall madly in love. Happily ever after. Boom. I'm a genius."

Chris's eyes widened. "Please don't."

Eli grinned. "Relax. I won't say a word. For now."

Before Chris could argue further, Sophie approached, catching just enough to be suspicious.

"Won't say what?" she asked, crossing her arms as she eyed them.

Chris fumbled. "Uh… what we thought about Vincent's speech."

She raised a brow, unconvinced but amused. "Right. So, what did we think?"

Chris sobered. "It was fine. But… I still don't understand why you'd want to join his squad. I know they're elite, but reporting to him? I couldn't do it."

Sophie's smile faded. Her thoughts turned inward, the weight of Chris's confession from the night before still fresh in her mind.

"I understand," she said quietly, her voice distant.

Eli sensed the shift and, as always, deflected. "Okay, how about this—we train after school. No demon invasions. No collapsing buildings. Just old-school sweat and effort."

Sophie brightened slightly. "Sounds good. I'll see you both at lunch?"

Chris nodded. "Definitely."

As she walked away, Eli leaned in again. "So… did I make it weird?"

Chris chuckled. "No, that was all me."

They shared a knowing grin and made their way down the hallway, ready to face the day.

The next four weeks at Eden Preparatory Academy passed in a relentless blur, each day sharpening Chris, Sophie, and Eli through the crucible of training. Mornings were consumed by lectures on soul essence—how emotions shaped power, both light and dark—while afternoons pushed their bodies and minds to the brink. They studied the seven corruptions— hatred, anger, greed, anxiety, fear, jealousy, and disgust— alongside the virtues meant to combat them: love, peace, charity, serenity, courage, kindness, and trust.

Chris trained with raw determination but struggled with control. During a sparring session, he overextended, unleashing a burst of energy that ricocheted wildly and knocked over half the training dummies. "You have the strength," the instructor said firmly, helping him to his feet. "But strength without focus is just destruction. Control your mind, and your power will follow."

Outside the classroom, he trained privately with his father. Giuseppe led him through visualization techniques, urging him to imagine his soul essence as a calm, flowing river rather than a raging storm—steady, controlled, powerful beneath the surface. But impatience lingered. One evening, after a failed focus exercise scorched the stone floor, Chris clenched his fists in frustration. "I'm trying! Why isn't this working?"

Giuseppe's voice was steady. "Because you're trying to force it. Power reflects the state of your heart, Chris. Find clarity within yourself, and your strength will become steady."

Meanwhile, Eli coasted on athletic talent, breezing through physical trials but often hamstrung by his own desire to seem effortless. During a soul energy channeling exercise, he smirked and half-heartedly went through the motions, causing his energy to sputter out mid-task. "This stuff is so boring," he muttered—until the instructor's voice sliced through his ego. "If you're too busy looking strong, Eli, you'll never be strong."

The words stuck. Eli began staying late after class, slipping into the gym when no one was around. He trained harder, quietly refining his technique. His jokes didn't stop, but something shifted—more control, sharper focus, even if he pretended it all came easy.

Sophie buried herself in every lesson. She stayed after class to study soul theory and practiced alone when the halls fell quiet. But as she trained, she compared herself to others—students with flawless alignments, more radiant soul auras. Each time she fell short, the doubts grew.

It came to a head during a soul alignment test. The room shimmered with radiant auras, but Sophie's flickered weakly. She held the glow as long as she could, jaw tight, breath measured. The instructor's gaze lingered on her, but Sophie said nothing—only nodding once, lips pressed in silent frustration.

"Stop measuring yourself against others," the instructor said gently. "Your strength is your own. Trust it."

Something shifted. She stopped chasing perfection and

started focusing on why she trained—to protect, to lead, to never freeze when someone she cared about needed her. Slowly, her aura grew steadier, no longer flickering under pressure.

The trio's growth was uneven but undeniable. Chris wrestled his emotions into shape. Eli balanced humor with discipline. Sophie found quiet confidence, even as uncertainty lingered. They pushed each other forward. Their bond became a shield.

Vincent watched them all. Especially Chris. His gaze lingered too long, sharp and unreadable. It wasn't fear he inspired—but pressure. Chris could feel it in every exercise, every lesson. A weight, as if waiting for someone to break.

Still, the three pushed forward. After one grueling session, they collapsed onto the grass outside, breathless and laughing beneath the low sun.

Sophie wiped her brow. "It feels like we've come a long way."

Chris nodded. "Every day we peel back another layer."

Eli grinned. "We're practically unstoppable."

Chris laughed. "And I wouldn't want to do this with anyone else."

That night, Chris sat with his mother on the back porch, the stars clear above them.

"You've been coming home late," Mariah said softly. "How's everything?"

"It's been… a lot," he said. "But it feels worth it. Like it's shaping me into someone I need to be."

"I'm proud of you," she said. "Just remember—strength isn't about power. It's about how you choose to use it."

In the days that followed, the leader board became a symbol of change. Chris's name soared from 900th to 81st. Sophie climbed from 23rd to 19th. Eli cracked into the 30s. Quietly, persistently, they rose.

One afternoon, they stood before the board together.

"Eighty-first," Chris murmured, stunned.

"You earned it," Sophie said.

Eli slapped him on the back. "And we're just getting started."

As they walked home, twilight settled over the path. Eli broke the silence. "So… which squads are we picking?"

Chris glanced at Sophie. "Gabriel's," he said. "It feels right."

Sophie hesitated. "I don't know anymore."

Eli grinned. "Then I'm picking Gabriel's too."

Later, when it was just Chris and Sophie, he turned to her. "It's okay if you still pick Michael's squad. We'll support you."

She paused, then looked at him. "I used to think I had to. But now… being with you and Eli, pushing each other—that matters more."

Chris smiled. "It does. No matter what, we're still a team."

They walked on in silence, the future rushing toward them like the wind. But for that moment, under the stars, they stood together—unshaken.

The following morning, the grand assembly hall buzzed with tension. Rows of students filled the chamber, their whispers echoing against the high ceilings. Some joked nervously about the reevaluations. Others fidgeted with their uniforms, glancing toward the double doors more often than usual.

Chris, Sophie, and Eli stood toward the back, shoulder to shoulder, trying to focus on the day ahead.

Then Vincent stepped onto the stage.

A hush fell instantly.

His posture was impeccable. His eyes unreadable. Yet there was a tension in his expression, like a taut string drawn too far.

"Good morning," he said, his voice ringing clearly through the hall. "Today marks the reevaluation of Eden Preparatory

Academy's top students. Your effort, resilience, and discipline are commendable."

Then came the shift.

"However, this year's selection will be different. You will not be choosing your squads."

A wave of shocked murmurs swept the room. Whispers flared into quiet protests, confusion rippling through the student body like static. Somewhere near the front, a parent—one of the few allowed to observe—leaned in and whispered harshly to a faculty member, who responded with an unreadable look.

Vincent waited. Let the discomfort build. Then continued, colder now:

"Squad placements will be assigned by me, under the guidance of Archangel Michael. The breach we suffered has forced a reorganization of priorities. Personal preference will no longer dictate survival."

As if summoned by his words, a divine shimmer appeared above the stage. A radiant projection of Archangel Michael manifested in a column of gold and white.

The room fell completely still.

"Students of Eden," Michael's voice boomed—measured, resonant, divine. "The rift has revealed cracks in our foundation. Cracks that must be mended. The darkness is no longer idle. To restore balance, we must respond with unity, not chaos. Squad distribution will be handled by Captain Vincent. Trust in his judgment, for it is my will."

The light faded, and Vincent stood silently for a moment longer before stepping down from the platform.

Chris felt his jaw clench. Sophie's arms crossed. Eli's brows furrowed.

No choice.

Later, in the sealed captain's chamber, tension spread like smoke. Vincent stood at the head of the polished marble table, the captains seated around him in a semicircle—Giuseppe, Maria, Mei, Nyla, Omari, and Jeffrey.

"This is a mistake," Maria said first, her hands flat on the table. "The reevaluation has always been based on choice. You're removing the students' voices. That creates resentment."

Mei nodded. "We're leaders, Vincent—not commanders of pawns. You're not distributing weapons. You're shaping young warriors."

Nyla leaned forward, arms folded. "You really believe you understand every squad dynamic better than the captains who've led them for years?"

Omari scoffed, frustration in his voice. "You're asking us to abandon structure. Trust built over decades. What if this weakens us instead?"

Jeffrey added, cool but firm, "Michael's guidance is one thing. But giving absolute placement authority to you—one man—is another. Why not involve the council?"

Vincent remained silent, absorbing it all. Then he stepped forward, voice low, deliberate.

"You're speaking from comfort. From precedent. Not necessity." He met each of their eyes. "The rift was no fluke. This academy was targeted. The enemy is adapting—and so must we."

Maria's gaze narrowed. "Adapting is one thing. Seizing control is another."

"I am following Michael's directive," Vincent said coldly. "This isn't ego. It's survival. We cannot allow outdated customs to hinder our evolution."

The room fell quiet.

Giuseppe had been silent, his arms crossed, his gaze unreadable. Now he spoke.

"I trust Michael. But if this backfires… it's on you, Vincent."

Vincent met his stare. "It won't."

The others exchanged reluctant nods, but doubt clung to the walls like ash. One by one, the captains filed out in silence—except Maria and Giuseppe.

She didn't speak at first. Neither did he. The tension crackled quietly between them—until finally, Maria broke the silence.

Maria let out a long breath, running a hand through her hair as she cast Giuseppe a weary look.

"You know how he gets," she murmured softly.

Giuseppe nodded, his face lined with the strain of the day. "He has his reasons. But that doesn't mean this was the right call."

He glanced toward the high chamber doors where the archangels had delivered their decree. His voice lowered, edged with quiet frustration.

"Letting Vincent decide squad placements without input from the council… It doesn't feel like Michael. Or any of them. It feels rushed. Forced. I don't like it."

Giuseppe exhaled, forcing the tension from his shoulders.

Together, they turned and moved down the marble corridor, their footsteps echoing against the stone walls as Eden Prep braced for its next great trial.

11

Reevaluations

The time had come for reevaluations, and anticipation buzzed in the grand assembly hall as students prepared to showcase their soul essence, create their weapons, and learn which squad they would join. The air was thick with a blend of excitement and nervous energy, every student eager to prove their worth.

One by one, the captains emerged from their chambers, taking their positions along the raised platform to oversee the ceremony. The golden banners of the seven squads hung high above, symbols of the ancient legacy each student hoped to become part of.

Giuseppe, clad in his captain's armor, scanned the crowd with a calm but watchful gaze. His eyes found Chris near the back, and with a nod, he beckoned him forward. Chris wove his way through the crowd, the knot of nerves tightening in his chest.

When he reached his father, Chris's voice was low but tight with frustration. "How is it possible that Vincent gets to assign the new members? Shouldn't we get a choice?"

Giuseppe's expression remained calm, but there was a flicker of concern in his eyes. He lowered his voice. "I'm not sure how he convinced Michael to give him that authority. But something doesn't sit right about it. We need to stay vigilant — something is going on, and I intend to find out what."

A muscle twitched in Giuseppe's jaw, betraying the calm mask he wore. His fingers tightened briefly on Chris's shoulder before relaxing again, a silent signal that he was holding back deeper fears he couldn't yet voice.

He paused, then placed a steady hand on Chris's shoulder, his voice softening with encouragement. "But today isn't about him. It's about you. You've worked hard, Chris. Now, it's time to see what element manifests from your soul essence. Remember, this is a reflection of your spirit, not just a test. Trust yourself."

Chris swallowed hard and nodded, feeling the weight of both his father's words and the moment pressing down on him. Determination flared in his chest, pushing back the lingering doubts. It was time.

The participants gathered, forming a line that stretched across the assembly hall. They stood in order, from rank one down to one hundred, each student stepping forward with a mixture of pride and tension, knowing the significance of this moment.

Sophie was the first of the trio to be called forward. She stepped into the large, circular chamber, its high ceilings and bare walls amplifying every sound, the space both vast and imposing. At the center of the room stood a sleek, glowing console, pulsating softly with energy.

"Please place your hand on the console and summon your full power until exhaustion," an automated voice instructed.

Taking a steadying breath, Sophie approached. She pressed her palm gently against the console, feeling a faint pulse against her skin. A soft hum filled the room as her energy stirred, a ripple of green light radiating from her fingertips. The glow intensified, spreading outward as her soul essence poured into the chamber.

Tendrils of emerald energy swirled around her, vibrant and alive, pulsing in time with her heartbeat. Her essence seemed to take root, the glow shifting as vines and leaves emerged from the energy, weaving through the air as if summoned from the earth itself. Sophie felt her strength draining rapidly, the pull deeper than anything she had experienced before. Her knees wavered, breath shallow, yet she held firm, focusing everything she had into the manifestation.

The light condensed, swirling faster, until it solidified into a small, radiant stone encased in delicate vines that gently curled around it. The amulet hovered in front of her, glowing with a rich, verdant hue. The Heart of Verdant Stone.

With trembling fingers, Sophie reached out and closed her

hand around the amulet. The moment her skin touched it, a warmth spread through her palm, steady and grounding, like the pulse of something ancient and powerful. It felt like a heartbeat, tethered not just to her body but to the life force of the earth itself.

But the effort had drained her nearly to collapse. Legs weak, she steadied herself against the console; the amulet clutched tightly in her hand. The task was complete, but she felt as if she had poured every drop of her strength into it.

The chamber doors slid open, and Sophie stepped through, still catching her breath, when she noticed Vincent waiting just beyond the threshold. His piercing gaze met hers, expression carefully composed yet unreadable.

"Congratulations," he said, his voice smooth but lacking warmth. "You've been assigned to Gabriel's squad."

The words landed strangely. For so long, Sophie had dreamed of joining Michael's squad, believing it was where she belonged. But now, with the Heart of Verdant Stone resting warm in her hand, that dream felt blurred, distant.

A sharp sting pricked at her chest. Had she fallen short somehow? Had she not been good enough for Michael's squad after all?

"Okay," she replied quietly, nodding, unsure of how to process the shift in her path.

Without another word, Vincent turned and left.

Before she could dwell on it further, Giuseppe approached, his expression calm but warm, a reassuring presence amid her swirling thoughts.

"Welcome, Sophie," he said gently. "We're proud to have you with us."

She managed a faint smile, though her mind still felt unsteady.

Giuseppe's eyes shifted to the amulet in her hand, the Heart of Verdant Stone pulsing softly with green light. His face softened with recognition.

"It seems your soul essence has unlocked earth and plant manipulation," he said, voice tinged with something close to awe. "Just like your mother."

Sophie blinked, a flicker of emotion crossing her face. She nodded, gripping the amulet a little tighter.

"Don't worry," Giuseppe continued, his voice reassuring. "We have some of the best elemental specialists here, and they'll help you develop your abilities. You're in excellent hands."

She looked around as other members of Gabriel's squad approached, their expressions welcoming. Though her path had shifted, their warmth offered a quiet sense of comfort she hadn't expected.

Sophie allowed herself a small smile, holding the Heart of Verdant Stone a little closer.

My new team, she thought, and for the first time in a long while, hope took root.

Eli was the second of the trio called forward. He stepped into the vast chamber, the sound of his footsteps echoing against the high ceilings as he approached the center console. The room felt impossibly large, its emptiness amplifying the weight pressing on his chest. For once, the ever-present humor was absent from his face. All that remained was quiet determination.

A soft hum filled the air as the console glowed faintly, waiting for him.

"Please place your hand on the console and summon your full power until exhaustion," the automated voice instructed, calm yet unyielding.

Eli inhaled deeply, pressing his hand against the cool surface.

Instantly, a pulse of warmth surged through his palm, igniting a flow of energy from deep within. His soul essence answered the call, spilling from him in a vibrant green radiance. The light coiled and danced around his body, illuminating the chamber in hues of emerald, rich and earthy.

The energy tugged harder, and Eli's breath quickened. The process wasn't just draining — it was overwhelming. He felt his strength ebbing as the console drew deeper, siphoning from his very core. Sweat beaded on his brow as the green energy twisted and condensed before him, morphing into something physical — tangible.

The essence solidified into a weapon.

A massive stone hammer hovered before him, its handle wrapped in living vines that shifted with life, pulsing in rhythm with his heartbeat. The head was rough, ancient, with jagged edges as if carved directly from the earth itself. Yet the vines softened the stone, intertwining with it like roots binding the power together, a balance of raw strength and control.

Eli's legs trembled, his breath ragged as he reached forward, his hand closing around the hammer's handle. The weight was immense — solid and grounding — yet it felt right. Familiar, as if it had been a part of him all along. Though his body was weakened, the weapon thrummed with untapped potential, a force waiting to be wielded.

His grip tightened. This wasn't just a weapon. It was a reflection of himself — raw strength harnessed by growth, wild power tempered by restraint. And as he held it, he felt a deeper connection — to the earth, to his spirit, to the truths hidden within his essence.

The console dimmed, the summoning complete, but Eli could barely stay upright. His knees threatened to buckle from the sheer exhaustion of the ritual. Still, he forced himself to stand tall, the hammer grounding him as he stumbled toward the exit.

The heavy chamber doors slid open with a low groan, and waiting just outside, Vincent stood, arms folded, his gaze as cold and unreadable as ever.

Eli blinked, the weight of the ceremony still pressing on his chest. Before he could speak, Vincent's voice cut through the silence.

"Congratulations. You've been assigned to Raphael's squad."

The words felt like a blow to the chest. Raphael's squad? The doubt struck before he could catch it. He didn't know anyone there. Why separate me from Chris and Sophie?

For a heartbeat, Eli considered asking why — but the set of Vincent's jaw, the way his eyes lingered, made it clear that questioning wouldn't yield answers.

Play it cool.

Eli forced a grin, masking the uncertainty. "Right… sounds good," he said, managing a nonchalant shrug. "Guess I'll go meet my new team."

As he turned away, the humor drained from his face for just a moment. What if I don't fit in with them? What if I'm not good enough? He pushed the thought aside and kept walking, his hammer a heavy reassurance in his hands.

Without another word, Vincent turned away, already focused on the next test, as if Eli were nothing more than a task checked off a list.

Exhaling, Eli tightened his grip on the hammer and made his way toward a group gathered near the far end of the hall. Captain Maria, with her dark hair neatly braided back, stepped forward, her face lighting up with a welcoming smile.

Without hesitation, she opened her arms and pulled him into

a quick, reassuring embrace. "Welcome to Raphael's squad, Eli. You did well. That hammer… it suits you."

The warmth in her voice caught him off guard, melting a sliver of the doubt coiling in his chest. He nodded, finally allowing a genuine smile to surface. "Thanks. It… uh, kind of feels like it chose me."

Maria stepped back, her eyes lingering on the Titanroot Hammer. "It did. And in time, you'll learn just how much strength you've drawn from within."

The other squad members offered him nods and subtle smiles, their friendliness chipping away at his earlier unease. This wasn't what he expected — but maybe, just maybe, it could work.

As he settled in among his new team, Chris, standing outside the chamber, watched his friend disappear into the crowd, gripping the stone hammer as if it were part of him. Chris clenched his fists, determination burning in his chest.

His turn was next.

The anticipation gnawed at Chris, a knot tightening deep in his chest as he stood among the gathered students. His eyes kept flicking toward the massive display above, where glowing letters revealed the names and squad placements of his peers. Each name felt like another heartbeat, steady, relentless — yet his own remained absent.

Sophie's name flashed next, her placement confirmed under his father's squad. Chris felt a wave of relief. Good. She'll be safe with Dad. Moments later, Eli's name appeared under Captain Maria's squad. Chris exhaled, forcing a nod to himself. Maria's solid. She'll take care of him.

But as the list continued to cycle, his name still missing, that knot in his chest tightened further. What about me? What does Vincent have planned? The question festered, cold and unwelcome, burrowing into his thoughts with each passing second.

The line crept forward. Time slowed. The quiet murmur of the crowd around him blurred into an indistinct hum. Finally, the heavy doors to the testing chamber groaned open, and a voice echoed through the hall.

"Chris Cronetti, step forward."

His chest tightened like a coil about to snap. This was more than nerves—it felt like fate pressing against his ribs.

He crossed the threshold, the chamber doors sealing shut behind him with a resounding clang. The room was vast, empty, the walls smooth and reflective, amplifying the faint hum of energy that pulsed from the central console. The silence felt heavier than it should have. It pressed against his skin, prickling like static.

A mechanical voice echoed, hollow and precise.

"Place your hand on the console and summon your full power until exhaustion."

Chris took a deep breath, then another.

This is it. Focus.

His hand pressed against the console.

A pulse of energy surged beneath his palm, thrumming in time with his heartbeat. The floor vibrated as the room came alive, golden threads of light spiraling outward from his fingertips, dancing like rivers of power. The energy flowed freely, his soul essence rushing forward as he let go of his restraint.

The light condensed, shifting and folding into something tangible.

A blade emerged.

Solid and whole.

A sleek black long sword, elegant and sharp, formed in the air before him. Veins of pale yellow energy crackled through the hilt like lightning, pulsing in rhythm with his heartbeat. It hovered, weightless, glowing with quiet power.

Chris felt the weapon — his weapon — call to him. It felt right. Balanced.

But the energy wasn't done.

A spark ignited.

The tip of the first blade flared suddenly, a burst of wild flame surging upward, searing orange and red. Chris flinched as the heat pulsed outward, engulfing the space in a blinding glow.

The fire twisted and coiled, taking shape, the beginnings of a second blade forming from the roaring heat.

But it was too much.

The heat pressed against his skin. His pulse spiked, the energy wild and uncontrolled, threatening to consume everything. The fire blurred, morphing into a different memory. Flames devoured the walls of his childhood home. Smoke so thick he could barely breathe. His father's lifeless body crumpled against the floorboards.

The heat pressed closer, the helplessness tightening around his throat.

Stay calm, a voice whispered within him. Trust it. Don't fight it.

Chris squeezed his eyes shut, trembling.

But fear was stronger.

The fire surged, and the second blade collapsed, breaking apart in a rain of dying embers before it could fully take shape.

The single black sword remained, trembling but intact.

He reached forward, fingers curling around the hilt. The black blade flared with a pulse of golden lightning along the edges, the flames simmering into a steady, controlled glow. It was still raw. Still dangerous. But now… it answered him.

Chris whispered the name that echoed in his soul.

"Eclipse Blade."

The connection solidified in that instant, binding the weapon to him in a way deeper than flesh, deeper than spirit.

The chamber dimmed as the console powered down, exhaustion crashing over him like a wave.

The heavy chamber doors groaned open.

And Vincent stood waiting.

Chris's footsteps echoed sharply as he stepped into the hall, the weight of the Eclipse Blade dragging slightly at his side. Vincent stood waiting, arms folded behind his back, expression carefully composed but cold.

Chris's grip tightened instinctively as he approached.

"Congratulations," Vincent said smoothly, his voice carrying across the hall. "You've been assigned to Michael's squad. I see you've inherited the power of lightning… just like your father."

The words twisted in Chris's chest — not encouragement, but a deliberate prod, a reminder of everything he hadn't lived up to yet.

Then Vincent's mouth curved into a thin, mocking smile.

"I know you wanted to be with your father. But don't worry… we'll take great care of you here."

The veiled mockery struck harder than any blade.

Chris's heart pounded. Anger rose up, hot and sharp, flooding through him before he could think. Lightning crackled along the Eclipse Blade, the air itself vibrating with the charge.

Without warning, Chris moved — the blade arcing through the air in a raw, furious swing.

But Vincent didn't even flinch.

With casual ease, he raised two fingers and caught the blade mid-swing. Frost bloomed from his fingertips, spreading instantly along the sword's edge and snuffing out the crackling energy. The blow was neutralized as if it had never existed.

A stunned gasp rippled through the crowd — students and captains alike frozen in disbelief.

Chris strained against the hold, his muscles trembling, but Vincent's grip was absolute.

Vincent's expression didn't change as he turned to address the crowd, his voice amplifying.

"Yes! This passion! This fire! This is the spirit we need to overcome our enemies."

Applause broke out — hesitant at first, then swelling as students and staff tried to make sense of what they were seeing.

Only Chris heard the words Vincent whispered next, low and cutting:

"But you… are not worthy of my blade."

With a flick of his wrist, Vincent shoved Chris backward, sending him stumbling. The Eclipse Blade clattered to the floor, the metallic sound ringing through the silence.

Chris knelt, breath ragged, shame burning hotter than the lightning that had failed him.

Vincent, composed as ever, continued as if nothing had happened.

"Let this serve as a reminder," he said to the assembly. "Strength without control is recklessness. Passion without discipline is ruin."

He turned toward Chris, his voice sharpening just enough for all to hear.

"Learn your place — and you may yet be of use."

Without another glance, Vincent stepped away, signaling the

reevaluations to continue.

Chris remained kneeling for a long heartbeat, the weight of every eye in the hall pressing down on him. Slowly, he reached for the Eclipse Blade, the frost still clinging stubbornly to its surface.

His fingers tightened around the hilt.

I'll show him, he vowed silently. I'll show them all.

He stood, his jaw set, and walked stiffly toward the section of the hall marked with the blue banners of Michael's squad.

Hiroshi, tall and composed, was waiting. The seasoned soul warrior bowed slightly—a gesture rarely offered to first-years. His gaze flicked briefly to the frost still clinging to Chris's blade, then to the tension in Chris's stance.

"You held your ground," Hiroshi said quietly. "That's harder than it looks—especially against him."

He offered a slight nod, his tone calm but firm. "Welcome to Michael's squad. I'm Hiroshi."

Chris returned the gesture, his reply clipped but sincere. "Thanks. I'll do my best."

"You'll do more than that," Hiroshi said simply. "Here, we rise — or we fall."

Chris met his gaze, a flicker of determination sparking in his chest.

"I'm ready."

Hiroshi gave a small nod of approval and stepped aside, allowing Chris to take his place among the elite warriors. Around him, Michael's squad members watched quietly, measuring him with their eyes, saying nothing. But Chris could feel the silent expectations thick in the air.

The final names were called, the reevaluations drawing to a close. Students were gathered with their new squads, buzzing with a mix of excitement and tension.

At the front of the hall, Vincent stepped forward one last time, his voice cutting cleanly through the murmuring crowd.

"Congratulations to all who have been placed," he said. "And remember — this is only the beginning. Your true tests lie ahead."

A heavy silence followed, charged with unspoken fears and hopes.

"Rest tonight," Vincent said. "Tomorrow… your real training begins."

The students began to disperse, breaking into smaller groups as they filed from the hall.

Chris lingered for a moment, his eyes locked on the empty stage where Vincent had stood.

The weight of the Eclipse Blade pressed against his back, a reminder of everything he had gained — and everything he had yet to prove.

The day was over.

But a far harder road had just begun.

12

Vincent Alone

As the ceremony ended and families gathered to leave, Chris walked silently beside his father, Giuseppe. The weight of the day's events clung to them, neither breaking the silence. Chris's grip tightened around the hilt of his blade, his mind echoing with Vincent's words, with the overwhelming pressure of expectations. Giuseppe stole a glance at his son but chose not to speak, sensing the storm Chris was wrestling with inside.

Nearby, Sophie lingered by her father's side, torn between excitement and apprehension. Her fingers toyed with the edge of her new squad emblem, the Heart of Verdant Stone still warm against her chest. The pride in her father's eyes should have been reassuring, but instead, it felt like a reminder of how far she still had to go.

Eli walked a few steps behind, flanked by his parents. His usual jokes and bravado were absent, replaced by a contemplative silence as Vincent's speech replayed in his mind. *Compassion. Courage. Unity.* The words were strong, but they sat uneasily with the lingering tension beneath Vincent's mask. Eli clenched his fists, unsure if he felt motivated or manipulated.

As the crowd thinned, Vincent slipped quietly into the shadows, his gaze sweeping the retreating families. His face remained calm, unreadable, yet something flickered beneath the surface—an emotion he refused to acknowledge. Guilt? Doubt? Or something darker. Ambition.

The torches outside Eden Preparatory dimmed as Vincent made his way home. The sight of the modest house was a welcome contrast to the intensity of the day. In the small garden, a woman knelt among the flower beds, carefully plucking weeds from the soil. The scent of lavender filled the air as the soft breeze rustled the leaves.

She looked up as he approached, her face brightening instantly. "Hi, Vinny. Welcome home! How was work today?" She wiped her hands on her apron, smudges of dirt streaking the fabric.

"It was good," Vincent replied, his voice warmer than it had been all day. "The new recruits were chosen. A lot of potential this year. How about yours Sam?" His smile softened as he closed the distance between them and pulled her gently into a hug.

"Vinny!" Samantha laughed, squirming. "I'm filthy! You'll get dirt all over your nice coat."

"I don't mind," he said softly, pressing a kiss to her forehead before letting her go. For the first time all day, the mask seemed to slip, and his features relaxed.

She shook her head with a playful smile, then gestured toward the house. "Veronica's upstairs. She's been waiting for you all day."

Vincent's expression softened even further. "I'll go see her."

Samantha brushed her hand over his cheek. "Take your time. I've got things covered here." She turned back to the flower beds, her presence a quiet comfort against the lingering storm in Vincent's mind.

He stepped inside the house, the warmth of home wrapping around him like a familiar embrace. The scent of freshly baked bread lingered, mingling with the faint scent of Samantha's flowers. The tension from the academy began to dissolve as he called up the stairs.

"Oh, Ronnie! Daddy's home!"

A tiny voice echoed back with sheer delight. "Daddy!"

Before he could react, a blur of blonde hair and boundless energy appeared at the top of the stairs. Veronica launched herself down, laughing, arms outstretched, fearless in her excitement.

"Veronica!" Vincent called out just as she jumped from the

top of the stairs. He rushed up, catching her midair, the force of her jump staggering him slightly, but he held her close. Her arms wrapped tightly around his neck, giggling as he steadied them both.

"I've been waiting for you all day, Daddy!" she squealed, her voice bright with excitement. "I have to show you something! Come on!"

Vincent's expression softened, the tension of the day melting away as he adjusted her in his arms. "All right, sweetheart. What is it?" he asked, carrying her up the steps as she eagerly pointed toward her bedroom.

Once inside, Veronica dashed to her small wooden desk, grabbing a stack of papers with crayon scribbles spread across them. She held one up triumphantly, beaming with pride. "Do you like it?" she asked, her wide eyes searching his face for approval.

The drawing was a colorful, heartfelt portrayal of their family—Samantha with long flowing hair tending flowers, himself standing tall with a sword in hand, and Veronica in the middle, clutching a bundle of pencils. She'd even drawn a sun with a smiley face in the corner, illuminating the scene with warm yellow rays.

Vincent knelt beside her, gently taking the paper into his hands, studying every detail. Each line was carefully placed, the colors vibrant, the effort behind it clear. "This…this is beautiful, Ronnie," he said, his voice soft with genuine pride. "You're so talented. Who taught you to draw like this?"

Veronica huffed, puffing out her chest in mock indignation. "No one, Daddy! I learned all by myself!" She folded her arms, clearly proud of her independent creativity.

Vincent grinned, a playful glint in his eyes. "Well then, my little artist, let's see what your old man can do."

He lowered himself onto the floor beside her, picking up a spare pencil and a blank sheet of paper from the desk. Veronica's eyes sparkled with excitement as she plopped down next to him, eagerly watching him draw. Together, they sketched side by side—clumsy animals, silly castles, and stick figure battles. Laughter filled the room as they playfully challenged each other to draw more creative scenes, turning their imaginations into shared masterpieces.

For a while, the worries of the academy, the burdens Vincent carried—everything else faded into the background. Here, in this small room filled with crayon marks and giggles, there was only them.

"Vinny! Ronnie! Dinner time!" Samantha's voice echoed gently from downstairs, breaking the spell.

Veronica pouted, holding up her newest creation—a fierce, smiling dragon breathing hearts instead of fire. "One last challenge after dinner?" she asked, hopeful.

Vincent ruffled her hair, pressing a kiss to her forehead. "Deal. But you'd better bring your best game," he teased, standing and offering her his hand.

She took it, clutching her drawing close, and together they headed down to join the warmth of their family table.

The aroma of roasted chicken, seasoned with fresh herbs, drifted through the house as Vincent and Veronica descended the stairs hand in hand. The comforting scent mingled with the crackle of the fireplace, wrapping the home in a cozy warmth.

In the dining room, Samantha moved with practiced ease, aligning the silverware perfectly along the plates, her usual attention to detail evident in every movement. She glanced up as they entered, her smile softening at the sight of her husband

and daughter together.

"Just in time," she said, carrying a dish of steamed vegetables from the kitchen and setting it gently on the table. "I was starting to think you two would be drawing all night."

Vincent chuckled, helping Veronica into her chair before taking his own seat. "She's been giving me some serious lessons. I think I'm ready to open my own art gallery," he teased, giving Veronica a playful wink.

Veronica beamed, cheeks flushing as she covered her mouth with a giggle. "Daddy drew a dog that looked like a potato!" she exclaimed, barely containing her laughter.

Samantha laughed, settling into her chair. "A potato dog? Now *that* I have to see."

"After dinner," Vincent replied with mock seriousness, unfolding his napkin and placing it on his lap. "Right now, let's eat. I'm pretty sure I could devour this entire chicken myself."

The family dug into their meal, the clinking of silverware mingling with the low hum of content conversation. The food was warm, comforting, and the shared company made it taste even better.

"So, sweetheart," Samantha began, turning toward Veronica, "how was school today? Anything fun happen?"

Veronica's eyes lit up instantly, her fork pausing mid-air. "We had art class! I drew a rainbow with clouds, and Mrs. Parker said it was so good she put it on the wall with the other best ones!"

Vincent grinned, leaning closer as if hearing the most important news of the day. "Of course she did. She knows real talent when she sees it."

Veronica beamed, practically glowing under the praise. "And during recess, I played hopscotch with Ellie and Mia! Ellie fell, but she got up and laughed, so we all laughed too."

"Sounds like a pretty fun day," Samantha said warmly, nodding in approval. "But…did you finish your math homework too?"

Veronica paused, wrinkling her nose slightly. "Yes… but fractions are hard. Why do we even need fractions anyway?"

Vincent raised a playful eyebrow. "To figure out how much of that cake you're eating later, of course."

Veronica gasped, eyes widening. "Then I *like* fractions!"

Laughter rippled around the table, the kind of easy, genuine joy that filled the room like sunlight. They traded stories—Vincent sharing a funny mishap with a recruit who mistook "fall back" for "fall *flat*," while Samantha recounted a chaotic battle with a particularly bold squirrel in the garden.

Veronica laughed so hard she nearly spilled her milk, which only made everyone laugh harder.

As the meal wound down, Samantha began clearing the dishes while Vincent, with a grin, scooped Veronica up onto his back.

"Hold tight, princess," he said with mock grandeur, "your royal steed is taking you to the fortress tower!"

Veronica squealed with delight, clinging tightly as Vincent galloped around the dining room, her laughter echoing through the house.

"Alright, off to bed, young lady," Vincent announced in an exaggeratedly stern voice, crossing his arms in mock authority.

Veronica pouted, hugging Mr. Flopsy tighter against her chest. "But I'm not tired!" she protested—only to ruin her argument with a massive yawn halfway through the sentence.

Samantha chuckled from the doorway, arms folded. "That yawn says otherwise, sweetheart."

Vincent raised an eyebrow, giving his daughter a knowing

look. "Busted," he teased, scooping her up gently despite her half-hearted squirming.

Upstairs, the bedtime routine unfolded as it always did—teeth brushed, tiny hands scrubbed clean, and Veronica dressed in her favorite star-and-moon pajamas that glowed softly in the dim light. She nestled under the blankets, clutching Mr. Flopsy close, the comforting plush worn from countless hugs.

"Daddy, can you read me a story?" she asked, her voice softer now, tinged with sleepiness but still hopeful.

Vincent smiled, already reaching for the familiar, worn book on the shelf. "Of course," he said, settling into the chair beside her bed. His voice was low and soothing as he read, painting the words into life with each gentle inflection. The rhythm of the story seemed to wash over Veronica like a lullaby, her eyelids growing heavier with every word, though she stubbornly fought to stay awake.

By the time he reached the final page, her breathing had slowed, her head resting against her pillow, eyes half-lidded. He closed the book gently and leaned over, brushing a kiss against her forehead.

"Goodnight, Ronnie," he whispered, voice hushed. "Sweet dreams."

"Goodnight, Daddy," she murmured, barely above a whisper as sleep finally claimed her.

Vincent rose quietly, turning off the overhead light. Only the faint glow of her night light remained, casting gentle patterns of stars along the walls. He lingered for a moment, watching the soft rise and fall of her breathing, a rare serenity settling over him.

Downstairs, the house was calm, the warmth of home pressing in gently as he descended the steps. Samantha sat curled up on the couch, a cup of tea resting on the coffee table, her legs tucked beneath her as she flipped through the worn pages of a novel. The only sounds were the occasional crackle from the fireplace and the quiet ticking of the clock.

Vincent sank onto the couch beside her, exhaling as the tension of the day finally ebbed. Samantha glanced up, smiling as she stretched her legs across his lap, her book resting lightly against her chest.

"You know," he said softly, watching the flames flicker, "she reminds me so much of you sometimes."

Samantha raised a brow, tilting her head in playful curiosity. "Oh? How's that?"

He hesitated, his gaze thoughtful. "That spark in her eyes when she talks about her art… It's the same way you look when you're working in the garden. Completely in your element."

Samantha laughed quietly, shaking her head. "She's got plenty of you in her too, Vinny. Especially that stubborn streak of yours."

He chuckled, resting a hand gently on her leg. "Yeah, well… that part's unstoppable, I guess."

The house felt peaceful—so effortlessly right. They sat in shared silence, the quiet rhythm of the moment wrapping around them like a soft blanket. Samantha eventually set her book aside, stretching with a yawn.

"Alright," she whispered, pressing a soft kiss to his cheek. "I'm heading to bed. Don't stay up too late."

"I won't," Vincent murmured, his hand lingering on hers as she rose. "Just finishing a few things."

She lingered for a heartbeat longer, studying him with quiet affection. Then, with a gentle smile, she headed upstairs, leaving him alone in the soft glow of the firelight.

As Samantha disappeared up the stairs, the warmth Vincent had worn so effortlessly moments before dissolved, leaving only a cold, impassive mask. His gaze lingered on the staircase for a heartbeat longer, but his focus shifted as the shadows at his feet began to twist unnaturally, writhing against the flickering firelight.

A voice, deep and mocking, slithered from the shadows, more felt than heard.

"Finally. I thought they'd never leave. How do you tolerate such... distractions, Vincent? There is still so much work to be done."

Vincent's jaw tightened, his voice cutting through the room like a blade. "Watch your tongue," he warned, his words icy. "Speak ill of my family again, and I'll leave you in worse shape than your foot soldier."

The voice chuckled, a rough, hollow sound that seemed to crawl along the walls.

"Ah yes... the last one. I admit, your methods impressed me. So thorough. So merciless. You broke him so easily—shattered his soul until he begged to lead you here."

Vincent's expression didn't flinch.

"I don't need your approval," he said coldly. "You exist because I allow it."

A twisted purr threaded through the gloom.

"And yet... here we are. You called for me, Vincent. Through him. Through the wreckage you made."

The memory cut sharp—brutal and unmerciful.

The battle at Eden Prep had ended. The demon's body turned to ash.

But something remained.

A flicker of essence, clinging like a parasite to Vincent's shadow.

Most would have missed it. Most would have succumbed.

Vincent had not.

The moment he felt it trying to worm into his soul, he acted. Not with fear—but with fury.

He bound the parasite using techniques no righteous warrior should have known. Forbidden sigils. Ancient soul-chains. Methods buried in blackened scrolls.

He crushed its will until it screeched and writhed—and finally, whispered the name:

Sargatanas.

The one whose voice now poisoned the air.

"And now look at you," Sargatanas crooned. *"Pulling strings in plain sight. No resistance from your oh-so-noble fellow captains, I presume?"*

Vincent moved with the same cold efficiency that had trapped the demon in the first place.

Turning without a word, he crossed the living room and headed for the far corridor.

"The word of an Archangel is absolute," he said, voice measured. "Their doubts mean nothing. Michael's blessing covers all sins."

The door slid open with a low hiss.

Vincent descended into the bowels of his home—the polished steel walls cold against the soft glow of etched sigils. Frost traced the edges where old magic fused with modern tech.

At the corridor's end loomed the secured chamber: reinforced doors inscribed with seals so ancient, even the academy archives no longer recorded them properly.

Vincent pressed his palm to the lock.

It scanned the scars burned deep into his soul—a price he willingly paid for access to powers no righteous man should wield.

The door groaned open.

Inside: a sterile sanctum of cold light and humming machinery.

At the center, the shattered demon hung limply in a ring of binding light, its essence flickering against the containment glyphs like a moth trapped against glass.

But it wasn't alone.

Against the far wall, two containment pods glowed—a woman and a man, both trapped in golden stasis fields. Angel Corps warriors. Their bodies were weakened, their soul signatures carefully extracted but left alive—barely.

Vincent crossed the room, his presence alone enough to make the demon shrink tighter into its chains.

Sargatanas spoke again, using the puppet body like a crude mouthpiece.

"Quite the collection you've started, Vincent. Tell me... do you keep them for leverage? Or just for the company?"

Vincent's gaze didn't waver.

"I needed their abilities," he said quietly. "Their light. Their sound."

The demon chuckled, rasping.

"But not for illusion alone. No, you crafted something far more delicate... you crafted faith."

Vincent's mouth tightened.

From these two warriors—one whose soul manipulation could bend sound into reverent echoes, and another whose light-casting could mimic the radiant presence of heaven itself—he had forged the perfect lie.

Not a simple illusion.

An embodiment of **Michael**.

Enough to silence doubt.

Enough to command obedience without question.

Enough to control.

Sargatanas hissed a satisfied laugh. *"Ahhh, Soulforger. You understand so well. The sheep must believe. Without it, they are nothing."*

Vincent said nothing for a long moment, staring at the trembling forms in the pods. Then he spoke, low and bitter.

"Better a righteous lie than the truth of despair."

The demon purred, pleased.

"Lie to them. Lie to yourself. It matters little. The rot has already begun."

Vincent ignored him.

His gaze shifted, sharp and cutting, to another name swirling in his mind:

Chris Cronetti.

"Your new recruit," Sargatanas crooned. *"There's something about him. Untouched. Untamed. Deliciously raw."*

Vincent's expression darkened.

"He's reckless. Dangerous. His power feels… wrong. Like a blade forged without a smith's hand."

His voice hardened into steel. "I'll understand it. I'll control it. And if I can't—I'll break it."

The voice coiled tighter around him, whispering from every corner of the chamber. *"And our arrangement? Control all you want, Vincent. But the shadows remember. You still owe me the full... count!"*

Vincent's eyes narrowed, a chill rippling outward as frost crept along the steel surfaces of the room. He turned back toward the withered husk, his voice sharp as steel.

"I will hold up my end. Just make sure you hold up yours."

The demon's twisted form convulsed, its decayed lips pulling into a jagged, unnatural grin. The containment sigils flared briefly, crackling with dark energy as the corrupted essence writhed beneath the surface.

The light dimmed, the pulsing energy receding to a faint glow as the chamber fell into a cold, tense silence.

Vincent remained where he stood, his face set in a mask of icy resolve. The frost thickened on the walls, the shadows lengthening as if drawn to him—waiting, watching.

Then, he turned and approached the centerpiece of his work—a small vial of black liquid, swirling with an unnatural fluidity. It wasn't merely a substance; it was a conduit, a key to unlocking what lay beyond his limits.

Without hesitation, he uncorked the vial and poured the liquid over himself. The moment it touched his skin, it moved with a life of its own, spreading like a sentient shadow, slithering over his body until it encased him. The dark substance tightened, solidifying into a harness-like structure that pulsed with raw, eerie energy.

Then, the true cost began. A deep hum resonated through the room as the harness did its work—siphoning his very soul essence. The pain was instant and unforgiving, sharp as razors slicing through his core. It wasn't just energy being drawn from him; it was something deeper, something vital. His face remained impassive, but his fingers twitched involuntarily as the liquid pulsed, feeding on his essence.

Agony followed. A biting pain as though his very essence was being unraveled, thread by thread. Vincent's face remained stoic, but his muscles trembled beneath the strain, fingers curling slightly as the glowing energy was siphoned from him. Wisps of light-blue essence flowed from his chest, surging through the conduits before collecting in the harness.

The process dragged on, relentless, until Vincent could feel the edges of emptiness creeping in—a void where his strength once resided. And yet, he endured. He *had* to endure.

When the harness ceased its extraction, Vincent staggered back, his breath ragged as he reached for another small vial resting on the workbench. Inside, a glowing, blue liquid shifted gently, the artificial soul essence he had created—born from stolen fragments of his own power, refined and condensed.

Without hesitation, he drank. The sharp, burning sensation surged through his veins, flooding back into his body. His skin prickled as strength returned, but it wasn't the same. Not natural. Not whole. It never was.

Still, he powered up the harness again.

Drain. Replenish. Record.

The notebook beside him lay open, the pages filled with cramped, precise handwriting. Every reaction. Every shift in his aura. Every trace of power lost and regained. Each session stripped another layer away, not just from his body but from something deeper. Something harder to measure.

The shadows grow stronger, he noted mechanically, the ink sharp against the paper. *Prolonged exposure is altering my essence composition. Maintain restraint.*

But even as he wrote it, he could feel it. The quiet shift. The cold lingering in his chest, long after the harness had dimmed.

Outside, the world remained untouched. Upstairs, Samantha slept soundly, and the soft creak of Veronica rolling over in her bed drifted faintly through the vents. They were safe. Blissfully unaware of what was happening beneath their feet.

"For them. For him," Vincent reminded himself, staring at a framed photo on his desk. With a steady breath, he powered

the harness once more.

The cycle continued, each round pushing his body further, testing the limits of both his endurance and control. The core swelled with stolen light, and with it, the edges of something darker.

By the time dawn's pale light filtered weakly through the narrow basement windows, Vincent was hollow. He felt it—more than physical exhaustion, but a void carved deep within his spirit. Yet, his hand remained steady as he scrawled his final notes.

Satisfied, he finally disengaged the harness and it returned to a liquid in the vial. The containment field pulsed one last time as the shadows recoiled, withdrawing from the room, but never truly gone.

Vincent ascended the stairs in silence. The house above was warm, still wrapped in the quiet calm of early morning. Samantha lay peacefully beneath the covers, her breathing soft and steady.

Careful not to disturb her, he eased into bed, the lingering cold clinging to his skin as he stared up at the ceiling. His mind refused to rest. Three hours. That was all he would allow himself before the cycle began again.

Vincent rose with practiced efficiency, his movements precise, every action measured.

He washed his face, the cold water numbing the lingering fatigue.

As he reached for the towel, the mirror above the sink shimmered — just for an instant.

In that brief, warped reflection, his eyes seemed darker, hollowed out, a faint coil of shadow pooling at his feet like a living thing.

He blinked, and it was gone.

Only his usual composed reflection remained: calm, charismatic, immovable.

Vincent dried his face and turned away without a second glance.

By the time he reached the kitchen, the scent of warm pancakes filled the air. Samantha stood at the stove, flipping them with easy familiarity, the golden edges curling perfectly. Veronica sat at the table, humming quietly, her brow furrowed over a workbook.

"Good morning, sleepyhead," Samantha teased, glancing over her shoulder.

Vincent smiled, warm and effortless, pressing a kiss to her cheek. "Good morning."

He ruffled Veronica's hair as he passed. "What's this?" he asked, peering at the neatly drawn shapes.

"A math puzzle!" she beamed. "I did it all by myself!"

"Better than me already," Vincent chuckled. "Maybe you'll be my tutor someday."

Samantha set a plate in front of him, rich with the scent of butter and syrup. A cup of black coffee followed.

He ate without hurry, listening as Veronica eagerly recounted her school project—a shoe box fairy garden—and Samantha gently reminded her to double-knot her shoelaces.

Yet even as he smiled, part of Vincent's mind drifted away, beyond the warm kitchen walls.

The warmth of home was a fragile shield.

Outside it, reality waited—cold, demanding, merciless.

Breakfast ended too soon. Veronica swung her backpack on, rushing for the door.

"Ronnie, slow down," Vincent called, crouching to fix the

tangled straps. He brushed a strand of hair from her face, his touch lingering a moment longer than necessary.

"Have a great day, sweetheart."

"I will! Love you, Daddy!" Veronica shouted, waving as the bus pulled away.

Vincent watched until the bus disappeared around the corner.

Back inside, Samantha was wiping the counters, humming softly.

Vincent moved behind her without a word, wrapping his arms around her waist, resting his chin lightly on her shoulder. She leaned into him, smiling without needing to look.

"Have a good day, Vinny," she murmured.

He lingered for a moment longer than usual, his hand brushing lightly along her wrist — as if memorizing the feel of it.

"You too," he whispered, pressing a kiss to her temple.

The warmth stayed with him only until the front door clicked shut.

Then the mask fell away.

Vincent's steps sharpened as he moved to the car, the world outside already colder in his eyes. The city stirred sleepily under a pale morning haze, but his mind was wide awake — honed, calculating, ruthless.

Today, the first day for the new recruits.

Today, Chris Cronetti.

Raw. Unfocused. Dangerous.

Vincent's grip tightened briefly on the steering wheel.

Chris would need to be watched closely—and Vincent would be the one to find out why his soul essence burned so violently.

And how it could be controlled.

The academy gates rose before him, stone and steel gleaming

pale beneath the rising sun. Vincent's presence drew nods and quiet bows from students and staff as he strode past, a force of command without a single spoken word.

The east wing lay in near silence. His chambers, his sanctuary of order.

The scent of wood polish and parchment grounded him as he stepped inside.

A large oak desk dominated the center, flanked by shelves of tactical manuals and soul essence theories. A sprawling map of the academy grounds stretched across one wall, annotated with crisp notes on rotations and training drills.

Vincent crossed to his desk and opened a sleek black notebook, flipping through precise, angular handwriting. His eyes drifted toward a steel table tucked into the corner—compact devices resting atop it. Tools designed for measuring, manipulating, and, if necessary, suppressing soul essence.

His thoughts circled back—inevitably—to Chris.

The boy's power was volatile. Potent.

But there was something else about it too—something Vincent couldn't quite place.

Before he could lose himself in analysis, a sharp knock broke the quiet.

"Enter," Vincent said, his voice smooth and composed.

Hiroshi stepped inside, bowing slightly. "Captain, the recruits are gathering in the training grounds. How would you like to proceed?"

Vincent closed the notebook with a quiet snap. "Today is about assessment. I want to understand what they're capable of—truly capable of. Their limits. Their flaws. What cracks beneath their strength."

"And Chris?" Hiroshi asked, his tone careful.

Vincent's expression darkened.

"Test him beyond his comfort zone. Push him. See where he breaks."

"And the others?"

"Start them in the resonance chambers," Vincent said, pointing toward the elemental zones marked on the academy map. "Establish their baselines first. Then stress them."

Hiroshi nodded, making brisk notes before bowing again and departing.

Vincent turned toward the window, his hands clasped behind his back.

The training fields stretched before him, golden morning light glinting off weapons and armor. Students milled about, some laughing, others tense.

His gaze narrowed, locking onto a single figure.

Chris.

Vincent studied the boy the way a surgeon studied a tumor—methodical, cold, detached.

You don't even know what you are yet, Vincent thought, a sliver of something between pity and contempt threading through him.

But soon, he would.

He had to.

Vincent's reflection darkened faintly in the glass, shadowed by the ambitions he could no longer fully control.

13

Three Elements

13

After the reevaluations and team assignments, Giuseppe and Chris drove home in silence so heavy it seemed to press against the walls of the car. The low hum of the engine was the only sound, steady, as neither father nor son spoke.

Chris stared blankly out the window, his thoughts a tangled storm of frustration and shame. His stomach churned, replaying the moment he had lashed out at Vincent—the reckless strike, the effortless way it had been deflected, and the cold humiliation that followed. Being assigned to Michael's squad under Vincent's command was bad enough, but the deeper wound ran beneath it all. The truth that Vincent had killed his father in another timeline gnawed at him, a secret so sharp it felt like a blade pressing into his chest.

Why hadn't he controlled himself? Why did it feel impossible to stay calm when it came to Vincent?

The car rolled to a stop in the driveway. Giuseppe cut the engine, his face as unreadable as it had been the entire ride. Without a word, he stepped out, closing the door with a soft thud. Chris lingered a moment longer, exhaling shakily before forcing himself to follow.

The walk toward the house was quiet, the tension between them palpable, each step heavier than the last. Chris could feel his father's disappointment without a single word exchanged.

As they neared the porch, the front door swung open, and Mariah stood there, her face lighting up in a warm smile. The softness in her eyes, the gentle welcome in her expression—it was such a stark contrast to the brooding silence that Chris felt his chest tighten further.

"Welcome home," she said, her voice tender, though her gaze immediately caught the unease lingering between them. Her smile faltered just slightly, her mother's intuition sensing the weight they both carried.

But neither Chris nor Giuseppe said anything.

The silence lingered, pressing just a bit heavier.

"How was the day, you two?" Mariah asked, her eyes shifting between them, her smile hopeful but cautious.

Giuseppe didn't slow his pace. "Not good," he answered curtly, brushing past her with the weight of unspoken tension in his voice. He headed straight for the staircase, already halfway inside when he added over his shoulder, "Chris, get cleaned up and meet me in the basement."

The sharpness in his voice left no room for argument.

Chris stood frozen for a moment, watching his father disappear deeper into the house. His chest tightened, the sting of disappointment pressing heavier now that they were home. He could still feel the weight of his earlier failure, as if it clung to him.

Mariah, still standing by the door, took a step closer, searching his face with quiet concern. "Chris?" she asked softly, her brow furrowing. "What happened?"

His throat tightened, words catching as he fumbled for an answer. He couldn't tell her. Not the full truth. Not the part where he'd lashed out and embarrassed himself—or why he had done it. If he told her the real reason, he'd have to explain everything: the memories of another timeline, the visions of Vincent standing over his father's lifeless body.

And he couldn't do that. Not to her. Not when she already worried so much.

"The squad assignments didn't go how I hoped," he finally muttered, keeping his voice carefully neutral. "I'm not on Dad's squad."

Mariah's expression softened, her gaze steady as she reached out and rested a gentle hand on his shoulder. "I know that must be hard," she said, her voice soothing, warm. "But just because you're not on your father's squad doesn't mean you won't excel. You've always wanted to be a soul warrior, haven't you? This is still your chance to do something special. To make a difference."

Chris swallowed, nodding stiffly, though her words barely touched the turmoil inside him. "Yeah," he mumbled. "You're right."

She offered a soft smile, though there was a flicker of worry behind it, the kind only a mother could feel. "Good. Now go get cleaned up. I'm starting dinner soon."

Chris gave a stiff nod and turned away, retreating upstairs as the weight of unspoken truths pressed against his chest. The moment he closed the bathroom door, he let out a shaky breath, bracing himself against the sink. Cold water splashed against his face, stinging his skin as he stared into the mirror, his reflection blurred by the droplets.

His mother's words lingered, soft and encouraging—but they barely scratched the surface of the turmoil churning inside him. How could they? She didn't know. She hadn't seen what he had seen. She hadn't watched his father die, hadn't lived through that nightmare the way he had. The images haunted him still: the fire, the smoke, the lifeless body on the ground. And Vincent, standing over it all.

He gripped the edges of the sink as the memory surged. *I can't tell her. Not yet.*

Wiping his face dry, Chris forced himself to move. His reflection stayed with him as he left the bathroom, fractured and uncertain.

The dread only grew heavier as he descended the stairs, each step echoing hollowly. The basement door loomed ahead, slightly ajar. The dim light seeping from the crack cast faint shadows that danced along the walls.

Pushing the door open, Chris was met by the cold stillness of Giuseppe's workshop. The air felt heavier here, thick with tension. A single overhead light flickered above, its pale glow barely reaching the edges of the cluttered space. Tools, crystals, and half-assembled devices littered the workbench—perfectly organized yet overwhelming, each piece a fragment of his father's relentless focus.

At the center of the room stood Giuseppe, arms crossed, his face unreadable. The usual warmth in his eyes was dulled, replaced by something harder, heavier. Disappointment? Expectation? Chris couldn't tell—but the weight of it filled the room, pressing in on all sides.

The silence stretched, and Chris felt the words forming at the back of his throat, but they wouldn't come. Not yet.

The stool scraped against the cold basement floor as Chris sat, the weight in his chest pressing heavier than the tools and devices crowding the workbench. Shadows stretched long and sharp, flickering with the dim light overhead, as Giuseppe paced in front of him. His face, normally calm, was set in hard lines, his arms crossed tight across his chest.

The silence lingered, thick and tense.

Giuseppe finally spoke, his voice low but firm, every word carrying the weight of his disappointment. "Your actions today were unacceptable, Chris. Swinging your blade on a captain? In front of the entire academy? What were you thinking?"

Chris felt his pulse spike, guilt tangling with the lingering ember of frustration that hadn't quite died since his clash with Vincent. He opened his mouth to defend himself, but his father's glare cut him off.

"No," Giuseppe snapped, his voice sharper now. "You *weren't* thinking. You let your emotions make the decision for you.

That makes you reckless. Predictable. And predictable?" He paused, stepping closer, his eyes boring into Chris. "That makes you easy to control."

The words cut deep, deeper than Chris wanted to admit. His fists clenched at his sides, nails digging into his palms as he stared down at the floor. His heart pounded against his ribs, a storm rising inside, pressing for release.

Giuseppe continued, his voice still edged but quieter now. "I'm telling you this not to hurt you, but because I need you to understand. Emotions are natural—anger, fear, grief. But they are tools, not guides. If you let them control you, you hand your power away. And in battle, that loss of control? It will get you killed. Or worse… someone else."

Chris felt the spark flare inside him, the weight of unspoken pain boiling too close to the surface. His head snapped up, eyes burning as he finally burst out, voice raw. "You don't understand! Living with the pain of those memories… going through what I went through… *seeing what I've seen.*"

His voice cracked on the last word, trembling as the emotions surged. His breath came faster, chest rising and falling as the past threatened to swallow him whole.

Giuseppe's face softened, the sternness giving way to something gentler—but Chris wasn't finished. He clenched his jaw, his voice quieter now but no less intense.

"The things I've seen in this lifetime…" He faltered, catching himself just as he neared the edge of revealing too much. He took a shaky breath, forcing the words back, his pulse slowing as he reined in the storm threatening to consume him.

The room was silent again, except for the faint hum of the overhead light and the unsteady rhythm of Chris's breathing.

Giuseppe nodded, his eyes searching Chris's face for a long

moment before he finally spoke, his tone softer now. "You're right," he said quietly. "I *don't* understand everything you've been through. I don't know the pain you're carrying. But I do know pain. I know the pain of losing someone close to me. The pain of feeling powerless. And I know this—letting that pain control you won't ease it. It won't make it right. It will only break you."

Chris looked away, shoulders tense, but the heat in his chest had dulled. His father's voice—still firm but gentle—filled the space again.

"I'm not asking you to forget. I'm asking you to *channel* it. Control it. Use it to sharpen your focus. Because you're stronger than you realize. And you can't afford to let that strength slip because of emotions you don't understand yet."

The words settled like a stone in Chris's chest. He exhaled slowly, nodding, not fully able to speak but hearing the truth in his father's words.

Giuseppe placed a hand on his shoulder, the weight grounding. "We'll work on it. Together."

Chris nodded slowly, swallowing hard. "I understand."

Giuseppe studied his son carefully, his expression unreadable. For a long moment, the only sound was the faint hum of the overhead light and the quiet rhythm of Chris's breathing. Finally, Giuseppe broke the silence, his voice low and measured.

"Good," he said, though his gaze remained hard. "Because Vincent has his eye on you now. He's sharp—too sharp. He knows something isn't adding up. He can sense we're hiding something."

Chris's head snapped up, pulse quickening. "There's… there's something else," he said hesitantly, his voice barely above a whisper.

Giuseppe's brow furrowed, his posture shifting, no longer just stern but wary. "What do you mean?" His voice was calm but edged, like he was bracing himself.

Chris swallowed hard, his hands curling into fists on his knees. "In the chamber," he began, his voice unsteady, "when my blade was forming… there was fire. It wasn't just lightning this time. Fire started forming a second blade." His words came faster now, as if saying them aloud might make sense of the memory. "Two blades, two elements—but I couldn't finish the second one."

Giuseppe took a step closer, the intensity in his eyes sharpening. "Fire?" he repeated, the word heavy with meaning. "You're saying your lightning—your core soul essence—wasn't alone?"

Chris nodded stiffly, the memory still raw. His shoulders sagged as he forced himself to continue. "Yeah, but… I stopped it. I pulled back before it could finish. I—" He broke off, his voice tight with shame.

Giuseppe's eyes narrowed further, his voice steady but pressing. "Why?"

Chris hesitated, his chest tightening as he tried to find the words. The images flooded back—the heat, the uncontrolled surge, the flames licking too close to his face. The memories of fire. *That* fire.

"Because I was afraid," he admitted at last, his voice hoarse. "It felt… wrong. Dangerous. Like it wasn't just power—it *wanted* to burn everything." His breathing hitched as the next words came out quieter, raw. "It felt like the fire from the original timeline. The one that… that destroyed the testing pod. The fire that took everything from me."

Giuseppe's face went still, a shadow passing over his features. The air between them thickened.

"The fire from your original timeline," he echoed, quieter now. Concern replaced the sternness in his voice.

Chris gave a small nod, his fists trembling at his sides. "It felt the same. Out of control. Like it wasn't even part of me—like it was something else. And it didn't just want to destroy… it wanted to take *me* with it."

Silence stretched between them, the weight of those words sinking in.

Giuseppe's expression shifted, not softening, but becoming more thoughtful, more measured. He knelt slightly, so they were eye level, his voice gentler now, though no less firm.

"Chris," he began carefully, "soul essence reflects who we are. Our strength. Our pain. Our fears. If your soul manifested two blades—fire and lightning—it means both elements *are* part of you, whether you want them to be or not. You're afraid of fire, and maybe for good reason. But fear doesn't mean you can't control it. It means you *must*."

Chris shook his head, his jaw clenched tight. "You *don't* understand," he said, voice cracking as he fought to keep it steady. "That fire… it *destroyed* everything. And when I felt it again in that chamber, I couldn't let it take control. I *won't* let it happen again."

Giuseppe exhaled slowly, then placed a firm hand on Chris's shoulder. His grip was steady, grounding.

"You think I don't understand?" he said, voice quiet but powerful. "I do. More than you know. But this isn't about running from what happened before. It's about *facing* it. Your soul essence—*your very spirit*—is trying to tell you something. And until you learn to face it, to *understand* it, it *will* control you. No matter how tightly you think you're holding it back."

Chris's gaze dropped, his mind racing with everything he had been holding in. But something in his father's words struck deeper than the shame or fear—something solid.

Giuseppe squeezed his shoulder once, steady but not forceful.

"You don't have to face this alone," he said. "But you do have to face it."

Chris gave a reluctant nod. He wasn't ready to face it yet—but for the first time, he knew he couldn't keep running forever.

Giuseppe's expression hardened as he turned toward the workbench, the dim light casting sharp lines across his face. His mind raced, tension tightening his jaw.

"Fire and lightning… two elements, two weapons." His voice was low, measured but firm. "That shouldn't be possible. If your soul essence can manifest both, we *have* to understand why. We can't ignore this."

Then, with sudden urgency, he spun back to face Chris, his voice sharper. "Quick—grab your blade from the car."

Chris hesitated, his breath catching. That same fear from the chamber threatened to rise again, a lingering whisper reminding him how close he had come to losing control. But the look in his father's eyes left no room for debate. This wasn't a request—it was a command.

With a reluctant nod, Chris turned and climbed the stairs, his heart pounding with each step. The walls seemed closer than usual, the house quieter, as if holding its breath. His mind raced, replaying the moment the fire had surged—the heat, the wild, uncontrollable force he'd barely stopped.

And then Vincent's words echoed in his mind. *Predictable. Reckless."*

Jaw tight, he shoved open the front door, the cool air hitting his face like a slap. His sword rested on the passenger seat where he'd left it, the hilt still crackling faintly with dormant energy. He hesitated for a heartbeat before grabbing it, the weight heavier than he remembered, as if reminding him how much he still didn't understand.

As he turned back toward the house, the door opened before he could reach it. Mariah stood there, his baby sister cradled in her arms, the soft light of the living room behind her. Her face was calm, but her eyes, warm and perceptive, took in the tension in his shoulders instantly.

"Uh-uh," she said, her tone a perfect blend of playfulness and command. "Dinner first. Set the table."

Chris blinked, confused. "But Dad—"

"*You take her,* and I'll take that," Mariah interrupted smoothly, shifting Genevieve into his arms as she reached for the sword. Her grip was gentle but steady, fingers curling around the hilt as her gaze met his with quiet understanding.

The baby let out a soft coo, kicking her feet as Chris instinctively adjusted his hold, balancing her awkwardly. She blinked up at him with wide, curious eyes, tiny hands grabbing at the fabric of his shirt.

Mariah's voice softened, though it left no room for argument. "I'll handle your father. *You*—keep her company and help with the table. We're a family, remember?"

Chris opened his mouth to protest but faltered. The blade felt lighter in her hands than it had moments ago, as if she were lifting more than just steel—lifting the weight pressing down on him. He watched her disappear down the basement steps, the door clicking shut behind her.

Genevieve let out a happy squeal, drawing his attention back to her. She waved her hands with a toothless grin, laughing as she kicked her feet against his chest.

Chris stared at her, a strange ache tightening in his chest. *I've been so focused on all of this—the training, the visions, the past...* His thoughts trailed as he watched her tiny fingers curl around his thumb, her joy so simple, so innocent.

I've barely even been a brother.

Letting out a slow breath, Chris shifted her more comfortably in his arms and made his way toward the dining room. Whatever his father was trying to unlock downstairs—whatever the fire meant—could wait.

For now, there was a table to set.

Alright, Genevieve," Chris said softly, adjusting his grip as he balanced his baby sister on one hip. "Let's set the table, okay?"

Genevieve responded with a delighted squeal, her chubby hands grasping at the air as she kicked her legs excitedly. Chris couldn't help but smile, the simple joy radiating from her momentarily easing the weight pressing on his chest. As he pulled plates and silverware from the cabinets, she babbled in her playful, wordless language, occasionally slapping her hands against his shoulder in giddy approval.

He worked carefully, placing each plate on the table while Genevieve watched with wide, curious eyes. Her giggles echoed through the room as Chris exaggerated his movements, pretending to take instructions from her. "This one here? Oh, you're right, it's way better next to the fork," he teased, earning more giggles.

For the first time in what felt like weeks, he allowed himself to breathe, the tension in his chest loosening ever so slightly. The overwhelming pressure of training, his failure, his mistakes—all of it blurred into the background in this rare, quiet moment.

Meanwhile, Mariah descended into the basement, the soft hum of Giuseppe's tools growing louder as she stepped into the dimly lit workshop. The scent of heated metal lingered in the air, mingling with the faint crackle of energy coming from the devices scattered across the workbench.

Giuseppe stood at the center of it all, hunched over a small mechanism, adjusting a delicate array of crystalline components with a steady hand. His face was tight with concentration, his usual composure marked by a furrowed brow and the slight clench of his jaw.

"Giuseppe," Mariah called gently, placing Chris's sword carefully on the workbench. "Dinner's ready."

He gave a curt nod, not looking up as he continued his work. "I'm almost done here. Just give me a minute," he muttered, voice clipped with distraction.

Mariah lingered, watching him in silence for a heartbeat longer. Then, with quiet determination, she stepped closer. "Giuseppe."

This time, he paused, setting down his tools with a sigh. His eyes met hers, guarded but tired.

"Is everything alright?" she asked softly, her gaze searching his face.

He hesitated. The practiced calm, the fortress he always built around his emotions, wavered for just a moment. Then, in a rare crack of vulnerability, he exhaled and admitted, "No. It wasn't a good day today."

Mariah's hand brushed his forearm, gentle but grounding. "Talk to me," she urged, voice steady. "This isn't just about a bad day. I can feel it."

Giuseppe's jaw tightened, but her touch anchored him. He nodded, lowering his voice. "It's Vincent. He chose Chris for Michael's squad… and I'm certain he's targeting him." His eyes darkened, the protective edge in his voice sharpening. "I can't prove it yet, but he's watching him too closely. Testing him."

Mariah absorbed his words, her face calm but serious. She didn't panic, but the slight press of her lips showed her worry. "Do you have a plan?"

Giuseppe nodded, the hardness in his eyes turning to quiet resolve. "I'm working on it. I'm not going to let anything happen to him."

She nodded, stepping closer to place both hands on his chest, her touch warm and steadying. "I know you'll protect him, Giuseppe. But promise me you'll protect yourself, too."

His posture softened, some of the tension ebbing as he leaned into her warmth. "I promise," he murmured, voice low but certain.

Mariah pressed a kiss to his forehead, lingering there for a heartbeat. Then she smiled gently. "Good. Now let's eat. You can save the world after dinner."

They ascended the stairs together, the scent of roasted vegetables and spices welcoming them back into the warmth of their home. Laughter echoed from the dining room— Genevieve's high-pitched giggles blended with Chris's playful voice as he proclaimed, "Yes, Captain Genevieve, I'll make sure the spoons are perfectly aligned."

The dining table sat in the soft glow of the kitchen lights, the remnants of their meal scattered across the plates. The gentle clinking of silverware had faded, replaced by the comforting murmur of conversation and the occasional burst of laughter.

Chris leaned back in his chair, a rare calm settling over him. For the first time in weeks, the weight of training, expectations, or the shadows of his past did not consume him. This—sharing a quiet meal with his family—felt normal. Safe. And he hadn't realized just how much he missed it.

Mariah pushed her chair back, lifting a sleepy Genevieve from her highchair. The little girl yawned, her tiny arms curling around her mother's neck as she nestled into her shoulder, eyelids already drooping.

"Alright," Mariah said softly, adjusting her grip on Genevieve, her voice warm but teasing. "I'm putting her to bed. That makes you two the cleanup crew."

Giuseppe raised an eyebrow, leaning back with exaggerated protest. "Cleanup crew? Since when do I take orders?"

Mariah's smile widened, unbothered by his playful defiance. "Since you'd rather do dishes than handle bedtime. Unless you're volunteering?" She gently kissed Genevieve's temple, already turning toward the stairs.

Giuseppe held up his hands in mock surrender. "Fine, fine. Dishes it is."

Chris grinned as he stood, gathering the glasses. "I'll start on the sink. Sounds like a pretty fair deal to me."

"Good answer, Chris," Mariah called over her shoulder, pausing briefly on the staircase. "And no cutting corners, either. I'll know."

Giuseppe scoffed under his breath, stacking plates with an exaggerated grumble. "Cutting corners? Me? She makes it sound like I'm some kind of slacker."

Chris shot him a smirk as he rinsed a glass. "I mean… she's kinda got a point."

Giuseppe narrowed his eyes, feigning offense. "Watch it, kid. You keep talking like that, and you'll be on dish duty solo."

They worked side by side, the peaceful rhythm of cleaning filling the kitchen. Chris scrubbed while Giuseppe dried, the sounds of running water and the soft clink of dishes blending with their quiet banter.

For a moment, it felt like nothing had changed—like they were just a family, sharing the kind of ordinary evening that once felt so routine. But Chris knew better. Beneath the laughter, the worries lingered. Shadows stretched beneath the surface, both unspoken and unresolved.

Still, for tonight, the warmth of home was enough.

The kitchen was spotless, the last dish dried and stored. Chris and Giuseppe exchanged a quiet nod before heading back toward the basement. The atmosphere shifted as they descended, the soft hum of machinery growing louder, casting a faint mechanical rhythm over the space. The warmth of the family dinner felt distant now, replaced by the cold focus of the work that lay ahead.

Giuseppe moved directly to his workbench, where Chris's sword rested. The blade gleamed under the overhead lights, its jagged edges still crackling faintly with residual lightning energy. He lifted it carefully, turning it in his hands with the eye of a craftsman—no, a scientist—studying something far more complicated than a simple weapon.

"I'm going to run some tests," he said, his voice thoughtful. "I need to compare your blade's energy signature with your soul essence. If you inherited lightning from me…" His brow furrowed as he traced a finger near the blade's edge, where a faint, singed line still lingered. "…then where did the fire come from?"

Chris hesitated, the question stirring something inside him. When he finally spoke, his voice was quieter. "Has Mom ever… used soul essence?"

Giuseppe blinked, as though the thought hadn't crossed his mind in years. His face softened, the edges of his usual stern focus blurring as a memory surfaced. "Once," he said quietly, setting the sword down with care. "She could wield wind essence—stronger than most recruits I trained with back in the day. But… she chose not to continue. It wasn't the life she wanted. And I respected that."

Chris blinked, surprised. "She never mentioned that."

"She doesn't talk about it much." Giuseppe's lips curved in a faint smile. "When she stepped away, it wasn't out of fear or failure. She knew what she wanted—this life, this family. But don't doubt her, Chris. Your mother's stronger than you think."

For a moment, the workshop was quiet, filled only with the rhythmic hum of the machines. Then Giuseppe's expression hardened back into focus. He reached across the bench, picking up a sleek, metallic device—thin, no larger than a stick of gum. Without a word, he pressed it into Chris's hand.

Chris turned it over, inspecting its smooth design. "What… is this?" he asked, eyebrows raised.

Giuseppe smirked, the inventor's edge returning to his voice. "That, my son, is an untraceable communication device. It's linked directly to our soul essences—yours and mine. As long as we're alive, we'll be able to stay connected over any distance." His gaze sharpened. "It's not just a tool—it's a safeguard. If anything happens with Vincent, you'll be able to contact me immediately. And if I learn something important… I'll reach you."

Chris stared at the device, its weight heavier than its size implied. The complexity of such an invention was beyond him. How does he come up with this stuff? He wondered.

"Go ahead," Giuseppe said, his voice calm but expectant as he extended a hand toward Chris. "Swallow it. It'll bind with your cells and integrate with your soul essence. Once it's activated, we'll be able to communicate instantly."

Chris eyed the small device in his palm—so simple, yet

impossibly advanced. He hesitated for only a heartbeat before nodding. With a swift motion, he placed it on his tongue and swallowed it. The cool surface slid down easily, followed by a strange warmth blooming deep in his chest, spreading like ripples through his core. His hand drifted instinctively to his stomach, feeling the strange sensation linger beneath his skin.

Giuseppe observed him closely, already scribbling into his ever-present notebook. "Anything feel different?"

Chris shifted his weight, rolling his shoulders. "Not really… just kind of warm. This is pretty crazy, even for you, Dad."

Giuseppe smirked, barely glancing up from his notes. "Crazy's what keeps us ahead of everyone else. Now," he said, nodding toward the sword resting on the workbench, "let's see what your blade has to say about your soul essence."

The weight of his father's words clung to Chris as he watched him turn back to the glowing instruments spread meticulously across the workspace. Despite the unease still lingering in the pit of his stomach—the fire he couldn't control, the second blade he'd failed to manifest—there was comfort in knowing his father was working tirelessly to figure this out. Whatever came next, he wouldn't have to face it alone.

Hours passed in the dim glow of the basement, the steady hum of machines filling the silence. Giuseppe worked with unwavering focus, running test after test, each one requiring small traces of Chris's soul essence. Delicate strands of energy siphoned from his core were drawn into crystalline chambers, analyzed under flickering screens that bathed the walls in pale light. The occasional scratch of pen on paper echoed as Giuseppe recorded each result with methodical precision.

Chris sat nearby, his gaze drifting between the swirling energy displays and his father's relentless work. Part of him felt like a science experiment—pricked, prodded, monitored—but a deeper part marveled at the focus Giuseppe poured into every detail. He wasn't just analyzing a weapon or a power. He was trying to protect him, to understand something neither of them could yet explain.

The door creaked open softly. Mariah stepped in, cradling a cup of tea as she scanned the cluttered workspace. "Everything alright down here?" she asked gently.

Giuseppe barely looked up from his notes, waving her off with a distracted nod. "Yeah… just a bit longer," he muttered, already back to adjusting the frequency dials on the console.

Mariah lingered for a moment, her gaze shifting to Chris. She offered him a small, knowing smile before retreating quietly, leaving them to their work.

Another hour passed. The machines continued to pulse, the occasional spark of energy crackling from the containment chamber where the Eclipse Blade rested. Chris was feeling the ache of fatigue when Giuseppe finally straightened, his eyes sharp with realization as he stared at the results on the screen.

"I think I've got it," he said, breaking the long silence, his voice a mix of exhaustion and triumph.

"Got what?" Chris asked, his curiosity sharpening as he straightened in his chair.

Giuseppe turned from the screens, holding up his notebook filled with dense, meticulous notes. His expression was thoughtful, intense. "Your blade," he began, voice steady, "is channeling your lightning soul essence perfectly. There's no trace of fire present within it. But when I tested your soul essence directly—" he paused, flipping a page, "—I found something… unusual. There's trace energy of lightning, fire, and a third essence. Something I've never seen before."

Chris blinked, his brow furrowing. "A third essence? What is it?"

Giuseppe shook his head, frustration flickering in his eyes. "I'm not sure yet. It's faint. But whatever it is, it's intertwined with your soul essence. I'll need more time to study it." His gaze sharpened, more serious now. "What I *do* know is this—your body is only actively channeling lightning and fire right now. And that's already… extraordinary." He paused, measuring his words. "Most soul warriors never unlock a second elemental channel, let alone a third. It can take years of refinement, if it even happens at all. But with you? It's already there. Latent, but present."

Chris stared at him, the weight of those words sinking in. "You're saying I could control three elements?" The idea felt impossible, overwhelming even.

"With proper training, yes," Giuseppe confirmed. Then his expression darkened, his voice lowering. "But Chris, I'm not sure this is something you should rush. The fact that fire manifested the way it did in your trial—and that it caused you to lose control—makes me think this isn't just raw power. It's tied to your emotions, your fears… Maybe even your experiences with the timeline shifts."

Chris felt his chest tighten at the mention of the other timeline, but he said nothing. His father had already figured out so much, it was only a matter of time before he pieced it all together.

Giuseppe set his notebook down and crossed the room, opening a small metal case on the workbench. He pulled out a sleek, black ring, the surface faintly gleaming under the dim basement lights. Holding it up, he extended it toward Chris.

"Here. Put this on," Giuseppe instructed.

Chris took the ring, rolling it between his fingers. It felt heavier than he expected, cool against his skin with a faint hum he could almost sense rather than feel. "What is it?"

"It's a soul essence inhibitor," Giuseppe explained, his voice calm but firm. "It's designed to suppress your elemental output. As long as you wear it, your fire essence—and anything else trying to manifest—will be locked down. You'll only be able to channel your lightning."

Chris hesitated, his grip tightening on the ring. "Why? I thought you said I needed to learn to control it."

"You do. But not like this," Giuseppe replied, his tone softening. "You're not ready, Chris. Not yet. Fire is unpredictable. Dangerous. And whatever this third essence is, it could be even more unstable. This will help you focus—master one power fully before you risk the others." He met Chris's gaze. "It's for your safety. You can't go into battle without control. Especially not with Vincent watching."

Chris exhaled slowly, feeling the weight of both the ring and his father's words pressing down on him. This wasn't just about caution—it was about keeping him from becoming a threat to himself. And yet, a part of him resisted. The fire was *his* too, wasn't it?

Still, he trusted his father. With a quiet nod, he slid the ring onto his finger. The metal adjusted instantly, fitting perfectly as the cool sensation spread through his hand and into his core. It felt like a lock clicking shut, a quiet but noticeable dampening of his energy.

Giuseppe watched closely. "Good. We'll keep monitoring your progress. The ring will suppress your fire essence, but as you train, we'll begin reintroducing it. Together."

For the first time that night, the tension in Chris's chest

loosened just a little. He wasn't sure what the third essence was or what it meant for his future. But with his father's guidance, the fear didn't feel quite so overwhelming. The road ahead was still uncertain—but he wasn't facing it alone.

14

Training Days

The morning sun stretched long shadows across the training grounds of Eden Preparatory Academy, bathing the stone paths in soft gold as Chris stepped onto the field. Beyond the academy walls, the world stirred with quiet joy—children laughed along the wide marble promenades, cafes buzzed with conversation and the scent of fresh bread, and people moved with the relaxed rhythm of a society at peace. There were no honking cars, no cries of hunger, no rush to survive—just the hum of fulfilled lives where every citizen contributed through passion, not obligation. Sculptors worked in open courtyards. Musicians played near public fountains. And at the heart of it all, the Council's decrees were obeyed not out of fear—but out of reverence. Their guidance had shaped a world without war, poverty, or deceit.

But here, within the stone arena of Eden Prep, the mood was far less serene.

Restless energy, an electric pulse of nerves and anticipation, filled the training grounds as recruits gathered beneath their assigned squad banners. The sharp clang of practice blades echoed in the distance, blending with the indistinct murmur of voices.

Chris's hand drifted toward the hilt of the Eclipse Blade at his side, its weight a steady reminder of the challenge ahead. Yet as he scanned the crowd, his focus wavered. His eyes moved over clusters of recruits, each wearing the colors of their squad—Gabriel's, Raphael's, Sariel's—but there was no sign of Sophie or Eli.

His chest tightened. They'd been his steady ground through everything—constant, unwavering. He knew they wouldn't be here, not with their separate assignments, yet their absence left a void heavier than he'd expected. It was only the first day, and already, the comfort of familiarity felt miles away.

Pushing the ache aside, Chris adjusted the blade on his back and shifted toward the assembly gathering under Michael's banner. The facade of the archangel rippled against the breeze, the deep blue standard stark against the sea of recruits. Some stood tall, their expressions calm and collected, while others fidgeted, whispering in hushed tones. A few already looked weathered—older students who had risen through the ranks and now wore the facade like a badge of pride.

Chris squared his shoulders and joined the formation, the unease still gnawing at him but buried deep beneath his resolve. He was here to prove himself. Not just to Vincent, not just to his father—but to himself.

A hush fell over the grounds as Vincent approached, his presence cutting through the tension like a blade. His eyes swept across the ranks, cold and calculating, and when they lingered on Chris—just for a second—it was like the air grew heavier.

"Today," Vincent began, his voice sharp, ringing out across the gathered recruits, "marks the beginning of your journey with Michael's squad. You were chosen not for who you are but for the potential you hold. And let me be clear—potential alone means nothing. It is a shadow without form, empty without the discipline to give it weight."

Chris swallowed hard, the words pressing down on his chest. He forced himself to meet Vincent's gaze when it passed over him again, the same relentless intensity in those eyes as during their confrontation days before. He wouldn't look away. He couldn't.

"You will be tested—physically, mentally, spiritually," Vincent continued. "Your soul essence is not merely a tool; it is a reflection of your will. And if you cannot master yourself, you will not remain here."

The tension in the air thickened, every recruit hanging on his words. Some straightened their posture, steeling themselves against the weight of the challenge. Others shifted uncomfortably, uncertainty etched across their faces. Chris felt both—the surge of determination, but also the ache of lingering doubt. He had to control it. He had to.

The squad was divided into smaller groups for the day's first drills. Chris was paired with two other recruits—each strong, capable—but none familiar. There was no comfort in shared history here. Just strangers bound together by the promise of proving themselves.

The drills were relentless. Weapon training, endurance sprints, soul essence channeling—the type of exercises meant to break down weakness piece by piece. Chris fell into rhythm, his blade moving with fluid grace, the weight feeling more natural with each swing. Yet every time his mind settled, it strayed— back to Sophie, to Eli. Were they struggling as he was? Were they thinking about him too?

No. Focus.

With a sharp inhale, Chris forced those thoughts down, channeling the discomfort into his movements. Every clash of steel, every step in the grueling sequence reminded him why he was here. Not to dwell on what was missing—but to fight for what still remained.

The sun hung lower as the day wore on, and as exhaustion set in, so did clarity. The ache of missing his friends wouldn't break him. The doubt wouldn't break him.

Not today.

Training for Michael's squad was an unrelenting gauntlet, each trial crafted to push the recruits to their breaking points. The focus was clear: harness your soul essence or fail trying. The day began in the resonance chambers, where recruits were instructed to channel their essence through their weapons to withstand the chambers' shifting frequencies.

The room hummed with intensity, energy crackling in the air as weapons glowed and vibrated. Chris gripped the hilt of the Eclipse Blade, the lightning running along its edge, casting sharp shadows on the walls. As the resonance intensified, his blade pulsed erratically, responding to his essence but not quite in sync. His jaw clenched, and sweat beaded on his brow as he fought to keep the energy steady, his blade flickering between control and chaos.

Nearby, a tall female recruit wielded a trident with smooth, deliberate movements. Her soul essence flowed like liquid through the weapon, streams of water coalescing around its prongs. The water twisted and danced in the air, forming spirals that absorbed the resonant pressure. Her face remained calm, her focus unwavering, as though she were one with the trident.

Across the chamber, a burly male recruit wielding a massive hammer struggled against the rising intensity. His soul essence took the form of earth manipulation, the hammer glowing faintly as rocks began to rise from the floor, orbiting him in uneven bursts. He gritted his teeth, his muscles straining as he fought to stabilize the heavy chunks of stone. The rocks wobbled and threatened to collapse, but with a determined roar, he slammed the hammer into the ground, sending the stones into a controlled arc toward a designated target. The impact was impressive, but far from refined.

Chris stole a glance at them, his frustration mounting. Their control, even under pressure, felt worlds apart from his own erratic attempts. He shook the thought away, refocusing on the blade in his hands. The frequencies climbed higher, and Chris pushed harder, forcing his essence into the weapon. Sparks flew wildly, some dissipating into the air, others barely hitting their mark. His arms ached, and his energy wavered, but he refused to stop.

Next came the endurance trials, where recruits were tasked with sustaining their essence through their weapons for as long as possible. The strain was immediate and brutal, draining not only their physical strength but their mental resolve. Chris gripped the Eclipse Blade, feeling the lightning within it surge and fade, as if testing his limits. Each second felt like an eternity as his arms trembled and his vision blurred with exhaustion.

The female recruit with the trident stood a few meters away, sweat streaming down her face as she maintained a steady flow of water essence. Droplets hovered around her in a shimmering halo, occasionally faltering but never fully losing their form. The male recruit with the hammer planted his feet firmly, his hands gripping the weapon's shaft as rocks rose and fell around him. He let out a low growl of effort, holding on with sheer determination even as cracks formed in the stones he manipulated.

Chris felt his energy slipping, the lightning in his blade sputtering like a dying flame. Gritting his teeth, he channeled every ounce of willpower he had, forcing the energy to stabilize. A faint crackle ran along the blade's edge, flickering, but alive. His body screamed for rest, but his mind refused to yield.

The final phase of the day took place in the elemental manipulation zone. Recruits faced an array of targets, each designed to test their precision and control. Chris stepped forward, gripping the Eclipse Blade tightly as he eyed the targets. The task was simple in theory: channel your essence through your weapon and hit each mark. In practice, it was anything but.

His first strike missed entirely, the lightning splintering off into the air. Frustration bubbled in his chest, but he adjusted his stance, breathing deeply to steady himself. The second strike was better—a bolt of lightning arced from the blade and struck the target dead-center. His confidence grew as he struck again, this time hitting a moving target. But just as he began to feel a rhythm, his control faltered. The next bolt fizzled out before it could reach its mark, leaving Chris gritting his teeth in frustration.

The female recruit with the trident was a stark contrast, her water essence slicing through the air in fluid arcs. Each strike hit its mark with precision, the water wrapping around the targets before dissipating. Her movements were graceful, her connection to the weapon seamless.

The male recruit wielding the hammer wasn't as precise, but made up for it with raw power. Each swing of his weapon sent boulders crashing into the targets with earth-shaking force. The rocks weren't always on point, but the sheer weight of his attacks left an undeniable impact.

By the time the day ended, exhaustion clung to every recruit like a second skin. Weapons were sheathed, and steps were heavy as they made their way toward the cafeteria.

"Man, I could eat a whole cow," the hammer-wielding recruit muttered, wiping sweat from his brow.

"Me too," another chimed in. "All that work has me completely drained."

Chris trailed behind, the weight of the Eclipse Blade on his back a constant reminder of the day's trials. His body ached, his energy was drained, but his resolve remained unbroken.

The group made it to the cafeteria and sat at one of the tables, eating their lunch in a thick, uncomfortable silence. The air was heavy with exhaustion from the morning's grueling training, and none of the recruits seemed eager to break the quiet. Chris toyed with his food, his mind still replaying the day's drills, when the sharp sound of footsteps approached.

Vincent's presence was unmistakable as he strode into the

cafeteria, his commanding aura cutting through the ambient noise. Stopping at their table, he gestured toward four recruits standing behind him.

"These are sophomore recruits," he said, his voice calm but firm. "They'll be joining you in your training."

The newcomers stepped forward and took empty seats among the group, their expressions ranging from wary to indifferent. Three boys and one girl now rounded out the squad, bringing their number to nine. Yet the silence persisted, the table feeling more like a collection of strangers than a team.

It wasn't until one of the sophomore boys spoke that the tension finally broke.

"Come on, you guys!" said a tall boy with sharp features, his voice slicing through the quiet. "What is this, some kind of rule against talking, or are you all just this boring?"

Chris glanced up from his tray as the words hung in the air.

"There's no rule," muttered one of the freshmen, his tone barely audible.

The sophomore girl rolled her eyes, her voice sharp with amusement. "No one wants to talk to you, that's why."

Unfazed, the tall boy smirked. "Ah, so there is life among us," he said, his gaze settling on Chris. His grin widened. "And you—I've heard about you. The lightning boy. So, are you capable of speech, or did all your training short-circuit your brain?"

Chris let the silence stretch a moment, glancing around the table with an exaggerated, thoughtful look. He set his fork down deliberately, leaning back in his chair as he met the boy's gaze with a lopsided grin.

"Talking is easy," he said, his tone light and tinged with humor. "It's knowing when to shut up that takes skill."

A ripple of laughter moved through the table, the tension loosening just enough to feel the shift. Even the girl cracked a small smile. The tall boy raised his hands in mock surrender, still grinning.

"Fair enough," he said, leaning back with a nod. "I'm Richard. Welcome to the squad."

Chris gave a small nod in return, appreciating the break in tension, brief as it was.

It didn't take long for Richard to jump back in. He leaned back in his chair, balancing it on two legs as he surveyed the group.

"Alright," he said, his voice cutting through the murmur, "let's just address the elephant in the room. A group of strangers at a table, all eating in awkward silence—what are we, a council meeting?"

The silence continued.

"If no one's going to take charge here, I will," Richard went on, clapping his hands once. "Let's get the introductions out of the way, huh? We're all stuck together, so we might as well know who we're stuck with."

Chris smirked but stayed quiet, while Allegra raised an eyebrow at Richard's brashness.

"Always so subtle, aren't you?" she said, amused.

"Subtlety is overrated," Richard shot back. "I'll start. Name's Richard, sophomore—obviously—and proud member of Michael's squad. My goal? To be the best there ever was, of course." He gave an exaggerated shrug, earning a few groans. "Oh, and I'm the one who's going to make sure you guys survive this madness. You're welcome."

"Someone had to claim that title," Lyra muttered dryly, glaring at him. "I'm Lyra. Also a sophomore. Also stuck dealing with him." She motioned toward Richard with a slight eye roll. "I'm here because I want to be. That's all anyone needs to know."

"Charming, as always," Richard said, earning a sharp look from her.

Allegra jumped in next, her tone light and warm. "I'm Allegra. Third-generation soul warrior," she said, resting her trident carefully against the table. "My parents were solid warriors, but I want to go further. Being on Michael's squad is my shot. Nice to meet you all."

"Third generation? I knew you had that 'destined for greatness' look," Richard teased, though Allegra's polite smile kept him in check.

Next was Deepak, who leaned forward with eagerness radiating off him. "I'm Deepak, freshman," he said, his voice bright with excitement. "I almost didn't try to be a soul warrior—thought I'd just follow my parents and become a farmer. But they pushed me to give it a shot, and it turns out I've got a crazy soul essence reservoir. So now, I'm here to see what I can do."

"That's awesome," Chris said with a nod. "Farming to soul warrior—big leap."

"Thanks," Deepak replied with a grin, his energy lifting the table's mood. "What about you?" he asked, turning to Chris.

Before Chris could respond, Richard leaned forward, eyes twinkling. "Yeah, we all heard about the lightning boy. Attacking a captain after reevaluations. How brash."

"Wait, that was you?" Lyra's voice cut in, her usually reserved demeanor breaking with surprise. She squinted, studying Chris more closely. "Is your last name… Cronetti?"

Chris sighed, already feeling the weight of the attention. "Yes," he said, keeping his tone measured.

Lyra's eyes widened. "You're Captain Giuseppe's son. You're

a second-gen," she added, now tinged with awe. "I've heard of you. Your dad's one of the best captains at the academy."

Chris shifted in his seat, uncomfortable beneath the scrutiny. "Yeah, that's me," he said neutrally.

"So why Michael's squad?" Ali asked, leaning forward. "If your dad's the captain of Gabriel's, why not stay with him?"

Chris hesitated. Before he could answer, Allegra spoke up, cutting through the moment with calm authority.

"You guys don't know?" she asked, glancing around. "None of this year's freshmen selected their squads. Vincent assigned all of us." She paused, letting the weight of her next words settle. "The Archangel Michael came down himself and gave him the authority to do it."

A stunned silence fell over the table. Even Richard, usually quick with a quip, blinked in disbelief.

"Wait," Lyra said skeptically. "Michael gave Vincent that much control? That's... not how it's supposed to work."

"It's not," Allegra confirmed. "It's unprecedented. Squad assignments have always been a choice."

Ali leaned in, brows furrowed. "Why change it now? What's so different about this year?"

Allegra hesitated, her fingers tracing the rim of her glass. She lowered her voice to a whisper, eyes flicking around to ensure no one else was listening.

"There's something they're not telling us outright," Allegra said quietly.

The words hit the table like a stone dropped into still water—sharp, jarring, and impossible to ignore.

Deepak sat forward, his voice low but steady. "The squads have been tightening control ever since. Changing squad protocols, enforcing stricter monitoring. They say it's about safety, but… it feels like containment."

"That's enough," Lyra said sharply, her voice cutting through the tension. "We can't spiral into paranoia."

But the silence that followed was heavy—not because anyone disagreed, but because no one could shake the feeling that something was still terribly wrong.

Chris swallowed hard, a new knot forming in his chest. Sophie. Eli. His parents. Everyone he cared about—they were all walking deeper into danger than they realized.

Allegra finally spoke again, her voice steady. "That's why Michael intervened. That's why he gave Vincent the authority. They're trying to stop something worse before it starts."

Lyra shook her head slowly, her brow furrowed as she tried to make sense of it all. "But for Vincent to assign all the squads… that's a lot of power to hand to one person. And if he personally chose you for Michael's squad, Chris, it means he's definitely keeping an eye on you."

Chris paused, his spoon halfway to his mouth. "Yeah, I've noticed," he admitted, taking a bite and chewing thoughtfully.

Richard leaned forward, his trademark grin returning. "Well, if Vincent's watching you, that just means you've got to give him a show. No pressure, though, lightning boy."

Chris rolled his eyes, but the corner of his mouth tugged upward in a small smile. "Thanks for the pep talk, Richard. Really inspiring."

Richard leaned back, satisfied with the reaction, while Allegra chuckled softly, shaking her head. The tension at the table began to ease, the heavy subject giving way to a lighter energy as the recruits shared small smiles and a few laughs. For a brief moment, the gravity of their situation felt less overwhelming, replaced by the beginnings of camaraderie.

Allegra shifted her attention to the next recruit, her gaze settling on Luke, who had been quietly observing the conversation. "What about you?" she asked, her tone warm but curious.

Luke straightened slightly in his chair, his hammer resting against the side. He met her eyes briefly before answering, his voice steady but quiet. "Luke," he said simply. "I thought I'd serve the Council of Elders like my parents, but when my soul essence manifested, I couldn't ignore it. It felt… like I was meant to be here."

Chris nodded, leaning forward slightly. "Makes sense," he said, his tone encouraging.

Ali, sitting beside Richard, offered a smile that lit up the space around him. "I'm Ali, sophomore," he said, a note of humor in his voice. "I'm just here to keep this guy"—he motioned toward Richard—"out of trouble. Someone has to."

Richard grinned, unfazed. "He's not lying," he added, shooting Ali a playful look.

The group chuckled, the shared laughter easing the tension that had lingered over the table. Allegra's gaze moved to Faith, who had been nervously fidgeting with her fork, her posture shrinking under the weight of being the center of attention.

"And you?" Allegra asked gently, her voice soft enough to coax without overwhelming.

Faith hesitated, her cheeks flushing as the others turned toward her. "I'm Faith," she said quietly, her voice barely above a whisper. "Freshman. I, um… I just wanted to prove to myself that I could do something meaningful."

Ali's expression softened, and he offered her a kind nod. "That's a good reason," he said sincerely. "You're here, aren't you? That's already a big step."

Faith's lips curled into a shy smile, gratitude flickering in her eyes. The brief moment of encouragement seemed to ground her, the tension in her shoulders easing.

The table turned toward Edward next, but he wasn't paying attention to the conversation. His focus was entirely on the dessert tray in the middle of the table, his sharp gaze locked onto the pastries as though they held the secrets of the universe.

"Edward," he said curtly, not bothering to lift his eyes from the tray. "Sophomore." There was a pause, the group waiting for him to continue, but instead, he gestured toward the tray. "Are you going to eat that?"

The abrupt shift in topic caught everyone off guard, drawing a ripple of laughter from the group.

"Not yet," Allegra replied, a smirk tugging at her lips as she slid one of the pastries his way. "Go ahead."

Edward took the pastry and scarfed it down quickly, his focus entirely on the dessert. Allegra blinked, a little startled by the speed and intensity of his action, but before she could say anything, Richard spoke up, leaning back with a grin.

"Don't mind Edward," he said, his voice dripping with faux sympathy. "He's from the Badlands and isn't really used to societal norms. We're still teaching him how to eat like a civilized person."

Lyra, seated beside him, shot Richard a glare and immediately punched his arm—not hard, but enough to make her point. "Stop saying that," she snapped, her tone sharp and unamused. "Edward means well and is getting adjusted to life here. If you let Richard tell it, you'd think he's an infant."

Richard rubbed his arm dramatically, wincing for effect. "Hey, I'm just saying the truth," he shot back, the grin still plastered across his face. "Is he not learning?"

Lyra rolled her eyes, clearly annoyed. "There's a difference between learning and being mocked," she said firmly. "You're always so quick to turn everything into a joke, and it's exhausting."

"Oh, come on, Lyra," Richard replied, leaning forward with an exaggerated look of innocence. "I'm just trying to lighten the mood. It's not like Edward cares."

Lyra crossed her arms, her frustration simmering just below the surface. "You're impossible. Every time you open your mouth, it's like you're trying to be the loudest person in the room."

"And every time you open yours, it's to remind me how much you don't like me," Richard shot back, smirking. "Admit it—you'd miss me if I stopped talking."

Lyra snorted. "Not likely."

The tension between them lingered for a moment before Allegra cleared her throat, cutting through the exchange. "Okay, okay," she said, raising her hands. "Let's not turn lunch into a sparring match. We're supposed to be bonding, remember?"

Richard leaned back with a grin, unbothered by the exchange. "I'm just saying, a little humor never hurt anyone. You all need to loosen up."

"Maybe there's a reason some of us aren't laughing," Lyra muttered, but her tone had softened slightly.

Chris leaned closer to Allegra and whispered, "What's the Badlands?"

Allegra turned to him, her eyebrows shooting up in surprise. "You don't know about the Badlands?!" she exclaimed, her voice loud enough for the whole table to hear.

"The Badlands is a place of corruption, greed, and death," Richard interjected in an overly dramatic tone, wiggling his fingers for effect. "None who journey out there return...

oooooh."

Ali couldn't help but laugh, joining Richard in his theatrics, while Lyra shot them both a withering glare. "The Badlands isn't a joke," she said sharply, her tone cutting through their laughter. "It's a place God's grace doesn't extend to. It's full of death and despair, and anyone who escapes and makes it here is lucky—and strong. But it's not something to make fun of."

Her eyes flicked toward Richard, her frustration evident. "That's why people shouldn't make jokes about those who come from there."

Richard raised his hands defensively, though his grin lingered. "Alright, alright. No jokes. Point taken."

Ali elbowed him lightly, chuckling. "Yeah, maybe dial it back, man."

The mood at the table grew a little heavier, and Chris shifted uncomfortably. He glanced at Edward, who, as usual, was silently focused on his food. The weight of Lyra's words settled on him. He didn't know much about the Badlands, but he could sense the reality of it was far from the exaggerated stories Richard had spun.

Hoping to lift the atmosphere, Deepak jumped in, his voice bright and eager. "So, uh, does anyone know what kind of training we're doing tomorrow?" he asked, glancing around the group. "I heard something about team exercises."

His attempt at redirection worked, drawing the group's attention back to the conversation. The tension eased as the recruits started speculating about the challenges they'd face, and the moment of discomfort gave way to cautious camaraderie.

"Team exercises probably mean combat drills," Chris said. "They'll want to see how we work together under pressure."

"That makes sense," Allegra added, nodding thoughtfully.

"Michael's squad is all about discipline and teamwork. They'll want us to prove we can handle real-world situations."

Richard leaned forward, his grin returning. "Teamwork, huh? Guess I'll have to carry all of you."

Lyra rolled her eyes again. "You're unbelievable."

"Thank you," Richard said, flashing her a wink.

The group chuckled, the earlier tension easing as the conversation shifted. Chris leaned back in his chair, a small smile tugging at his lips as he watched the recruits interact. It wasn't perfect, but it was starting to feel like something close to camaraderie—a tentative step toward becoming a real team.

15

Team Building

The next morning Chris's group gathered for another grueling session. Vincent strode toward them with Hiroshi following closely behind.

The recruits stood in a tense line, the training grounds transformed into a dark, sprawling simulation of chaos. The massive Stone of Eden pulsed faintly in the center of the field, encased in shimmering barriers of light. Beyond it, twisted demon constructs lurked, snarling and circling like predators sensing prey.

Vincent's cold gaze swept over the team, his presence cutting through the tension like a blade. "You've made progress," he began, his voice icy and measured. "As expected. But today's task will push you beyond anything you've faced. This is not about individual strength—it's about synergy, trust, and execution. From now on, your team will be known as Team Ten of Michael's Squad and your task is to protect the Stone of Eden at all costs."

The recruits exchanged glances. The gravity of Vincent's words settled heavily over them. Faith clenched her fists nervously, her plant essence gauntlets creaking faintly as her fingers flexed. Deepak spun his staff absently, a nervous tick that belied his usual excitement. Chris tightened his grip on the hilt of his blade, the faint arcs of electricity crackling along its surface betraying his unease.

"Begin."

The simulation roared to life as the barriers dropped. Demons surged forward, snarling and hissing, their twisted forms clawing hungrily toward the Stone of Eden.

Without hesitation, Richard grinned and elbowed Ali. "Alright, partner. Let's make this interesting."

"What do you have in mind?" Ali asked.

"Whoever takes down the most demons wins. Let's go!" Richard declared, dashing toward the nearby forest.

"Wait—what?" Chris called after him, watching in disbelief as Richard and Ali sprinted into the woods, their laughter fading into the distance.

Lyra's eyes narrowed as she drew her bow, the light string shimmering as she notched a glowing arrow. "Idiots," she muttered. "If they're not taking this seriously, I'll handle it myself." She veered to the left, breaking away from the group with precision and purpose.

"Lyra, wait!" Chris shouted, but she was already gone, her bow drawn as she unleashed a beam of light into the approaching swarm.

The team began to splinter. Deepak rushed to the front, his staff spinning as he conjured gusts of wind to hold back the advancing demons. Luke moved beside him, his massive hammer swinging in wide arcs as he smashed through the creatures with sheer brute force. Faith hung back nervously, her gauntlets glowing faintly as vines snaked from the ground, but her movements were hesitant, unsure.

Chris groaned in frustration. "Everyone, stay together! We're stronger as a team!" But his voice was drowned out by the chaos.

Near the front line, Allegra held her trident defensively, water swirling around its prongs as she speared a demon construct and sent a torrent crashing into another. But more demons poured in, overwhelming her position. She stumbled, her breath hitching as claws reached for her—

Then the ground shifted beneath her. A sudden force yanked the demons back, and they collapsed into a heap as if crushed by an invisible weight. Allegra turned to see Edward standing a few feet away, his posture calm as his weapon—a sleek, dark staff—glowed faintly. He flicked it again, and gravity rippled outward, slamming more demons into the dirt.

"Thanks," Allegra breathed, regaining her composure. She moved to his side, her water essence coiling like serpents as the two began to fight in tandem.

Chris spotted them from a distance, his mind racing. He couldn't let this chaos continue. His lightning blade sparked to life as he sprinted forward, clearing a path through the horde. Electricity arced wildly from the blade, striking demons in wide, crackling bursts. He pushed through to where Faith was struggling near the Stone, frozen by indecision.

"Faith! Focus!" Chris shouted, his voice cutting through her panic. "Use the vines to shield the Stone. We need to keep it protected!"

Faith nodded shakily, her confidence building as she thrust her gauntlets forward. Thick, thorny vines erupted from the ground, forming a defensive wall around the Stone of Eden. Chris gave her a nod of encouragement before charging toward the others.

He skidded to a halt near Deepak and Luke, who were holding the line. "We need to regroup!" Chris shouted, his voice commanding.

Deepak spun his staff, creating a gust of wind to knock back an incoming wave of demons. "What's the plan?"

Chris glanced around, his mind piecing together what he had seen of their abilities. Allegra and Edward were already working well together, their water and gravity essences complementing each other. Deepak's wind could keep enemies at bay, and Luke's hammer had the raw power to hold the line. Faith's vines were a natural shield, and Lyra's light essence could strike with precision. If only Richard and Ali hadn't run off…

"Luke, Deepak, hold the front and keep them from advancing. Faith, keep reinforcing the barrier around the Stone. Allegra and Edward, we need you to hit their flanks—work together like you were before. Lyra—" He hesitated, realizing she was still fighting alone.

"I'll bring her back," Chris muttered to himself. He dashed toward where Lyra's arrows of light were streaking through the air, leaving blazing trails as they struck demons with precision.

"Lyra!" Chris called, dodging a demon as he slid beside her. "We need you with the team."

She fired another arrow, her frustration still evident. "I'm not leaving the flank exposed. Someone has to deal with this mess."

"We're all dealing with it," Chris said firmly, his blade crackling with electricity as he slashed through a demon lunging toward her. "But we can't win if we're all scattered. You're too good a shot to be out here alone."

Lyra glanced at him, her bow lowering slightly as his words sank in. She exhaled, nodding reluctantly. "Fine. Let's go."

Together, they made their way back to the group. Chris's lightning and Lyra's arrows created a path of destruction, clearing the way for their retreat.

When they rejoined the others, Chris barked out commands, his confidence growing. "Allegra, Edward—collapse the flanks and push them toward the center. Deepak, give Luke cover with wind. Lyra, take high ground and pick off anything that gets through. Faith, keep that barrier strong. We've got this."

The recruits moved as one, their teamwork clicking into place. Allegra's water surged in powerful waves, forcing demons into Edward's gravitational traps, where they were crushed or immobilized. Deepak's windstorms kept the enemies at bay, while Luke's hammer smashed through any that dared get too close. Lyra's arrows rained down from above, each shot precise and devastating.

The sounds of battle roared from the dense forest—gusts of wind tearing through trees, the sharp hum of sound waves slicing the air, and the guttural growls of demons. The ground shuddered as the first wave of grotesque, shadowy forms burst from the treeline. Their jagged claws gleamed in the eerie red glow of their eyes, and their chaotic movements honed in on the Stone of Eden.

"Lyra, light them up!" Chris shouted, his voice cutting through the chaos.

Without hesitation, Lyra notched an arrow in her glowing light bow, drawing the string until it hummed with radiant energy. She released, and the arrow burst into a brilliant flash midair, illuminating the clearing in a cascade of shimmering gold. The demons recoiled, their snarls turning to panicked howls as the light seared their senses, throwing them into disarray.

"Allegra, corral them!" Chris commanded, his grip tightening on the hilt of the Eclipse Blade.

Allegra stepped forward with calm precision, planting her trident firmly into the ground. Water erupted from its prongs, spiraling outward in fluid arcs. The streams twisted and surged, her movements guiding the liquid like an extension of herself. The rushing water coiled around the demons, funneling them into a tighter formation as they thrashed against its unyielding current.

"Chris, now!" Allegra called, her voice steady despite the mounting tension.

Lightning crackled along the length of Chris's blade, illuminating his determined expression. With a powerful swing, he sent a surge of electricity racing through the water. The current arced instantly, shocking the trapped demons. Their snarls turned into agonized shrieks before their forms disintegrated into black smoke, fading into the night.

"Nice one," Allegra said, pulling her trident free and twirling it expertly as she readied for another attack.

"We've got more incoming!" Luke warned, his deep voice steady as he hefted his massive hammer. He brought it crashing to the ground, and jagged spikes of earth erupted in a straight line, impaling several demons that attempted to flank the group. Their bodies crumbled into ash as the earth swallowed them whole.

Lyra darted forward, her light bow shimmering as she fired a rapid volley of arrows. Each shot struck true, piercing through the demonic forms with surgical precision. "That's all you've got?" she called out, her voice laced with both adrenaline and confidence as she drew another arrow, its tip glowing with concentrated energy.

From the far side of the battlefield, Faith extended her gauntleted hands, vines snaking out from the ground at her command. The plants surged forward, wrapping around a cluster of demons and immobilizing them. She clenched her fists, and the vines constricted, crushing the creatures with a resounding crack.

"Keep it up, Faith!" Deepak shouted, spinning his staff in a wide arc. A powerful gust of wind swept across the field, knocking another wave of demons off balance and scattering their ranks. He grinned, his confidence growing as he adjusted his stance for the next attack.

Edward, standing a few paces behind the group, moved with an eerie calm. With a flick of his hand, the weapon he wielded glowed faintly, bending gravity around it. He thrust it forward, and the space in front of him warped. A group of demons froze mid-lunge, their forms suspended in the distorted field. Edward's expression remained unreadable as he twisted his wrist, sending the creatures hurtling backward into a jagged rock formation.

Allegra, fighting side by side with Edward, glanced at him briefly. "Not bad," she said with a faint smile, her water surging forward to strike down a few stragglers. "You're precise—I like that."

Edward didn't respond, his focus unwavering, but his actions spoke volumes as he continued manipulating the battlefield with calculated efficiency.

Chris took a moment to survey the group. They were holding their own, but he knew this wasn't sustainable. The demons kept coming, and their scattered efforts, while effective for now, wouldn't hold against a prolonged assault.

"Everyone, regroup!" Chris yelled, slashing through another demon as he ran toward the center of the field. "We need to work together!"

His voice carried over the chaos, and slowly, the recruits began to rally around him. Allegra and Edward covered the left flank, their water and gravity essences combining to drive the demons into a bottleneck. Deepak and Luke held the front, with wind and earth creating a nearly impenetrable wall. Faith reinforced their position, her vines weaving into barriers that held back the relentless horde. Lyra took to higher ground, her light arrows raining down with deadly accuracy.

When they were finally gathered, Chris raised his blade, its lightning crackling brightly. "Here's the plan," he began, his voice steady despite the tension.

Suddenly, the sound of hurried footsteps and snapping branches drew everyone's attention. Richard and Ali burst through the tree line, their faces flushed and their movements frantic.

"Uh, guys," Richard called out, his usual bravado tinged with urgency.

"We have a problem," Ali added, his tone low and serious.

Chris's eyes shifted to Ali, and the flames dancing along the edge of his blade caught his attention. The fire roared like a living thing, casting flickering shadows that twisted in the dim light. Chris froze, his stomach churning as his gaze locked onto the fiery blade. A chill ran down his spine, and his surroundings began to blur.

The fire wasn't just on Ali's blade anymore—it grew, spreading uncontrollably in Chris's mind. The edges of his vision darkened, and he was back in his original timeline. Flames consumed his childhood home, their heat oppressive and suffocating. He could hear the roar of the fire, the splintering of wood, and the desperate cries of his mother as she pulled him through the chaos. The memory burned as vividly as the flames, and then he saw his father—still and lifeless, silhouetted against the inferno.

His breath came in short, shallow bursts. The fire on Ali's blade seemed to mock him, daring him to confront it. His grip on the Eclipse Blade faltered, trembling as the fear and pain of that night threatened to pull him under.

"Chris!" Allegra's voice cut through the haze like a splash of cold water. She stepped closer, her tone sharp and commanding. "Snap out of it!"

Her words jolted him back to the present. Chris blinked rapidly, his vision clearing as the battlefield came back into focus. The trees, the team, and the tense atmosphere grounded him once more. His gaze darted to Allegra, whose piercing eyes were fixed on him.

"What's going on?" Chris managed, his voice unsteady as he tried to regain his footing.

"Titans," Ali said grimly, his blade still aflame.

Chris blinked, his brow furrowing. "Titans?"

"Titans," Richard confirmed, his usual humor absent as he pointed toward the tree line.

Chris followed his gaze, and his stomach sank. Emerging from the shadows of the forest were two massive demons, their hulking forms towering over the smaller demons surrounding them. The Titans moved with a terrifying purpose, their glowing red eyes fixed on the Stone of Eden. The ground seemed to shake beneath their enormous, clawed feet as they advanced.

Behind the Titans, a swarm of lower-level demons surged forward, their guttural growls echoing ominously. The sight was enough to send a ripple of unease through the group.

The recruits fell into a tense silence, their earlier panic threatening to resurface. Chris shook his head, forcing the lingering fear of the fire and his memories to the back of his mind. He gripped the hilt of the Eclipse Blade tightly, its lightning crackling in defiance.

Chris raised his voice, his tone steady and commanding as the team began to gather themselves. "Alright, everyone, focus!" he called, his eyes scanning each of them, measuring their resolve. The Titans were closing in, their massive forms shaking the ground with every step, and the swarm of smaller demons surged behind them, snarling and chaotic.

Chris gripped the hilt of the Eclipse Blade, lightning crackling along its edge as he quickly pieced together a plan. His mind raced, assessing their strengths and how they could work together to turn the tide.

"Okay, listen up," Chris began, his voice cutting through the tension. "Here's the plan. Deepak, Edward—you two are up front. Use your wind and gravity to push the small ones back and keep them away from the Stone. Create as much distance as you can."

Deepak nodded, gripping his staff tightly. Edward, as stoic as ever, gave a curt nod, his eyes narrowing in focus.

"Faith," Chris continued, turning to the timid girl whose eyes widened at the sound of her name. "Use your vines to wrap the Titans' legs. Slow them down and keep them from advancing."

Faith swallowed hard but clenched her fists, the gauntlets on her hands sparking faintly with green energy. "I'll do my best," she said softly, determination flickering in her voice.

"Luke," Chris said, locking eyes with the quiet recruit. "Use your hammer to create holes in the ground—trip them up. We need to keep them off balance."

Luke hefted his hammer, its weight solid and reassuring in his grip. "Got it," he said simply.

Chris's gaze shifted to Ali and Richard, who were already catching their breath from their earlier skirmish. "Ali, Richard— you're on the smaller demons. Clear as many of them as you can. Keep the pressure off the rest of us."

Richard smirked, his cocky demeanor returning. "Finally, the fun part," he quipped, earning an eye roll from Lyra, who stood beside him.

"Lyra," Chris continued, ignoring the jab, "blind the Titans with your light. We need to disorient them long enough to make our move."

Lyra nodded, her bow already drawn. "Consider it done," she said, her voice calm and focused.

Finally, Chris turned to Allegra. "You take the one on the left, and I'll take the one on the right. When they fall, go for the neck. We'll take them out together."

Allegra spun her trident in her hand, the water swirling around it in shimmering arcs. "I'm with you," she said, her voice resolute.

Chris took a deep breath, looking at each of his teammates,

their faces a mixture of determination and nerves. "We've got this," he said, his voice steady. "Ready?"

"Ready," they said in unison, their voices strong and unified.

"Go!" Chris commanded, and the group broke into action.

Deepak and Edward rushed forward, taking position at the front. Deepak twirled his staff, the air around him swirling into a fierce gust that pushed back the swarm of demons. Edward followed, his weapon humming with spatial energy as he manipulated the gravity around the smaller demons, crushing some and pinning others in place. The combination of wind and gravity created a barrier that slowed the horde, giving the rest of the team room to move.

Faith ran toward the Titans, her gauntlets glowing green as vines burst from the ground, coiling around the massive demons' legs. The Titans roared in frustration, their movements hindered as the vines tightened, pulling them closer to the ground.

Luke followed closely behind, slamming his hammer into the earth with a resounding crack. The ground split beneath the Titans, forming jagged holes that made it difficult for them to keep their footing. One of the Titans stumbled, its massive body lurching as it struggled to regain balance.

"Now!" Chris shouted, his voice carrying over the chaos.

Lyra drew back her bow, the light arrow glowing brightly before she released it. The arrow burst in a blinding flash, forcing the Titans to reel back as their vision was consumed by the brilliant light.

Ali and Richard charged into the swarm of smaller demons, their movements fluid and coordinated despite their earlier recklessness. Ali's blade erupted in flames as he sliced through the advancing creatures, while Richard's sound waves rippled through the battlefield, disorienting the demons and sending them crashing into one another.

Chris sprinted toward the Titan on the right, lightning coursing through his blade. He dodged the sweeping claws of the massive demon, his movements quick and precise. Allegra mirrored him on the left, her trident glinting as water surged around her, slamming into the Titan's side and throwing it off balance.

The Titans began to falter, their enormous forms struggling under the combined assault of the recruits. Chris leaped into the air, lightning crackling along the edge of his blade as he aimed for the Titan's neck. Allegra's trident glowed with power as she thrust it forward, water slicing through the air like a blade.

"Now!" Chris and Allegra shouted in unison, their voices ringing out as their weapons struck true. The Titans roared one last time before collapsing, their massive bodies disintegrating into ash.

The battlefield fell silent for a moment, the recruits catching their breath as the last remnants of the demon swarm faded away. Chris lowered his blade, the lightning dissipating as he looked around at his team. They were battered and exhausted, but they had done it—together.

The battlefield fell silent as the team cautiously scanned their surroundings. The air, once thick with tension, now felt still and weightless.

"Is it…?" Ali began, his voice trailing off, still uncertain.

Before anyone could respond, the world around them shimmered and shifted, the eerie landscape dissolving back into the familiar training grounds. The towering trees, the clawed earth, and the ominous sky were replaced with the neat, controlled environment they had started in.

"Yeah," Chris said, lowering the Eclipse Blade as the last traces of the simulation faded. "It's over."

"And that," Richard said, breaking the silence with his trademark grin, "is what teamwork looks like." His tone was playful, but there was genuine pride beneath his words.

The group broke into scattered cheers and relieved laughter, their exhaustion momentarily forgotten in the glow of victory. Lyra, who had been quietly catching her breath, even allowed herself a small smile as she glanced at Richard—a rare moment of camaraderie between the two.

Faith, her gauntlets still faintly glowing, raised her hands in celebration. "That was amazing! Great plan, Chris," she said, her voice bright with excitement. "How'd you know that would work?"

Chris rubbed the back of his neck, his smile modest. "I just thought if the Titans were that big, we needed to bring them down to our level. Make it a fair fight."

"And that is exactly what you did," a familiar voice cut through the celebration, sharp and commanding. Vincent's presence seemed to drain the air of its lightness, but his words carried an unusual undertone of approval.

The team turned as Vincent approached, his gaze sweeping over them with an unreadable intensity. "Excellent job, everyone," he said, his tone steady, though there was a faint edge of satisfaction. "Teamwork, communication, and trust were all on display today. You've proven that you can work as a unit."

The recruits stood a little taller at his words, the weight of his rare compliment sinking in. Even Chris, who often felt the brunt of Vincent's scrutiny, couldn't help but feel a flicker of pride.

"The day is over," Vincent continued. "Go home and rest. You've earned it."

The squad exchanged relieved glances, the lingering adrenaline from the simulation fading into the contentment of a job well done. Small smiles appeared across the group, and even Luke, usually reserved, looked quietly pleased.

"Thank you, Captain," they said in unison, their voices filled with respect and gratitude.

As Vincent turned and walked away, the recruits began to gather their things, the glow of their success still palpable. Richard slung an arm over Ali's shoulder, grinning. "See, that wasn't so bad. We're practically legends already."

Lyra rolled her eyes but didn't bother hiding her smirk. "Let's just see if you can keep up next time, Richard."

"I think I did just fine," he shot back, puffing out his chest dramatically.

Faith laughed softly, her shy demeanor starting to thaw in the warmth of the group's camaraderie. "I can't believe we actually did it," she said, her tone almost incredulous.

Allegra twirled her trident with a satisfied smirk. "Believe it. We're a team now."

Chris looked around at his teammates, each of them glowing with a mixture of pride and relief. For the first time since joining Michael's squad, he felt a true sense of belonging. This wasn't just a team—they were becoming something more. And for now, that was enough.

The group exited the training grounds, their chatter and laughter filling the air as they walked toward the academy cafeteria. The simulated battle had worn them out, and the thought of a hot meal was enough to make even the usually reserved recruits loosen up.

"I don't know about you guys," Richard said, stretching his arms dramatically, "but I feel like I just fought a hundred demons single-handedly. Someone better feed me before I collapse."

Deepak smirked, nudging him. "You didn't fight anything single-handedly. You ran into the woods and nearly got us all killed."

Richard feigned offense, placing a hand on his chest. "Untrue! I was strategically testing the waters. You're welcome, by the way."

Lyra, walking a few paces ahead, rolled her eyes but couldn't suppress a small grin. "Strategic recklessness isn't exactly a virtue, Richard."

Chris, walking beside her, chuckled. "I think that's just his way of saying he panicked and got lucky."

Richard pointed dramatically at Chris. "Seriously, Lightning Boy? I thought we were bonding back there!"

"Bonding over what? Your terrible strategy?" Chris shot back with a teasing smirk.

The group burst into laughter as they approached the cafeteria. Allegra held the door open for everyone, her trident resting casually over her shoulder. "Come on, let's get food before Richard starts eating the table."

Inside, the cafeteria buzzed with the usual hum of recruits swapping stories and theories about their training sessions. The scent of roasted meats, fresh bread, and warm spices filled the air. The group grabbed trays and lined up at the buffet, their conversation continuing as they piled their plates high.

Chris's eyes scanned the cafeteria, weaving through the sea of faces in search of Sophie or Eli. His chest tightened slightly when he realized they weren't there. It was a small hope, fleeting and fragile, but he had held onto it anyway. No luck.

"Chris?" Lyra's voice pulled him from his thoughts, and he turned to see her standing a few steps away, her gaze questioning but patient. "You coming?" she asked, tilting her head slightly toward the group.

He blinked, refocusing, and nodded. "Yeah, I'm coming," he said, shaking off the lingering disappointment as he followed her back to the others.

"I'm just saying," Deepak said as he loaded his tray with pasta, "if we keep this up, we might actually stand a chance against real demons. That plan today? Genius, Chris."

Chris shrugged modestly. "It was a team effort."

Allegra, standing beside him, nodded. "True, but someone had to take the lead. You did good."

Lyra, reaching for a bowl of soup, glanced at Chris out of the corner of her eye. "Yeah, you're a natural at this," she said softly, her tone sincere. "It's easy to see why Vincent's keeping an eye on you."

Chris glanced at her, slightly taken aback by her directness. "Thanks, Lyra. That means a lot."

Allegra caught the exchange and raised an eyebrow but said nothing, a small smile playing at her lips as she turned back to the food.

Once everyone had their plates filled, they claimed a large table near the windows. The late afternoon sunlight streamed in, casting a warm glow over the group as they settled in and began eating.

"So," Allegra said, breaking the comfortable silence as she twirled her fork in her pasta, "if today was a test of teamwork, what do you guys think tomorrow will be?"

"Hopefully something less exhausting," Faith said, her voice still shy but carrying a note of hope.

"Don't count on it," Ali said, biting into a piece of bread. "If Vincent's involved, it'll only get tougher from here."

Lyra leaned forward slightly, her elbows resting on the table. "It's not just about the training. It's about seeing how we handle pressure—how we adapt. I think that's what Vincent's looking for."

Chris nodded, his fork paused midair. "Yeah. And after today, I think we're starting to figure it out. We just need to keep building on that."

Lyra smiled, her gaze lingering on him for a moment longer than necessary. "You really think so?"

"I do," Chris said, meeting her eyes. "We've got a long way to go, but we're getting there."

Richard, oblivious to the subtle exchange, leaned back in his chair and stretched. "As long as I'm not the one doing all the heavy lifting, we'll be fine."

"You mean as long as you're not the one running off into the woods," Lyra quipped, her sharp wit cutting through his bravado.

"Touché," Richard admitted with a grin. "But come on, admit it—I make things interesting."

Allegra laughed. "Interesting isn't always a good thing, Richard."

The group chuckled, the tension from earlier dissipating further with each passing moment. Faith, who had been quietly listening, finally spoke up. "I think… I think we're starting to feel like a real team."

Everyone turned to her, and her cheeks flushed under the sudden attention, but she smiled. "I mean, today was hard, but we worked together. Even when it didn't seem like we could."

"Well said, Faith," Allegra agreed, lifting her glass in a mock toast. "To teamwork."

The group raised their glasses, even Edward, who seemed more interested in his dessert than the conversation. Lyra, however, glanced at Chris again as she clinked her glass against his. "To teamwork," she said softly, her voice carrying an undertone that made Allegra glance between them again, her suspicions growing.

As the meal wound down, Deepak leaned back in his chair, a satisfied grin on his face. "Okay, best part of the day? Definitely when Luke and Faith dropped that Titan. That was incredible."

Faith blushed and Luke, ever the quiet one, simply nodded, his expression calm. "It was a team effort."

"Come on, give yourself some credit," Richard said, nudging him.

Luke shrugged modestly, and the group laughed at his understated reaction.

"Speaking of credit," Ali said, turning to Chris, "how do you come up with plans like that on the fly? Is it just instinct?"

Chris hesitated, caught off guard by the question. "I don't know," he admitted. "I just try to think about what everyone's good at and how we can work together. It's not just me—it's all of us."

Lyra smiled, her eyes softening. "It's a good trait to have. Not everyone can do that."

Chris met her gaze, a flicker of uncertainty passing through him. "Thanks," he said quietly.

As the group began clearing their trays and preparing to leave, Allegra leaned toward Chris with a playful smirk. "You've got quite the fan club," she teased under her breath, her eyes darting toward Lyra.

Chris blinked, confused for a moment, before following her gaze. Lyra was helping Faith with her tray, her usual reserved demeanor relaxed. "What are you talking about?" he asked, his voice low.

Allegra just chuckled, shaking her head. "Nothing. Forget I said anything."

As the recruits filed out of the cafeteria, their laughter echoing in the hall, Chris felt a warmth settle over him. The day had been exhausting, but moments like this—where they could just be themselves—reminded him why he was here. For the first time in a long while, he felt like he belonged. And that was enough.

16

Team Ten

The weeks that followed their first major training session were grueling, intense, and, oddly enough, rewarding. Each day, Team Ten of Michael's squad honed their skills under Vincent's watchful eye, their sessions designed to push them beyond their limits. Despite the exhausting routines and the occasional clash of personalities, the recruits began to find their rhythm—not just as individuals but as a team.

The mornings always started in the resonance chambers, where the recruits were pushed to deepen their connection to their soul essence. The training was as much mental as it was physical, and Vincent left little room for error. Yet, as the days passed, the group's focus sharpened, their abilities growing stronger.

One crisp morning, the team stood outside on the training grounds, weapons in hand, as Vincent gave his usual stoic instructions.

"Today, you'll run a synchronized strike drill," he said, pacing in front of them. "The objective is simple: incapacitate the target while protecting your squad mates. Any lapse in coordination will result in failure." He paused, his piercing gaze moving over them. "Begin."

As the group took their positions, Chris turned to the others. "Alright, same formation we talked about. Deepak and Edward, control the movement of the targets. Lyra, keep us covered with suppressive light shots. Faith, you're on support with your vines—trap anything that gets too close. Allegra and I will go in for the strikes."

Lyra gave him a subtle nod as she pulled back her light bow. "Got it. Let's keep it tight."

"Ready when you are," Allegra said, twirling her trident, a confident smile playing on her lips.

Deepak, standing at the front with his staff, grinned. "I'll send them flying before they even know what hit them."

With a whistle, the targets—a collection of glowing, fast-moving dummies—shot forward. Deepak swept his staff, summoning a powerful gust of wind that scattered the incoming targets, while Edward used his gravity manipulation to pull them back into a tight cluster.

"Lyra, now!" Chris shouted.

Lyra shot off a series of glowing arrows, each finding its mark and momentarily stunning the targets with bursts of radiant light. The coordinated strikes bought enough time for Faith to lash out with her vines, ensnaring the dummies' legs and pulling them to the ground.

Allegra charged forward, water swirling around her trident as she struck with precision, while Chris followed up with a lightning-quick slash from his Eclipse Blade. The synchronized assault was seamless, the group moving like a well-oiled machine.

When the last dummy hit the ground, Vincent stepped forward, his expression as impassive as ever. "Better," he said simply, though there was the faintest hint of approval in his tone. "Reset and do it again."

Outside of training, the group spent most of their time together, sharing meals, walking the academy grounds, and even sneaking in the occasional laugh. Their dynamic, once marked by hesitance and unfamiliarity, had transformed into a sense of camaraderie.

Later that evening, they gathered in the cafeteria after another long day, their exhaustion evident as they slumped into their seats.

"I'm pretty sure Vincent's secretly trying to kill us," Richard said dramatically, dropping his tray on the table. "No one runs that many drills unless they have a personal vendetta."

"You just don't like running," Allegra teased, taking a bite of her food.

"True," Richard admitted, pointing his fork at her. "But it's still excessive."

"It's working, though," Faith said quietly, her voice gaining confidence with each passing day. "We're getting better."

Ali grinned. "See? Even Faith thinks you're complaining too much, Richard."

"Hey!" Richard protested, but the table broke into light

laughter.

Chris, sitting beside Lyra, shook his head with a small smile. "He's not wrong, though. The drills are brutal."

"Yeah, but they're paying off," Lyra said, glancing at him. "We're actually starting to look like a team out there."

Chris met her gaze, and for a moment, something unspoken passed between them. Allegra, seated across from them, caught the brief exchange and raised an eyebrow but said nothing, a knowing smile tugging at her lips.

"Alright, since we're all so close now," Richard said, leaning forward with a mischievous grin, "I think it's time for some team bonding. Let's share our most embarrassing moments. Who's in?"

"Not it," Luke said immediately, crossing his arms.

Faith giggled. "I'll go first," she said, surprising everyone. "When I was eight, I tried to climb a tree to impress some older kids… and got stuck. They had to call my mom to get me down."

The table erupted in laughter, even Luke cracking a small smile. "Classic," Ali said, shaking his head.

Chris chuckled, leaning back in his chair. "Alright, Faith set the bar. Who's next?"

By the end of the second week, the group's progress was undeniable. During a midweek sparring session, they were paired off to test their individual skills.

Chris faced Allegra, their weapons clashing in a controlled yet intense exchange. She moved with fluidity, her water essence enhancing her strikes, while Chris countered with precise arcs of lightning.

"You're fast," Allegra said, grinning as she parried a strike.

"You're not bad yourself," Chris replied, stepping back and feinting to the side.

Across the training grounds, Lyra and Richard sparred, their dynamic as competitive as ever.

"Try to keep up, Lyra!" Richard taunted, sending a blast of sound toward her.

Lyra dodged gracefully, pulling back her light bow and firing an arrow that struck the ground at his feet. The burst of light made him stumble, and she smirked. "Maybe you should focus more on your aim, Richard."

"You're lucky I like you," Richard quipped, shaking his head.

Meanwhile, Luke and Deepak sparred nearby, their contrasting styles creating a unique spectacle. Luke's hammer sent shock waves through the ground, while Deepak used his air essence to glide around the arena, avoiding the strikes with ease.

"Nice one!" Deepak said, narrowly dodging a swing. "But you're going to have to be quicker than that."

Luke grunted, a small smirk betraying his amusement. "We'll see."

After another successful training session, the group lingered on the field, the sun setting behind the academy. The golden light bathed the grounds, and for a moment, everything felt calm.

"I hate to admit it," Richard said, breaking the silence, "but I think we're actually getting good at this."

"We've come a long way," Lyra agreed, her gaze briefly flicking to Chris. "And we've still got more to learn."

Chris nodded, the weight of leadership settling comfortably on his shoulders now. "As long as we keep pushing, we'll be ready for whatever comes next."

Allegra smiled, twirling her trident idly. "Well said, Lightning Boy."

The group laughed, the sound carrying into the quiet evening air. Though challenges surely lay ahead, for now, they were a team—and that was enough.

The next day another routine training session came to an end. The recruits dispersed from the field, laughing and chatting as they gathered their gear. Allegra, however, was distracted. She watched as Lyra lingered, her movements slow and deliberate as she adjusted the quiver on her back. Allegra's eyes narrowed slightly. Over the past few weeks, she couldn't help but notice the subtle glances Lyra sent Chris's way during drills, the way her tone softened when she spoke to him, the small smiles she offered when he gave instructions. It wasn't just friendly—it was something more.

It didn't help that Chris, though seemingly oblivious, had started spending more time with Lyra, talking strategy or refining techniques after the group had broken off for the day. Allegra tried to ignore the feeling that twisted in her chest whenever she saw them together, but tonight, it was impossible to push aside.

As Lyra adjusted her gear and glanced toward the path leading away from the training grounds, something in her demeanor struck Allegra as… unusual. Lyra wasn't heading toward the group or back to the common area where the team often gathered after practice. Instead, she took a sharp turn down a quieter path leading to the east wing of the academy.

Allegra hesitated, her fingers tightening around her trident. What's she up to? she wondered, her curiosity and jealousy mingling into something undeniable. Without giving herself time to overthink, she followed.

Allegra stayed far enough behind to avoid being seen, her steps light and careful. Lyra moved with purpose, her eyes fixed ahead as the path narrowed. Allegra's heart thudded in her chest as they approached a shadowed corridor near the academy's administrative wing. She slowed her pace, ducking behind a pillar as Lyra came to a stop outside a dimly lit office.

To Allegra's surprise, two figures were already waiting: Richard, leaning casually against the wall, and Vincent, standing tall with his arms crossed. The sight of the captain sent a chill through Allegra. There was something about his presence that always felt unsettling, as though he carried the weight of unspoken intentions.

Lyra approached the two figures waiting near the shadowed corner of the grounds. Her expression was unreadable, her shoulders squared, and her movements purposeful. Vincent stood tall, his arms crossed, his piercing gaze sweeping the area like a predator surveying its domain. Beside him, Richard leaned casually against the wall, though the tension in his posture betrayed the unease beneath his usual bravado.

"Is everything ready?" Vincent asked, his voice low and commanding.

Allegra crouched behind a pillar a safe distance away, her breath shallow as she strained to hear. She watched Lyra nod, her tone measured but laced with something unspoken. "We're making progress," she said. "But we need more time."

Richard shifted, glancing between Lyra and Vincent. His usual cocky grin was nowhere to be seen. "We're being careful," he said, his voice unusually serious. "No one knows."

Vincent's gaze sharpened, and the air seemed to grow colder, as if the very shadows around him were responding to his presence. "See that it stays that way," he said, his tone as cutting as a blade. "I don't tolerate mistakes."

Allegra's grip tightened on her trident as she peeked out from her hiding spot. She could feel the weight of Vincent's words, the ominous energy radiating from him, even from where she was hidden. Her instincts screamed that something wasn't right, though she couldn't yet piece together what.

Vincent turned abruptly and opened the heavy door to his office. Without hesitation, Lyra and Richard followed him inside, their expressions serious. The door clicked shut behind them, sealing the trio inside. Allegra's heart raced as she stared at the closed door, her thoughts spinning wildly. Whatever they were discussing wasn't meant for anyone else to hear— that much was clear.

The energy around the office felt heavy, almost suffocating, as if it had its own presence. Allegra shivered, the sensation of being watched prickling at the back of her neck. She knew better than to linger. Quietly and carefully, she slipped away, her steps light and deliberate, ensuring she didn't make a sound. As she moved farther from the office, the oppressive energy began to lift, but the questions in her mind only multiplied.

By the time Allegra reached the open grounds again, her thoughts were a whirlwind. What could Lyra, Richard, and Vincent possibly be discussing in secret? Why the secrecy? And why did it feel so wrong?

She glanced back one last time at the darkened windows of Vincent's office before continuing on her way, her resolve hardening. Whatever was going on, she couldn't ignore it. She would need to talk to Chris—but first, she needed to figure out how to approach him without sounding like she was jumping to conclusions. One thing was certain: this wasn't over.

The next day Chris stood near the edge of the training grounds, stretching under the golden morning sun. The cool air carried a sense of calm as the team began to trickle in, their voices low and spirits high after weeks of progress. He rolled his shoulders, mentally preparing for another rigorous session, when Allegra's voice broke through his thoughts.

"Chris," she called, her tone clipped and serious.

He looked up, surprised by the urgency in her steps. "Allegra? What's going on?"

Glancing around to ensure no one was within earshot, Allegra stopped in front of him, her grip tightening on her trident. "We need to talk," she said quietly, her voice firm.

Chris frowned, his posture straightening. "About what?"

Allegra took a breath, meeting his eyes. "Lyra and Richard," she began. "Last night, after training, I followed Lyra. She slipped away from the group, and I saw her meet up with Richard—and Vincent. They went into his office."

Chris blinked, his confusion quickly shifting to a mix of disbelief and mild annoyance. "Wait, you *followed* her? Allegra, what are you doing?"

"I know how it sounds," she said sharply, cutting him off. "But something felt off, Chris. I couldn't ignore it. They were talking about keeping something quiet, about making sure no one found out. Captain Vincent was giving them orders. It wasn't just a casual conversation."

Chris folded his arms across his chest, his jaw tightening as he processed her words. "The team's been doing really well lately," he said defensively. "Why are you jumping to conclusions? Lyra and Richard might've been discussing strategy, or who knows— maybe something Vincent assigned them. Yeah, I'm not the biggest fan of his, but he's still our captain. If he's giving them orders, there's probably a reason. They have been on the squad for a year."

Allegra's frustration bubbled to the surface, but under it,

something colder stirred. Something she hated to admit. "Chris, think about it. Lyra and Richard hate each other—and now they're sneaking off together. Doesn't that strike you as wrong?"

Chris exhaled sharply, running a hand through his hair. "No, I don't," he said, his tone edged with irritation. "We've all been working hard, and the team's finally starting to click. Why would I start tearing apart what we've built because of a hunch?"

Allegra's chest tightened. It wasn't just a hunch—and it wasn't just suspicion. But how could she say that without sounding like a jealous fool?

Allegra's eyes narrowed, her grip on her trident tightening. "Because it's not just a hunch. You didn't see the way they were acting—Richard wasn't even joking around like he always does. And the energy around the Captain's office? It wasn't normal. As the leader of this team, you should at least be aware of what's happening."

Chris scoffed, his frustration boiling over. "I'm *not* the leader. We are a unit."

"Yes, you are," Allegra shot back, her voice firm but not unkind. "You can run from the title, but it doesn't change the fact that everyone sees you that way. Ali, Deepak, Faith, Luke—heck, even Edward—they all look to you. Whether you like it or not, you set the tone for this team."

Chris fell silent, her words hitting him harder than he cared to admit. His gaze dropped briefly before he shook his head. "I get what you're saying," he said after a moment, his tone softer but still guarded. "But accusing Lyra and Richard of something without proof? That's not how we keep this team together. The last thing we need is paranoia."

Allegra took a step back, exhaling slowly. "I'm not asking you to accuse anyone, Chris. I'm just saying—be careful. Lyra's...

not right. I don't know how else to explain it, but something about her isn't adding up."

Chris hesitated, glancing over Allegra's shoulder toward the rest of the group assembling on the field. Lyra stood near Deepak, her light bow resting on her shoulder as she laughed at something he said. Richard stood by Ali, cracking jokes as usual. They looked… normal. Relaxed. For a moment, Chris felt like he could dismiss Allegra's words entirely. But then he looked back at her, at the resolute determination in her eyes, and something about it stuck.

"Fine," he said finally, his tone resigned. "I'll keep an eye on things. But I'm not going to jump to conclusions, Allegra. The team needs trust right now, not suspicion."

Her lips pressed into a thin line, but she nodded. "I just thought you should know," she said, stepping back and lowering her trident.

He nodded reluctantly, watching as she turned and made her way toward the others. The weight of her warning lingered as he adjusted his blade, the familiar hum of its lightning resonating faintly in his grip. He glanced toward Lyra again, her easy smile lighting up her face as she spoke with Richard.

"Trust," he muttered to himself, trying to shake the unease creeping into his chest.

But Allegra's voice echoed in his mind, refusing to be ignored: *"Be careful. Lyra's not right."*

After another grueling day of training, the team began to gather their things, their chatter low but relaxed. The routine had become almost second nature by now, their movements fluid and synchronized. Chris had just slung his blade over his shoulder when Vincent's sharp voice cut through the air like a whip.

"Chris, stay behind for a moment."

The group froze, their heads turning toward Chris. Allegra caught his eye, her brows knitting with concern. She gave him a small, reassuring nod. "We'll see you later," she said softly before joining the others as they made their way toward the academy gates.

Chris turned to Vincent, his fingers instinctively tightening around the hilt of the Eclipse Blade. "Yes, sir?"

"Come with me," Vincent said, his tone leaving no room for hesitation.

Chris swallowed his apprehension and followed Vincent into the academy. The sun's golden rays faded behind them, replaced by the dim, flickering glow of the corridor lights. The walk was silent, each of Vincent's steps measured, each echo unsettling. When they reached Vincent's chambers, the door creaked open, and Chris stepped inside.

The room was exactly as he expected: cold, sparse, and unwelcoming. A large desk stood at the center, papers neatly stacked, a single lamp casting long shadows across the space. Vincent gestured for Chris to sit in a rigid wooden chair opposite his desk. Chris hesitated for a moment before lowering himself into the seat, the weight of the room pressing down on him.

Vincent paced slowly behind his desk, his hands clasped behind his back. "Each squad," he began, his voice calm yet cutting, "is composed with precision. The right balance of strengths and weaknesses. Normally, after a few weeks, rookie groups like yours are dissolved and redistributed into more seasoned squads."

Chris tilted his head slightly, unsure of where this was leading. "But...?" he prompted.

Vincent stopped pacing and turned to face him, his eyes narrowing. "But your group has shown accelerated growth. Remarkable chemistry. It's rare. Tell me, Chris, why do you think that is?"

Chris shifted uncomfortably in his seat, trying to gauge Vincent's intent. "I think it's because we've built trust," he said cautiously. "We support each other, on and off the field. That bond makes us stronger."

Vincent's lips curled into a faint, almost mocking smile. "Trust? Bond?" he echoed. "How quaint." He leaned forward slightly, his piercing gaze locking onto Chris. "You're wrong."

Chris blinked, startled by the bluntness. "Excuse me?"

"Your group is excelling," Vincent continued, "because I hand picked each of you. Every strength, every flaw, every nuance of your personalities—I accounted for all of it. You're performing exactly as I expected you to because I designed it that way."

The words hung heavy in the air. Chris's stomach twisted. Was this supposed to be a compliment? A warning? He couldn't tell.

Vincent's piercing gaze fixed on Chris as he leaned back in his chair, his presence filling the sparsely lit chamber. His words were deliberate, each syllable chosen with precision. "After seeing the development of your team, do you still have doubts about Archangel Michael giving me the authority to assign squads? Because I can assure you, Chris, each and every squad is experiencing the same level of success as Team Ten."

Chris didn't flinch under Vincent's scrutiny, though his jaw tightened. He forced himself to stay calm, his mind racing with Allegra's words from the previous day. The unease she had planted refused to dissipate. "You say 'rookie squads,'" Chris began, his tone careful but pointed, "yet we have four sophomores on our team. Was that part of your plan as well?" He kept his expression neutral, though his question hung in the air like a dagger, hinting at the information Allegra had shared.

Vincent's lips curved into a faint smile, one that didn't reach his eyes. "Yes," he said smoothly, his tone measured. "You must understand something, Chris. The battles we have faced—and the ones we will face—are not just about strategy or brute strength. They reveal who we truly are. They expose our essence, the power we wield, and what we're truly made of."

Chris narrowed his eyes, his grip tightening on the armrest of the chair. "And what happens when people don't rise to your expectations?" he asked, his voice sharper than he intended. "What happens when they fall short?"

Vincent's smile faded, and the room seemed to grow colder. He leaned forward, resting his hands on the desk between them. "Some people cower. Some people run," he said, his voice low and cutting. "And some people rise. The question, Chris, is which type are you?"

The tension in the room was palpable, the silence that followed heavy with unspoken challenges. Chris felt the weight of Vincent's words pressing down on him, but he refused to look away. "You sound like you're testing me," Chris said finally, his voice steady despite the knot tightening in his stomach. "But I'm not sure what the point is. We're a team. If we fail, we fail together."

Vincent straightened, his sharp gaze never leaving Chris. "A noble sentiment," he said, almost mockingly. "But battles don't always leave room for nobility. Sometimes, survival depends on individual strength—and individual choices."

Chris's chest tightened as he read between the lines. There was a subtext to Vincent's words, something veiled but deliberate. He thought back to the moments in training when Vincent's attention seemed to linger on him, scrutinizing him in ways that felt almost personal.

"And what happens when those choices conflict with the team's survival?" Chris asked, his voice laced with suspicion.

Vincent's smile returned, colder than before. "That, Chris, is what these trials are meant to reveal. You'll find out soon enough."

Chris studied Vincent carefully, searching for any crack in the man's composed exterior, but Vincent offered none. Instead, the captain's words lingered, filled with an ominous weight that left Chris unsettled.

Vincent straightened, his gaze scrutinizing Chris like a hawk circling its prey. His eyes flicked to Chris's hand, where the black ring rested snugly on his finger. "And that ring," Vincent said, his tone sharper now. "What is it?"

Chris's heart skipped a beat, but he kept his expression neutral. "A gift from my dad," he said smoothly, twisting the band as though it were an idle habit. "He gave it to me when I formed my weapon. Said it matched my blade."

Vincent leaned back in his chair, his gaze steady and inscrutable as he finally broke the silence. "Interesting," he murmured, his tone unreadable.

After a moment, he folded his hands together, his voice taking on a conversational edge. "Giuseppe, your father, is a very smart man. I've known him for years. Did you know we were both rookies together on Raphael's squad? Back then, he had a saying he was particularly fond of: *Knowledge is power.* I wonder… did he instill those same sentiments in you?"

Chris hesitated for the briefest of moments before nodding. "Yes," he said carefully. "Knowledge is power. When you know a problem, you have the ability to do something about it."

Vincent's lips curled into a faint smile, though it didn't reach his eyes. "I couldn't have said it better myself."

The silence that followed was heavy, the air thick with something unspoken. Vincent's gaze lingered on Chris as if weighing every word, every gesture. Finally, with a flick of his hand, Vincent dismissed him. "You may go."

Chris stood, his movements slow and deliberate. He gave Vincent a polite nod before turning and leaving the room. The soft click of the door shutting behind him echoed in the stillness, a sound that sent a faint shiver down his spine.

The hallway was dimly lit, the glow from distant sconces casting long shadows that stretched across the walls. As Chris walked, his hand instinctively brushed over the ring on his finger, the smooth surface grounding him as his thoughts raced.

Dad, he thought through the device, his mind buzzing. *He asked about the ring.*

Giuseppe's response was immediate, his voice steady but tinged with concern. *What did you tell him?*

Chris exhaled slowly, keeping his pace measured as he descended the corridor. *The truth,* he replied. *Just... not the important part.*

There was a brief pause before his father's voice came through again, calm yet firm. *Good. Stay sharp, Chris. He's watching you closely now.*

Chris reached the end of the hallway, the faint hum of the training grounds filtering through the air. He paused, leaning against the cool stone wall for a moment as his thoughts churned. Why had Vincent summoned him? Was it simply to test him, or was there something deeper? Was Vincent probing for weaknesses, looking for cracks in the armor Chris tried so hard to maintain?

His mind drifted to Allegra's warning from earlier, her voice urgent as she insisted that something was off about Lyra and Richard.

Be careful, Chris. She's not right, Allegra had said.

Chris shook his head, trying to push the thought away. *Trust,* he reminded himself. *The team needs trust.*

The sun dipped low on the horizon, casting hues of orange and pink across the sprawling grounds of Eden Prep. Chris stepped out of the school gates, the quiet crunch of gravel beneath his boots breaking the stillness. He adjusted the strap of his blade across his back, ready to head home after another long day, when a familiar figure caught his attention near the edge of the courtyard.

He froze for a moment, a grin breaking across his face. "Sophie?"

She turned toward him, her hair catching the golden glow of the sunset. The smile that spread across her face was immediate and warm. "Chris!" she called back, her voice carrying across the quiet space.

When they reached each other, Sophie wrapped him in a quick but tight hug, one that spoke of familiarity and time apart. "It feels like it's been years," Chris said, stepping back but keeping his grin.

"It's been three weeks," Sophie corrected with a laugh, "but yeah, it feels like forever."

Chris chuckled, running a hand through his hair. "Three weeks feels like an eternity with everything going on. How've you been holding up?"

"Oh, you know," Sophie said, her tone teasing but fond. "Your dad's training is brutal. The first week, I thought my arms were going to fall off. But he's a great teacher—relentless, but fair. Honestly, I can see where you get your stubborn streak."

Chris laughed, shaking his head. "Yeah, that sounds about right. He always says, 'If you don't push past your limits, you'll never find your true strength.' Come to think of it, he has a lot of sayings." He mimicked his father's deep, authoritative tone, earning another laugh from Sophie.

"Exactly, he has a quote for everything." Sophie said, her laughter fading into a warm smile. "But, honestly, it's been good. He's been teaching us more advanced techniques—stuff I never thought I'd be ready for."

Chris chuckled knowingly. "Yeah, sounds about right. How bad is it?"

"Bad," Sophie said, though her tone was more amused than bitter. "First week, I thought I was going to pass out during sparring drills. He's relentless, Chris. Like, 'You will hold this stance until your legs give out' relentless."

Chris laughed, a genuine, hearty sound that made Sophie smile despite her exaggerated complaints. "Yeah, that's Dad. He's all about pushing you past your limits."

"And you're just as bad," Sophie said, nudging him playfully. "You inherited his stubbornness."

Chris raised a brow. "Oh, really?"

"Really," Sophie said, her grin widening. "But, honestly... It's been good. I feel like I'm getting better every day. Your dad's tough, but he's also... fair, I guess? He doesn't just push us to break—he pushes us to rebuild stronger."

Chris nodded, pride flickering in his expression. "That sounds like him. And you're one of the hardest workers I know. If anyone can handle his training, it's you."

Sophie blushed slightly as she looked down, her voice softening. "Thanks, Chris. That means a lot."

The two of them fell into step together, leaving the academy gates behind as they walked along the path bathed in the warm light of sunset. The quiet hum of the world around them set a peaceful tone for their conversation.

"So, how's your squad?" Sophie asked, glancing at him. "I heard you've been making waves."

Chris shrugged, though a small, almost sheepish smile tugged at his lips. "They're great. Tough, a little stubborn, but talented. We've been getting better every day."

"Let me guess," Sophie said, her voice teasing. "You're the glue holding everyone together."

Chris snorted. "Hardly. I'm just trying to keep up."

"Oh, please," Sophie said, rolling her eyes. "You've always been a natural leader, even if you don't see it. Trust me—your team knows it."

Chris's gaze drifted to the horizon, his voice thoughtful. "I don't know. Everyone's pulling their weight. It's starting to feel like we're actually a team, but… I don't know if I'd call myself the leader."

"Maybe not officially," Sophie said, "but I'd bet your team sees you that way anyway. You've got this way of pulling people together, Chris. It's one of your best traits."

Chris glanced at her, surprised by the sincerity in her tone. "Thanks, Soph."

They walked in companionable silence for a moment before Chris broke it. "Hey, have you heard from Eli?"

Sophie shook her head, her expression dimming slightly. "No, not since he left. His squad and a couple others got sent to Celestia Academy for training and I haven't had much time to check in."

Chris sighed, his fingers brushing against the strap of his blade. "I hope he's okay. I miss having him around."

"Me too," Sophie admitted. "But knowing Eli, he's probably throwing himself into training and getting stronger every day. You know how he is."

"Yeah," Chris said with a small smile. "Always trying to outdo himself."

Their conversation was interrupted by a sharp vibration in their pockets, followed by the shrill tone of an academy-wide alert.

Chris froze, pulling out his phone. Sophie did the same, her face tightening as she read the message:

Squad Members: Assemble with your teams immediately.

Chris slowly lowered his phone, feeling the weight of the words settle like a stone in his gut. Across from him, Sophie's brow furrowed, the easy warmth she'd carried a moment ago now stripped away.

They turned back toward the academy without another word, the fading sun casting long, skeletal shadows across the path. The lightheartedness they'd shared moments ago was gone, swallowed by a quiet dread.

As they walked, Chris glanced sideways at Sophie—grateful she was here, even if neither of them could fix what was coming.

"You ready for whatever this is?" he asked, his voice low, steady despite the unease gnawing at him.

Sophie managed a small, fierce smile. "Always. You?"

Chris smirked faintly, though it felt heavier than usual. "You know me. Too stubborn to back down now."

They quickened their pace, the academy looming ahead, its walls bathed in the last blood-red light of sunset.

Behind them, the shadows stretched longer.

17

The Defense of Celestia Academy

Sophie and Chris quickened their pace, the academy gates coming into view as the sun dipped low on the horizon, casting a warm glow across the sprawling grounds. The weight of urgency hung between them, but Chris managed a faint smile as he glanced at Sophie.

"Try to meet up later?" he asked, his tone hopeful despite the tension.

Sophie nodded, her expression softening. "Yeah, see you later."

With that, they parted ways, Sophie heading toward her squad, her figure disappearing into the bustle of activity near

Gabriel's section, while Chris veered toward the assembly area for Michael's squad. His thoughts lingered briefly on Sophie before refocusing. There was no room for distraction now.

When Chris stepped into the briefing room, the atmosphere was thick with anticipation. Allegra, Richard, Lyra, Luke, Faith, Edward, Ali, and Deepak were already seated or standing in small groups, their conversations low but charged. Around the room, other members of Michael's squad, many of whom Chris had never interacted with, were scattered in clusters, their faces serious.

Chris approached the core group, his hand resting lightly on the hilt of the Eclipse Blade. "What's going on?" he asked, his eyes sweeping over them.

"We don't know yet," Richard replied, leaning casually against the wall. "We're still waiting on Vincent."

The group murmured amongst themselves, speculating about the sudden call to assemble, their chatter filling the space with nervous energy. It wasn't long before the door burst open, and Hiroshi stepped in, his expression grim.

"This Briefing will be short so pay attention," Hiroshi announced, his voice cutting through the room like a blade. "In the past four weeks, smaller rifts have been appearing all across the region. Ever since the attack on Eden Prep, the Shadow Key has been used to contain them, however as the Angel Corps pushed the artifact to its limit, it lost its potency. It is no longer able to close these new rifts. There are too many. These new ones have been dangerous, but manageable. Teams like yours have been able to close them using sealing rituals—a technique that combines your elemental powers to temporarily stabilize the breaches."

Chris sat forward in his chair, his fingers brushing over the hilt of the Eclipse Blade. The mention of sealing rituals wasn't new, but the way Hiroshi spoke hinted at something far worse.

One of the unnamed recruits raised their hand. "Sir, if the rituals are temporary, what's stopping the rifts from reopening?"

"They're not permanent solutions," Hiroshi admitted, his expression darkening. "The rifts are unstable—tearing at the fabric between our world and theirs. Each time we seal one, it's like patching a leak in a dam. It holds, but the structure weakens with every new breach."

Another recruit chimed in. "Why are so many rifts opening now? What's causing them?"

Hiroshi's jaw tightened. "We don't know for certain, but what we do know is this: the rifts are allowing demons to break through and wreak havoc. The smaller ones have been containable so far, but five new rifts have opened near Celestia Academy. These are not minor breaches. They are massive and growing, and the demons pouring out of them are overwhelming our forces."

Chris's stomach tightened at the mention of Celestia Academy. Eli was stationed there, training as part of Raphael's squad. His mind raced, picturing his friend caught in the chaos. **Eli... Are you safe?**

Hiroshi stepped closer to the map pinned to the wall, the glowing markers representing the rifts casting an eerie light over the room. He pointed to five large red dots clustered near Celestia Academy. "These rifts are not like the ones you've faced. They're larger, more unstable, and heavily defended by demonic forces. Squads at Celestia have been trying to contain the situation, but their numbers are dwindling. That's why all squads have been called to converge there immediately."

Hiroshi's voice hardened. "Squads are spread thin across the region. We are not receiving reinforcements. Everyone available is already engaged in containment missions or recovery efforts. That's why this operation matters. If Celestia falls, the entire defense line collapses."

The room erupted with murmurs of concern, but Hiroshi silenced them with a sharp gesture. "Listen carefully. This is not just about closing rifts. This is about survival. If these breaches are not sealed, the damage will spread far beyond Celestia. The entire region could fall."

Chris's chest tightened. The thought of Celestia overrun with demons—and Eli in the middle of it—made it hard to focus. He clenched his fists, forcing himself to stay present. **He's strong. He can handle himself.**

"Lieutenant Hiroshi," a member asked hesitantly, "what happens if we fail to seal the rifts?"

Hiroshi's gaze darkened, his voice lowering. "If we fail, the rifts will expand. The demonic energy will destabilize the surrounding area, and more powerful entities will break through. It will become a war zone—one we cannot win."

The room fell silent, the gravity of his words settling heavily over them. Allegra glanced at Chris, her trident resting across her lap. "What's our role in this?" she asked, her voice steady despite the tension.

Hiroshi turned to her, pointing to the northernmost rift on the map. "Michael's squad will be assigned to this rift. It's one of the most volatile and heavily guarded. Your combination of powers makes you the best fit for this mission. You'll work alongside squads from Gabriel and Raphael."

Richard let out a low whistle. "The big leagues. Guess we're not just playing with the rookies anymore."

Lyra shot him a glare. "This isn't a joke, Richard."

"It's never a joke," Richard retorted, though his usual smirk faltered under Lyra's sharp gaze.

"What about the sealing rituals?" another recruit asked. "If the rifts are this big, can they even work?"

Hiroshi nodded grimly. "The rituals will be more complex, requiring multiple squads to channel their essence in tandem. Think of it as a chain: one squad begins the ritual, weakening the rift, while others follow to stabilize it. It will demand precise coordination, and every squad member must push themselves to the limit. If even one link in the chain falters, the entire ritual could collapse."

Faith's voice was barely above a whisper. "And if it collapses?"

"Then the rift will grow," Hiroshi said bluntly. "And so will the chaos."

Chris sat back, the weight of the mission pressing down on him. He glanced at his team, seeing their determination mixed with unease. Allegra's countenance was unreadable as she gripped her trident. Lyra's light bow rested against her leg, her expression unreadable. Even Richard, for all his bravado, seemed unusually quiet.

Chris broke the silence. "When do we leave?"

"Immediately," Hiroshi said. "Gather your weapons and supplies. You'll receive further instructions when you arrive at Celestia. Remember: this is bigger than any one of you. You'll need to trust your teammates and the other squads to succeed."

As the squad began to rise, Hiroshi's voice cut through the room once more. "One more thing," he said, his tone sharp. "Do not underestimate the rifts. They reveal who you truly are—your strength, your fears, your limits. You may think you're ready, but the battles ahead will test every part of you. Keep that in mind."

The squad nodded, their determination growing despite the weight of his words. As they exited the chamber, the glow of the map fading behind them, Chris's mind lingered on Hiroshi's warning. The same sentiment Vincent left him with. **Reveal who we truly are...**

Allegra walked beside him, her gaze flicking to his tense expression. "You okay?"

Chris nodded, though his thoughts remained on Eli and the chaos waiting for them at Celestia. "Yeah. Let's just get this done."

But as the sun dipped lower on the horizon, casting long shadows over the academy grounds, Chris couldn't shake the unease creeping into his chest. Whatever lay ahead, he knew this mission would change everything.

The transport ship loomed in the center of the academy's launch bay, its sleek frame gleaming under the harsh overhead lights. Gabriel's and Michael's squads filed inside, their weapons clutched tightly and their expressions set with grim determination. The hum of the ship's engines filled the cavernous bay, a low, constant reminder of the urgency pressing down on everyone.

Chris and his team took their places near the rear of the ship, the weight of the mission hanging over them like a storm cloud. Allegra leaned her trident against the wall beside her, her brow furrowed in thought, while Richard fiddled with his sound-based weapon, his usual jokes replaced by a rare, tense silence. Faith and Deepak exchanged a nervous glance, their weapons resting awkwardly in their hands. Lyra sat across from Chris, her light bow balanced delicately on her lap, her eyes distant but sharp.

The last of the recruits boarded, the heavy clang of the ship's ramp closing echoing through the bay. Giuseppe, Captain of Gabriel's squad and Chris's father, strode toward Hiroshi with an air of authority, his sharp gaze cutting through the tension.

"Where is Captain Vincent?" Giuseppe asked, his voice calm but clipped, betraying a hint of irritation.

Hiroshi's expression darkened, and he shook his head. "I've been trying to contact him," he said, his tone edged with frustration. "None of my messages are getting through."

Giuseppe's jaw tightened, his fingers flexing slightly as he processed the situation. For a brief moment, his eyes flicked toward the recruits, as if measuring the weight of their collective uncertainty. After a pause, he exhaled sharply and turned back to Hiroshi with a decisive nod.

"Fine," Giuseppe said firmly. "We'll go without him."

He didn't wait for further discussion. His commanding presence filled the space as he turned to the ship's pilot. "Kojo! Get us to Celestia Academy now."

The pilot, a tall man with steady hands and an unwavering focus, nodded and began inputting the coordinates. The ship's engines roared to life, a deep vibration running through the floor as it lifted off smoothly. Outside, the sprawling grounds of Eden Prep blurred and disappeared as the vessel tilted forward, cutting through the sky with precision.

Chris sat silently near the rear, his hand resting on the hilt of his Eclipse Blade. The hum of the engines blended with the faint murmur of uneasy whispers from the recruits. The mission's gravity weighed on all of them, but Chris felt an added layer of tension clawing at his thoughts. His eyes drifted to the window, where streaks of orange and pink from the setting sun painted the horizon. **Where is Vincent?** The question echoed in his mind, refusing to let go.

"Something's off," Allegra muttered beside him, her voice just loud enough for Chris to hear. She glanced around the cabin, her fingers tapping absently on the shaft of her trident. "Vincent doesn't just disappear. Not like this."

Chris turned to her, his expression guarded. "I know," he said quietly, his grip tightening on his blade. "But whatever's going on, we don't have time to worry about him right now. We have a mission."

Allegra nodded reluctantly, but her unease didn't fade. Across from them, Lyra shifted in her seat, her sharp eyes darting between the two. "You think it's deliberate?" she asked, her voice calm but tinged with curiosity. "Captain's absence, I mean."

Chris hesitated, his mind racing through the possibilities. He didn't trust Vincent—not entirely—but he also knew the captain wasn't careless. Every move Vincent made was deliberate, calculated. But what kind of calculation left a squad heading into battle without their leader?

"I don't know," Chris admitted finally, his tone clipped. "But speculating isn't going to help. Right now, we have to focus on what's ahead."

"Chris is right," Giuseppe's voice cut through the cabin as he approached the group, his expression stern. He looked at the gathered recruits, his presence commanding but not unkind. "Vincent or no Vincent, this mission is critical. The rifts at Celestia are unstable and growing. The squads already there are holding the line, but they won't last without reinforcements. That's where we come in."

Faith swallowed hard, her hands fidgeting with her gauntlets. "What kind of demons are we expecting?" she asked softly.

Giuseppe's gaze softened slightly as he addressed her. "Waves of lower-class demons, mostly. But the rifts are also drawing in titans—massive, destructive creatures. The squads stationed there have been able to hold them back so far, but their numbers are increasing. Our job is to seal the rifts and neutralize the threat."

"And if we can't seal them?" another recruit from Gabriel's squad asked hesitantly, his voice carrying the weight of the question.

"Then we make sure Celestia doesn't fall," Giuseppe said firmly. "No matter what."

The recruits exchanged uneasy glances, the gravity of the mission sinking in. Chris kept his eyes on his father, his respect for the man mingling with his own rising anxiety. Celestia Academy wasn't just another battleground—it was where Eli was stationed. **He's holding the line right now. What if—**

Chris cut the thought off before it could spiral. He needed to focus.

"Stick together," Giuseppe continued, his voice steady but commanding. "Trust your training, trust each other, and trust your captains. We've faced worse odds before, and we've always come out on top."

Chris caught Allegra's glance, the faint worry in her eyes mirrored in his own. As the ship continued its flight toward Celestia Academy, the weight of what awaited them pressed heavily on his shoulders. The mission was clear, but the unanswered questions about Vincent—and the ominous feeling gnawing at his mind—refused to be silenced. **We'll handle it,** Chris told himself, his grip tightening on his blade. **We have to.**

The transport ship cut through the sky like a blade, its engines roaring as the battle ahead came into view. From the windows,

Celestia Academy emerged on the horizon—a once-proud stronghold now marred by fire and destruction. Smoke curled in thick plumes, blotting out sections of the sky, and the distant clash of weapons against demonic flesh carried through the air even before the ship began its descent.

Inside the cabin, tension thickened. Warriors checked their weapons, hands glowing with barely contained soul essence, their expressions grim but resolute. Chris's fingers flexed over the hilt of his Eclipse Blade, the weight of the battle settling deep into his chest. His heart pounded, not just from the impending fight, but from the unshakable thought of Eli down there.

The ship lurched as it descended, and the scene below became clearer. The academy grounds were a war zone. The rifts, jagged tears in reality itself, pulsed with eerie light, spilling forth an endless stream of demons. Smaller, twisted creatures scuttled across the battlefield, their claws slashing at defenders. Towering titans lumbered in the distance, their guttural roars shaking the earth. Teams of soul warriors were already engaged, holding the line—but barely.

The moment the ship's doors hissed open, the squads surged out into the fray.

"Gabriel's Teams 1-6, head toward your designated rift and join the teams already stationed there! Pool your soul essence— we need maximum energy output if we're going to seal them!" Giuseppe commanded, his voice unwavering amid the storm of battle. "Teams 7-12, move to reinforce the main rift with Michael's Teams 1-10! We need to thin out the assault! Earth and water users, coordinate to stabilize the battlefield and hold the line!"

Squads moved with military precision, splitting toward their objectives. In the chaos, Chris caught a familiar flash of motion—Sophie. She was among a group sprinting toward the northern rift, her amulet already glowing green with soul essence. Their eyes met across the battlefield. There was no time for words, but her look spoke volumes: **Be careful.**

Chris gave a sharp nod before turning back to his own team. "Let's go!" he ordered, his grip tightening around his blade.

Team Ten rushed forward, plunging straight into the thick of battle.

The battlefield was a storm of clashing steel and raw power. Soul warriors from Celestia Academy fought valiantly, their weapons lighting up the haze of smoke and ash. But they were strained—fatigue clear in their movements, wounds slowing their strikes. The demons pressed forward relentlessly, their grotesque forms clawing and slashing through the defenses.

Chris cut down a smaller demon lunging toward him, the crackle of lightning illuminating its contorted face before it disintegrated into smoke. "Stay together!" he shouted over the chaos.

Allegra pivoted beside him, her trident swirling in an elegant arc as a torrent of water crashed into a group of approaching demons, knocking them back. Deepak followed with a powerful gust of wind, lifting them off their feet before Luke slammed his hammer down, causing jagged earth to rise and impale them midair.

Faith dodged between attacks, her gauntlets glowing as vines erupted from the ground, entangling the legs of a massive demon attempting to charge the defensive line. "I've got this one restrained!" she called, sweat dripping from her brow as the beast snarled and thrashed against her hold.

"Hold it down!" Ali shouted, his blade engulfed in spiraling flames as he lunged forward. With a swift, decisive slash, his fire carved through the demon's chest, the flames spreading like a living entity, consuming the creature in an instant. The heat radiated outward, the flickering orange glow reflecting in Chris's -eyes.

He froze.

The battlefield blurred, his vision tunneling on the fire. It was everywhere—curling around weapons, streaking across the sky, licking at the charred remains of fallen demons. His breath quickened, his pulse hammering in his ears. His grip on his sword slackened. The present unraveled at the edges, and in its place, a memory clawed its way forward.

The fire had taken everything.

A shadow lunged at him from the corner of his vision, claws poised to strike.

"Chris!" Allegra's voice cut through the haze, sharp with urgency.

Water erupted in a fierce torrent, swirling around him like a protective barrier before crashing into the charging demon. The creature recoiled, momentarily stunned, before Allegra's trident shot forward, impaling its chest with lethal precision. Its body convulsed once before dissolving into nothing.

She turned to Chris, her brow furrowed in alarm. "Chris!" she called again, stepping closer.

No response.

His eyes were unfocused, locked onto something far beyond the battlefield. His breathing was uneven, his body stiff, unresponsive.

Allegra didn't hesitate. She grabbed his shoulders, shaking him hard. "Chris, **snap out of it!**" When that didn't work, she slapped him across the face.

Still nothing.

Lyra caught sight of the commotion as she loosed a beam of light into a demon's skull. Wiping sweat from her brow, she sprinted toward them, her bow still crackling with residual energy.

"What's going on?" she demanded, skidding to a stop beside them.

Allegra kept a firm grip on Chris, her frustration evident. "I've got him."

Lyra frowned, studying Chris's vacant stare. "Doesn't look like it. He's completely out of it."

"I can handle it," Allegra snapped, tightening her hold on him.

Lyra's gaze hardened. "Yeah? Because from where I'm standing, it looks like whatever's happening is **beyond** you."

But Chris couldn't hear them anymore.

The battlefield, the voices, the chaos—it all faded into a deafening silence. His surroundings twisted, warped, until they were no longer Celestia Academy, no longer **now.**

It was happening again.

Chris stood frozen, his body unmoving as the battlefield around him raged on. His vision was swallowed by flickering flames, the searing heat curling around his senses, suffocating him with memories of a past that refused to die. The screams of his original timeline echoed in his mind, the crackling inferno consuming everything.

A demon lunged toward him, claws poised to strike.

Allegra reacted first, her trident spinning as a torrent of water crashed into the creature, hurling it backward. Lyra shot a piercing beam of light, cutting through another that tried to flank them. Edward, standing just behind them, lifted his hand, his gravitational essence shifting the space around them, forcing several demons to stagger as if the weight of the world had doubled upon them.

"Hold the line!" Allegra commanded, her voice tight with strain. She stole a glance at Chris, her expression twisting with worry. He was still out of it, his breathing shallow, his eyes locked onto something unseen.

"Chris!" Lyra barked, not bothering to hide the frustration laced with concern. She knocked an arrow, its tip glowing with radiant energy. "Snap out of it! We can't hold them off forever!"

Edward, his gaze unreadable, stood slightly apart, glancing at Chris between managing the distortions in gravity. "He's talking," he muttered under his breath.

"What?" Allegra asked.

Edward's eyes narrowed as he concentrated. "He's saying something… but not to us."

Within the depths of his mind, Chris stood in an endless void—black, weightless, silent. Yet ahead of him, fire burned. It flickered and swayed, inching closer, its glow casting long shadows across the nothingness. The heat licked at his skin, familiar yet unwelcome.

A voice called to him from within the flames.

"Do not be afraid."

Chris stiffened. The voice was soft but commanding, distinctly feminine, carrying a strange sense of familiarity that sent a shiver through him.

His heart pounded. "I know you," he whispered, his voice raw with confusion. "You're the voice from the garden."

The flames pulsed, as if acknowledging his words, but the voice did not answer the question.

"Embrace the flames, Christopher."

Chris's hands clenched into fists. The fire surged forward, coiling around his arms, creeping toward his chest. He flinched, expecting pain, expecting it to devour him like before.

But it didn't.

It settled—not consuming, not scorching—just there.

Chris swallowed hard, his breath uneven. "No," he muttered, shaking his head. "The flames—" His throat felt dry, his words brittle. "They're too much. Too uncontrollable."

"They are within you." The voice was steady, unwavering. **"They are not your enemy. They are your ally."**

The fire danced, growing more intense. It twisted upward, encircling his torso and legs like a living thing. The heat deepened—not from without, but from within. The power of the flames bubbled up inside him, surging through every nerve, rising fast toward an unbearable crescendo. It clawed at the walls of his control, demanding release, threatening to explode outward.

His black ring pulsed violently on his finger—and then cracked, ever so slightly.

From nearby, Lyra's eyes widened. She saw it. The fracture. The fire he was trying to hold back.

Chris's breathing quickened as the inferno wrapped tighter. It wasn't burning him, but that didn't mean it wouldn't. He knew what flames like these could do. He had seen them take everything from him once before.

"They destroyed my home," he whispered, his voice hollow. **"They took everything."**

"They did not take. They revealed."

The words struck something deep inside him, but he wasn't ready to accept them. Not yet.

The fire curled higher, wrapping around his body, waiting. Not attacking. Not forcing.

Just waiting.

Chris squeezed his eyes shut. *I can't.*

But the fire didn't retreat.

You will have to.

Chris gasped as reality slammed back into him, his lungs heaving as though he had been drowning. His knees buckled—but Allegra caught him, her grip tight around his arm.

Lyra, frozen beside them, was still staring at the faint crack in the ring.

"Chris!" she shouted, her voice laced with worry.

Lyra was already at his side, her bow still in hand. "What just happened? You were—" she hesitated, searching for the right words. "Talking. But not to us."

Edward, maintaining his gravity field to keep demons at bay, studied Chris with a measured expression. "It sounded like a conversation," he remarked. "Something about flames."

Chris staggered upright, his chest still rising and falling with uneven breaths. He could feel warmth lingering inside him, buried deep, but it wasn't steady. It wasn't something he could trust yet.

Allegra's grip on his arm tightened. "Chris," she said firmly, her eyes searching his. "Who were you talking to?"

Chris exhaled, his fingers flexing involuntarily. A flicker of orange sparked across his hand before disappearing, leaving only the ghost of heat behind.

"I don't know," he admitted, his voice low.

Chris shook his head. "Don't worry about it," he muttered, his tone sharper than he intended. He wasn't sure if he was telling them or himself.

Allegra didn't look convinced, but she didn't push. Lyra's expression tightened with frustration. Edward merely observed, unreadable as always.

Chris turned away from them, forcing himself to focus on the battlefield. The fight wasn't over. He wasn't over this.

But he had to move forward.

"I'm good now," he said, even as doubt curled in his stomach.

Without waiting for a response, he charged back into the fight.

As Chris reentered the fray, a towering demon lunged at a group of Celestia Academy defenders, its claws poised to rip through them. His instincts took over—before the creature could strike, he surged forward, lightning crackling along the length of his blade. With a single decisive slash, the Eclipse Blade carved through the demon, the force of the strike sending a shock wave through the air as the creature dissolved into ash.

"Allegra, keep their flanks covered!" Chris called out, eyes darting across the battlefield. "Lyra, light the field so we can track their movements!"

Without hesitation, Lyra raised her bow, summoning a burst of radiant light that spread across the battlefield. The shadows retreated under the glow, exposing the demons' erratic movements. Allegra took position on the left, her trident spinning as she unleashed torrents of water to drive back incoming threats.

Chris exhaled sharply, steadying his stance. His mind sharpened, instinct kicking in. *Patterns. Openings. Make every move count.*

He tapped into his soul essence, channeling a neural boost to enhance his reflexes and speed. The battlefield stretched before him in razor-sharp clarity—movements slowed, threats became obvious, and gaps in the demons' defense revealed themselves like an open book.

With a burst of speed, he darted between the swarming

creatures, the Eclipse Blade humming with electric energy. He struck with ruthless efficiency—each precise swing severing limbs, tearing through dark essence, leaving nothing but smoke and ruin in his wake.

Behind him, Deepak twirled his staff, summoning a powerful gust of wind. The concentrated blast ripped through a cluster of demons, flinging them into the air before slamming them against the ruined stonework of the academy grounds. Several Celestia warriors who had been cornered took the opportunity to regroup, their exhaustion replaced by renewed determination.

"Finally, some backup!" one of them called out, relief thick in his voice.

"We're here to help!" Lyra responded, stepping forward and activating her ability, Mirage. Ghostly duplicates of soul warriors flickered across the battlefield, moving in synchronization with their real counterparts. The demons snarled in confusion, their attacks wasted on illusions.

Luke seized the distraction. With a fierce grunt, he swung his hammer, the ground beneath him trembling as spikes of earth erupted in a controlled shock wave. The creatures caught in the attack screeched in agony before their bodies dissipated into nothingness.

"Nice work, Luke!" Lyra shouted, drawing her bow and shooting a bolt of concentrated light. The projectile soared through the chaos, piercing through the skull of a demon lunging toward a wounded Celestia defender.

"Keep moving!" Chris commanded, eyes scanning the battlefield. His squad was holding their ground, executing their roles with precision. Allegra and Edward anchored the flanks—her water weaving through the ranks of demons while Edward manipulated gravity, pulling some enemies into the ground and crushing others under immense pressure. Their combined synergy held back the tide, preventing the creatures from overwhelming their forces.

Ali and Richard fought like a chaotic storm on the far right, working off each other's unpredictable energy. Richard's sound-based attacks sent shock waves through the air, disorienting the demons, while Ali's fire blade seared through the stunned creatures with swift efficiency.

Faith moved swiftly through the battle, her gauntlets pulsating with life essence. Vines burst from the earth at her command, wrapping around the limbs of larger demons, holding them long enough for others to land killing blows.

"Chris!" Allegra called from the side, barely dodging a lunging creature. "We need to push forward!"

Chris clenched his teeth. *They had to keep going.*

He launched forward, the crackling of his lightning blade echoing across the battlefield as he cut through another demon. His squad followed, their movements precise and relentless.

The tide of battle shifted. What had seemed like an overwhelming onslaught minutes ago was now turning in their favor. The combined efforts of Team Ten and the Celestia warriors steadied the front lines, giving them a fighting chance against the creatures still pouring through the rift.

Chris took a brief moment to glance at his team.

They weren't just recruits anymore.

They were warriors.

And they weren't done yet.

As Chris and his squad pressed forward, carving through the chaos with a calculated blend of speed and power, Giuseppe led his own team with the unwavering precision of a seasoned warrior. Every movement was deliberate, every strike devastating. His blade pulsed with raw lightning essence, each arc of energy leaping from his sword to the creatures around him, electrocuting them mid-lunge. The scent of scorched demon flesh filled the air as their bodies disintegrated under the force of his relentless assault.

"Get with the others and begin the process!" Giuseppe commanded, his voice cutting through the cacophony of battle.

His squad surged forward with unwavering focus, closing the distance toward the rifts. Sophie sprinted ahead, her amulet glowing faintly against her chest. With a deep breath, she thrust her hands forward, channeling her essence into the earth. Thick vines shot out from the ground, twisting and coiling around the approaching demons. The creatures roared in frustration, their limbs bound as they thrashed violently against the restraints.

Kim followed closely behind, her staff humming with wind essence as she moved with fluid precision. With a single, powerful sweep, she unleashed razor-sharp gusts that sliced cleanly through the immobilized demons. Their shrieks echoed as their dark forms were cleaved apart, vanishing into the ether.

Despite the steady advance of Giuseppe's squad, an unsettling feeling tugged at Sophie's thoughts. Her gaze flickered across the battlefield, searching frantically amidst the flashing soul essence and chaotic melee. *Where is Eli?* The question gnawed at her, a persistent weight in the back of her mind. She shook it off—*Focus. We need to get to the rift first.* But the worry lingered, pressing down like an unseen force.

Giuseppe led from the front, cutting a clear path through the mass of demons with near-effortless efficiency. His squad moved as a single unit, their coordination seamless, honed through relentless training. Though the battle raged on around them, their rhythm never faltered.

Yet, as they neared the first rift, Sophie's unease deepened. The ground trembled beneath her feet, and an unnatural chill clawed at the edges of her awareness. Something about this fight felt... different.

Something wasn't right.

The battlefield roared with the clash of soul essence and steel, the cries of warriors mixing with the guttural snarls of demons. Despite the chaos, two rifts had already been sealed, but the battle was far from over. The Celestia Academy warriors had suffered heavy losses—too many fighters had fallen, their soul essence depleted from the relentless assault.

Sophie pushed forward, her amulet pulsing faintly against her chest as she weaved through the chaos. The weight of the mission bore down on her, but there was no time for hesitation.

That's when she saw him.

Eli stood amidst the fray, his massive hammer gleaming with energy. Every swing sent demons flying or crumbling into ash, his strikes precise and relentless. Sophie felt a flicker of relief at the sight of him—if Eli was still standing, there was still hope.

"Eli!" she called, her voice cutting through the chaos.

He heard her just as he brought his hammer down in a devastating arc, sending a shock wave rippling through the battlefield. For a brief moment, the demons around him staggered. He turned at the sound of her voice, recognition flashing in his eyes.

"Sophie!" He jogged toward her, his hammer resting against his shoulder, his armor smeared with ash and blood. "You're here. Good. We need more essence at the rift—the flow isn't strong enough yet."

"That's why I'm here," Sophie said firmly.

Eli gave her a nod. "Then let's move. We're sealing two rifts at once."

Her eyes flickered toward the nearest rift, its swirling darkness spewing out creatures even as warriors desperately fought to hold the line. Beyond it, the second rift loomed, its energy even more unstable.

Without hesitation, she followed Eli, the ground beneath her trembling with the force of battle.

At the first rift, a cluster of warriors had formed a protective barrier while another group worked on the sealing ritual.

Lieutenant Hiroshi stood at the center, his blade planted in the ground, guiding the energy with a firm, steady presence. But despite their efforts, the rift still pulsed violently, resisting their attempts to shut it.

"Get the fortification team in position!" Hiroshi ordered.

Sophie wasted no time, scanning the battlefield for fellow plant users. She spotted two others—both warriors from Celestia Academy—channeling their energy to restrain demons rather than reinforce the barrier.

"We need to focus on containment!" Sophie called, rushing toward them. "We can't let anything through while they finish the seal!"

The two plant wielders exchanged a glance before nodding. Together, they pressed their hands to the earth, their soul essence surging into the ground. Sophie mirrored their stance, feeling her amulet pulse in sync with their energy.

The earth trembled beneath them, and from the soil, massive vines erupted. They coiled and wove together, forming a towering barrier of thick roots around the rift, sealing off any chance for demons to escape. The creatures inside scratched and clawed at the walls, but the roots only tightened, suffocating them within.

"We need ten more seconds!" one of the sealing warriors shouted.

"Hold it steady!" Sophie gritted out, reinforcing the structure with another surge of power.

Eli moved in front of them, his hammer raised. "I've got the front," he said. "Nothing's getting through."

The demons outside the barrier snarled and launched themselves toward the fortification team, but Eli met them head-on. With a single, brutal strike, he shattered the ground beneath them, sending them tumbling into a crater. More demons surged forward, but Eli swung his hammer in a wide arc, obliterating them in one powerful burst.

Behind them, the sealing warriors released their final surge of energy.

The rift crackled violently, twisting inward. Then, with a thunderous snap, it collapsed—gone in an instant.

A brief silence fell over the battlefield.

Then Hiroshi's voice cut through. "The second rift! Move now!"

The second rift was far worse.

It pulsed aggressively, its energy thick and suffocating. Unlike the first, it wasn't just spewing demons—it was actively pulling at the world around it, as if trying to devour everything in its grasp.

"Damn it," Eli muttered. "This one's worse than the first."

"Focus!" Hiroshi snapped. "We seal it, or we all die here."

The sealing warriors formed their circle again, their hands trembling from exhaustion, but they pressed on. Sophie turned to the plant users she had worked with before.

"Same plan," she said. "But we need stronger roots this time."

They nodded, and together, they knelt to the earth once more.

The vines that erupted this time were massive, thicker than trees. They coiled like living fortresses, forming a dome around the rift to keep anything from escaping.

But something was wrong.

The rift pulsed violently, and the energy surged outward in a shock wave, shattering part of the barrier.

The sealing warriors cried out in pain, some collapsing under the pressure.

"We're losing control!" one of them gasped.

Sophie gritted her teeth, pouring more energy into the roots. "No! Hold it together!"

Eli rushed forward, slamming his hammer into the ground. "Everyone, brace yourselves!"

A shock wave rippled outward, reinforcing the barrier just enough to buy them time.

"More energy!" Hiroshi barked, his voice strained as he held his sword firm.

The sealing warriors gathered their strength, soul essence surging. The rift twisted, fighting against their power.

Sophie reached for her amulet, drawing from every last reserve of energy she had left.

"Come on," she whispered. "Close."

The rift howled, its resistance at its peak.

Then—finally—it cracked, then twisted inward, folding into itself.

With one final pulse, it vanished.

Meanwhile, Captain Giuseppe and the other captains spearheaded the protection detail, ensuring the warriors had the space they needed to close the two remaining smaller rifts. With each one sealed, the battlefield thinned slightly, but the true fight remained at the largest rift—a churning, chaotic tear in reality where the demonic presence was strongest.

Chris and the rest of Michael's squad stood as the last line of defense for the sealing team. But the demons were relentless. With every warrior that fell, the line weakened, and the creatures pushed forward with renewed ferocity.

Chris gritted his teeth, cutting through a demon lunging toward the sealers, but there were too many. His squad was holding, but barely. They needed more support.

"We're losing ground!" Allegra called out, using a wave of water to force a group of demons back, but it wasn't enough to break their advance.

Hiroshi, from his position near the front line, took one look at the battlefield and knew the line wouldn't hold much longer.

"We need to reinforce them!" he commanded. Without hesitation, he signaled to his team. "All units, fall in! Michael's squad needs support now!"

With that, Hiroshi's forces surged forward, joining the fray, determined to hold the line long enough for the rift to be sealed.

Across the battlefield, Chris spotted Sophie and Eli moving towards him. Relief washed over him as he saw them safe and unharmed, at least for now. "Glad to know they're okay," he thought, his grip tightening on the hilt of his Eclipse Blade.

Chris turned his attention back to the battle around him, cutting down demons with sharp, calculated strikes. His speed and precision were unmatched, each move a display of the training that had brought his team this far.

But even as he fought, his gaze drifted toward his friends. He couldn't help it—they were a reminder of what was at stake. With renewed focus, Chris began to push through the waves of demons.

Chris slashed through another demon, its twisted form disintegrating into smoke as he pressed forward. His breaths came heavy, but his focus remained razor-sharp. Across the battlefield, he caught sight of Sophie and Eli, their figures unmistakable in the sea of warriors. Relief flooded him—both of them were still standing, still fighting.

"Sophie! Eli!" Chris called out, his voice cutting through the chaos.

Eli, mid-swing, drove his hammer into the ground, sending a shock wave that blasted a group of demons backward. He turned at the sound of Chris's voice, a grin breaking through the grime and exhaustion. "Took you long enough!" he shouted back.

Sophie, her hands still glowing with energy as her vines wrapped around a demon's legs, yanking it into the earth, glanced up with relief. "Chris!" she breathed, her focus momentarily shifting from the battle. "You okay?"

"Still in one piece," Chris called as he reached them, Allegra and Luke flanking him. Allegra's trident dripped with demon ichor, her eyes scanning the battlefield, always assessing. Luke remained silent, but his presence was solid, his hammer held at the ready.

Chris didn't waste time. "We're holding the line while the rift is being sealed, but the demons just keep coming. We need to reinforce the defenses—now."

The battlefield was a storm of chaos and unrelenting force as the captains pushed toward the front lines, their presence like a wave of raw power surging through the ranks of defenders.

Giuseppe led the charge, his lightning-infused blade crackling with energy, each swing cutting through demons like a bolt from the heavens. Beside him, Maria moved with effortless grace, her twin fans whipping up powerful gales that sent clusters of demons hurtling backward. Mei's fire whip cracked through the air, wrapping around a demon's throat before she yanked, incinerating it in a burst of flames. Nyla's resonant chimes rang out across the battlefield, her sound essence creating rippling waves of force that disoriented the enemies, throwing them off balance. Omari's stone breaker mace shattered the ground beneath him, sending jagged spikes of rock skewering through the oncoming horde. And above them all, Jeffrey's light bow shimmered as arrows of pure radiance shot across the sky, each one finding its mark with deadly precision.

The captains' arrival reinvigorated the warriors of the Angel Corps, their movements fueled by renewed determination. Chris, Sophie, Eli, and Allegra fought their way toward the ritual site, where the sealers were desperately attempting to contain the rift.

But the rift was fighting back.

Dark energy pulsed violently from its core, sending tremors across the battlefield. Demons poured out in endless waves, their grotesque forms clawing at the defenders with relentless fury. And then, the air shifted. A new weight, a new presence pressed down on them like an impending storm.

From the depths of the rift, the ground quaked violently.

A low, guttural growl rumbled across the battlefield.

Then, five massive figures stepped through.

Titans.

The battlefield seemed to freeze as they emerged, towering above the warriors, their hulking frames exuding pure malice. Their glowing eyes bore into the ranks of the Angel Corps, their presence alone sending a ripple of fear through even the most seasoned warriors.

Chris's breath caught in his throat. "No," he muttered.

Eli tightened his grip on his hammer. "You've gotta be kidding me," he said, his voice edged with both frustration and determination.

Sophie stepped closer, her hands already glowing with her soul essence. "We don't have time to be afraid," she said. "We end this. Now."

Giuseppe's voice cut through the tension, sharp and unwavering. "Angel Corps, listen up!"

The battlefield roared back to life, warriors snapping to attention as he continued.

"We have one objective: Close that rift!" His lightning blade sparked as he pointed toward the swirling vortex of darkness behind the titans. "But we need more power. We don't have enough soul essence to seal it as we are."

Maria's voice rang out next. "We have to split up! One group will continue pooling soul essence to shut it down—the rest of us will hold off the demons and the titans. If we lose control of the front, this battle is over."

Omari swung his mace, shattering the skull of a demon attempting to break through. "All earth and water users, fortify the ground around the sealers! Give them as much protection as possible!"

Jeffrey pulled back his bowstring, his glowing arrow illuminating the night sky. "Light users, disorient the titans! Sound users, keep them off balance!"

Mei's flames flared around her, casting shadows across the battlefield. "Fire and lightning wielders, we're on offense. Hit them hard, hit them fast!"

Giuseppe turned back to the warriors before him, his gaze sharp. "Anyone not engaged in battle—get to the rift and pour everything you have into sealing it!"

The Angel Corps mobilized in perfect synchronicity.

Chris turned to his squad, his heart hammering. "You heard them! Allegra, Luke—help reinforce the sealers' defenses. Lyra, keep the titans disoriented. Deepak, Edward, Faith, Ali—we need to contain the smaller demons. We hold the line until that rift is closed."

Allegra nodded. "We've got this."

Chris took a breath, his grip tightening around the Eclipse Blade.

The final battle for Celestia Academy had begun.

18

The Final Rift

The battlefield was a relentless storm of chaos.

The titans roared, their massive forms moving with terrifying speed despite their size. The ground trembled with every step they took, their powerful limbs smashing through structures and sending warriors flying with every swing. The captains of the Angel Corps stood firm, their weapons blazing with raw soul essence, the only line of defense between the colossal beasts and the ritual site where the sealing team struggled to stabilize the rift.

Giuseppe darted between two of the titans, his lightning-infused blade flashing through the darkness as he slashed deep into one's armored hide. Sparks crackled across its body, stunning it momentarily, but it roared and swung a clawed hand at him. He barely dodged in time, rolling beneath the swipe before retaliating with another strike, sending a jagged bolt of electricity surging through its massive frame.

Mei's fire whip cracked through the air, coiling around another titan's leg. With a sharp yank, she sent flames searing up its body, the heat intensifying until the creature bellowed in rage. It swung wildly, trying to rid itself of the burning pain, but Nyla stepped in, ringing her resonant chimes. A powerful shock wave of sound erupted from her instrument, distorting the air and causing the titan's movements to stagger.

Maria, moving like a blur, twisted her twin fans, summoning a powerful cyclone that engulfed one of the titans. "Omari, now!" she called.

Omari, standing firm with his massive stone breaker mace, lifted it high and brought it down with immense force. The earth beneath him cracked and exploded upward, jagged rock spears impaling the trapped titan's legs. It shrieked in pain, falling forward as Maria's winds intensified, trapping it in place.

Jeffrey, perched on higher ground,shot a barrage of radiant arrows from his light bow. The golden streaks of energy struck with deadly precision, piercing the weak points in the titans' armored hides. His shots were relentless, aiming to blind and slow the behemoths down so the captains could strike harder.

But despite their efforts, the titans pressed forward.

Chris, Luke, Eli, and Richard were locked in battle with the smaller demons, their movements fluid and relentless.

Chris's Eclipse Blade crackled with lightning, each swing slicing through the grotesque creatures that swarmed toward the sealers. He moved like a storm, fast and unpredictable, his blade cutting through one demon before arcing into the next. But for every one he felled, two more took its place.

"Keep pushing!" Chris shouted, dodging a clawed strike before sending a lightning-infused kick into the demon's chest, sending it flying back.

Luke stood his ground like an immovable fortress, his hammer crashing down and sending tremors through the battlefield. Each strike sent demons crumbling, but the sheer volume of enemies was becoming overwhelming. "There's no end to them!" he grunted, swinging his hammer into another group, the ground beneath them rupturing with the force of his blow.

Eli fought with brutal efficiency, his hammer a blur of motion. Every swing crushed through bone and sinew, sending demons flying in all directions. His power was immense, but even he couldn't ignore how their numbers weren't thinning. "We're barely holding them back!" he yelled.

Richard, his dual daggers glowing with sound essence, moved between enemies with nimble precision. Each strike sent reverberating shock waves through the demons, staggering them long enough for him to land a finishing blow. He dodged effortlessly, flipping over an incoming strike before jabbing his dagger into a demon's throat.

Chris glanced toward the sealing team. Allegra, Lyra, Deepak, Faith, Ali, and Edward stood in formation around the rift, their hands raised, soul essence pooling together as they attempted to seal the breach. The energy around them pulsed and flickered, but it wasn't enough.

"We need more power!" Lyra called out, sweat dripping down her face from the strain.

"We're already giving everything we have!" Deepak gritted his teeth, his wind essence flaring as he struggled to hold his part of the ritual steady.

Allegra clenched her jaw, her trident glowing as she funneled more water essence into the barrier. "We need time! But if we stop to help, we'll be overrun!"

Faith's vines twisted and curled around the rift, reinforcing the barrier as best she could. "They just keep coming!" she gasped.

Chris's mind raced. If the defenders shifted to help power the seal, the demons would break through and slaughter them before they could finish. But if they kept fighting, the sealing team wouldn't have enough strength to close the rift in time.

They were outnumbered.

And time was running out.

The titans pushed forward, one breaking free from its restraints and charging toward the sealers.

Maria threw up a wind barrier to slow it down, but it wouldn't hold for long.

"We need a plan now, Chris!" Eli shouted, knocking back a demon before stepping beside him.

Chris clenched his fists, his mind cycling through every option. His lightning flared around him, the energy coursing through his veins, his heart pounding in his chest.

There had to be a way.

There had to be something.

Then it hit him.

His gaze shot to Eli and Luke. "What if we force them back?"

Eli wiped his brow, his stance never wavering. "We've been trying to do that."

"No, not just fighting them—pushing them away." Chris turned to Luke and Eli. "You can manipulate the earth. Can you create a fault line, make the ground split beneath them?"

Luke's eyes flickered with realization. "I can try."

Chris nodded. "Luke and Eli, you'll use your shock wave to drive them into it. Richard, you and I will clear out the demons near the ritual site."

Richard smirked, twirling his daggers. "Now that sounds like a plan."

Chris turned back to the sealing team. "Allegra, Deepak, Faith, Ali, Edward—hold on a little longer! We're about to give you the time you need!"

Allegra gave a determined nod. "Just hurry."

Chris tightened his grip on his blade, exhaling sharply. This had to work.

Giuseppe and the captains continued their battle against the titans, their strikes powerful, but the creatures refused to fall.

The battlefield was at a breaking point.

The final rift loomed, pulsing with dark energy, feeding the chaos.

Everything was about to come down to this last push.

Chris took his stance, eyes burning with determination.

"Let's finish this."

Chris stood at the center of the chaos, heart pounding as he locked eyes with Luke and Eli. They both gave him a sharp nod—there was no hesitation now. The plan had to work.

"Alright," Chris said, gripping his Eclipse Blade tightly. "Luke, crack the ground. Eli, you'll send them straight into it. Richard, we clear a path for the sealers."

"Got it," Luke rumbled, already shifting his stance.

Eli adjusted his grip on his hammer, his eyes flickering with a fierce determination. "I'll hit them with everything I've got."

Richard twirled his daggers, grinning despite the exhaustion weighing on them all. "Time to make some noise."

Chris turned back toward the sealing team. "Just hold on! We'll give you the time you need!"

Allegra, sweat beading on her forehead, forced a strained smile. "We don't have much choice, do we?"

Deepak, Faith, Lyra, Ali, and Edward were visibly struggling to keep the seal from collapsing under the relentless force of the rift, their bodies trembling as their soul essence poured into stabilizing the energy. They didn't have long.

"On my mark!" Chris shouted.

Luke slammed his hammer into the earth, and with a deafening *crack*, the battlefield trembled. Jagged fissures split open beneath the demons' feet, swallowing several into the gaping chasms below. The others staggered as the ground shifted violently beneath them.

"Now, Eli!" Chris roared.

Eli took a deep breath, lifted his hammer high, and brought it crashing down. The impact sent a devastating shock wave across the battlefield, a seismic pulse that knocked entire hordes of demons off balance, sending them stumbling straight into Luke's fissure.

Chris and Richard wasted no time. They cut through the remaining demons blocking the path to the sealers, blades flashing, footwork relentless. It was working. The demons were losing ground.

For the first time since the battle began, hope ignited in Chris's chest.

But then—

The demons surged.

Like a tide that had only been momentarily forced back, they retaliated with renewed ferocity. Even as some of their forces fell into the fissures, more emerged from the rift, their monstrous forms clawing through reality, spilling onto the battlefield in horrifying numbers.

And then, the titans pushed forward.

One of the massive creatures roared, shaking the air with its deafening bellow before lunging straight for Luke and Eli.

Chris's eyes widened in horror. *No—!*

The plan was falling apart before it had fully taken shape.

The titans were adapting. The demons weren't being pushed back—they were pressing harder.

The sealing team was losing energy. The warriors on the field were barely holding on.

And Chris—Chris felt helpless.

His breath came in ragged gasps as the weight of failure crashed over him. He could feel himself slipping, the battle spiraling beyond his control.

They weren't strong enough. They weren't fast enough. They weren't—

BOOM.

A bone-chilling wave swept across the battlefield.

Chris barely had time to process what was happening before it hit him—the sharp, piercing sensation of raw, unrelenting *cold.*

The very air seemed to freeze.

Demons screeched as their bodies were encased in layers of ice, jagged frost consuming them whole before shattering them into shards.

From seemingly nowhere, *Vincent* appeared.

His presence was as sharp and unyielding as the ice he wielded.

With a sweeping motion of his sword, frost erupted outward, crystallizing entire hordes of demons in place. The battlefield, once ablaze with chaos, was momentarily silenced under the chilling power of his arrival.

Chris felt his breath catch.

Vincent didn't hesitate—he *never* hesitated.

Moving like a ghost, he cut through the enemy ranks with brutal efficiency. Every motion was precise, every strike devastating. Ice followed his blade like an extension of himself, freezing demons mid-attack, leaving them helpless before he shattered them into nothingness.

Then, in a blur, Vincent turned toward the nearest titan.

With a flick of his wrist, ice coiled around the creature's limbs, locking it in place. It roared, thrashing violently, but the frost only deepened, spreading through its massive form like an unstoppable force.

Vincent leaped, blade glinting under the pale battlefield light. He landed on the titan's shoulder, his cold, calculating gaze never wavering.

With one merciless strike, he *drove* his sword deep into its neck.

The ice followed.

A sharp *crack* echoed through the battlefield as the titan's entire body stiffened, its movements faltering. The frost consumed it from the inside out, crystallizing its very essence until it was nothing more than an immobile statue.

And then—Vincent twisted his blade.

The titan shattered into a thousand frozen fragments.

The battlefield stood still for a brief moment.

Then—chaos erupted once more.

Chris barely had time to think. He could feel the sheer intensity of Vincent's power radiating across the field, the shift in battle undeniable.

But more than that, he could *feel* Vincent's gaze land on him.

"Move," Vincent ordered coldly, not sparing Chris a second glance. "Back to the ritual. Now."

Chris swallowed, adrenaline roaring back into his veins. He turned on his heel, sprinting toward Luke, Eli, and Richard.

"Let's go!" he shouted.

With Vincent holding the line, the four of them raced back toward the sealers. Allegra, still standing firm in her stance, looked up as they approached.

"You *better* tell me what just happened later," she snapped, her trident glowing as she reinforced the ritual.

Chris didn't respond—there was no time. He took his position alongside the others, soul essence flaring as he focused everything on finishing what they started.

Vincent had bought them a chance.

Now, it was up to them to end this.

"Everyone, get ready!" Hiroshi's voice rang out, steady and commanding despite the chaos that had consumed the battlefield moments ago. "Four... three... two... one... NOW!"

Chris felt a sudden squeeze around his hand. He glanced down in surprise—Lyra. Her fingers wrapped tightly around his, her grip firm yet trembling. The contact caught him off guard, but for some reason, he didn't pull away.

Instead, he focused.

A collective surge of soul essence erupted from the warriors, merging into a brilliant wave of golden light. It flooded the battlefield, sweeping through the remaining demons as it surged toward the gaping rift. The air crackled with power, humming with the resonance of so many fighting as one.

For a single, breathless moment, everything froze.

The rift twisted violently as the energy collided with it. The dark, seething vortex convulsed inward, folding upon itself before detonating in a blinding explosion of radiant force. A shock wave rippled outward, tearing through the remaining demons like they were nothing more than shadows vanishing at dawn.

The battlefield fell deathly silent.

Chris stood frozen, breath heaving, the weight of exhaustion finally catching up to him. The war cries, the monstrous shrieks, the clash of metal against flesh—it was all gone. The only thing left was the eerie stillness, the stunned realization that the battle was over.

They had won.

Slowly, he loosened his grip on Lyra's hand, but she didn't immediately let go. Chris felt a flicker of uncertainty, his mind still trying to catch up to what had just happened.

Then he caught sight of Sophie.

She was staring at him—more specifically, at his hand still linked with Lyra's. Her expression was unreadable, but there was something in her gaze that made Chris shift uncomfortably. Then, just past Sophie, he noticed Allegra. Her eyes flicked from his hand to his face, her usual easy confidence replaced by something sharper, something unreadable—but unmistakably cold.

Chris cleared his throat, finally pulling away.

His pulse was still racing, but now, it wasn't just from battle.

The distant sound of shifting boots against the stone made him turn.

Vincent was striding toward the gathered warriors. His expression, as always, was unreadable—sharp, calculating, and unaffected. The way he moved, without hesitation or exhaustion, made him stand apart from the rest. The battlefield had left everyone else breathless and worn, but Vincent?

It was as if he had never even been in a fight.

The battlefield was settling into a heavy quiet, the aftermath of war weighing on the warriors like a suffocating fog. Scattered across the grounds, the wounded groaned softly, some barely conscious as they clutched their injuries. Vincent's voice rang clear through the somber air.

"All healers, tend to the injured."

At his command, water and plant essence users moved swiftly, seeking out those in need. Among them was Sophie, who immediately knelt beside a fallen warrior, her hands glowing faintly as she channeled her soul essence into the wound.

Chris, catching sight of her, strode over. "You can heal now?" he asked, surprised as he fell into step beside her.

Sophie looked up, offering a small but tired smile. "One of the new skills I've picked up," she said, pressing her hands to the wound and watching as tendrils of green light wove the torn flesh back together. The warrior beneath her exhaled sharply, relief washing over his features.

Chris nodded, impressed but not entirely shocked. Sophie had always been quick to adapt, always seeking new ways to make herself useful. It was one of the things he admired most about her.

Meanwhile, near the entrance of the academy, Giuseppe turned toward Vincent, his expression unreadable but his tone edged with suspicion. "When did you arrive?"

Vincent, standing still amidst the wreckage, exuded an aura of calm detachment. "Since the beginning of the assault," he replied, voice even, measured. "I've been researching the rifts, trying to determine their cause."

Giuseppe's eyes narrowed slightly. "So, you sat out the entire battle in the name of research?"

Before Vincent could answer, another voice cut through the tension.

"Must be nice," Mei snapped, stepping forward with arms crossed. Her fire essence still flickered faintly around her fingertips, the embers of battle not yet fully extinguished. "Watching from the sidelines while the rest of us fought for our lives."

Vincent's expression remained unmoved, but there was a sharpness in his gaze as he turned to face her. "Would you rather I wield my blade like every other warrior on this field? Or find a way to stop these rifts from ever opening again?" His voice darkened, his frustration barely restrained. "I assume, Captain Mei, you would prefer the latter."

Mei didn't back down, but the words hit their mark. Around them, the other captains shifted, glancing at one another as the tension in the air thickened.

Vincent took a step forward, his gaze sweeping across the battlefield. "Look around," he said, his voice low but commanding. "Look at our fallen comrades, our wounded. If we continue as we are, this moment will repeat itself again. And again. And again." His eyes flickered with something unreadable as he continued. "My research has given me answers. I know the cause of these rifts. And," he turned sharply toward Giuseppe, "he does too."

A ripple of shock went through the gathered captains.

Giuseppe's expression didn't waver, but Chris caught the subtle tightening of his jaw.

"What is he talking about?" Omari demanded, his deep voice heavy with suspicion. "You know what's causing the rifts?"

Giuseppe's gaze flickered to Vincent, but he didn't respond immediately.

"I don't," he finally said, his tone firm but controlled. His eyes locked onto Vincent's. "What exactly are you getting at?"

A slow smirk tugged at the corner of Vincent's lips, but there was no amusement behind it—only sharp calculation. He took a slow step forward, and Giuseppe mirrored him, the two circling each other with the deliberate tension of predators testing the waters before striking.

"You know why, Giuseppe," Vincent said, his voice dipping into something quieter, more dangerous. "You know exactly why their blood stains this battlefield tonight."

The air crackled faintly with residual energy, a reminder of the battle that had only just ended. Around them, the captains stiffened, their wariness deepening as they watched the exchange unfold.

Giuseppe's fists clenched at his sides, his stance subtly shifting, the weight in his expression turning darker. "If you've got something to say, Vincent," he said, his voice carrying an edge of warning, "then say it."

Vincent stopped moving. His expression was cold, calculating, but beneath it, there was something else. Something deeper.

The battlefield, once alive with chaos and combat, had now settled into an eerie silence. The only thing more suffocating than the smoke lingering in the air was the tension between Vincent and Giuseppe.

Vincent's grip tightened around the hilt of his sword, his knuckles stark white against the dark metal. His gaze, sharp and unrelenting, bore into Giuseppe with an intensity that sent a cold ripple through the gathered warriors.

"When you picture our relationship, Giuseppe," Vincent began, his tone cutting through the silence like a blade, "you think of it as a friendly rivalry, built on mutual respect. Isn't that right?"

Chris stiffened, something about Vincent's words sending a jolt through his body. A flicker of a memory surfaced, one not from this timeline. His mind was thrust back into the fractured remnants of another reality—images of Vincent, darker, more menacing, flashing through his consciousness. He wasn't sure if it was just a trick of his thoughts, or if, somehow, the Vincent standing before him was truly capable of becoming the monster he had once known.

Instinctively, Chris's fingers clenched around the hilt of the Eclipse Blade, a faint crackle of lightning dancing along its edge.

Vincent took a slow step forward, his eyes locked onto Giuseppe with something venomous behind them. "But when I think of it," he continued, his voice taking on an almost mocking edge, "all I see is someone who belongs in my shadow."

The weight of his words hung heavy in the air, and the captains and warriors around them stilled. The battlefield had become something else entirely—no longer a place of physical combat, but of veiled threats and unspoken truths clawing their way to the surface.

"For years," Vincent pressed on, his voice like a slow, deliberate blade slicing through the space between them, "you've been celebrated—praised for your intellect, your strategies, your precision. Ever since that fateful day, you were the one they turned to. Even now, as captain of the highest archangel's squad, the others still seek your wisdom first." His jaw clenched, the emotion slipping through despite the icy exterior. "And me? I am still forced to prove myself."

A murmur passed through the ranks of warriors. The captains exchanged tense glances, understanding that they were now spectators to something deeply personal.

Giuseppe remained still, his face unreadable, his eyes watching Vincent carefully. But Chris could see the subtle tension in his father's posture. He wasn't unaffected by these words.

Vincent let out a quiet breath, as if steadying himself. But when he spoke again, his voice was lower, sharper. "I gave you a chance," he said. "Multiple chances. A chance to tell the truth. A chance to spare your son."

Chris's stomach dropped.

Giuseppe's expression finally shifted, his eyes narrowing ever so slightly. "What are you getting at, Vincent?" His voice was steady, but Chris could hear the edge beneath it—Giuseppe already knew that whatever came next would be dangerous.

Vincent's smirk returned, razor-sharp and cold. "You played coy, Giuseppe," he accused. "All this time, you've hidden behind your cleverness, thinking you could outmaneuver me."

Chris felt his pulse in his throat as Vincent's gaze flickered toward him. A chill settled over him as their eyes met, something in that cold stare making his breath feel too shallow.

"I know your secret," Vincent said, the words deliberate, heavy with meaning.

Chris's blood ran cold.

Vincent turned his gaze back to Giuseppe, his smirk deepening, his presence suffocating. "I know your *son's* secret."

Silence. Thick, deafening silence.

The weight of the accusation bore down on them like the heavens themselves had split open. Chris's mind raced. How much did Vincent know? How much of the truth was he holding over them? And how far was he willing to go to expose it?

Giuseppe's fists remained at his sides, but his entire being radiated something unreadable. A challenge. A warning.

Chris barely heard the murmurs beginning to rise among the warriors, the shifting movements of uncertainty. All he could feel was the invisible pressure bearing down on him, the storm that Vincent had just unleashed.

The tension in the air was suffocating, pressing down on everyone present like an invisible force. Sophie stood beside Chris, her expression tight with worry, her hand instinctively gripping his arm as if trying to tether him to reality. But Chris barely registered her touch. His eyes were locked on Vincent, his muscles coiled with anticipation, every fiber of his being bracing for what was about to happen.

Wait.

His father's voice echoed suddenly in his mind, calm but firm through their telepathic link.

Chris's grip on the Eclipse Blade tightened, his fingers trembling against the hilt. Every instinct screamed at him to act, to fight, but Giuseppe's voice cut through the storm raging in his head.

Not yet.

The warning settled like a weight in Chris's chest. His breaths came slow, measured, but his pulse pounded like a war drum in his ears.

Then, without a word of warning, Vincent moved.

His sword flashed in a deadly arc, ice lancing from the blade and streaking toward Chris with terrifying speed. The attack was instantaneous, catching even the captains off guard.

Shards of frozen death.

Chris's body reacted before his mind could. He stepped forward, instinctively shielding Sophie as he slashed his blade in an upward arc.

Flames erupted.

A violent surge of fire exploded from the Eclipse Blade, incinerating the incoming ice in a furious clash of elements. The heat pulsed outward, warping the air with its intensity.

Silence followed.

Chris stood there, breathless, his blade still alight with fire, his fire.

He felt it crackling along his skin, not burning, but alive—dangerous, untamed, waiting.

Waiting for him to accept it.

The battlefield had stopped. Everyone was staring at him.

Shock rippled through the ranks of warriors, captains, and recruits alike. Even Vincent, his expression normally unreadable, had a flicker of something behind his cold gaze.

Then Chris noticed.

His inhibitor ring.

It was **gone.**

His eyes darted down to his hand, his fingers feeling bare where the dark band should have been. His gaze snapped to Lyra—and there it was. In her hand.

She had taken it.

Betrayal seared through him. He barely found his voice.

"Lyra...?"

She didn't speak. She only tightened her grip on the ring, her eyes unreadable.

Vincent took a slow, measured step forward, his voice cutting through the stunned silence.

"You see, everyone. He's been hiding his full power."

Murmurs spread through the crowd, the weight of Vincent's words sinking in.

"And that…" Vincent's voice turned sharp, his tone almost hungry. "That is not just fire soul essence. That is the power of the Ethereal Flame, a demon's power source."

Chris's breath caught in his throat. No.

"He is the reason we face these threats. The reason the testing pod went up in flames. And he is the beacon that has drawn these demons here. He is solely responsible for these rifts."

The statement sent a shock wave through the gathered warriors. The captains, even those who had fought beside him, stiffened at the implication. Their reactions varied—Mei's fiery rage, Omari's cautious hesitation, Nyla's wary gaze.

Chris felt exposed, as if his entire existence had just been peeled apart layer by layer in front of everyone.

Then Vincent's gaze turned back to Giuseppe.

"You," he said, his voice dropping lower, more venomous, "think you can hoard power, Giuseppe. You think you can hide behind your principles while making your son a vessel for a demon's power. But I won't allow it. Not anymore."

Giuseppe took a step forward, his voice sharp and laced with fury. "What do you plan to do, Vincent?"

The smirk that curled across Vincent's lips sent an icy shiver through the air. "I'm taking your son."

Before anyone could react, the shadows surged.

Chris barely had time to register the movement before the darkness consumed him.

It came from everywhere—unnatural, suffocating, alive.

Sophie's scream barely had time to leave her lips before she, too, was swallowed.

One moment, Chris was standing among his allies.

Next, there was nothing.

"NO!"

Giuseppe's roar split through the stunned silence.

His blade crackled with lightning as he moved, his instincts screaming kill as he swung with all his force toward Vincent.

The ground shook with the force of his attack.

But Vincent was ready.

With a calculated step, he raised his icy blade, meeting Giuseppe's strike head-on.

The clash sent a deafening shock wave rippling through the battlefield, kicking up dirt, ice, and embers. The sheer force of their collision sent warriors stumbling backward, their soul essence flickering under the intensity of the two captains' power.

The captains sprang into action—Maria's wind howled as she shot forward, Mei's fire lashed outward, Omari's stone breaker mace slammed into the earth, shaking the battlefield beneath their feet.

But Vincent didn't waver.

Even as he held Giuseppe's blade locked in place, his icy smirk never faltered.

The storm had only just begun.

19

Vincent vs. Giuseppe

The battlefield trembled under the weight of their battle, every strike of Giuseppe's lightning-infused blade against Vincent's frost-laden sword sending shock waves rippling through the academy grounds. The very air crackled and hissed as opposing forces clashed—heat against cold, fury against calculation.

The warriors of the Angel Corps stood at a distance, weapons gripped tightly, watching the duel unfold with a mixture of awe and trepidation. Even the most seasoned captains hesitated to step in. It wasn't just a battle—it was a reckoning, years of tension and hidden resentment manifesting into an elemental storm before their very eyes.

"Where are they?!" Giuseppe's voice was raw with fury as he lunged forward, his movements fueled by desperation. His blade arced like a thunderbolt, slamming against Vincent's in a brilliant cascade of sparks and icy mist.

Vincent met each strike with unnerving composure, his feet gliding across the frost-covered ground with a precision that made the fight seem more like a dance than a battle. Cold. Calculated. Unshaken.

"You're reckless, Giuseppe," Vincent said, deflecting another blow with a sharp parry. His voice was steady, yet beneath the calm was something more—a hint of satisfaction, a knowing certainty. "And that recklessness blinds you."

Giuseppe growled, his grip tightening on his sword. "Enough of your riddles!" Lightning surged along his blade as he struck again, the sheer force behind the attack sending a visible tremor through the ground. But Vincent was faster.

With a single fluid motion, Vincent sidestepped, his icy blade coming down to meet Giuseppe's with a deafening crack—sending both men skidding backward. Frost and lightning clashed violently in the space between them, forming a whirlwind of energy that sent loose debris spiraling into the air.

The other captains sprang into action.

"Stand down, both of you!" Mei roared, her fire whip crackling to life as she advanced. Maria and Nyla flanked her, their own weapons glowing with power.

"You're tearing the battlefield apart!" Maria shouted, her dual fans of wind essence snapping open as she prepared to intervene.

Omari and Jeffrey weren't far behind. Omari's massive stone breaker mace pulsed with energy, while Jeffrey's light-infused bow was already drawn, his sharp gaze locked onto Vincent.

But as soon as they neared, a wave of frost erupted from Vincent's position, expanding outward in jagged spikes—forcing them all to stop in their tracks.

Mei barely managed to pull back in time, her flames keeping the encroaching ice at bay. "Damn it!" she hissed.

Maria gritted her teeth. "This is madness. We need to get to the root of the issue, not fight each other!"

Vincent and Giuseppe didn't even glance their way. Their focus remained locked in on each other.

Giuseppe's breath came heavy, his chest rising and falling in sharp, uneven intervals. But his rage had not diminished.

"Where are they, Vincent?! What did you do?! Answer me!"

Vincent exhaled through his nose, almost as if he was disappointed. "You still don't see it, do you? You let your emotions control you. That's why you'll never understand the truth."

Giuseppe lunged again, but this time—Vincent was waiting.

In a flash, Vincent's blade sliced through the air faster than anyone could follow. The ice-infused steel clashed against Giuseppe's weapon with such force that the shock wave sent dust and frost exploding outward, obscuring the battlefield for several seconds.

Through the haze, Nyla's chimes of resonant sound echoed, trying to disrupt Vincent's movements, but even her frequency manipulations seemed to falter against the sheer intensity of the battle.

Maria pressed forward despite the icy terrain, her wind-infused attacks attempting to break through the growing storm of Vincent's essence.

But the battle between the two captains had reached a level beyond interference.

Giuseppe snarled, stepping into Vincent's range again, lightning pulsing off his body in erratic, unstable waves.

"You gave me no choice, Vincent!" His blade crackled as he swung.

Vincent's eyes flashed with something unreadable. "No, Giuseppe. You gave yourself no choice."

Their battle raged, sending shock waves across the ruined battlefield. The captains surrounding them attempted to intervene—Omari slammed his stone breaker mace into the ground, sending jagged earth shooting up to separate them, but Giuseppe shattered it instantly with a pulse of electricity. Maria sent slicing gusts of wind between them, hoping to force them apart, but Vincent's icy barrier absorbed the attack without so much as a flinch.

"You can't stop them!" Nyla called out, gripping her chimes tightly, her sound essence reverberating through the air. "They're too locked in!"

Jeffrey drew his light bow, an arrow crackling with divine energy poised at the ready, but even he hesitated. One wrong move could tip the fight into something far worse.

In the midst of the chaos, the unnatural shadow that had swallowed Chris and Sophie pulsed with a life of its own.

The battlefield blurred around them as they fell, their screams lost in the void.

It was like tumbling through an endless abyss—weightless, cold, and disorienting. The world above seemed to vanish completely, leaving nothing but darkness. Chris reached out instinctively, his fingers grasping at nothing but empty space.

Then, with a jarring impact, they crashed onto a cold, unyielding surface. The shock knocked the wind out of Chris, pain flaring along his back as he groaned and tried to regain his bearings.

"Chris?" Sophie's voice cut through the thick silence, shaky but sharp. "Are you there?"

"Yeah," Chris groaned, pushing himself up onto his hands and knees. "I'm here."

"Ow!" Sophie yelped as she bumped into him, her head colliding with his shoulder.

Chris winced, rubbing the sore spot where they hit. "Seriously?"

"Well, it's not like I can see anything," Sophie shot back, her breath unsteady.

Chris forced himself upright, blinking into the suffocating darkness. It was absolute, not a sliver of light breaking through. The air was damp and cold, carrying a metallic tang that made his skin crawl.

"Where are we?" Sophie asked, her voice rising slightly as panic seeped into her tone. "What's going on?"

Chris exhaled slowly, trying to push down the unease twisting in his gut. "I don't know," he admitted, frustration lacing his voice. "Vincent's lost his mind."

"Lost his mind?" Sophie's breathing turned uneven as she cut him off. "Chris, he said you're a vessel for demon powers! What does that mean? Why would he say that? What aren't you telling me?"

Her voice cracked—an uncharacteristic sign of fear.

Chris clenched his fists. He could barely make sense of what was happening himself, let alone explain it to her. The flames, the visions, the whispers that had followed him for weeks. And now, Vincent's accusations—saying he was the beacon drawing the demons in.

He forced himself to take a deep breath. "Sophie, calm down," he said, his voice firm but steady. "We have to stay focused. Panicking won't help us right now."

Sophie swallowed thickly. "Calm down?!" she echoed, her voice sharp before she caught herself. She sucked in a shaky breath and exhaled slowly. "You're right. You're right… I just—what's happening?"

Chris hesitated before answering, running a hand through his hair. "I don't know why Vincent said those things," he said, his voice quieter but resolute. "I don't know. But we need to figure out where we are and how to get out of here. That's all that matters right now."

Sophie nodded, though he could tell she was still shaken. "Okay," she said softly. "What's the plan?"

Chris pushed himself fully to his feet, his boots scraping against the cold, uneven ground. He reached out blindly, trying to feel anything solid around them. "First, we figure out what this place is," he muttered. "Then, we find a way out."

Sophie followed suit, her own movements cautious. "And if we can't?" she asked hesitantly.

Chris exhaled, determination hardening his gaze even in the dark. "Then we make a way out."

The oppressive blackness seemed to press closer as they moved cautiously, each step uncertain. Shadows loomed, shifting unnaturally in the void around them.

Chris couldn't shake the feeling that something was watching.

That whatever was waiting in the dark—

Was waiting for him.

Chris exhaled sharply, trying to steady the pounding in his chest. The silence was suffocating, the darkness pressing in on him like a living entity. His grip tightened around the hilt of his Eclipse Blade, his fingers twitching with the instinct to fight—even when there was nothing to fight against.

"Okay, think, Chris," he muttered under his breath, his voice barely more than a whisper in the void. "What did he catch us with?"

Sophie, standing close beside him, responded without hesitation, her voice steady but laced with unease. "It was the shadow of the building," she said, the realization settling heavily between them.

Chris frowned. "How is that even possible?" His mind raced, trying to make sense of what had just happened. He had seen Vincent wield ice, had fought against his relentless precision before—but this? This was something else entirely.

Sophie took a deep breath, her tone shifting to something more thoughtful. "You know how there's soul essence that manifests light, right?"

"Yeah," Chris said, nodding slightly, though she couldn't see him.

"Well, there's also soul essence that manifests darkness," she continued. "It allows users to manipulate shadows, even the void itself. They can attack with shadows, hide within them... even move through them."

Chris's brow furrowed. "And Vincent can do that?" His stomach twisted. "That doesn't make sense."

Sophie hesitated before lowering her voice. "It's supposed to be a lost art, only attainable through... dark energy."

Chris stiffened, his breath catching in his throat. Dark energy. The very thing they had been trained to avoid, to destroy, to purge from existence. His fingers curled tighter around his blade.

"How can Vincent do it?" Sophie asked, her voice hushed as if speaking the thought aloud made it more real. "And why does this feel different? This isn't just shadow manipulation, Chris. We can't hear anyone. Can't sense anything. We've been transported somewhere else entirely."

She turned her head slightly. "And look."

Chris blinked, instinctively scanning his surroundings, but there was nothing to see—no horizon, no light, no movement. Just an endless abyss. The darkness was so thick it felt tangible, clinging to his skin like smoke.

"I can't see anything in here," he admitted, frustration creeping into his voice.

"Exactly," Sophie said, her voice sharp with tension. "Whenever I use my power, my amulet glows—it reacts to the plants and earth around me. But here…" She lifted her amulet, but there was no light, no warmth. "There's nothing. No plants. No earth. Nothing for my power to connect to."

Chris inhaled deeply and closed his eyes, focusing inward, reaching out through the mental link he shared with his father.

Nothing.

He pushed harder, searching for the steady, familiar presence of Giuseppe's soul essence. But there was only silence—an empty void where his father's voice should have been.

Chris clenched his jaw, frustration creeping in as he instinctively tried to summon his lightning. A surge of determination coursed through him as he willed the familiar energy to respond, to crackle along his fingertips, to hum with the electric current that had always been a part of him.

But again—nothing.

His heart pounded. His soul essence, the core of his strength, felt distant, unreachable. His connection to his own power severed, just like the link to his father. It was as if this place had stripped him of everything—his strength, his instincts, his very identity.

Chris's eyes snapped open. "I can't hear my dad," he said, his voice quieter now, edged with something dangerously close to worry. His grip on the Eclipse Blade tightened as his mind raced. "If this isn't just shadows, then what is it? And how do we fight it?"

Sophie exhaled slowly, her fingers clenching around the dimly glowing amulet. "We might not be able to fight it. Not yet," she admitted. "First, we need to figure out what this place is—and how to get out of it."

Chris nodded, his jaw tightening. "Then let's start looking. There has to be something, even here."

Together, they began to move cautiously, their steps slow and deliberate. The silence pressed heavier against them with each passing second, and though they couldn't see the ground beneath their feet, it was solid—cold and smooth, like polished stone.

Then, after what felt like an eternity, she reached out and grabbed his wrist.

"Chris," she whispered, urgent but controlled.

He stopped instantly, his body tensing. "What is it?"

Sophie didn't answer right away. Instead, she took a cautious step forward, stretching her hand into the empty space ahead of them. Her breath hitched.

"The air changes here," she said quietly.

Chris frowned. "Changes how?"

She shook her head. "I don't know. But something's different."

Chris reached out, testing the air in front of them. At first, it felt no different—cold, stagnant. But then he felt it. A pulse. Faint, distant, but unmistakably there.

It wasn't just an empty void.

There was something here.

Meanwhile, back at Celestia Academy, the duel between Vincent and Giuseppe raged on. The battlefield had become a fractured wasteland, torn between frost and lightning as Vincent and Giuseppe clashed with relentless fury. Their duel was more than a battle—it was a storm, each strike reverberating across Celestia Academy like thunder crashing against ice. The ground beneath them bore the scars of their battle, half frozen over in jagged crystalline formations, half scorched with deep fissures of charred earth. Every impact sent shock waves rippling through the air, forcing the onlookers to retreat further for fear of being caught in the crossfire.

Giuseppe's blade sparked with volatile electricity as he lunged forward, his strikes fast and unyielding. "Where are they, Vincent?!" he roared, his voice laced with fury and desperation. "What did you do to them?!"

Vincent sidestepped the attack with unnerving precision, his frost-laden sword intercepting Giuseppe's next strike with a sharp clang. "You let your emotions cloud your judgment, as always," he said coolly. "Do you even know what you're fighting for anymore?"

Giuseppe gritted his teeth, surging forward again. Sparks flew as he swung, lightning crackling through the air, but Vincent moved as though he had anticipated the attack long before it came. With a fluid motion, he twisted his blade, sending a wave of frost spiraling outwards. The bitter cold spread rapidly, creeping toward Giuseppe's feet, forcing him to shatter the encroaching ice with a burst of raw soul essence.

"You're hiding something!" Giuseppe snapped, his attacks becoming more aggressive, his frustration palpable. "Tell me where they are!"

Vincent's expression remained unreadable, his icy gaze holding none of the urgency Giuseppe was demanding. His silence, his measured movements—it was maddening. It was as if the fight was nothing but an inconvenience to him.

"Enough!" Mei's voice cut through the battlefield like a whip—both figuratively and literally. A crack of flame lashed between the two captains, forcing them apart, the fire scorching the frozen ground between them.

Giuseppe staggered back, his chest heaving, while Vincent merely stepped away, the frost on his blade still untouched by the heat.

Nyla was the next to act, her Resonant Chime Gauntlets pulsing with an ethereal glow as she raised her hands. With a sharp motion, she clapped them together, sending a sound wave that rippled between the two men. The vibrations were enough to force them further apart, a jarring disruption in the midst of their deadly dance.

"What in the world is going on here?" Nyla demanded, her sharp gaze darting between the two combatants. "You're supposed to be captains, not two reckless brutes tearing through the academy."

Omari followed suit, his massive Stone breaker Mace slamming into the earth with a thundering impact. The ground trembled beneath him as he stepped forward, his voice deep and commanding. "This fight isn't solving anything. Both of you—stand down before you bring more destruction to our own ranks."

Jeffery stood behind them, silent but poised, his Luminous Bow drawn. An arrow of pure light shimmered at his fingertips, its glow casting an almost holy radiance over the battlefield. His stance was steady, and though he did not speak, his message was clear—he would not hesitate to fire if this madness continued.

Mei took another step forward, her fiery whip still in hand, her gaze burning with anger. "This needs to end," she said firmly. "Giuseppe, what the hell is going on? Why are you fighting like this?"

Giuseppe's grip on his sword tightened, his breath still ragged. His voice, however, held no hesitation. "He took my son," he said, his words raw with emotion.

Vincent raised an eyebrow, his cold demeanor unshaken. "I didn't take him." He turned his gaze to the gathered captains and warriors, his voice steady but carrying the weight of something far more damning. "Chris has been hiding his true power. The ethereal flame was just the beginning. He's shown his ability to manipulate the shadows, vanishing into them like the demons we've fought to destroy."

A murmur rippled through the ranks, the implications of his words settling uneasily over the battlefield.

Then, a sharp voice cut through the growing tension.

"Captain Vincent is right!"

The statement came from Lyra, her voice ringing out above the murmurs. All eyes snapped to her as she stepped forward, her expression resolute. The warriors who had just barely begun to process Vincent's accusations now turned to Lyra, waiting for what she would say next.

Giuseppe's gaze darkened, his jaw clenching. "What did you just say?"

Lyra lifted her chin, standing firm despite the weight of the moment. "Chris's power is not normal," she said, her voice steady but unwavering. "You've all seen it now. The flames, the shadows... we can't ignore this. If he truly has demon power within him…"

Gasps spread across the battlefield, warriors exchanging uncertain glances. The captains, though seasoned and hardened, could not ignore the growing concern etched into the faces of their forces.

Mei's whip curled at her side, her brows furrowed in deep contemplation. "Are you saying you believe Chris is responsible for the rifts?"

"Yes," Richard finally spoke, stepping forward, his voice firm but measured. "After training with him, being on the same team, I've always felt something… off about Chris. An energy around him. Something he's kept hidden. He's always been guarded—like he was afraid of what we'd find out."

"All lies!" Allegra's voice cut through the quiet, sharp with fury. She turned, her gaze burning with defiance. "I don't know what you two are up to, but smearing Chris like this? Accusing him of something this insane? That's not the way forward!"

Lyra exhaled, shaking her head. "Allegra, think. Really think," she said, her tone edged with something close to pity. "He hid his fire abilities from us for weeks. Then suddenly, he disappears into a shadow? And during the battle, we all heard him talking—to someone. He was saying things about the flames, about control. Who was he speaking to, Allegra?" Her eyes narrowed. "Was it a demon? Is that what's been guiding him this entire time?"

Allegra opened her mouth to respond, but no words came. She searched for a rebuttal, something—anything—to counter Lyra's claims. But the questions lingered, heavy and damning.

"I know you care about him," Lyra continued, voice softer now, almost regretful. "But open your eyes. He's betrayed the Angel Corps, our laws, our very creator."

Allegra's chest tightened. "No," she whispered, shaking her head. "No, you're wrong. Chris—he wouldn't do that. He wouldn't." She turned desperately toward the rest of Team Ten. "Guys—back me up. You know him. You know this isn't true."

Silence.

Not a single one of them spoke.

Their faces were grim, torn between doubt and loyalty. And that silence cut deeper than any blade.

"Enough," Mei's voice rang out, final and absolute. "We will get to the bottom of this once and for all." Her gaze flickered toward Giuseppe, who stood rigid, his body still charged with barely contained fury. "Giuseppe, stand down."

His eyes widened in disbelief. "You can't seriously believe them," he spat, his voice trembling with anger. "Vincent planned this! He's been playing this game from the very start!"

Mei's expression didn't waver. "Planned or not, these claims are serious. If Chris is connected to demonic power, we have to treat it as a potential threat. Stand. Down."

Giuseppe's hands clenched into fists, his mind racing. This wasn't how it was supposed to go. The words he had spoken to Chris not long ago echoed in his head: *Don't let your emotions make you predictable.* And now, standing there, surrounded, he realized—Vincent had played him perfectly. He had let his desperation turn into a weapon against him.

For a long moment, Giuseppe didn't move. Then, slowly, he exhaled and loosened his grip on his blade, lowering it ever so slightly. His expression was unreadable. "Fine," he said, his voice quiet, restrained. "You want me to stand down? I'll stand down."

The tension in the air seemed to ease slightly. The captains exchanged glances, their grips on their weapons relaxing, just for a moment.

And that was all he needed.

In a flash of pure lightning essence, Giuseppe struck.

His blade lashed out in a sudden arc, the crackling energy illuminating the battlefield. Mei reacted first, snapping her fiery whip forward, barely managing to deflect his first attack. Nyla's Resonant Gauntlets glowed as she absorbed the brunt of his shock wave, the vibrations rippling through her armor. Omari swung his Stone breaker Mace, blocking Giuseppe's next strike with a thunderous impact that sent cracks splintering across the ground.

Jeffery, ever the precise marksman, shot a glowing arrow of light, forcing Giuseppe to shift his stance and dodge, retreating a few paces.

The skirmish was brief but explosive—each movement a calculated strike, each defense an instinct honed from years of experience. The gathered warriors could only watch in stunned silence, unable to intervene.

Mei's voice rang out, furious. "Giuseppe, *stop!*"

But he was already moving.

With a final burst of lightning, he turned and sprinted toward the academy's outer edge. The crackling energy propelled him forward in an instant, his figure a blur as he reached the rocky mountainside.

And then, just like that—he was gone.

Vanishing into the descending shadows, leaving behind nothing but the smoldering battlefield and the stunned faces of those who had once stood beside him.

Mei exhaled sharply, her grip on her whip tightening before she finally lowered it. Her expression was grim, her gaze lingering on the jagged path Giuseppe had disappeared down.

"We need to find him," she said, her voice firm, leaving no room for argument. She turned to Vincent, her eyes sharp with suspicion. "And we need to get to the bottom of what's really going on with Chris."

Vincent met her gaze with an unsettling calm. With a smooth motion, he sheathed his frosted blade, the lingering chill dissipating into the air. A ghost of a smirk tugged at the corner of his lips, but his tone was measured. "I already told you the truth," he said, his voice steady. "Now, it's up to us to act on it."

The weight of his words settled over the gathered captains. Silence stretched between them, heavy and unresolved. No one spoke, but the unspoken tension rippled through the group like an oncoming storm.

Maria crossed her arms, her jaw set. "So what now?" she asked, her voice low, wary.

Omari glanced toward the distant mountains, where the last traces of Giuseppe's presence had vanished into the night. His massive arms tensed at his sides. "We have two problems," he said. "One: a rogue captain. Two: a potential demonic threat. If Vincent's right, and Chris is tied to the ethereal flame and umbral manipulation, then we're dealing with something beyond any normal rogue recruit."

Jeffery, ever composed, ran a gloved hand over his bowstring, his gaze calculating. "We need to separate emotion from fact," he said plainly. "Giuseppe is gone, but he won't stay hidden forever. And as for Chris… if he really is the source of these rifts, we can't afford to ignore it."

Nyla's expression was unreadable, but her fingers drummed lightly against her gauntlets, the resonant chimes humming faintly. "If," she echoed. "There's still too much we don't know."

"Then we find out," Mei declared, her voice cutting through the uncertainty like a blade. She turned to Vincent, her gaze unyielding. "If you have any more information, now's the time."

Vincent's smirk deepened just slightly. "Patience, Mei. The pieces are already moving." His gaze flickered toward the fading moonlight, something unreadable in his expression. "And soon enough, everything will fall into place."

The captains exchanged glances, unease settling like a thick fog around them.

Somehow, none of them felt any closer to the truth.

And yet, they all knew—whatever was coming next, there was no turning back now.

20

The Void

The suffocating darkness wrapped around them, stretching endlessly in every direction. Each cautious step Chris and Sophie took echoed faintly, though the ground beneath them felt neither entirely solid nor weightless. It was as if they were suspended in a realm where the rules of reality had been rewritten.

Chris's grip on Sophie's hand tightened, his other hand wrapped around the hilt of his Eclipse Blade. The blade thrummed softly, a muted pulse of energy that reassured him he was still tethered to his soul essence. He kept his breathing steady, though his mind churned, trying to make sense of where they were—and why.

"This place," Sophie murmured, her voice barely above a whisper, "it doesn't just feel empty… it feels alive."

Chris turned slightly toward her, though he could barely see more than her outline against the void. "What do you mean, alive?"

Sophie hesitated, as if the words themselves would make the feeling more real. "Like it's watching us," she admitted. "Waiting."

A cold prickle ran down Chris's spine. He scanned the endless darkness around them, his eyes sharp, but there was nothing. No shapes, no structures—just the oppressive black, pressing in from all sides.

"We can't just stand here," he said, forcing certainty into his voice. "There has to be a way out."

Sophie's fingers curled around his, gripping tighter. "What if there isn't? What if this is Vincent's way of trapping us forever?"

Chris exhaled slowly, forcing himself to think past the rising unease. "No," he said. "If he wanted us dead, we'd already be dead. This isn't about killing us. It's about proving something."

Sophie swallowed, her other hand resting lightly on the amulet at her chest, as if drawing strength from it. "Then what do we do?"

Chris took a step forward, pulling her gently with him. "We move," he said. "We find something—anything. Standing still isn't an option."

They pressed on, their footsteps impossibly loud in the silence. The void around them seemed to shift, warping at the edges of their vision. It was subtle at first—just a flicker, a movement darker than the surrounding blackness—but when Chris turned to look, it was gone.

His jaw tightened. "We're not alone."

Sophie stiffened. "What do you mean?"

Chris kept his voice low. "I saw something. I don't know what, but it was there."

Sophie hesitated before nodding. "Then we keep moving," she echoed.

And so they did, venturing deeper into the abyss, where the silence wasn't empty—it was waiting.

Back at Celestia Academy, the war room was thick with tension. Maps, hastily scrawled notes, and battle reports littered the long table, their edges curled from hurried handling. A single lantern flickered, casting shifting shadows across the faces of the captains gathered around.

Nyla broke the silence first, her resonant chime gauntlets tapping against the table in a slow, rhythmic pattern. "So," she said, her voice cutting through the heavy air, "what's the plan? We have a captain on the run, two recruits missing, and now you're telling us there's demon involvement."

Before anyone could respond, Maria burst into the room, her expression grave. "A head count was just done," she announced, her voice strained with urgency. "We took heavy casualties. forty-nine lives were lost. We're also missing sixty others. They've just vanished."

A stunned silence followed, broken only by Mei, whose fiery whip coiled tighter at her side, radiating increased heat. "Sixty? That many can't just vanish unnoticed."

Omari leaned forward, his massive frame imposing even seated. "If it's sixty people, this isn't random. It's coordinated. Vincent, do you think Chris and Sophie's disappearance is connected to this?"

Vincent stood rigid, his fingers gripping the hilt of his frosted blade tightly. "Almost certainly. Their use of umbral manipulation points directly to demonic involvement."

Mei's sharp gaze locked onto Vincent, suspicion deepening. "If Chris is somehow involved in the disappearance of sixty people, then we're not just dealing with recruits gone astray. What aren't you telling us?"

Vincent's gaze hardened as he studied each captain carefully. "Everything I've told you is the truth," he said smoothly. "But it appears the threat is larger than we initially thought. The technique Chris and Sophie used ties directly into these disappearances. We're dealing with something far more dangerous than mere rogue behavior."

Jeffery, usually calm, now showed visible agitation. "We can't afford to chase ghosts blindly. Giuseppe might hold answers about Chris's involvement. We need to find him immediately."

Vincent tilted his head slightly, his lips tightening. "Giuseppe is predictable. His emotions rule him; he'll slip up soon enough. But finding Chris is paramount—he's the linchpin connecting these disappearances to the demonic threat."

Maria exhaled sharply, eyes narrowing. "Then we split our focus. One team hunts Giuseppe for answers, another searches for Chris and Sophie, while the rest of us strengthen defenses. If sixty have vanished, more could follow."

Mei nodded slowly, her fingers flexing instinctively around her whip's handle. "Agreed. And Vincent, if you're wrong about any of this, the responsibility is yours."

A heavy silence blanketed the room once more, each captain absorbing the magnitude of their next steps. The lantern flickered again, the shifting shadows deepening their collective resolve. The hunt had just intensified.

The void stretched endlessly before them, a suffocating abyss that seemed to devour every sound, every breath. Chris and Sophie moved cautiously through the oppressive darkness, their steps hesitant and unsteady on the formless ground beneath them. There was no way to tell where they were going—or if they were even moving at all.

The silence was unbearable, broken only by the faint sound of their breathing and the occasional shuffle of movement. Every now and then, Chris thought he caught a flicker of something in the corner of his vision, but when he turned to look, there was nothing. Just the abyss.

"Chris," Sophie said, her voice trembling slightly. "Can you use your lightning? Maybe it can light the way."

Chris hesitated, gripping the hilt of his Eclipse Blade tightly. He had already tried to summon his lightning essence, but each attempt had yielded nothing—no spark, no surge of power, just an empty void where his connection should have been. "It's not working," he admitted. "I thought I felt something before, but now… nothing."

Sophie exhaled, her breath shaky as the cold seeped into her skin. She wrapped her arms around herself, her voice quieter now. "It's freezing, Chris. We won't survive long if we stay in this place."

Chris clenched his jaw, the weight of her words settling in his chest. She was right—this place felt like it was slowly consuming them, draining their strength, their resolve. The darkness was more than just an absence of light; it was a living thing, pressing against them, waiting for them to break.

But he wouldn't let that happen.

"We'll get through this," he said, his voice firm despite the doubt creeping into his mind. He glanced around, though there was nothing to see. "There has to be something—a way out, a weak point, anything. We just have to keep moving."

Sophie nodded faintly, though her grip on his arm tightened as they continued their slow, cautious trek through the void. The chill deepened with every step, wrapping around them like unseen tendrils, making it harder to move, harder to think. The silence between them grew heavier, thick with uncertainty.

Then, Sophie spoke again, her voice quiet but pointed. "The ring," she said. "The one Lyra took. What was it for?"

Chris stiffened, his grip on the Eclipse Blade tightening. His mind raced, debating how much to tell her. The ring—his father's creation—had been meant to suppress his fire essence, to keep something inside him contained. And now that it was gone…

Chris hesitated, choosing his words carefully. "Sophie… I don't want to say I've been hiding this, but I only just found out recently."

She stopped abruptly, turning toward him even though she couldn't see his face in the suffocating darkness. "What's going on?" she asked, her voice steady but tinged with worry.

Chris exhaled slowly, realizing there was no point in holding back now. "According to my father," he said, his tone measured, "my body holds three forms of soul essence. One that manipulates lightning, one that manipulates fire, and a third that we haven't identified yet."

Silence. Then—

"What?" Sophie's voice shot up, disbelief laced with something sharper. "Three forms of soul essence? Chris, that's impossible! That's—" She cut herself off, frustration bleeding into her tone. "And you didn't think to tell me this before?"

Chris sighed, rubbing the bridge of his nose. "I didn't even know until recently!" he said, his voice taut with frustration. "I'm still figuring it out myself."

Sophie's breath came fast, uneven. "So… Vincent's right, isn't he?" Her voice turned rigid, like she was trying to force herself to stay calm. "About you? Did you summon the shadow?"

Chris froze. The accusation stung deeper than he expected.

He turned to face her fully, his voice low but firm. "No, Sophie. I'm trapped here just like you." His hands clenched at his sides, his pulse hammering in his ears. "I don't know what Vincent's talking about, but I didn't summon anything."

For a long moment, neither of them spoke. The darkness pressed in, cold and relentless, but it was nothing compared to the weight of Sophie's silence.

Sophie's words hung between them, sharp and unrelenting. "So, is your fire essence really the power of a demon, or is that another lie from Vincent?"

Chris clenched his jaw. "I don't know," he admitted, the weight of uncertainty pressing on him. "Even my father doesn't know how it manifested."

"Then you have to try." Sophie's voice was firm, unwavering.

Chris frowned. "What do you mean?"

"If we're cut off from our normal soul essence, maybe your fire is still connected," she said, stepping closer. "You could try to summon it."

Chris hesitated, gripping the hilt of his Eclipse Blade tightly. "I can't just—"

"Yes, you can," Sophie cut him off, planting herself directly in front of him. Her voice was steady, but her eyes burned with urgency. "You said fire is a different part of your soul essence. If nothing else is working, then use it. Light the way. Warm us. What's stopping you from at least trying?"

"It's not that simple," he muttered. "It's not like my lightning."

"Exactly," Sophie pressed. "It's not like your lightning, which means it might still work."

"I said it's not that simple!" Chris snapped, stepping back from her.

Sophie didn't flinch. "You keep saying that, but you're not explaining anything! What's holding you back? Why can't you help us?"

Chris turned away, his hands curling into fists at his sides. "Just drop it, Sophie. Let's keep moving."

"No, Chris!" she shot back, her voice rising. "Why can't you—"

"Because I'm afraid!"

His voice erupted into the void like a crack of thunder, reverberating through the oppressive darkness. The admission stunned them both into silence. Chris stood there, his chest rising and falling, his fists trembling.

Chris dropped to his knees, the weight of his emotions crashing down on him like an unrelenting wave. His shoulders slumped, his head hung low, and his trembling hands gripped the hilt of his Eclipse Blade as though it was the only thing tethering him to reality.

"I'm afraid," he admitted, his voice barely above a whisper. "Just thinking about the fire… of what it did… of what it means." His breath hitched, and for a moment, he couldn't speak, as if the memories themselves were suffocating him. Then, the words spilled out, raw and unfiltered.

"In the timeline I came from, everything burned. My entire world. My life—it all turned to ash. And no matter what I did, I couldn't stop it." His voice cracked, the pain seeping through every syllable. "I was powerless. The fire… it destroyed everything."

His hands trembled as he slowly raised them, staring at his fingers as if they still carried the embers of his past. "I was supposed to die in that fire. If my mom hadn't pulled me out… I wouldn't be here. The flames, the power—I can't even look at it without seeing what I lost. Without feeling it all over again. And now I'm afraid of what it means," he admitted. "Afraid that Vincent might be right."

That the fire inside him wasn't just another soul essence—but something darker. Something he couldn't control.

The silence that followed was suffocating, the weight of his confession hanging heavy in the void. Then, Sophie moved.

She knelt down beside him, her presence steady, unwavering. She didn't try to offer empty reassurances, didn't tell him he was wrong to feel the way he did. Instead, she placed a hand on his shoulder, her grip firm and grounding.

"Chris…" she said, her voice soft, yet filled with quiet strength.

"That fire," Sophie said, her voice steady and unwavering, "isn't the fire that destroyed your past. It's yours, Chris. It's part of you. And it's not just destruction—it's warmth, light, and power. You've fought so hard to be here. You're stronger than your fear."

Chris let out a shaky breath, his hands still clenched at his sides. He wanted to believe her, wanted to accept her words as truth, but the weight in his chest refused to lift. His voice came out hoarse, raw with something deeper than pain—exhaustion.

"You don't understand, Sophie," he muttered, his gaze still

locked on the empty void around them. "No one does. No one can. Not in this timeline, at least."

Sophie frowned, but she didn't interrupt.

"The loss," he continued, his voice tightening. "The emptiness. Watching everything you love be ripped away, burned to nothing. And then to be thrown into a world where it all still exists—but it's not the same. It's real, but it isn't mine." His fingers twitched, as if gripping something invisible, something lost. "And no matter what I do, I carry it all with me. A constant reminder. A memory of everything that was taken."

Sophie's heart ached at his words. She had known Chris for years, had fought beside him, trusted him, but she realized now—she had never truly understood the weight he carried. The past wasn't just something he remembered. It lived inside him, intertwined with his very being, a ghost that refused to let go.

"I carry pain every day," Sophie said, her voice quieter now but no less firm. "I never really talk about it, but when I lost my mother… my whole world stopped."

Chris's head lifted slightly, his ears tuning in as a memory surfaced—one he had nearly forgotten. A younger Sophie, standing at the edge of the schoolyard, her face streaked with tears, eyes red and distant. He remembered the way she had clutched her books to her chest like they were the only thing holding her together.

"Your mom," he murmured, his throat tightening. "Sophie… I'm sorry. I didn't mean to—"

She shook her head, cutting him off gently but firmly. "No. I need to say this, and you need to hear it."

Chris hesitated but said nothing, sensing the weight behind her words.

Sophie took a slow breath, steadying herself. "When she died, I felt like I lost a part of myself. Like I'd never be whole again. People would always tell me that I should carry on, but it felt like the pain was all I had left of her. That if I let it go, I'd be letting her go too."

Her fingers curled slightly, as if grasping at something unseen. "But I was wrong. The pain is real, but so is everything she left behind—everything she gave me. Her love, her lessons, her strength… those don't disappear just because she's gone."

Chris watched her closely, the way her shoulders tensed as she spoke, the quiet tremor in her voice. But then Sophie let out a shaky exhale, her hands tightening at her sides.

"But even now, I still struggle," she admitted. "Because no matter how much I want to honor her memory, no matter how much I push myself… sometimes, I wonder if I'll ever measure up. My mom was a warrior—a great one. People looked up to her. And when I was growing up, it felt like I was always chasing a shadow I could never reach." Her voice wavered for a second, but she kept going. "Like no matter what I did, I was letting her down."

Chris's chest ached at her words, at the raw honesty in her voice. He understood that feeling all too well.

Sophie took a slow breath, steadying herself before meeting Chris's gaze. Her voice was quiet but firm, carrying a weight that pressed through the darkness between them.

"I may not have lived through what you did, but I know what it's like to be afraid of something inside you," she admitted. "To feel like it's bigger than you, stronger than you. Like if you lose control, even for a second, everything could fall apart."

Her fingers curled slightly at her sides as she exhaled. "I've been there, Chris. I know what it's like to carry something that feels like it could break you. And I know how easy it is to let fear tell you who you are."

Her words settled over him, weaving into the cracks of his fractured resolve like a thread pulling him back together. For the first time, Chris didn't recoil from the fear clawing at his chest—he faced it. He let himself feel the weight of his past, the fire that had once swallowed everything he loved. But this time, he wouldn't let it consume him.

Chris closed his eyes, drawing in a deep, steadying breath. His fingers tightened around the hilt of his Eclipse Blade, its familiar weight grounding him. He had spent so long resisting the flames, fearing what they meant, what they could do. But Sophie was right. The fire wasn't just destruction. It wasn't just pain.

It was his.

Exhaling slowly, he focused—not on controlling the fire, but on accepting it. He didn't try to force it into submission or suppress it. Instead, he willed it to move, to flow, not through his hands, but through the blade itself.

A low hum vibrated through the sword, resonating deep within his core. The edges of the blade shimmered faintly, pulsing like a heartbeat. Then, in a single moment of release, the fire erupted.

A brilliant, golden-orange blaze surged along the length of the weapon, illuminating the void with a warmth that pushed back the suffocating cold. The heat rippled outward, banishing the lingering chill that clung to their skin. The darkness that had surrounded them retreated, recoiling from the sudden burst of light.

Sophie took a step back, her breath catching. "Chris…" she whispered, the awe in her voice unmistakable.

Chris opened his eyes, watching the flames dance along his blade, steady and controlled, no longer wild and unpredictable. He had always feared that fire would destroy him. But now, as it pulsed in his grip, for the first time, he realized—this fire didn't control him.

He controlled it.

Sophie smiled, the firelight casting a soft glow on her face, her eyes reflecting the warmth that now surrounded them. Chris looked down at his blade, watching the flames dance along its surface—not erratic, not uncontrollable, but steady, responding to him. For the first time, the fire didn't feel like a threat. It felt like something more. Something he could wield. Something that belonged to him.

Possibility.

He exhaled slowly, the tension in his chest easing as he let himself accept that truth.

"Thanks to you," he murmured, his voice quieter but steadier than before.

Sophie reached out, her fingers wrapping around his free hand, her grip firm and reassuring. She gave a gentle tug, urging him upward. "Come on," she said, her smile small but certain. "Let's keep moving. This time, we'll find our way out."

Chris met Sophie's gaze, nodding as he tightened his grip on the Eclipse Blade. With a deep breath, he raised the weapon, willing the flames to burn brighter. The fire surged along the length of the blade, its glow expanding outward, pushing back the suffocating darkness.

Then, for the first time, they saw it.

The flickering light cast jagged shadows along the uneven walls around them. They weren't standing in an endless void— this was a cave, its towering rock formations coated in thick layers of frost. The air hung heavy with moisture, their breaths visible in the cold. Stalactites loomed above them like frozen fangs, and the ground beneath them was slick with ice, uneven and treacherous.

Sophie exhaled, her shoulders sagging with the realization. "It's not endless," she murmured. "We're somewhere. We can find a way out."

Chris turned slowly, taking in the walls, the craggy ceiling, the jagged tunnel stretching forward. The darkness had lied to them, had tried to convince them they were lost in an abyss with no escape. But now, with the fire illuminating their surroundings, they could see the truth.

It wasn't an empty void.

It was something they could overcome.

Chris set his jaw. "Then let's keep moving."

Together, they pressed forward, the firelight carving a path through the cold, unyielding dark. Each step carried them away from fear, away from doubt, and toward whatever awaited them on the other side.

Back at Celestia Academy the air was eerily silent, the weight of loss hanging over the gathered warriors like a thick, suffocating fog. The once-proud field, now scarred with the remnants of battle, bore witness to the sacrifices made that day. The remaining squads stood in formation, their bodies weary, their faces marred with soot, sweat, and grief. Among them, hushed murmurs passed between shaken recruits, whispers of the fallen, of the horrors they had faced, and of the uncertainty looming ahead.

At the front, the captains stood in a solemn line, their presence commanding. Each bore the weight of responsibility in their stances, their expressions grim and unreadable. Vincent stepped forward, his movements slow, deliberate. Even without speaking, his presence was enough to silence the quiet hum of conversation, all eyes shifting to him. The icy energy that always accompanied him now carried something heavier—finality.

"We've suffered an immense loss today," Vincent began, his voice unwavering, cutting through the silence like a blade. "forty-nine of our own have fallen. Brothers and sisters who stood beside us, who fought with everything they had to protect this academy, this realm, and the balance we hold sacred."

The words sank in like stones dropped into a still lake. Some warriors closed their eyes, others bowed their heads in mourning. Even the wind seemed to hush, as if honoring the fallen.

"But because of your bravery," Vincent continued, his tone shifting, sharpening, "we have held the line. We have forced the enemy back and learned more about the threat we face. That knowledge comes at a cost, but it is necessary if we are to win the battles ahead."

A murmur of unease rippled through the crowd at his words. The battle had been hard-fought, but many still felt the sting of loss outweigh the relief of victory. Yet, even in mourning, they needed direction. They needed purpose. Vincent knew this.

His expression darkened. His next words fell like ice into the air.

"Unfortunately, the greatest threat we face does not come from beyond these walls," he said, his voice now edged with something colder, heavier. "It comes from within."

The tension in the air shifted instantly. Warriors exchanged uncertain glances, confusion flickering across their faces.

Vincent took a measured step forward, his eyes scanning the gathered squads. "Captain Giuseppe," he continued, his tone even but cutting, "has betrayed the Angel Corps."

A sharp intake of breath swept through the crowd, followed by hushed voices of disbelief. Gasps, muttered protests, shocked expressions—it was as if the very foundation beneath them had cracked.

"Impossible," someone whispered.

"That can't be true…"

Vincent raised a hand, silencing them with the sheer authority in his gesture.

"He harbored demonic power within his son, Chris," Vincent stated, his voice unrelenting. "Power that was unleashed today. That power allowed both Giuseppe and Chris to escape justice."

The murmurs shifted, turning from disbelief to something more uncertain, more volatile.

Vincent's piercing gaze swept over them. "Their actions have jeopardized everything we stand for. The balance we swore to protect, the lives that were lost today—they are the ones responsible."

Some warriors, still grappling with the weight of the revelation, averted their eyes. Others, their faith in the Angel Corps unshaken, hardened their expressions, nodding in grim acceptance.

"As of this moment," Vincent declared, his tone final, "Giuseppe and Chris are fugitives. They are threats to the peace and balance of this world. And we have one mission—" his voice dropped, but the weight of it pressed upon every chest like an unspoken vow.

"We will find them. And we will bring them to justice."

A chilling silence followed, the impact of his decree sinking deep into the hearts of all present. Some nodded, duty-bound to follow orders. Others hesitated, doubt creeping in like an unwelcome shadow.

Allegra stood among the gathered warriors outside Celestia Academy, her mind still reeling from Vincent's accusations. The cold night air did little to cool the heat of her frustration. Warriors whispered among themselves, some too shaken to question Vincent's words, others nodding in grim agreement. Allegra could hardly stomach it.

Chris—a traitor? A danger to their world? It was ridiculous.

Yet as she looked around at her squad, she saw the doubt beginning to creep in. Lyra stood near the front, her arms crossed, her expression unreadable. Richard wasn't cracking jokes. Deepak and Luke exchanged uncertain glances, while Faith's hands were clasped tightly together, her eyes downcast. Even Ali, who was normally so brash, looked like he was second-guessing everything.

Allegra clenched her fists. How could they just accept this?

Then, out of the corner of her eye, she saw it.

Eli.

He was slipping through the crowd, his movements careful, deliberate. His shoulders were tense, his hands clenched at his sides. Allegra's brows furrowed. Something about the way he moved set off an alarm in her mind.

Where are you going?

Without a second thought, she stepped away from the group, keeping her distance as she followed. The murmurs of the crowd masked the sound of her steps, and as she weaved through the outer edges of the assembled warriors, she saw him break away completely.

Allegra hesitated for only a second before moving after him.

Eli didn't look back. He just kept walking, his pace increasing the further he got from the others. As soon as he reached the tree line beyond the academy's walls, he took off into a full sprint.

Giuseppe.

Allegra's heart pounded. That had to be it. He was going after Giuseppe.

She exhaled sharply and took off after him, keeping to the shadows as she ran. The crisp night air bit at her skin, but she ignored it. The ground beneath her feet shifted from soft grass to rough, uneven dirt as they moved further from the academy, the mountains rising in the distance.

Eli was fast, but Allegra was faster. She stayed just far enough behind to avoid detection, her eyes locked onto his silhouette in the dim moonlight. He wasn't slowing down.

Allegra's mind raced.

Eli didn't believe Vincent.

Neither did she.

But the fact that he was willing to run off alone meant he had doubts—doubts he needed to silence.

Fine. If he wanted to find out the truth, she would be right there with him.

Back in the void, Chris and Sophie stumbled out of the cave, their breaths coming in ragged gasps as they emerged into a frozen wasteland. The transition was jarring—the pitch-black abyss behind them giving way to an expanse of jagged ice and endless frost. The air was razor-sharp, biting at their skin with each breath. Snow swirled in violent gusts, carried by an unforgiving wind that howled through the barren land like a mournful wail.

Chris steadied Sophie as she nearly lost her footing on the uneven ground. "We're out," he muttered, though there was no relief in his voice. The landscape before them was just as hostile as the void they had escaped.

Sophie shivered, pulling her arms around herself. "Where are we?" she whispered, eyes scanning the frozen horizon. Ice stretched as far as they could see, fractured and broken in places, revealing endless darkness beneath. It was as if the very ground threatened to swallow them whole.

Then, a sound pierced through the wind.

A guttural growl.

Sophie's grip on Chris tightened. "What was that?"

Chris turned sharply, eyes narrowing as the firelight from his blade flickered against the moving shadows beyond the ice. The darkness wasn't just a lack of light—it was alive. Figures slithered and shifted, circling just beyond the reach of the flames, their glowing eyes peering hungrily at the two intruders.

"We're not alone," Chris said grimly.

And then, they charged.

The first demon lunged from the shadows, its skeletal frame covered in patches of frostbitten flesh, jagged claws swiping for Chris's throat. He reacted instinctively, swinging his fire-lit blade in a sharp arc. The flames roared to life, carving through the creature in an explosion of embers. The demon shrieked as it crumbled into ash, but no sooner had it fallen than two more took its place.

Chris barely had time to register the movement before another lunged from the left. He twisted, his blade igniting with a surge of fire that roared through the icy battlefield. The demon shrieked as it was engulfed in flame and disintegrated, but more shapes rushed forward, their grotesque figures illuminated in the glow of his fire.

"There's too many," Sophie gasped, stepping back as the dark shapes circled them.

Chris gritted his teeth. "Stay behind me."

Another creature leaped forward, but Chris was faster. He slashed downward, the fire bursting outward in a ferocious explosion. The blast detonated on impact, sending a shock wave rippling through the frozen wasteland. Ice cracked beneath them, and for a moment, the advancing demons hesitated.

Chris exhaled heavily, his breath visible in the frigid air. His arms ached, his body burning from the exertion of channeling so much fire at once. He could handle a fight, but this wasn't a battle—it was a war of attrition.

And they were losing ground.

A sharp, pained cry made his heart lurch. He turned in time to see Sophie stumble backward, her foot catching on the uneven ice. One of the demons had broken past his defenses, its twisted form closing in on her with terrifying speed.

Chris didn't think—he just moved.

In an instant, his fire flared brighter, roaring to life as he shot forward. His blade cut through the demon just before it reached Sophie, slicing it in half with a burst of flames. He spun, stepping between her and the encroaching horde, his pulse hammering in his ears.

"Stay close," he commanded, his voice firm but laced with urgency.

Sophie nodded, her hands clenched into fists at her sides. "We need a way out, Chris," she said, her voice laced with desperation. "We can't keep this up forever."

Chris didn't stop running. His legs burned, his breaths came in short, ragged gasps, but he pushed forward, driven by pure instinct. The frozen wasteland stretched endlessly before him, jagged ice formations rising like skeletal remains in the darkness. The fire from his blade barely cut through the overwhelming void, casting flickering shadows against the frost-covered terrain.

Sophie clung tightly to his back, her arms wrapped around his shoulders as the wind howled past them. "Chris, they're still behind us!" she yelled, her voice barely audible over the deafening roars of the demons chasing them.

"I know!" Chris shouted back, forcing himself to move faster. Every step sent icy shards scattering beneath his boots, but he didn't dare slow down. The guttural snarls of the creatures grew louder, their clawed feet pounding against the frozen ground as they closed in.

Then—just as Chris prepared to push himself even harder—the noises behind them suddenly stopped.

The roars, the snarls, the heavy thudding of pursuit... gone.

Chris's pulse pounded in his ears as he dared a glance over his shoulder.

The demons had halted.

They loomed just beyond the edge of his firelight, their grotesque forms shifting restlessly. Their glowing eyes still burned with hunger, but none of them moved forward. It was as if an invisible wall held them back.

Chris slowed, then stopped completely, his chest rising and falling in sharp, labored breaths. Sophie unwrapped her arms and slid off his back, stumbling slightly as she turned to look behind them.

"What... why aren't they following us?" she asked, her voice still breathless from the escape.

Chris didn't answer immediately. He took a cautious step forward, blade still crackling with fire. The demons twitched but didn't advance. It was like something was physically preventing them from moving any closer.

"They're not just stopping on their own," Chris murmured, still gripping his sword tightly. "Something's keeping them back."

A chill crawled down Chris's spine as the voice echoed behind him. It was soft yet unwavering, carrying a weight that sent shivers through his entire body.

"Chris... is that you I hear?"

He froze mid-step, every instinct screaming at him to move, to run—to do anything but turn around. His grip on the Eclipse Blade tightened, firelight flickering weakly against the endless shadows. That voice... He knew that voice.

No.

It wasn't possible.

His breath caught in his throat. The last time he had heard it was when he was in the Garden of Eden.

The sound of footsteps—light and deliberate—approached from the darkness behind him.

"Is that you?"

Sophie stiffened beside him, instinctively shifting closer. "Chris?" she whispered, concern laced in her voice. But he barely heard her. His entire world had shrunk down to the voice that had haunted his thoughts, a name that clawed its way out of his throat in a breathless whisper.

"Lilith?"

The void ahead of him flickered, the firelight barely piercing the suffocating blackness. And then... a figure began to emerge.

Chris's breath hitched as he watched, his body locked in place, torn between disbelief and the creeping realization that whatever was happening—it was real.

21

Eli's Pursuit

Eli stood on the rugged mountainside, his boots gripping the uneven rock as the wind howled through the jagged cliffs.

Below him, the dense forest stretched into darkness, swallowed by the shadows of night. Overhead, clouds drifted across a moonlit sky, casting fleeting silver light across the stone. The world was quiet save for the wind's low moan—but none of that mattered to him now.

All that mattered was finding the truth.

Vincent's words still echoed in his mind, twisting like thorns in his thoughts. *Chris... a threat?* It didn't add up. Not after everything they'd been through together. Not after all the battles they'd fought side by side.

"I have to find out for myself," Eli muttered under his breath, his jaw set with determination. He adjusted the strap of the Titanroot Hammer on his back, its weight familiar and reassuring. With one last glance toward the academy behind him, he turned and stepped forward, disappearing into the brush.

The terrain was rough, but Eli moved with purpose, his steps sure and steady. He could feel the pulse of the earth beneath him, a steady rhythm that connected him to the land. When he reached a narrow clearing, he crouched low, his sharp eyes scanning the area. If Giuseppe had fled this way, there had to be a trail.

Gripping the Titanroot Hammer, Eli planted its head firmly into the dirt and closed his eyes. Channeling his soul essence, he sent a controlled pulse into the earth, feeling it ripple outward like invisible waves. The ground whispered back to him, revealing subtle disturbances—heavy footprints leading deeper into the mountains.

He exhaled sharply. *I'm coming, Captain.*

Just as he was about to move, a voice rang out behind him.

"Hey."

His grip tightened on his hammer as he turned, instantly on guard. Allegra stood at the edge of the clearing, her trident resting lightly in her hand, her expression unreadable.

"Where do you think you're going?" she asked, stepping closer.

Eli's stance remained firm, his body tense, prepared to fight if it came to that. "I don't have time for this," he said evenly. "I'm going to find the truth myself. Chris is my best friend, and I refuse to just sit around while Vincent twists everything. If you think you can stop me from doing that, then I wish you the best of luck." He rolled his shoulders, preparing to engage if necessary.

Allegra didn't flinch. She met his gaze head-on, her expression unwavering. "I don't think I can stop you," she said, her voice steady. "Because I agree with you."

Eli blinked, momentarily caught off guard. "What?"

"I believe Vincent is lying too," Allegra continued, stepping closer. "I'm Allegra and Chris is my teammate, and none of this makes sense. I think he's being set up. That's why I followed you. I want to help."

Eli studied her for a moment, looking for any hesitation, any sign that she might be trying to mislead him. But there was none. Just determination. Just the same fire that burned in his own heart.

Slowly, he relaxed his stance and exhaled, nodding. "Alright," he said, shifting his hammer onto his back. "Then let's work together. I'm Eli."

A small smile ghosted over Allegra's lips. "Nice to meet you."

Eli returned the smirk, then turned back to the trail. "Let's move. Captain Giuseppe couldn't have gotten far ahead."

Together, they disappeared into the mountains, their shared

purpose binding them in silent understanding. The truth was waiting, and they would find it—no matter what it took.

Eli moved carefully through the thickening brush, Allegra keeping pace beside him, her trident resting lightly against her shoulder. The journey had been mostly silent, save for the sounds of their boots crunching against the forest floor and the occasional gust of wind rustling through the trees. But the tension between them—born from the uncertainty of their mission—was palpable.

Eli's Titanroot Hammer pulsed faintly with his soul essence as he pressed it into the ground again, channeling another pulse. The vibrations rippled outward, mapping the terrain in ways only he could sense. He exhaled as the information returned to him—a faint trail, a familiar energy signature buried beneath layers of earth and stone.

"There," Eli murmured, his eyes snapping open. "Captain Giuseppe's definitely been through here."

Allegra nodded, her sharp gaze scanning the path ahead. "Then we're on the right track." She glanced at him. "How sure are you that we'll actually find him?"

Eli adjusted the strap of his hammer, standing to his full height. "I'm sure. The earth doesn't lie." He started forward again, Allegra following without hesitation.

For a while, they moved in silence, weaving through towering trees and jagged cliffs. The sun had fully set now, leaving only the pale glow of the moon to light their way. The night air was cold, crisp with the scent of damp earth.

Eventually, Allegra broke the silence. "You're really willing to go this far for Chris, huh?"

Eli didn't hesitate. "Yeah. I'm pretty sure he'd do the same for me."

Allegra watched him, her expression unreadable. "I believe in Chris too," she admitted. "But I can't pretend Vincent's accusations don't have people questioning him. Even me questioning."

Eli scoffed. "Yeah, well, Vincent can manipulate a room with just his words. But just because he's confident doesn't mean he's right."

Allegra exhaled, kicking a loose stone ahead of her as she walked. "What do you think he's really after?"

Eli frowned, the weight of the question settling over him. "I don't know. He's been watching all of us—manipulating things behind the scenes. Chris, Captain Giuseppe…they're just pieces on the board to him."

Allegra's grip on her trident tightened. "And you think Chris is just another piece?"

"No," Eli said firmly. "I think Chris is the one thing Vincent can't control."

Allegra fell silent at that, mulling over his words. The wind picked up slightly, rustling the branches above them.

After a few more minutes, they came upon a shallow stream cutting through the forest. Eli crouched down, pressing his fingers into the damp soil near a faint footprint. His pulse quickened.

"Captain Giuseppe was here recently," he confirmed.

Allegra scanned their surroundings, but before she could speak, a rustling in the underbrush made them both tense. Eli's grip shifted to his hammer instinctively, his muscles coiling for a fight. Allegra mirrored him, her stance firm.

From the shadows, a pair of glowing eyes emerged.

A large lynx padded forward, its golden gaze fixed on them with an unreadable expression. It moved with effortless grace, its fur blending into the dry foliage around it.

Eli knelt slowly, keeping his movements deliberate. "Hey, big guy," he said softly. "Not here to hurt you."

The lynx growled low, its ears flattening slightly as it crouched, ready to spring. Eli froze, his eyes meeting the piercing golden gaze of the creature. The tension in the air was palpable as the lynx's sleek, tawny fur rippled with every subtle movement.

Then Eli noticed something—its stance, its size, the way it moved. A faint smile tugged at his lips. "Okay, big girl," he said gently, correcting himself.

The growl softened, but the lynx's muscles remained taut, its gaze locked onto him. Slowly, Eli reached into his pack and pulled out a small piece of beef jerky, holding it out in an open palm. "Here," he said softly. "A peace offering. What do you say?"

The lynx sniffed the air cautiously, her golden eyes narrowing. After a tense moment, she took a slow step forward, then another, until she was close enough to sniff the meat in his hand. Eli stayed perfectly still, letting her decide.

With a quick motion, the lynx snatched the meat and backed away, chewing it as she watched him warily. Eli let out a slow breath, his muscles relaxing slightly. "See? Not so bad, right?" he said, his voice calm and soothing.

The lynx finished the meat and hesitated, her ears twitching as she considered him. Eli reached into his pack again and pulled out another piece, holding it out. This time, the lynx stepped closer, her growling completely gone.

"There you go, big girl," Eli said softly as she took the second piece of meat from his hand. Encouraged by her calm demeanor, he slowly extended his hand, palm up, letting her sniff it. Her nose twitched, and after a moment, she leaned her head forward, brushing against his hand.

Eli grinned faintly. "Guess we're friends now," he said, running his hand gently over her soft fur. The lynx let out a low rumble, not quite a purr but not a growl either. It was a sound of cautious acceptance.

He stood slowly, brushing off his knees. "Thanks for the company, big girl," he said, giving her one last pat. The lynx watched him as he adjusted the Titanroot Hammer on his back and resumed following the trail. As he moved on, he glanced back to see her sitting in the brush, her golden eyes still fixed on him.

"Take care of yourself," he said with a small smile before turning his attention back to the path ahead. The faint vibrations of Giuseppe's trail still pulsed beneath his feet, and Eli's determination reignited.

Eli nodded, forcing his focus forward. The faint vibrations of Giuseppe's trail still pulsed beneath his feet, leading them deeper into the unknown.

Far from the mountains, back at Celestia Academy, the war room was thick with tension. Vincent stood at the head of the long table, his frosted blade resting before him. The dim light from the lanterns cast sharp shadows across his face, making his cold expression even more unreadable. The other captains sat in silence, their eyes locked on him as he spoke.

"Giuseppe's betrayal has left us vulnerable," Vincent began, his voice measured, each word deliberate. "He has abandoned the Angel Corps, choosing to flee rather than face the consequences of his actions. But Chris and Sophie…" He paused, his gaze darkening. "They are an even greater threat."

Mei's fiery whip coiled at her hip, her arms crossed as she

leaned forward. "You think Chris is already lost?" Her tone was skeptical but edged with concern.

Vincent's eyes remained unwavering. "I think his power is dangerous," he stated, his voice sharp. "The technique he and Sophie used to vanish was demonic in nature. That alone proves they cannot be ignored." He let the weight of his words settle before continuing. "Hiroshi, Jeffery, and I will lead a squad to locate them. Their presence is a risk we can't afford."

Nyla, standing near the table with her resonant gauntlets faintly glowing, let out a slow breath. "And what of Giuseppe?" she asked. "If he's still out there, he's not going to just stand by and let us capture Chris."

"That's why Mei, Nyla, and Omari will take their squads and track him," Vincent said. "He's heading into the mountains, but he can't stay hidden forever. His betrayal runs deep, and we will not allow him to slip through our grasp."

Omari, his massive arms folded across his chest, frowned. "Even if we find him, do you really think Giuseppe is going to surrender? We all saw him fight. He isn't going down without a war."

Vincent's fingers drummed against the table, his gaze unwavering. "Then we bring him down."

A heavy silence fell over the room. Each captain exchanged glances, but no one argued. The decision had already been made, and there was no turning back.

Nyla nodded firmly. "Very well. We all have our missions. Let's not waste time—let's move," she said decisively, already turning toward the door.

With that, the captains moved into action, their hesitation buried beneath duty. There was no turning back now.

Eli pressed onward through the dense forest, his steps careful yet determined. He could still feel the faint traces of Giuseppe's soul essence pulsing beneath his feet, a subtle vibration in the earth that led him forward. The path was winding, weaving through thick underbrush and over jagged terrain, but Eli knew he was close. He'd been tracking Giuseppe for hours, and now the trail led straight to a massive, ancient tree. Its gnarled roots twisted like the veins of the earth, sprawling out across the ground, stretching deep into the forest floor.

Eli crouched, pressing his hand against the cool, damp earth. He closed his eyes and sent a controlled pulse of his earth soul essence outward, letting it ripple like a sonar wave. The vibrations returned almost instantly—strong, direct, and leading straight to the base of the tree.

He stood, frowning slightly. "The trail…" he muttered, glancing around at the empty clearing. "It just stops here."

"You sure?" Allegra's voice came from behind him as she stepped into the clearing, her trident resting against her shoulder.

Eli turned toward her, his expression unreadable. "Yeah. No doubt about it. He came through here, but I don't see any other tracks leading away."

Allegra exhaled, scanning the area with narrowed eyes. "Then he's still close." She walked forward, placing her own palm against the bark of the massive tree, as if searching for something. "Or he's hiding."

Before Eli could respond, the air shifted.

A sudden jolt of energy shot through the ground. Instinct kicked in—Eli grabbed Allegra's wrist and yanked her back just as a bolt of lightning struck where she had been standing moments before.

The two of them spun toward the source of the attack,

weapons raised.

Standing a short distance away, blade crackling with electricity, was Giuseppe.

Eli's face lit up with a mix of relief and excitement. "Yes! I found you!"

Giuseppe, however, did not look relieved. His eyes were cold, his stance sharp and deliberate. "I'm sorry you're the first one who did," he said, his tone laced with something unreadable.

Before Eli could process the words, Giuseppe lunged.

His blade streaked through the air, charged with raw lightning essence. Eli barely managed to bring up his Titanroot Hammer in time to block the blow, the impact sending a sharp vibration through his arms. Sparks flew with every clash, illuminating the clearing in bursts of light.

"Hey! Whoa! I'm not here to fight!" Eli shouted, his voice strained as he struggled against the force of Giuseppe's strikes. "I came to help you! Chris is my friend!"

Giuseppe hesitated for just a second, his blade still humming with residual energy. He stepped back, studying Eli's face with cautious intensity.

"You're Eli?" he asked, his voice quieter, less hostile.

Eli let out a heavy breath, lowering his hammer slightly. "Yeah, I'm Eli. And I've been tracking you for hours, man. I'm on Chris's side."

Giuseppe's stance finally relaxed, the energy around his blade dissipating as he exhaled deeply. "I didn't recognize you," he admitted, his expression softening. "I'm sorry."

Allegra, still standing behind Eli, stepped forward, her grip on her trident loosening. "We both are," she said firmly. "And I want to make one thing clear—I don't believe Vincent. I think he's setting Chris up."

Giuseppe turned to her now, his gaze scrutinizing. "You're Allegra, right? You're on Chris's squad?"

She nodded. "Yeah. And I've seen enough to know something isn't adding up."

Eli crossed his arms, glancing between them. "Look, the three of us are on the same page. We all know Vincent's up to something, and we know Chris isn't the monster he's making him out to be." He turned back to Giuseppe. "So let's stop wasting time and figure out our next move."

Giuseppe considered them for a long moment before nodding. "Alright. But we can't stay here. If I found this place, others will too." He gestured for them to follow. "We need to move."

The trio navigated deeper into the forest, stepping over gnarled roots and dodging low-hanging branches. The air was thick with tension, but their pace never faltered.

"You know you're leaving a trail, right?" Eli asked after a few minutes. "That's how I found you."

Giuseppe glanced back at him, his expression unreadable. "Yes. I wanted to lure in whoever was tracking me and take them out before they could report back."

Allegra shot him a look. "Well, that explains the lightning to the face."

Giuseppe ignored the remark. "But since it's you two, we can use this to our advantage. If Vincent and the others are expecting me to run, we need to make them believe I'm still on the move while we regroup."

Eli gave a small grin. "So we *want* them to keep tracking you?"

"Exactly," Giuseppe confirmed. "We mislead them, buy ourselves some time. But first, we need a safe place to strategize."

Allegra glanced at Eli. "We could go to your place."

Eli shook his head immediately. "No way. Vincent knows I'm friends with Chris. My place is probably under surveillance."

Giuseppe nodded in agreement. "Same with mine."

Eli frowned. "Then where do we go?"

Giuseppe's sharp eyes scanned the terrain, calculating. "We'll figure it out," he said. "But wherever it is, it has to be somewhere Vincent would never expect."

Allegra glanced between the two of them, her mind already working through possibilities. "Then we better start moving fast."

And with that, the three of them disappeared into the forest, leaving behind nothing but the whisper of wind through the trees.

The dense canopy of the forest loomed overhead, casting shifting shadows as Mei, Nyla, and Omari led their squads deeper into the terrain. The thick foliage muffled their movements, but the tension was palpable. Every warrior present knew the weight of their mission—finding and apprehending Captain Giuseppe, a man who had not only evaded pursuit but could easily turn the tide against them if they weren't careful.

Omari's deep voice carried through the rustling leaves, steady and commanding. "Listen up," he called, pausing to scan the surrounding area. "We're dealing with a captain here. If you find Captain Giuseppe, do not engage him alone. Call for backup immediately. He's too dangerous to take on by yourself. If we work together, we can bring him in cleanly and without unnecessary risks."

His squad nodded, their grips tightening on their weapons, their breaths controlled but tense.

Mei adjusted the handle of her fiery whip, the coiled weapon pulsing faintly with heat as she surveyed her team. "We track, we locate, and we report," she added. "Don't get reckless. If Captain Giuseppe planned this escape, he's already ten steps ahead of us. We don't move unless we're sure."

Nyla flexed her fingers, the faint hum of her resonant gauntlets cutting through the hushed atmosphere. "He's fast, and he knows how we operate," she said. "That means we need to be unpredictable. My squad, with me." She gestured sharply, and her warriors peeled off toward the northern stretch of the forest.

"Mine, follow," Mei ordered, leading her group toward the eastern perimeter.

Omari rolled his shoulders, his massive Stone breaker Mace shifting as he motioned for his warriors to move west. "Spread out, keep your soul essence controlled. We don't let him slip through."

The squads dispersed, moving like shifting currents through the forest, their presence nearly imperceptible beneath the thick cover of trees. They moved in calculated formations, canvassing every break in the foliage, every exposed track in the dirt, searching for even the faintest sign of their target.

The deeper they pushed into the wilderness, the heavier the silence became. Even the natural sounds of the forest seemed to hold their breath as the Angel Corps advanced.

Back at Celestia Academy, the dimly lit halls felt colder than usual. The usual bustle of the stronghold was subdued, whispers of recent events spreading like wildfire, leaving unease in their wake.

Jeffrey stood near a narrow hallway, his luminous bow strapped across his back, his expression unreadable as he adjusted the quiver at his hip. Across from him, Hiroshi leaned against the wall, arms crossed, his gaze distant but sharp. Both were waiting.

Footsteps echoed down the corridor.

Vincent emerged from the shadows, his presence as commanding as ever, though there was something different in his posture—something more rigid, more deliberate.

Hiroshi straightened, pushing off the wall. "Everything's in motion. Mei, Nyla, and Omari are in the forest now."

Vincent exhaled quietly, his posture rigid as he turned away from the others. "I need a moment," he said, his voice even but distant. Without waiting for a response, he gestured toward a nearby room. "Just some time to decompress before we leave. Wait here."

Jeffrey studied him for a second before nodding. "Alright. Take what you need."

Without another word, Vincent stepped inside, the door clicking shut behind him. The hallway fell into an uneasy silence, the lingering tension thick in the air.

Jeffrey shifted his weight, glancing toward Hiroshi. "He's been like this a lot lately?" His voice was low, cautious.

Hiroshi's eyes remained locked on the closed door, his expression unreadable. "Yeah," he replied, the single word carrying layers of meaning.

Jeffrey didn't press further. He adjusted his bow, glancing down the long corridor where dim lanterns flickered against the stone walls. "We'll be ready when he is," he muttered, more to himself than anyone else.

Hiroshi gave a small, almost imperceptible nod. Neither spoke again as they stood in the stillness, waiting for Vincent to emerge.

Vincent stepped into the dimly lit room, shutting the door behind him with measured force. The air was unnaturally cold—the kind of chill that gnawed at the bone, bypassing skin altogether. Even cloaked in his frost-forged aura, he felt it: a creeping, unnatural presence that saturated the space.

A single flame flickered weakly in the corner, casting jagged shadows along the walls. But the shadows didn't behave as they should. They pulsed. They writhed. They watched.

Vincent's jaw tightened. He wasn't in the mood for theatrics.

His voice sliced through the silence like a blade of ice. "What have you done?"

For a moment, there was only the oppressive stillness pressing against him—thick as tar. Then, from the shifting dark, a low chuckle slithered forth, curling around him like smoke. The flame flared—brief and violent—before dying again, plunging the room into a deeper gloom.

"I have done nothing but as you asked," a voice purred from the abyss—smooth, knowing, laced with mockery.

Vincent's patience was already thin, and the demon knew it. His fingers twitched at his side, breath slow and measured as he reined in the frost gathering at his fingertips.

"Don't play games with me," he warned, tone sharp as tempered steel. "We had a plan. Chris was supposed to be under my control. Your meddling has jeopardized everything."

The chuckle deepened, curling into something richer, more entertained. The shadows in the corner thickened, pooling together into a tall, angular form. Twin embers burned where eyes should have been—predatory, gleaming with cruel amusement.

Meddling?" the demon echoed, tilting its head, as if the very word amused it. "I merely did what I promised—delivered the boy to the shadows, just as agreed. Where he ended up…" It grinned, sharp teeth gleaming like daggers. "Well, let's just say the shadows have a will of their own."

Vincent's fists clenched. His frosted blade hummed faintly, reacting to the storm building beneath his still exterior.

"You went back on your word," he growled. "You agreed to transport him to the location I designated—where I could control the outcome. Now he's vanished, and only you know where he is."

The demon let out a contented sigh, savoring Vincent's frustration like fine wine.

"Oh, I know exactly where he is," it said, voice dripping with satisfaction. "But why should I tell you? Information like that… comes at a price."

Vincent's eyes narrowed, his fury coiled just beneath the surface. "You want to renegotiate? After breaking our deal?"

"Deals," the demon mused, stepping forward as its form shifted with the surrounding darkness, "are fluid, Vincent. Adaptable." The space seemed to shrink as the air grew heavier, pressing against his skin like a second atmosphere.

"And let's not forget—it was you who sought me out. You who begged for help. Without me, you'd still be fumbling in the dark like everyone else."

Vincent inhaled sharply, the frost creeping along his fingers reluctantly retreating. The demon wasn't wrong—but that didn't mean it was in control.

Ice slithered from the base of his blade across the floor— silent, deliberate, a warning. The room's temperature dropped further, air brittle enough to snap.

"Do not mistake my presence here for submission," Vincent said, voice calm, lethal. "You need me more than I need you. And don't forget—I can exorcise you from this plane whenever I choose."

The demon chuckled—a low, guttural sound that rippled through the room. It stepped closer, the darkness folding and shifting around it like living smoke. The embers in its eyes burned brighter, narrowing with malice and delight.

"Oh, Vincent," it purred, grin widening to something unnatural, "do that, and you'll never see those wretched humans again. Your precious boy? Lost forever. Your grand ambitions? Scattered like ash." It leaned in, savoring the crackling tension.

"I am but a whisper in your world. A nudge of chaos. A harbinger of what's to come." The flame in the corner flickered again, casting its face in angular relief.

"But let's not allow wounded pride to dictate our next steps."

It took another step, its presence pushing against Vincent like a tide of black smoke.

"Just listen to my new proposal," it murmured, voice syrupy, "and keep an open mind." The shadows along the walls twisted, stretching like claws as the demon's ember-gaze bore into him.

"You might find I'm offering something… mutually beneficial."

Vincent didn't respond. He stood unmoved, gaze like frozen steel. The ice beneath him thickened, a crystalline mirror of his inner war—rage clashing with reason, pride battling necessity.

At last, he spoke. His voice was glacial.

"Speak. But choose your words carefully. My patience wears thin."

22

Hell

The cold pressed against them, relentless and suffocating, as Chris's firelight flickered against the desolate landscape. Jagged ice formations jutted from the ground like the remains of a shattered world, and the darkness beyond the reach of the flames stretched endlessly, shifting and twisting as if alive. A heavy silence hung in the air, broken only by the distant howl of a wind that carried no warmth.

Chris's breath hitched, his mind racing between disbelief and wariness. Lilith's sudden appearance wasn't just unexpected—it felt impossible.

"Lilith?" His voice was barely a whisper, uncertainty lacing his words. "Is that really you?"

The woman standing before him offered a faint smile, her sharp features catching the glow of the fire. Ruby-red hair cascaded over her shoulders, and her piercing eyes gleamed with an unsettling familiarity. She looked almost unchanged from the last time he had seen her.

"You remember me," Lilith said, her voice smooth, yet carrying an undercurrent of something unreadable.

Beside him, Sophie stiffened. Her gaze darted between Chris and Lilith, suspicion tightening her expression. "Is this the Lilith you told me about? Adam's wife?" she asked warily.

Chris hesitated for only a second before nodding. "Well…first wife," he corrected cautiously.

His grip on the Eclipse Blade tightened as he studied her. The vibrant, almost celestial energy she had radiated before was gone. There was no divine presence, no commanding aura. Instead, the darkness clung to her like a second skin, threading through her very essence. She seemed diminished, yet somehow more dangerous.

"You look different," Lilith said suddenly, tilting her head slightly. Her piercing gaze locked onto him, as if seeing something beyond the surface. "Changed."

Chris exhaled sharply, shaking off the unease creeping down his spine. "This is what I normally look like," he said, brushing off the comment. "Never mind that—what are you doing here? And where is here?"

Lilith's smirk deepened, something almost amused flickering

behind her eyes. "In over 10,000 years, I'm still explaining your surroundings to you. Some things never change," she said, her voice dripping with both familiarity and exasperation.

She stepped forward, slow and deliberate, her presence pressing against them like an unseen force. Sophie instinctively tensed, her fingers grazing the amulet around her neck as she kept a wary eye on Lilith.

Lilith stopped just short of them, the weight of her aura almost suffocating. "I don't have a map for you this time," she said, gesturing vaguely to the oppressive darkness. "But I've been here long enough to know exactly where you are."

Sophie's unease only grew. "Where is here?" she demanded, her voice firm despite the chill creeping up her spine.

Lilith's expression remained impassive, almost indifferent. "You," she said simply, "are standing in the center of Hell."

Chris and Sophie froze, their breath catching in their throats. The words settled over them like a suffocating fog. Sophie took a half-step closer to Chris, as if his presence alone could anchor her against the impossible.

"Hell?" Sophie whispered, her voice barely audible. "We're in Hell?"

Lilith nodded, as if she had just stated the weather. "Not the fire and brimstone version you've been fed, but Hell nonetheless," she clarified. "And not just anywhere—this is its core."

Chris's grip on his blade tightened as his mind raced. "If this is Hell," he said, forcing his voice to steady, "then we need to find a way out. Fast."

Lilith let out a soft chuckle, but there was no amusement in it. "Easier said than done," she mused. "But lucky for you, you have me."

Sophie's eyes narrowed. "Why help us?" she asked, her suspicion unwavering. "You don't strike me as the charitable type."

Lilith's gaze shifted solely to Chris, her expression sharpening. "Because I've been trapped here ever since the Tree of Knowledge was destroyed," she said, her voice carrying a weight of bitterness. "By him."

Chris stiffened. A lump formed in his throat as Lilith's piercing eyes bore into him, accusation dripping from every syllable.

"You owe me your life, Chris," she continued, her tone low and unwavering. "And now, you owe it to me to get me out of here."

Chris met her stare, his thoughts a storm of confusion, guilt, and doubt. "How did you even get here?" he asked, his voice steady but cautious.

Lilith's features hardened, the faintest flicker of pain flashing in her eyes. She exhaled, a slow and deliberate breath, before speaking.

"After our little duel—if you can even call it that—the Garden of Eden was in ruin. Fire and death consumed the place Adam and I once called home. The trees burned, the rivers ran dry, and the wildlife was wiped away. I stood amidst it all, condemned for something beyond my control."

Her voice darkened, venom laced in every word. "The Creator cast me into the deepest pit of Hell, delivering me into the hands of His son—Lucifer." She let out a humorless laugh. "He made me his prisoner. Chained me in the abyss for eternity. Left me to rot here, forgotten."

Chris swallowed hard, but Lilith wasn't finished.

"Do you know why?" she asked, her voice sharp as a blade.

She stepped closer, close enough that Chris could see the burning resentment in her eyes.

"Because of you."

Chris flinched, Lilith's words cutting deeper than he had expected. He opened his mouth to respond, but nothing came. The weight of her accusations settled between them like an unshakable presence, pressing down on his chest. He couldn't meet her eyes.

Beside him, Sophie watched the exchange, unease tightening her features. She wasn't sure she wanted to understand the full story Lilith was weaving, but the pieces were coming together all the same.

Lilith took another step closer, the firelight flickering across her sharp features. "Now, with your help, I can finally escape this pit of Hell," she said, her voice even, but beneath it lay an undercurrent of something raw—desperation, determination, or perhaps something darker.

Chris frowned, his grip tightening around the hilt of his Eclipse Blade. "Escape?" he echoed cautiously. He didn't trust this—not yet.

Lilith held his gaze, unwavering. "Yes," she confirmed.

His jaw tensed. "Why do you think I can help you?" His tone sharpened, suspicion creeping into his words.

A slow, knowing smile tugged at Lilith's lips, though it never reached her eyes. "Because," she said smoothly, "you have the power to unlock the seal and free us from this world."

Chris's breath hitched, his mind racing. The idea that he was somehow the key to escaping this abyss unsettled him in ways he couldn't yet define. Sophie shot him a sidelong glance, concern evident in the furrow of her brow.

"What seal?" Chris asked after a long pause, his voice lower now, more wary.

Lilith studied him for a moment before stepping back, as if allowing the weight of her words to settle. "The one keeping us trapped here," she said simply. "You don't fully understand your power yet, but you will."

Chris hesitated, his heart pounding. The firelight danced along the edges of his vision, making the shadows around them seem restless. Was this a trick? A manipulation? Or was she telling the truth?

Lilith's expression remained calm, but there was something behind it—an impatience, an expectation. "So, what do you say?" she asked, tilting her head slightly.

Chris and Sophie exchanged glances. The choice before them felt heavier than anything they had faced before. Trusting Lilith—especially in a place like this—was a risk, a dangerous one. But as they looked around, taking in the vast emptiness, the suffocating darkness, they knew the truth.

They had no other options.

Chris exhaled, fingers flexing around the hilt of his blade. Finally, he gave a small nod. "We're in," he said, his voice steady despite the knot of uncertainty in his chest.

Sophie hesitated, her gaze locked onto Lilith. Every fiber of her being screamed at her not to trust this woman. But she wasn't blind to reality—they were stranded in the heart of Hell. If Lilith really knew a way out, they had no choice but to follow her lead.

"We're in," Sophie echoed, though her voice was edged with distrust.

Lilith's lips curled slightly. "Very well," she said, turning toward the path ahead. Her movements were deliberate, graceful, as if the darkness itself parted for her. She gestured for them to follow. "Stay close. I know the way."

Chris cast one final glance at Sophie, who nodded reluctantly. Together, they stepped forward, their silhouettes stretching in the flickering firelight as they followed Lilith into the unknown.

The suffocating void pressed in around them as they moved deeper into the abyss, their footsteps muffled by the thick silence. Whatever lay ahead, one thing was certain—there was no turning back now.

And far from the depths of Hell, back at Celestia Academy, the quiet corridor outside Vincent's isolated chamber remained still, heavy with expectation.

Jeffrey leaned against the wall, his luminous bow resting casually at his side, but his eyes flickered with impatience. Across from him, Hiroshi stood with arms crossed, silent and unmoving, his gaze fixed on the closed door in front of them.

The faint sound of shifting footsteps broke the quiet as the door creaked open. Vincent stepped out, his frost-laced aura subdued, yet his presence still commanded attention. His expression was unreadable, but there was something sharper in his eyes—something resolute, unwavering.

"It's time," Vincent said, his voice steady, void of hesitation. He adjusted his blade at his side, glancing between the two captains. "We're leaving now. Chris won't evade us for long."

Jeffrey pushed off the wall, stretching his shoulders. "Finally. We're ready," he said, his tone carrying both relief and anticipation.

Hiroshi gave a slight nod, falling into step behind Vincent without a word.

Just as Jeffrey turned to follow, there was a blur of movement—silent, efficient. Vincent flipped his sword in an almost casual motion, catching it by the blade and striking the base of Jeffrey's skull with the hilt. The force was precise, calculated, and the impact landed cleanly. Jeffrey's body tensed, then crumpled, unconscious before he could register what had happened.

Hiroshi instinctively took a step back, his eyes narrowing in alarm. "What was that for?" His normally composed voice carried an edge of disbelief.

Vincent turned to him, his expression as cold as the frost beneath his fingertips. "We have a new objective," he said evenly. His voice was calm—too calm. It carried no explanation, no justification, only command. "Follow me."

Without waiting for a response, Vincent bent down, gripping Jeffrey's collar and hoisting his limp body off the ground as if he weighed nothing. He dragged him toward a side room, the scrape of Jeffrey's boots echoing in the dim corridor.

Hiroshi hesitated, glancing between Vincent and the unconscious captain. He wasn't easily shaken, but something about this moment unsettled him in a way that lingered.

Vincent pushed open the door to a storage room cloaked in deep shadows and unceremoniously deposited Jeffrey inside. He knelt briefly, shifting the body so it was hidden from immediate view before standing and shutting the door with a quiet, deliberate click.

Hiroshi's fingers twitched at his side, his body tensed as if preparing for the next unpredictable move. "You going to tell me what this is about?" he asked, his voice low, unreadable.

Vincent turned to face him fully, his gaze steady and unyielding. "Not yet."

Hiroshi exhaled through his nose, forcing his hands to remain loose at his sides. He could press further—but he already knew it would be futile. He'd known Vincent long enough to recognize when the man had made up his mind.

"Let's go," Vincent said, as if that were the end of it.

And perhaps, for now, it was.

Hiroshi cast one last glance at the closed door before falling into step beside Vincent. The tension in the air thickened, unspoken questions circling between them like vultures.

But Hiroshi knew better than to push Vincent when he was like this.

For now, he would watch.

And wait.

Vincent and Hiroshi moved through the dimly lit corridors of Celestia Academy with quiet precision, their footsteps barely breaking the silence. The air was thick with something unspoken, something heavy. It wasn't just the weight of the mission that lingered between them—it was the unease, the unanswered questions pressing against Hiroshi's chest like an unseen hand.

They reached the massive library, its towering shelves stretching endlessly into the shadows. Rows upon rows of ancient tomes stood in eerie stillness, their bindings whispering of forgotten knowledge, secrets buried beneath dust and time. A place meant for learning, for understanding. But tonight, it felt like something else entirely.

Vincent stopped abruptly in front of a particular bookshelf, his gaze fixed, unreadable. Hiroshi lingered a step behind, watching, waiting. The air grew colder—not just metaphorically, but physically. Frost coiled around Vincent's fingers, a telltale sign of his rising soul essence.

"Please, Hiroshi," Vincent said, his voice even, yet carrying an unmistakable finality. "No questions."

Hiroshi's jaw tensed, but he remained silent, the tension in his shoulders evident. He knew Vincent well enough to recognize when his mind was set. This was one of those moments.

Before Hiroshi could react, Vincent moved. With a fluid motion, he drew his blade, and in the blink of an eye, a surge of icy energy exploded from its edge. The frost-laced attack struck the bookshelf with pinpoint precision. Wood splintered, ice crackled, and an eerie silence followed the impact as the wall behind the shelf fractured, revealing a hidden passageway.

Dust swirled in the air, mingling with the lingering mist of frozen debris. Hiroshi took a step back, his eyes narrowing as he took in the now-exposed entrance—a narrow, spiraling staircase plunging downward into darkness.

Vincent didn't hesitate. He stepped forward, his blade still drawn, his expression as cold and sharp as the ice he wielded.

"Let's get this over with," he muttered, his tone devoid of anything but purpose.

Hiroshi lingered for a moment, glancing back at the wreckage Vincent had left behind. The destruction felt… excessive. Unnecessary. But more than that, it felt intentional.

He exhaled slowly, his fingers flexing at his sides before he finally followed. The shadows of the staircase swallowed them whole, the weight of the unknown pressing heavier with each step they took into the hidden depths below.

Back in Hell, the oppressive darkness pressed in around them as Chris and Sophie followed Lilith through the jagged, frozen wasteland. The landscape was treacherous—sharp, uneven terrain stretching endlessly before them, littered with blackened spires of stone and deep fissures that pulsed with an eerie crimson glow. The air was thick, heavy, as if the very atmosphere sought to suffocate them. Shadows moved at the edges of their vision, too fast to track but too close to ignore.

Faint whispers and guttural growls echoed in the distance, a constant reminder that they were not alone.

Lilith navigated the treacherous path with unsettling ease, her steps light, almost effortless. She moved like a phantom, gliding over the cracked ground, her crimson hair flowing behind her as if caught in a phantom wind. Chris and Sophie, in contrast, struggled to keep up, their bodies weighed down by exhaustion and the suffocating unease creeping into their bones.

Chris's grip tightened around the hilt of his Eclipse Blade. Every step forward felt like another plunge into the unknown, and his nerves were wearing thin. He glanced over his shoulder, his voice hushed but urgent. "How much farther?"

"Not much," Lilith answered, her voice devoid of emotion. She didn't slow her pace, didn't even look back. There was an exhaustion in her tone, not physical, but something deeper. "But we need to stay quiet. The closer we get, the worse it gets."

Sophie shot Chris a wary look before returning her attention to the shifting darkness around them. She clutched her amulet tightly, its familiar warmth a small comfort against the unnatural cold seeping into her bones. "Dangerous how?" she whispered.

Lilith finally turned her head slightly, just enough for her sharp eyes to meet Sophie's. "The demons here don't just hunt you for sport," she said, her words carrying a weight that made the air feel even heavier. "They devour your soul. And the farther we go, the stronger they become."

Chris swallowed hard, exchanging a glance with Sophie before continuing in tense silence. His senses were on high alert, his muscles taut as he walked. The sound of something scraping against stone grew louder behind them, then faded again, like a predator toying with its prey.

Sophie hesitated before speaking, her voice quieter than before. "How did you survive here?"

Lilith's step faltered for just a moment—so brief that if Chris hadn't been watching closely, he would have missed it. When she spoke, her words were measured, clipped. "I did what I had to," she said. "I killed. I ate demons. That's how I stayed alive. That's how anyone survives here." She turned her head slightly, her expression unreadable. "And even then, it's never enough. This place doesn't let you live. It just lets you… exist."

Sophie stopped mid-step, her breath catching in her throat. "You… ate demons?"

Lilith finally slowed, glancing back at Sophie with something that wasn't quite regret, but wasn't pride either. "Do you know what it's like to starve for centuries?" she asked, her voice quiet but laced with something raw, something jagged. "To have no choice but to fight, to kill, just to make it through another day? I didn't ask to be cast down here, but I adapted. I had to."

The words hung between them like a blade suspended in midair. Chris and Sophie exchanged a look, both unsure of how to respond. Lilith's confession was horrifying, but at the same time, it made one thing painfully clear.

She wasn't lying.

Chris's grip on his Eclipse Blade tightened. There were still too many questions, too many uncertainties. But there was one question he couldn't keep buried any longer.

"And Lucifer?" His voice was low but steady. "What about him?"

At the mere mention of the name, Lilith's entire demeanor changed. Her steps slowed, her shoulders tensed, and when she finally turned to face them, her expression twisted into something darker—pure, unfiltered hatred.

"Lucifer is the reason I've endured so much," she said, her voice colder than the frozen ground beneath their feet. "He is evil, Chris. Not just in his actions, but in his very being. He doesn't just rule over this realm—he is this realm." Her jaw clenched, and when she spoke again, her voice was lower, carrying the weight of centuries of suffering. "For millennia, he's tortured me, breaking me piece by piece, not for any purpose, not to teach me a lesson—just because he could. Because he enjoys it."

Silence settled between them. The weight of her words was suffocating, and for the first time, Chris truly looked at her—not just as a guide through this nightmare, not just as a being with power, but as someone who had endured something unimaginable.

Sophie swallowed hard, her earlier suspicion of Lilith fading into something else—something close to sympathy. "He punished you?" she asked hesitantly.

Lilith let out a humorless laugh, sharp and bitter. "Punishment?" she repeated. "No. Punishment implies an end. A consequence with an eventual relief. That's not what Lucifer does." Her gaze hardened, her fists clenching at her sides. "It wasn't enough for him to cast me down here. He needed me to suffer. To remind me, every single day, that I'm nothing more than a prisoner in his eyes."

Sophie looked away, her fingers tightening around her amulet as if searching for some kind of comfort in its familiar presence. "Then… how did you escape?"

Lilith's lips curled into a faint, bitter smile. "Even Lucifer isn't all-seeing," she said. "He's powerful, yes, but he isn't omnipotent. There are moments, however rare, when his attention is divided—when he can't watch every corner of his kingdom at once." Her voice took on a sharper edge. "So I waited. Centuries passed before I had my chance. When it came, I took it."

Her gaze shifted to the darkness ahead, and for the first time, a flicker of something almost like vulnerability crossed her face. "I've been hiding ever since, moving deeper and deeper into the shadows to avoid his gaze." She exhaled, the breath visible in the unnatural cold. "But even here, I'm not safe. No one is."

Chris exhaled slowly, processing everything she had just told them. "I had no idea…" His voice trailed off, unsure of what else to say.

Sophie nodded weakly beside him, her voice barely above a whisper. "Neither did I. It's horrible."

Lilith glanced back at them, her gaze unreadable. Then, her expression hardened. "Don't pity me," she said sharply. "Pity will get you killed here. It's useless." She turned and continued walking. "Just focus on what matters—getting out."

The group pressed on in silence, the weight of her words lingering between them. The air seemed colder now, the darkness pressing in closer. The landscape grew more hostile— towering spires of blackened stone loomed around them, and the distant, bone-chilling wails of suffering souls carried through the wind.

Sophie moved a little closer to Chris, her voice barely audible. "Do you trust her?"

Chris didn't answer right away. His eyes remained fixed on Lilith's back as she moved through the desolate terrain, never slowing, never hesitating.

Finally, he exhaled and murmured, "I don't know." He glanced at Sophie. "But what choice do we have? If she can get us out of here, we need to try."

Sophie nodded reluctantly, though her grip on her amulet remained firm. "I just hope we're not walking into something worse."

The oppressive silence weighed down on them as Lilith came to an abrupt stop. Chris and Sophie followed her gaze, their breath hitching at the sight before them.

An enormous structure loomed in the distance, carved directly into the obsidian cliffs, its darkened stone veined with eerie, pulsating red light. It was as if the fortress itself was alive, its presence radiating a suffocating dread that settled deep in their bones.

Chris swallowed, tightening his grip on his Eclipse Blade. "This is it?" he asked, his voice hushed.

Lilith nodded slowly, her expression unreadable. "This is it."

Sophie took a cautious step forward, her eyes scanning the fortress's jagged, towering spires. "What... What exactly is this place?" she asked, barely above a whisper.

Lilith exhaled sharply, as if the very thought of it repulsed her. "Lucifer's lair," she said, her tone clipped, but heavy with something deeper—resentment, hatred. "And at its center lies the portal to the other realms."

Chris exchanged a wary glance with Sophie. "The portal? Can we actually use it?"

Lilith's jaw tightened. "It's locked," she admitted. "Sealed with ancient magic—stronger than anything ordinary soul essence can break." She turned to Chris then, her piercing gaze seeming to burrow into him. "But your fire..." she said, her voice lowering with something close to reverence. "The Ethereal Flame."

Chris stiffened. The name sent a chill through him, not from fear, but from recognition. He had heard it before—spoken in hushed whispers, in riddles and warnings. And now Lilith was saying it like it was an answer.

Lilith took a slow step toward him. "That fire of yours doesn't just burn—it transforms. It's tied to the essence of life and death itself. That's why it's special, why it's feared. It's the only thing capable of unlocking the portal."

Chris turned his gaze to the massive stone doors at the fortress's entrance. Etched across their surface were intricate, glowing runes, pulsing faintly in the surrounding darkness. But as he stepped closer, something strange happened—the symbols reacted, shifting slightly, their dull red glow flickering as though recognizing his presence.

The heat from the seal resonated deep within his core, the same way his fire did when he called upon it. It wasn't just a door—it was a boundary, one woven into the fabric of this realm itself.

Sophie must have noticed the way he tensed. She placed a hand lightly on his arm, grounding him. "Do you think you can do it?" she asked softly.

Chris hesitated, staring at the runes that seemed to pulse in time with his heartbeat. Could he do it? The Ethereal Flame— it wasn't just his power. It was something ancient, something dangerous. Something even he didn't fully understand.

Lilith studied him closely, her voice quieter but no less intense. "The seal will resist you, but you have the strength to break it," she said. "You just need to trust yourself. Trust the power inside you."

Chris exhaled slowly, forcing himself to push past the fear, the uncertainty. This was it. Their way home. Their only chance.

Sophie squeezed his arm gently. "You've got this," she said, her voice steady, unwavering. "We're with you."

Chris clenched his jaw, his resolve hardening. He stepped forward, raising his blade, feeling the familiar warmth of fire crackling beneath his skin.

And then, he let it ignite.

The fire surged, consuming the length of Chris's blade in a radiant glow. Sophie watched in awe as the flames intensified, the heat pressing against her skin. There was something undeniably different about this fire—something raw, untamed, and ancient.

"It really is different," she whispered, more to herself than anyone else.

Chris exhaled slowly, steadying himself. His grip tightened around the hilt of his Eclipse Blade as he stepped forward, the runes on the massive stone doors pulsing violently in response to his presence. The moment the ethereal flames licked the surface of the seal, the portal trembled, its glowing symbols flaring in resistance.

"Push through," Lilith commanded, her voice unwavering. "Don't hold back!"

Chris gritted his teeth, summoning every ounce of power he could muster. The runes fought back, their crimson glow intensifying as if resisting his fire, but he refused to yield. The flames along his blade roared, burning hotter, brighter, consuming the ancient magic woven into the seal. The stone groaned under the force, deep cracks forming like lightning across its surface.

The air thickened, heavy and suffocating, pressing down on them as Chris drove his blade forward. The pressure built to a breaking point until—

CRACK.

The runes shattered in a blinding explosion of energy, their light extinguished in an instant. The stone doors groaned, the sound reverberating through the expanse like the final breath of something ancient. Slowly, they began to part, revealing a swirling vortex of shadow and fire—a gateway pulsing with unrestrained power.

Chris staggered back, the glow of his blade flickering as exhaustion settled over him. Sophie was at his side in an instant, steadying him with a firm grip.

"You did it," she said, her voice filled with quiet, undeniable pride.

Chris nodded, still catching his breath, his heart hammering against his ribs.

Lilith stepped forward, her lips curling into a knowing smirk. "I told you," she said, a hint of satisfaction in her tone. "The Ethereal Flame… it was the key."

The vortex loomed before them, its endless swirl of darkness shifting like a living thing. Lilith stood at its threshold, her expression unreadable as she regarded the portal. "On the other side of this… is Earth," she said, her voice steady but heavy with meaning.

Chris met Sophie's gaze, his grip tightening around his blade. There was hesitation in her eyes, fear of the unknown, but beneath it burned something stronger—resolve.

"Are you ready?" Lilith asked.

Chris took a deep breath, his exhaustion momentarily forgotten. He reached for Sophie's hand, his fingers lacing through hers.

"We're ready," he said firmly.

Without another word, they stepped forward together. The portal flared, swallowing them whole as the world around them dissolved into oblivion.

23

The Key to Chaos

The darkness of the vortex peeled away like a dissipating fog, unraveling into the crisp night air of Earth. Chris, Sophie, and Lilith stumbled slightly as they emerged, their senses reeling from the abrupt shift. The scent of pine and damp earth filled their lungs, a stark contrast to the oppressive void they had just escaped. The towering trees of a dense forest stretched around them, their leaves rustling softly in the night breeze.

Chris exhaled, his breath visible in the cool air. "We're back," Sophie whispered, almost as if saying it aloud would confirm that they had truly returned.

Without hesitation, she turned and threw her arms around

Chris, gripping him tightly. The warmth of her embrace caught him off guard, and for a moment, he stood frozen. Slowly, he wrapped his arms around her in return, the reality of their survival sinking in. But as the moment stretched, awareness settled over them, and they awkwardly pulled away, their gazes flickering elsewhere.

Chris cleared his throat, shifting his focus. "Let's see if this works," he muttered, closing his eyes and reaching out through the mental link he shared with his father. He concentrated, directing his thoughts outward.

Dad, can you hear me?

For several agonizing moments, there was nothing but silence. Then, faintly, a voice cracked through the distance.

Where are you? Giuseppe's tone was strained but unmistakably alive.

Chris opened his eyes, relief washing over him as he prepared to answer his father. But before he could even take in their surroundings, Sophie's sharp inhale made him pause.

Her fingers twitched against the ground, her plant soul essence woven into the earth beneath them. A sudden shift—a tremor that didn't belong—rippled through her connection, like something unnatural disturbing the flow of life.

Her eyes widened in alarm.

"Chris, move!" she shouted.

Before he could process her warning, she lunged toward him, shoving him aside just as a set of razor-sharp claws slashed through the space where he had been standing. The air cracked with the chilling sound of ice scraping against stone as Lilith's attack missed by mere inches.

Chris hit the ground hard, rolling onto his back just in time to see Lilith standing a few paces away, her posture eerily calm.

Frost shimmered along her extended claws, sharp and gleaming like crystalline daggers.

Sophie scrambled to her feet, her amulet glowing as she positioned herself between them. "Lilith, what are you doing?" she demanded, her voice sharp with disbelief.

Lilith tilted her head slightly, her expression unreadable—until the corners of her lips curled into a slow, predatory smile. "Taking back what's mine," she said, her voice smooth yet dripping with venom.

Chris scrambled to his feet, gripping the hilt of his Eclipse Blade tightly. His heart pounded in his chest, the weight of the moment pressing down on him. The relief of their return to Earth had vanished in an instant.

Chris froze. "What are you talking about?" he demanded, his breath coming in short, sharp bursts.

Lilith's eyes gleamed with malice, her nails lengthening into razor-sharp talons as frost shimmered faintly along their edges. She took a slow, deliberate step forward. "The ethereal flame," she hissed, her voice laced with bitter rage. "You stole it from me, and I intend to take it back."

Before Chris or Sophie could respond, Lilith lunged. Her claws slashed through the air with deadly precision, and Chris barely managed to raise his blade in time. The force of the impact sent him stumbling backward, his boots digging into the damp earth.

"Lilith, stop!" Chris shouted, parrying another strike, his blade sparking as it clashed with her frost-covered talons. "We helped you escape!"

Lilith laughed, a hollow, humorless sound. "And you think that makes us even?" she spat, her next attack coming faster, more aggressive. "The flame was mine long before you even existed! You're nothing but a thief wielding power you don't deserve!"

Sophie stepped forward, her amulet pulsing with a vibrant green glow as she slammed her hands to the ground. Thick, twisting vines erupted from the soil, lunging toward Lilith like serpents. "Stay back!" Sophie commanded, the vines surging forward, trying to ensnare her.

But Lilith moved with an unsettling grace, her claws slicing through the vines as frost spread along their severed edges, turning them brittle and lifeless. "You think this will stop me?" she sneered, swiping her hand through another wave of plant life as if it were nothing.

Chris gritted his teeth, stepping protectively in front of Sophie. "Lilith, whatever you think I stole, you're wrong! I don't even understand this power yet!"

"Lies," Lilith growled, lunging again. Chris barely had time to brace himself before their weapons collided once more—his blade against her claws.

But this time, something was different.

As their attacks met, a burst of energy erupted around them. The flames coating his blade roared to life, but instead of burning alone, they crackled with something more.

Lightning.

A blinding arc of fire and lightning surged from his sword, illuminating the battlefield in an explosion of raw energy. Chris's eyes widened in shock. He hadn't expected that.

Lilith reeled back, her expression flickering with something between surprise and irritation. She hadn't expected it either.

Chris exhaled sharply, trying to push past his own astonishment. He didn't have time to process it now—he had to fight.

"We need a way to subdue her!" Chris shouted, shifting into

a defensive stance, the electricity and fire still pulsing along his blade. His body trembled slightly from the energy coursing through it, but he steadied himself.

"She's too powerful!" Sophie called back, summoning another wave of vines in a desperate attempt to create some kind of barrier. "I don't know if we can stop her!"

Lilith let out another sharp, cold laugh as she effortlessly shattered Sophie's defenses, frost creeping further along the battlefield. The temperature around them dropped, and Chris could see his breath mist in the air. "You don't have to do anything," she purred, stepping forward. "Just give me the flame."

Chris's jaw clenched. The energy surging through him was still unstable, still new, but it was his.

"This isn't yours, Lilith!" he shouted, raising the Eclipse Blade high. Fire and lightning swirled together, merging, amplifying, until they were nearly indistinguishable.

Then he swung.

A blinding bolt of fiery lightning shot from the blade, crackling as it tore through the air toward Lilith. She dodged with unnatural agility, her claws slashing upward in retaliation.

The collision of their forces ignited the battlefield—flames and frost meeting in a violent explosion of heat and cold. The ground beneath them split from the impact, sending shards of ice and burning embers scattering in every direction.

Chris barely had time to recover before Sophie's voice rang out. "Chris, behind you!"

He spun, instinct taking over, and slashed his blade in a tight arc. Another surge of fire and lightning spiraled outward, scorching the ground and forcing Lilith back.

Chris's breaths were heavy, his limbs burning from the raw

power he was channeling. It was working. He was controlling it.

But he wasn't sure how long he could keep this up.

"We can't hold this forever!" he panted, his grip tightening around his blade.

Sophie's face was pale, but her resolve was firm. "We don't have a choice. Just keep her at bay—I'll think of something!"

Lilith's expression darkened, her icy claws elongating further. The frost spreading around her deepened, coating the ground beneath her feet in a thick layer of ice. She wasn't backing down.

"You can't stop me," she said, her voice low and steady, filled with eerie certainty. "This flame belongs to me. And I will take it—no matter what."

The battle raged miles away, its chaos distant in the eerie stillness of the canyon. Here, in this desolate place, another confrontation was brewing—one far more calculated, woven in secrecy and shadow.

Vincent and Hiroshi arrived at the canyon's edge, their transport settling into the dust with a low hum before falling silent. The towering cliffs loomed above them, jagged spires of rock cutting into the moonlit sky. The shadows stretched unnaturally long across the barren expanse, as though the canyon itself was holding its breath.

Vincent dismounted first, his movements precise, methodical. The frost clinging to his blade pulsed faintly, a subtle warning to anything that dared lurk in the dark. His sharp gaze swept over the lifeless terrain, searching, waiting. Behind him, Hiroshi hesitated before stepping forward, his unease barely masked beneath his composed demeanor.

"Sir..." Hiroshi started, his voice breaking the silence.

Vincent raised a hand, halting him mid-sentence without so much as a glance. His focus remained fixed on the canyon ahead, as if listening to something only he could hear.

Then, the silence shifted.

A whisper of movement, a ripple in the shadows. The darkness along the canyon walls stirred, stretching unnaturally, coiling like smoke given shape. The air grew heavy, dense with unseen power, and the temperature dropped as a faint, sinister hiss echoed through the canyon.

The shadows deepened, folding in on themselves, condensing into a form that towered over them both. The figure that emerged was impossibly tall, its elongated limbs draped in writhing darkness. Crimson eyes flared to life, gleaming with wicked amusement as the demon's angular face twisted into a knowing smirk.

"Well, well," Sargatanas purred, his voice rich with mockery. "I thought you humans knew how to follow directions."

Vincent stepped forward, the frost of his aura intensifying. His breath curled in the air like mist, but his expression remained impassive, unreadable. He met the demon's glowing eyes without hesitation, his voice calm, controlled.

"We're here," he said, his tone carrying the weight of purpose.

The shadows around them thickened, the canyon itself seeming to shrink beneath the presence of something far older, far more dangerous than the simple void of night.

Hiroshi remained motionless, his grip tightening on his staff as the demon's piercing gaze flicked to him, lingering for only a moment before returning to Vincent. The weight of the demon's presence was suffocating, the air thick with a tension that seemed almost alive.

A slow, jagged grin stretched across the creature's face, revealing teeth like shards of broken glass. "Let's hope you've come prepared to deliver, Captain," it purred. "I don't appreciate wasted time."

Vincent's expression was ice, his tone razor-sharp. "And I don't appreciate you changing the terms of our deal," he said coolly. "Yet, here we are."

The demon chuckled, the sound like gravel scraping against stone. "So direct. So impatient." It waved a clawed hand lazily in the air. "Fine, then. Let's get to it." The glow of its crimson eyes flared as it tilted its head, mock curiosity dripping from its words.

"Where is Chris? That's what I want to know," he said, his voice measured, deliberate.

The demon's grin widened further, its elongated fingers flexing idly. "You came here for answers," it mused, "and yet you arrive empty-handed. Tell me, Vincent—did you really think I wouldn't notice?" It tsked, shaking its head with exaggerated disappointment. "I gave you simple instructions."

Vincent remained unmoved, his glare unwavering. The frost at his feet thickened, tendrils of ice creeping over the canyon's cracked ground.

"I thought you were smarter than this," the demon sighed, its tone taking on a more menacing edge. "To waste my time so carelessly…"

Before it could continue, Vincent's voice cut through the air like a blade. "Oh, I have it." His words were calm, almost casual, but the shift in the atmosphere was immediate. "The precious shadow key you wanted so badly." He took a slow step forward, his grip tightening on his sword. "But the only way you get it is if you turn over Chris."

The demon's grin faltered, just for a fraction of a second,

before it curled back into something darker. Its amusement now carried an edge of hunger, of something far more dangerous lurking beneath its theatrics.

"Oh, Vincent," the demon murmured, stepping closer, its towering form eclipsing the pale moonlight. "You have this situation confused." The air around them turned deathly cold, the shadows stretching unnaturally as the creature's presence pressed against them. Hiroshi tensed beside Vincent, his fingers clenching around his staff, his pulse hammering against his ribs.

"I'll say this once more," the demon hissed, its voice dropping into something almost inhuman, a vibration that sent a chill down Hiroshi's spine. "Hand over the shadow key… and I will give you Chris."

For a moment, there was silence.

Then, Vincent exhaled slowly, his expression unreadable, his tone heavy with what sounded like resignation. "Very well," he said, his voice low but firm. He turned slightly, not taking his eyes off the demon. "Hiroshi."

Hiroshi hesitated only a moment before reaching into his bag, his fingers brushing against the cold, unyielding surface of the small black box. He pulled it free, holding it firmly as he stepped forward. The demon's crimson eyes gleamed with something close to satisfaction, and a deep, guttural laugh rumbled from his chest.

"Ah," the demon murmured, his grin stretching unnaturally wide, revealing rows of jagged teeth. "Very nice. Very nice indeed." His clawed hand reached out, the shadows at his fingertips seeming to curl hungrily around the box before he even touched it. "You have done well, humans. You have exceeded my expectations."

The black box creaked open in his grasp, revealing the small, intricately carved shadow key nestled inside. Sargatanas lifted it delicately, turning it between his fingers as if weighing its significance. A low hum of dark energy pulsed from the artifact, its presence a void against the night.

Vincent remained motionless, his cold gaze fixed on the demon, unreadable yet piercing. Then, his voice cut through the demon's gloating like a blade through ice. "Enough. We upheld our end. Now," he demanded, his frosted blade pulsing subtly at his side, "where is Chris?"

Sargatanas tilted his head slightly, his grin unwavering, though something deeper flickered behind his crimson eyes— amusement, calculation. The tension in his massive form seemed to ease as he relaxed, letting the silence stretch between them.

"I must admit," the demon finally said, his voice low and almost reverent, "I respect your ambition, Vincent. Your relentless drive. You are not unlike me in that way." He paused, his gaze locking onto Vincent's with something that almost resembled admiration. "Your hunger for control, for certainty… it is admirable."

Vincent's expression remained impassive, but the temperature around him dipped slightly. "Spare me your empty flattery," he said icily. "Where is Chris?"

Sargatanas chuckled softly, the sound vibrating in the cold canyon air. "Ah, but you see," he said, taking a slow step forward, his presence towering, suffocating, "Chris is no longer your concern."

Hiroshi stiffened, his grip on his staff tightening as Vincent's frosted aura flared ever so slightly. "We had a deal," Vincent said, his voice sharp, his patience dangerously thin.

The demon let out a mock sigh, shaking his head as if chiding a foolish child. "Yes, yes, the deal," he mused. "The thing about deals, Vincent… they are not always as binding as you believe. They evolve. They change. They are subject to the whims of those who truly hold power." His grin deepened, his eyes glowing like embers in the dark. "And, unfortunately for you, Chris has outgrown your grasp."

Vincent didn't move, his gaze unwavering, but Hiroshi could feel the shift in his aura—a barely restrained fury, a glacial storm waiting to be unleashed. "You dare go back on your word?" Vincent's voice was quieter now, but there was venom in every syllable.

Sargatanas spread his clawed hands in an exaggerated gesture of false regret. "I merely choose to… adjust the terms." His voice was laced with condescension, each word a careful needle meant to provoke. "Chris is beyond your reach now. And that is simply the way of things."

Before Vincent could react, the shadows around Sargatanas began to churn and writhe violently, thick tendrils of darkness curling up and around him. The shadow key gleamed for one final moment before the abyss swallowed it whole. With a final, mocking grin, the demon let the void consume him.

The air grew deathly still, the heavy silence pressing down on them as the last echoes of the swirling shadows faded into nothingness.

Vincent and Hiroshi stood alone in the canyon, the cold wind cutting through the emptiness.

The deal had been made.

And they had been left with nothing.

Hiroshi's breath came fast, his grip tightening on his staff as he tried to steady himself. "Captain… Was that really the Shadow Key?" His voice wavered, uncharacteristically shaken.

"How could you give it to him? He can unlock the realm of Hell! This could destroy everything—what are we supposed to do now?"

Vincent remained silent, his frosted blade humming faintly at his side. The cold radiating from him seeped into the air, an eerie contrast to the rising panic in Hiroshi's voice. Slowly, he turned, his expression unreadable, his tone razor-sharp but maddeningly calm.

"Hiroshi," Vincent said, his voice measured, "sometimes, I don't tell you everything—because I need your reaction to be real. Genuine responses, unclouded by bias or pretense."

Hiroshi blinked, confusion flickering across his face. "What…?"

Vincent's gaze drifted to the spot where Sargatanas had vanished, his expression distant yet calculating. "This was one of those moments." His voice was steady, but beneath it, there was something sharper—a quiet confidence, a certainty that cut through the unease in the air. "That fool thinks he's won. That he's outmaneuvered me." His fingers flexed over the hilt of his blade. "But he's mistaken. His arrogance will be his undoing."

Hiroshi frowned, processing Vincent's words, the tension in his stance slowly ebbing. "You… you planned this?"

Vincent didn't answer right away. Instead, he lowered himself to the ground, sitting precisely where he had stood moments before, his blade resting across his lap. The frozen aura around him pulsed faintly, tendrils of ice creeping into the dust beneath him. He exhaled slowly, his tone calm, controlled.

"The idiot believes he has the upper hand, but he's already begun unraveling his own plan," Vincent continued, his gaze still fixed on the empty space where Sargatanas had disappeared. "And when the moment is right, we will strike."

Hiroshi swallowed, his earlier panic dissipating into something else—something closer to reluctant trust.

"So… what now?" he asked after a moment, his voice quieter.

Vincent's eyes flicked up to meet his, the hint of a smirk tugging at the corner of his lips.

"Now?" Vincent said, settling in. "Now, we wait."

Hiroshi hesitated for only a moment before nodding. He let out a slow breath and lowered himself to the ground beside Vincent.

The canyon stretched endlessly around them, the silence vast and unbroken. But they remained still, unmoving, patient—like the stone itself, waiting for the inevitable moment when the tides would turn.

Meanwhile, far from the stillness of the canyon, the hunt for Captain Giuseppe continued. The forest was alive with movement as Nyla, Omari, and Mei led their squads through the dense terrain, their pursuit relentless. The faint trail of Giuseppe's soul essence flickered like a beacon to the captains, growing stronger as they closed in on their elusive target.

The dense forest stretched endlessly as Giuseppe, Allegra, and Eli moved with purpose, each step calculated. The pursuit was relentless, but Giuseppe's sharp mind had already turned the tables. The plan was clear: isolate the squads and incapacitate their captains, one by one.

"They're closing in," Eli said, his Titanroot Hammer resting heavily on his shoulder. He pressed it to the ground, sending a pulse of soul essence through the earth. His brow furrowed. "Omari's squad is right behind us—maybe a minute or two away."

"Perfect," Giuseppe murmured. He knelt, drawing a crude map in the dirt with the tip of his blade. "We hold them at this ridge. Omari's mace is powerful, but without it, he's just another fighter."

Eli frowned. "How are we gonna separate him from it?"

Giuseppe smirked. "Leave that to me. You and Allegra focus on sealing the pass once the squad enters. We're not fighting to win—we just need to contain them."

Allegra crossed her arms, watching the terrain ahead. "I can buy us extra time," she said. "If they start breaking through, I'll keep them off-balance."

Giuseppe nodded, satisfied. "Then let's get to work."

Omari's squad pushed forward with precision, their weapons ready as they closed in on their target. The faint trail of Giuseppe's soul essence had led them here, and the massive warrior's determination was evident in the tight set of his jaw. His stone breaker mace gleamed faintly, its sheer weight enough to level anything in its path.

"Stay sharp," Omari commanded, his deep voice steady. "He's a captain for a reason. No mistakes."

As if on cue, Giuseppe stepped into view, standing at the mouth of the ridge with a casual confidence. His blade rested lightly in his hand, and a faint smirk played at his lips. "You've been chasing me all day, Omari. Are you getting tired yet?"

Omari's eyes narrowed. "Your tricks won't save you. Surrender now, and maybe we'll make this quick."

Giuseppe chuckled, the sound echoing through the ridge. "Quick? Where's the fun in that?" His free hand gestured to the rocky terrain around them. "Come on, Omari. Show me what you can do."

Omari had enough. "Move in!" he barked, leading his squad forward.

Giuseppe was already in motion. With a flick of his blade,

a burst of lightning shot toward Omari. The captain raised his mace, deflecting the attack with a powerful swing, the air rippling with the force.

"That's all you've got?" Omari taunted.

Giuseppe smirked and sent another crackling burst, this time at Omari's feet. The ground erupted in dust and sparks, forcing Omari to shield his face.

Omari surged forward, swinging his mace in a wide arc. Giuseppe ducked, weaving past the strike, leading Omari deeper into the ridge.

Hidden in the shadows, Eli crouched, his Titanroot Hammer poised. He locked eyes with Allegra, who gave him a curt nod, already preparing her next move.

Omari swung again, but this time, Giuseppe sidestepped and slashed downward. His blade sliced cleanly through the strap securing the massive weapon to Omari's arm. Sparks flew, and before Omari could react, Giuseppe followed up with a sharp kick, sending the mace skidding across the rocky ground.

Omari's eyes flicked toward it, realization dawning.

"You—"

Before he could finish, Eli slammed his Titanroot Hammer into the earth. The ground rumbled violently, and jagged stone pillars shot up, cutting Omari off from his squad.

Allegra sprang into action, releasing a burst of soul energy. A wave of force rippled outward, knocking back the nearest members of Omari's squad and widening the gap between them.

Omari glared at Giuseppe, his fists clenching as the trap fully set in around him.

As the dust settled and the last echoes of the collapsing ridge faded, Allegra emerged from the shadows, her stance firm as she joined Giuseppe and Eli. Her golden eyes flicked toward

Omari, now trapped behind layers of stone and rubble, his shouts muffled but still full of fury.

"That should keep him busy for a while," Allegra said, crossing her arms. "Though I wouldn't count him out just yet."

Giuseppe smirked, backing up toward the edge of the ridge. "I don't need to stop him," he said, glancing at Omari's buried mace. "I just need to slow him down."

Omari's fists clenched, his chest rising and falling with restrained fury. "This won't hold me forever."

Giuseppe tilted his head slightly, the amusement never leaving his face. "I don't need forever. Just long enough."

Eli wiped the sweat from his brow and rested his hammer on his shoulder. "That's one down," he said, exhaling. "Think the others will be as easy?"

Giuseppe chuckled. "They'll be trickier, but we've got the advantage. Let's move before anyone catches on."

A knowing look passed between the three of them before they melted back into the trees, their footsteps silent against the damp earth. Behind them, Omari's frustrated shouts continued, but they didn't look back. The next phase of their plan was already in motion.

Not far from them, Nyla's squad moved with relentless precision. They had heard the commotion from the ridge, but they didn't falter. If Omari had been compromised, then they needed to move faster—outmaneuver Giuseppe before he could set another trap.

But Giuseppe, Eli, and Allegra were already watching them, waiting for the perfect moment to strike.

The forest pulsed with tension as Nyla's squad moved swiftly through the dense foliage, their footfalls barely making a sound against the damp earth. The echoes of the collapsed ridge still hung in the air, but they didn't slow their pursuit. If Omari had been compromised, then it was up to them to bring Giuseppe in.

"He's toying with us," Nyla muttered, her resonant chime gauntlets gleaming faintly in the filtered moonlight. "Stay sharp. If we keep pressing forward, we'll cut him off before he sets another—"

A voice rang out from up ahead, smooth and deliberate. "Nyla! Still trailing behind? I expected more from you."

The squad came to an abrupt halt, and Nyla raised a hand to still them. Her sharp eyes scanned the darkened trees, searching for the trap she knew was waiting. "He's leading us somewhere," she murmured. "Be ready."

They moved cautiously, following the sound of Giuseppe's taunts until they reached a clearing just before the river bend. The ground here was unusually soft, damp from the nearby water, and the canopy above cast eerie shadows across the area.

"Fan out," Nyla ordered, her voice firm. "He's close."

The moment the words left her lips, the earth beneath them trembled.

"Move!" Nyla shouted, but it was too late.

Eli, positioned in the dense underbrush behind them, swung his Titanroot Hammer down with all his strength. The ground responded instantly, shifting and cracking before completely giving way. The squad let out startled cries as the earth collapsed beneath them, sending them plummeting into a deep sinkhole. Dust and debris filled the air as the forest swallowed them whole.

As Nyla and her warriors scrambled to their feet within the pit, Allegra and Giuseppe made their move. They descended with blinding speed, weaving through the panicked soldiers as they severed weapon straps and kicked blades and staffs out of reach. Nyla barely had time to react before Giuseppe's blade was upon her, separating her from her weapon.

Nyla clenched her jaw, fury burning in her eyes as she took in their situation. The squad was disarmed, trapped in the pit with no easy way out. Above them, Eli raised his hammer once more, the ground shifting as he reinforced the walls, sealing them in.

"This won't hold me forever," Nyla growled.

Eli exhaled, resting his hammer against his shoulder. "That's two squads down," he said, eyeing the sealed sinkhole.

The air in the forest felt charged, thick with anticipation as Giuseppe, Eli, and Allegra moved swiftly through the under-brush. The scent of damp earth mixed with the distant crackling of torches carried by the advancing squad. They had stalled Omari and Nyla, but Captain Mei was a different challenge entirely.

"Come on, let's get ready for what's next. Can you feel who's coming?" Giuseppe asked, his voice low but focused.

Eli closed his eyes briefly, sending a pulse of his earth soul essence through the ground. The vibrations echoed back to him, steady and deliberate—footsteps, at least ten, moving with precision. His eyes snapped open. "Yeah, it's Captain Mei and her squad."

"She's sharp," Allegra added, her arms crossed as she scanned the terrain. "She won't fall into the same traps as the others."

Giuseppe nodded. "Then we adjust. Let's prepare."

The three of them moved deeper into the forest, their movements swift but controlled. Every step, every rustle of leaves was deliberate. They had turned the relentless pursuit into a battle of strategy, and so far, they were winning.

"You know," Eli said, glancing over at Giuseppe, "this is actually kind of fun."

Giuseppe smirked. "It's always fun when you're not the one being cornered. But don't get cocky. Mei's different. We'll need to be smart."

Allegra rolled her eyes. "You sound like you're enjoying this too much."

Eli chuckled. "I'll follow your lead, Captain," he said with a mock salute.

Giuseppe was about to reply when he suddenly froze mid-step. His entire body went rigid, his sharp senses picking up something—no, someone—he hadn't felt in what seemed like an eternity.

A voice echoed faintly in his mind.

Dad, can you hear me?

His breath hitched, and for a moment, he stood completely still. The forest, the chase, the plan—all of it faded away as he focused on the telepathic link igniting in his mind.

"I hear him," Giuseppe whispered, almost in disbelief. His voice carried something rare—relief, hope. "It's Chris. He's okay."

Eli and Allegra exchanged glances. "Wait, what? You hear him?" Eli asked, stepping closer.

Giuseppe didn't answer. His entire focus was on strengthening the link. He closed his eyes, shutting out the world, reaching through the vast distance between them. **Where are you?** His thoughts pulsed with urgency.

Allegra shifted uncomfortably. "Is he answering?" she asked, her usual confidence tinged with worry.

But there was nothing. No response. No further connection. Just silence.

Giuseppe's jaw tightened. **Chris, answer me.** Still nothing.

"Captain?" Eli's voice broke through the heavy stillness.

Giuseppe exhaled sharply, his eyes snapping open, frustration flickering across his face. "Nothing," he muttered, more to himself than the others.

Allegra frowned. "That's not good. If he reached out, something must have happened."

Eli pressed his palm to the ground again, his earth essence spreading outward. His expression darkened. "Um… Captain, we've got another problem. That squad is almost here."

Giuseppe pushed aside his worry for Chris, his mind snapping back into battle mode. His son was alive. That had to be enough for now.

He looked at Eli and Allegra, already formulating their next move. "We stick to the plan," he said, his voice regaining its usual steel. "We make sure Mei's squad ends up just as trapped as the last one. But stay sharp—she won't fall for the same tricks."

Eli nodded, his grip tightening on his Titanroot Hammer. Allegra unsheathed her daggers, rolling her shoulders as she assessed the battlefield ahead.

Giuseppe cast one last glance toward the distance, silently willing Chris to respond. But there was nothing.

He turned away, his focus now locked on the approaching squad. The chase wasn't over yet.

The forest trembled beneath the weight of their battle, the once-tranquil wilderness now a battleground of fire and frost. Chris and Sophie stood their ground, backs against the thick trees, their breath visible in the unnatural cold spreading with every step Lilith took.

The moonlight barely pierced through the thick canopy

above, casting eerie shadows that danced in the wake of their clashing powers. The ground beneath them was a battlefield of contradictions—ice creeping across the earth where Lilith moved, fire-scorched patches marking where Chris had struck.

Chris tightened his grip on the Eclipse Blade, its twin elements crackling in his hands—fire roaring along one edge, lightning sparking violently along the other. "We have to end this," he muttered, jaw clenched as he steadied himself.

"We can't keep this up, Chris!" Sophie's voice carried urgency, her amulet pulsing faintly as she struggled to summon her abilities. She pressed a hand to the frozen ground, willing the earth to respond, but the frost had spread too far, sealing the soil in an unbreakable grip. "The ground's frozen—I can't get anything to grow!"

Lilith chuckled darkly, the sound sharp as the glacial wind that swirled around them. Her long, jagged claws gleamed with icy malice as she circled them like a predator. "You're wasting your time," she mocked, her voice smooth yet laced with venom. "Your tricks won't work here. The moment you stepped into this fight, you were already mine."

Chris stepped protectively in front of Sophie, his blade flaring brighter as his resolve solidified. "This power isn't yours!" he shot back, his voice unwavering.

Lilith's cold laughter sent a fresh chill through the air. "You poor, naïve child," she sneered. "You think power is about ownership? That flame isn't just some tool—it's a key. And in your hands, it's nothing but wasted potential."

With a burst of unnatural speed, she lunged, her claws arcing toward Chris in a blur of silver and frost. He barely had time to react, bringing up his blade to meet her strike. Fire and ice collided, erupting in a blinding flash that sent shock waves through the clearing. Chris was forced back, his boots skidding over the ice-coated ground as he struggled to hold his stance.

Sophie rushed forward, grabbing his arm before he could stumble. "Chris, she's playing with us," she said urgently, her green eyes flashing with worry. "You have to focus."

Chris exhaled sharply, frustration boiling beneath his skin. "I know," he muttered, eyes locked onto Lilith as she straightened, her expression still eerily calm.

Lilith tilted her head, a slow, predatory smile stretching across her lips. "What's wrong?" she mused, stepping forward with measured grace. "Is the power too much for you? You don't deserve it—you never did." The temperature around them plummeted as she extended her claws, frost crawling up the bark of the trees. "That flame was never yours. And I will take it back."

Chris felt the fire within him surge, responding to the challenge. The blade in his hands pulsed as both fire and lightning crackled along its surface. Without hesitation, he raised it high and slashed through the air, sending a surge of fiery lightning racing toward her.

Lilith barely moved, sidestepping at the last second, the attack colliding with a nearby tree. The massive trunk splintered and cracked, breaking apart in a deafening explosion of embers and ice.

Sophie took the opening, summoning the last reserves of her power. Her amulet glowed with renewed intensity as thick vines shot from the ground, forming a protective barrier between them and Lilith. "You're not taking anything!" she shouted, her stance unyielding.

Lilith's eyes glowed like molten silver in the moonlight as she slashed through the vines effortlessly, frost spreading over the broken remains. "Then you leave me no choice," she hissed.

In a single motion, she lunged again, faster than before. Chris barely had time to react as her claws came within inches of his chest. With instinct overriding thought, he twisted his grip on the Eclipse Blade, channeling both fire and lightning at once. The combined energy erupted outward in a blinding arc of power, colliding with Lilith mid-air.

The forest exploded with light and fury as the two forces met, the ground quaking beneath them. Sophie stumbled back, shielding her face from the sheer force of the impact, her heart hammering in her chest.

Lilith landed a few feet away, the ice cracking beneath her feet. She steadied herself, her breathing even, her expression unreadable. Then, slowly, she smiled.

Chris tightened his stance, gripping his blade even harder. Sophie's breathing was ragged beside him, but she stood firm.

The battlefield crackled with energy, fire and frost colliding as Chris and Lilith clashed in a deadly dance. Sophie stood back, her breath coming in short, panicked bursts as she tried to think of a way to turn the tide.

"Chris, we can't win like this!" she shouted, her desperation cutting through the chaos. "We need a plan!"

Chris barely spared her a glance, his mind racing. The ethereal flame burned within him, pulsing like a wild, untamed beast in his veins. He could feel its power, raw and boundless, but controlling it was another matter entirely. "I just need a second!" he called back, dodging another of Lilith's vicious strikes.

Lilith was relentless, her icy claws flashing as she pressed her attack. Sparks flew as her talons met Chris's blade, a storm of fire and ice swirling around them. The ground trembled beneath their feet, the trees around them groaning under the force of their battle.

Lilith sneered, her silver eyes glinting with cruel amusement. "You're wasting your strength, boy," she taunted, her voice laced with venom. "The longer you fight, the weaker you'll become. Just give me what belongs to me, and I'll make this quick."

Chris clenched his jaw, pushing against her with every ounce of strength he had. "You're not taking anything!" he snarled, his blade blazing with fire and crackling lightning.

Sophie stood rigid a few feet away, clutching her amulet tightly. The weight of the battle pressed down on her, and an uneasy feeling coiled in her chest. "Chris…" she whispered, her voice barely audible. "We need to end this before it's too late."

And then, the forest changed.

The darkness that had clung to the edges of their fight began to move, writhing unnaturally like living shadows. The air thickened, turning cold and heavy, and an eerie silence settled over the battlefield. Even the trees seemed to recoil, their leaves shivering in an unseen wind.

A new presence stirred in the blackness.

From the depths of the inky void, a figure emerged—tall, angular, and wreathed in shadows that curled around him like living smoke. His crimson eyes burned with an unsettling calm as he surveyed the battlefield. First, he looked at Lilith. Then, his gaze flicked to Chris and Sophie.

Lilith's posture stiffened, her claws flexing instinctively as she took a wary step back. For the first time since the fight began, her cold confidence wavered.

"Sargatanas," she hissed, her voice laced with both anger and unease. "What are you doing here?"

Chris felt his blood run cold. The name echoed in his mind, carrying a weight he didn't yet understand. The demon's presence was suffocating, the very air around them bending under his power.

Chris swallowed hard, lifting his blade, though even he wasn't sure if it would be enough.

The fight had just changed.

And he wasn't sure they were ready for it.

24

Convergence

The demon halted mid-step, his towering form exuding both menace and confusion. His crimson eyes narrowed as he studied Lilith, suspicion flickering behind his piercing gaze.

"I sensed dark energy, but never thought it'd be you that I'd run into," Sargatanas said, his voice low and smooth, carrying an edge of disbelief. "Especially not here." His gaze flicked between her and the two humans. "How are you here, Lilith? On Earth? And what," he gestured toward Chris and Sophie with a slow, clawed hand, "are you doing with them?"

Lilith stiffened, a flicker of something unreadable crossing her face before she masked it behind her usual icy demeanor. "That's none of your concern," she snapped.

Sargatanas tilted his head, his expression darkening. "You escaped Hell?" His voice was laced with both astonishment and anger. "You didn't tell me you were planning this. You said you needed me to send them to you! So together we could punish these wretched humans—the ones who betrayed you."

Chris's grip on his blade tightened as his eyes darted between the two demons. He could feel the shift in power between them, the sudden turn of events altering the very air around them. "What's going on?" he muttered under his breath, more to himself than anyone else.

Before anyone could answer, the shadows around Sophie came alive, twisting and writhing unnaturally. Without warning, they shot up and coiled around her arms and legs, yanking her off balance and pinning her in place.

She gasped, struggling as the tendrils of darkness constricted around her limbs. The cold seeped into her skin like living ice, paralyzing her in an instant.

"Sophie!" Chris shouted, instinctively stepping forward.

Sargatanas raised a hand, his gaze never leaving Lilith. The shadows around Sophie responded immediately, tightening with unnatural precision, locking her in place.

"You can stay where you are, boy," Sargatanas growled, his voice carrying an unmistakable finality. "You're not part of this."

Chris gritted his teeth, frustration and fury bubbling beneath the surface. His blade crackled with fire and lightning, but he didn't move—yet.

Because for the first time since the battle began, Lilith looked uncertain. And that terrified him more than anything.

The battlefield had shifted. The once-blazing clash between Chris and Lilith was now drowned in the suffocating weight of an entirely new presence. The air had turned thick and cold, shadows creeping unnaturally along the ground, coiling around trees and stones like hungry serpents.

Chris's heart pounded in his chest as he quickly scanned his surroundings. His eyes caught a break in the dense canopy, a sliver of moonlight piercing through the darkness. Without hesitation, he sprinted toward it. The moment his boots landed in the patch of light, the shadows around him recoiled, hissing like wounded beasts. Safe. At least for now.

Sophie wasn't as lucky. She thrashed against the inky tendrils wrapped around her limbs, glaring daggers at the demon who held her captive. "Let me go, you coward!" she spat, her voice sharp with defiance, though Chris could hear the strain in it.

Sargatanas's burning gaze flicked to her, his lips curling into something that was neither a smile nor a snarl. "Waste your breath if you must, girl," he said, his voice cold and smooth as glass. "But you are right where I need you to be."

Lilith, who had held herself with cold arrogance all this time, suddenly looked different—tense, wary. Her silver eyes flicked toward the demon, her stance shifting as if preparing for something unseen. "Sargatanas," she said carefully, her voice losing its usual edge. "Let her go. This is between me and you."

The demon's gaze snapped fully to her, and whatever amusement had lingered in his expression vanished, replaced by something raw—fury laced with unmistakable betrayal.

"Me and you?" Sargatanas echoed, his voice quieter now, but far more dangerous. "How dare you say that to me, Lilith? After everything I've done for you. After everything we've done together." His claws twitched, his shadows curling tighter around Sophie, making her gasp as they constricted.

Lilith took a slow step back, her usual sharp confidence faltering. "You don't understand," she said quickly. "I had no choice—"

"No choice?" Sargatanas's voice trembled, and for the first time, it wasn't just rage that colored it. It was hurt. "You used me. You made me believe we were in this together." His crimson eyes burned, his shadows lashing out against the ground like a wounded animal's tail.

Lilith flinched, her breath hitching. "Sargatanas, listen—"

"No," he snarled, stepping closer, his towering form radiating an energy so suffocating that even the air around them seemed to bend under the weight of it. "You *lied* to me. You played me like a fool." His voice wavered, as if the very admission disgusted him. "I sent them to Hell for you. I gave you everything I had, and you—you just leave."

Chris, standing just at the edge of the shadows, his Eclipse Blade pulsing with crackling energy, finally pieced it together. His grip tightened on the hilt as he glared at Lilith. "You used him," he said coldly, his voice cutting through the thick air. "You had him send us to Hell so you could escape."

Lilith turned sharply to Chris, her silver eyes flashing with anger, but there was something else beneath it now—something dangerously close to regret. "You don't know anything, boy," she snapped, her claws flexing. "This was never about *you*."

Sargatanas's shadows lashed violently around him. "He's right, isn't he?" The demon's voice was softer now, almost hollow. His burning eyes searched Lilith's face as though begging for some other answer. Some reason to believe she wasn't as heartless as her actions had made her seem.

Lilith swallowed, but her lips parted without an answer.

Sargatanas's face twisted, heartbreak flickering across it for the briefest moment before something colder took its place. "You *never* cared," he murmured, and the realization alone seemed to fracture something deep within him. "Not about me. Not about what we could have built together." His voice grew heavier, a tide of darkness swelling within it. "It was always about *you*. I don't know how he got you out but it's no matter."

Lilith's silver eyes widened, genuine fear flashing across her face. "Sargatanas—wait."

Lilith opened her mouth, but before she could speak, Sargatanas raised his clawed hand, and the shadows around him swirled violently. From the shifting blackness, an object began to take shape—a small, black key, its surface veined with streaks of twisting darkness.

Chris's stomach dropped.

Sargatanas's lips curled into a cruel smile. "I'm sorry to inform you," he said, his voice dripping with malice, "that whatever little plan you thought you had is over."

Lilith took a step back. "What…" Her voice wavered, disbelief thick in her tone. "How did you—"

"Oh, Lilith," Sargatanas interrupted, his mock sympathy laced with venom. "You really thought you could deceive me? That I wouldn't notice your pathetic little schemes? Did you truly believe I'd let you use me without securing my own advantage?" He took another step forward, his overwhelming presence suffocating. "I wanted to believe our love was real, but something in me knew better. So while you clawed your way back to this world, I ensured that whatever plan you were weaving would serve my purpose instead."

He lifted the shadow key higher, letting its unnatural essence bathe the forest with darkness. "With this," he continued, his voice swelling with triumph, "I will open the gates. Astaroth and Beelzebub will rise, and they will erase your treachery from existence."

Chris gritted his teeth, his grip tightening around the hilt of his Eclipse Blade. The energy pulsing from the key sent chills through him, like an unholy force pressing against his very soul. He darted a glance at Sophie, who struggled against the shadows constricting her. Her vines fought to break free, but they withered under Sargatanas's overwhelming power.

Then, against all odds, Sophie lifted her head, her green eyes burning with defiance. "You're going to unleash two of the highest demons on Earth?" she spat, her voice cutting through the suffocating tension. "Do you have any idea what that'll do to this world?"

Sargatanas chuckled, low and knowing. "Oh, little girl," he murmured, his glowing eyes locking onto hers. "I know exactly what it'll do."

"I thought the Shadow key lost its power? That the Angel Corps overused it." Chris said.

"You fool, you really know nothing. This key does not belong to you humans. You all pour your pathetic soul essence into it until it has no use but that is a misuse of the key. It is made for us demon kind, and the true power of a demon can open any portal to our homeland." Sargatanas said "and when I open that portal, Earth will burn. Balance will crumble. And from the ashes, we will rise. A new order forged in power." He gestured toward Lilith, his claws flexing. "And she will pay for her betrayal."

Lilith snarled, her icy aura flaring. "You fool," she spat. "You think Astaroth and Beelzebub will view you as an equal? They'll devour you the moment they step into this realm!"

Sargatanas let out a low, menacing laugh. "That's where you're wrong, my dear," he said, his voice dripping with confidence. "With the shadow key, I am the one who decides who enters this world—and under what terms. I've played your game, Lilith, and now it's my turn to win."

Chris and Sophie exchanged a glance, their minds racing. The key, glowing ominously in the demon's grasp, was clearly the centerpiece of everything. Chris's fiery blade crackled faintly as he stepped forward, his resolve hardening.

The tension in the clearing reached its breaking point as the glow of the shadow key intensified, its ominous light bathing the forest in an unnatural hue. Sargatanas stood tall, triumphant, as Chris, Sophie, and Lilith prepared for what could be their only chance to stop him.

The forest was eerily still, the usual hum of nocturnal life muted beneath the weight of anticipation. Hidden among the dense underbrush, Giuseppe crouched low, his sharp gaze sweeping the treeline. Beside him, Eli pressed his palm against the cool earth, his Titanroot Hammer pulsing with a faint glow as he sent subtle waves of soul essence through the ground.

"They're close," Eli whispered, tension laced through his voice. "Mei's squad is moving toward the clearing—maybe two minutes out."

Giuseppe gave a small nod, his expression unreadable. "Good. We stick to the plan: split them up, isolate Mei, and neutralize her squad before they realize what's happening. Her fire whip is powerful, but if we keep her away from her team, we'll have the advantage."

A soft rustle signaled Allegra's approach as she slipped into position beside them. "You sound confident," she murmured, eyes scanning the shadows ahead. "But Mei isn't just powerful—she's smart. She won't walk blindly into this."

Giuseppe smirked. "That's exactly why she will. She'll think she's the one springing the trap, not the other way around."

Allegra glanced at Eli, exchanging a skeptical look. "And if she doesn't take the bait?"

Giuseppe's gaze flickered toward her, steady and sure. "Then we adjust. But trust me—she will."

As they settled in, ready to spring the ambush, a strange glow flickered against the horizon. It wasn't the orange hue of Mei's fire essence but something more intense, something unnatural. A pulse of energy followed, rippling through the ground beneath them. Eli's connection to the earth flared in response, and he sucked in a sharp breath.

"What is that?" Allegra whispered, her usual confidence wavering.

Giuseppe's brow furrowed as he rose slightly from his crouch, his grip on his blade tightening. "It's not Mei."

Before anyone could respond, the forest exploded with light. A massive pillar of pure soul essence surged into the sky, its brilliance cutting through the darkness like a beacon. The very air trembled, the force of it sending a pulse of energy through the trees. Leaves rustled violently, branches creaked, and the earth itself seemed to vibrate beneath the raw power radiating from the distant source.

Eli staggered back, eyes wide. "What in the—"

Giuseppe was already moving, his instincts screaming that whatever had just happened was bigger than their current mission. "That's soul essence," he said, voice low and grim. "Dark soul essence."

Allegra stood beside him, her usual sharpness replaced with unease. "Is it Chris?" she asked, almost hesitantly.

Giuseppe didn't answer immediately. His connection to his son was still there, but distant—like trying to hear a whisper through a storm. "I don't know," he admitted. "But we're going to find out."

Before they could act, the sound of approaching footsteps shattered the moment. From the shadows of the forest, Mei and her squad emerged, their weapons drawn and their expressions tense. The faint embers of her fire whip flickered at her side, casting an eerie glow over her face.

Her sharp eyes landed on Giuseppe, Eli, and Allegra. "So," she said, her voice cool but alert, "I take it that wasn't one of your tricks?"

Giuseppe straightened, his usual smirk absent. "No," he said simply. "And unless you somehow managed to summon a god-tier soul essence blast, I'm guessing it wasn't you either."

Mei's squad shifted uneasily behind her, their attention flicking between their former targets and the still-radiating pulse in the distance.

"Whatever's happening," Allegra said, stepping forward, "it's bigger than this fight."

Mei studied them for a long moment before exhaling sharply, the embers on her whip dimming. "Truce?" she asked.

Giuseppe nodded. "Truce."

Eli slung his hammer over his shoulder. "So… we're all heading toward the giant soul explosion, then?"

Giuseppe smirked, a flicker of excitement creeping back into his eyes. "Looks like it."

Without another word, the uneasy alliance took off into the forest, the glow of the distant energy calling them forward.

The two groups converged, their hurried steps barely making a sound against the forest floor. The deeper they went, the more the air thickened with an unnatural weight. A suffocating pressure settled over them, the oppressive chill sending a shiver down even the most seasoned warriors' spines.

Giuseppe's senses sharpened, every fiber of his being alert. He could feel it—the raw, immense energy pulsing ahead, an overwhelming force that set his instincts on edge. His grip tightened around his blade as they broke through the final line of trees and into a clearing bathed in eerie, shifting light.

The sight before them brought the entire group to a stunned halt.

Chris stood at the heart of the battlefield, his Eclipse Blade ablaze, wreathed in fire and crackling lightning. The ground beneath him scorched and trembled, barely able to contain the energy radiating from his weapon. Beside him, Sophie struggled, her limbs bound by writhing tendrils of living shadow, her amulet flickering weakly as she fought against their grip.

And standing across from them, towering and wreathed in darkness, was Sargatanas.

The demon's crimson eyes gleamed with malevolent amusement, his jagged grin stretching wide as he raised the small black key.

A deep, guttural laugh rumbled from Sargatanas's chest, filling the air with a sound that was both mocking and triumphant.

"Chris!" Giuseppe's voice cut through the tension, urgent and sharp.

Chris whirled around, his eyes widening in shock. "Dad?!"

The moment of recognition hung between them, a fleeting second of relief before Sargatanas's gaze shifted toward the newcomers. His smirk widened as his piercing eyes took in the sight of the reinforcements.

"Well, well," he purred, his voice dripping with condescension. "The family reunion grows larger. How delightful."

Mei, standing rigid with her whip coiled tightly in her grip, narrowed her eyes. "Is that…?" she asked, her voice low with unease.

"That is Sargatanas," Giuseppe confirmed grimly, stepping forward. His gaze locked onto the key in the demon's clawed grip. "And that key… it's the Shadow Key."

Mei's breath hitched. "The Shadow Key? That's impossible!"

Sargatanas chuckled, a slow, reverberating sound of cruel satisfaction. With deliberate ease, he lifted the key higher, its glow intensifying as if feeding off the chaos around it.

"Oh, it's very possible," he said smoothly. "And soon, it will open the gates for Astaroth and Beelzebub. You should all be honored—after all, you'll be the first to witness the birth of a new world."

Chris stepped forward, his blade crackling with renewed energy, fire and lightning swirling along its edge. His grip tightened, his stance unwavering despite the fear that lingered in his chest.

"Not if we stop you first," he said, his voice steady.

The tension in the clearing was suffocating as Sargatanas held the small black key aloft, its surface glistening like obsidian beneath the moonlight. It pulsed with an eerie glow, waves of raw power radiating from it, sending tremors through the ground. Chris, Sophie, Giuseppe, Mei, and the others stood frozen, their weapons drawn, watching in silence as the demon poured his soul essence into the artifact.

"It's already too late," Sargatanas growled, his voice reverberating through the trees. His crimson eyes burned with triumph as another surge of energy shot from the key, tearing into the sky with a blinding radiance. The earth trembled beneath their feet, a low hum vibrating through the air.

Then, the key began to change.

The black surface writhed in his grasp, shifting unnaturally, like liquid metal unraveling itself. The intricate etchings along its form pulsed violently before dissolving into a viscous, inky substance, twisting and curling like living tendrils. The black liquid spread rapidly, crawling up Sargatanas's clawed fingers, slithering over his wrist, then surging up his arm.

For a fleeting moment, his face lit up with exhilaration. "Yes," he hissed, his voice filled with unrestrained hunger. "The power is mine!"

But his triumph was short-lived.

The inky blackness didn't stop at his arm—it spread faster, coating his chest, winding around his torso like a sentient force with a will of its own. The demon's grin faltered, replaced by confusion as the liquid solidified into an intricate structure, tightening around his body. What had once been a key was now a harness—sleek, black, and etched with faint golden inlays that shimmered ominously.

Sargatanas's claws scraped against the metal-like plating, his movements frantic as realization set in. "What... what is this?" he snarled, his voice laced with sudden panic. He flexed his muscles, attempting to break free, but the harness only tightened, locking into place with a final, decisive snap.

The moment it sealed, the sigils engraved upon it flared to life, and a surge of energy pulsed through his body—not power, but something far worse.

Draining.

A strangled roar tore from Sargatanas's throat as dark streams of energy bled from his form, twisting through the air like smoke being siphoned from a dying fire. His once-commanding presence wavered as his strength was ripped away, his dark soul essence flowing out in torrents that the harness greedily absorbed.

From the depths of the forest, Vincent and Hiroshi emerged, their figures cutting through the moonlit haze like phantoms. Vincent's frosted blade gleamed in the dim light, his icy aura trailing behind him like a specter of death. Hiroshi followed in silence, his expression unreadable, his presence a shadow to Vincent's storm.

Vincent's voice sliced through the clearing with smooth precision. "Well, well…" His cold gaze swept over Chris, Sophie, and Lilith before settling on Sargatanas, who writhed against the harness draining his essence. "What do we have here?"

The demon turned sharply, crimson eyes ablaze with fury and desperation. He snarled, his voice trembling with rage as the harness pulsed, drawing more of his power. "You!" His claws scraped against the device, but it held firm, a prison of his own making. "What… Did you do?"

Vincent smirked, stepping forward with slow, deliberate strides. "Oh, Sargatanas…" His tone dripped with mock sympathy. "I simply gave you what you asked for: the Shadow Key." He flicked his blade toward the harness. "Though, I must admit… it doesn't seem to be working in your favor."

The demon staggered, his claws curling into fists as he let out a guttural growl. "You… tricked me!" he roared, voice thick with anguish. "This wasn't the deal!"

Vincent's smirk deepened, his frozen aura swirling in the air. "The deal?" His voice was as cold as the frost licking at his blade. "I don't think you're in a position to lecture me about honoring deals."

He raised a hand, and the streams of dark energy siphoned from Sargatanas shifted course. The stolen essence coiled toward Vincent, wrapping around his arm like living shadows, seeping into his frosted blade. Crimson streaks pulsed through the ice, the weapon glowing with a twisted fusion of power.

Lilith, who had remained silent until now, took a step forward, her usual composure cracking as she glared at Vincent. "You fool," she spat. "Do you really think you can control a demon's power?"

Vincent didn't break his gaze from Sargatanas, his smirk unwavering. "Watch me."

The harness pulsed again, and Sargatanas groaned, his knees buckling as his strength was torn from him. He looked up at Vincent with something close to horror. "You… used me…" His voice was weaker now, the fire in his eyes fading.

"Don't take it personally," Vincent said, his tone almost casual. "You're not the first to fall victim to your own arrogance." He turned to Hiroshi, who remained still at his side, an unshaken observer of the scene unfolding.

"This," Vincent continued, gesturing to the harness, "is one of my most prized creations. It doesn't just steal power—it refines it, reshapes it, makes it mine."

Chris stepped forward, his blade igniting in a burst of fiery light. "You can't just steal power like this!" His voice was thick with anger.

"Vincent, stop this!" he shouted.

Vincent's gaze flicked to Chris, his smirk never wavering. "Can't I?" His tone was razor-sharp, cutting through Chris's desperation. "You, of all people, should understand that power belongs to those strong enough to wield it." He turned back to Sargatanas, the dying demon slumped against his fate. "And Sargatanas," he added, "has proven himself unworthy."

Sophie gasped as the shadows binding her unraveled, her amulet flaring to life as she regained her freedom. She staggered forward, her voice laced with disgust. "You're no better than the demons you claim to fight, Vincent!" Her hands clenched into fists. "This isn't justice—it's greed!"

Vincent's icy veneer cracked. His expression twisted, his voice rising with something raw, something furious.

"This is what is necessary!" he roared. "We humans take our gifts from God and His angels and use them to fight their war. And for what?" His fingers tightened around his sword, the crimson energy pulsing brighter. "To be slaughtered every time? To watch our people die because we're weaker?" His breath was ragged, his glare seething with defiance.

"I'm done being weak."

Sargatanas collapsed to his knees, his once-imposing form now withered and frail. The harness pulsed weakly, siphoning the last remnants of his essence into Vincent. His crimson eyes, once burning with fury, were now dull, filled only with hatred and the bitter sting of defeat.

"You… won't get away with this," he rasped, his voice barely more than a breath.

Vincent knelt beside him, the air growing colder as his icy

aura wrapped around them like a noose. "Oh, but I already have," he murmured, his tone almost gentle. "Your essence will fuel my cause, and your failure will serve as a warning to anyone who dares to stand against me."

The clearing fell into an eerie silence. A gust of wind carried away the last traces of Sargatanas, his body reduced to nothing but ash. Vincent rose to his feet, his frosted blade shimmering ominously in the moonlight. Hiroshi stepped forward without a word, his nod an unspoken acknowledgment of what had just transpired.

Vincent turned his gaze toward Chris and Sophie, his faint smile sending an involuntary chill down Chris's spine.

"Now," he said, his voice smooth yet heavy with intent, "let's talk about that flame of yours."

The temperature around them shifted. Vincent's body tensed, then began to twist and contort, his frosted aura dissipating as something darker, far more menacing, took its place. Shadows slithered around him like living things, and then—with a sickening crack—massive, leathery wings erupted from his back, their blackened expanse blotting out the moonlight. His frame stretched, growing taller, more monstrous. His features sharpened with an unnatural malice, his glowing eyes burning with something beyond human comprehension.

The air thickened, crackling with raw energy as tendrils of living shadow coiled at his feet, writhing like hungry beasts.

Chris instinctively gripped his sword tighter, his pulse hammering in his ears. His instincts screamed at him to move, but his body felt frozen in place. "What... what are you?" he finally managed, his voice strained with both confusion and dread.

Vincent's lips curled into a slow, chilling smile. "Something far beyond what you can comprehend," he replied, his voice a deep, resonant growl that sent a shiver through everyone in the clearing.

With a flick of his hand, the shadows obeyed, swirling and solidifying into grotesque figures—twisted, humanoid forms with hollow, glowing eyes. Shadow demons, bound to his will.

Before anyone could react, Vincent moved.

In a blur of motion, he was upon Chris, his clawed hand wrapping around his throat. With terrifying ease, he lifted him off the ground, Chris's sword slipping from his grasp as he struggled against the crushing force of Vincent's grip.

"Chris!" Sophie's scream cut through the chaos, her amulet igniting in a brilliant light as she willed the earth to fight back. Vines surged forward, twisting toward Vincent in an attempt to ensnare him—but the shadows devoured them before they could even reach.

The other warriors barely had time to raise their weapons before Vincent's wings unfurled with a powerful beat. The sheer force sent a shock wave through the clearing, debris and dust exploding outward as he launched into the sky, carrying Chris with him.

Below, the others were forced to shield their eyes against the sudden wind, their shouts drowned out by the roaring air.

High above, the cold night air stung Chris's skin as they ascended, the ground growing smaller beneath them. He thrashed against Vincent's grip, his fingers clawing at the iron hold around his throat.

"Let… me go!" he gasped, his breath coming in ragged, desperate gulps.

Vincent's dark laughter echoed through the sky. "Why would I do that?" he mused, his tone rich with mockery. His glowing eyes bore into Chris with an intensity that sent a cold dread sinking into his bones.

"You've been running from your power for far too long, boy." His grip tightened, his wings cutting through the night like blades.

"It's time to see what you're truly made of."

Meanwhile, below, the clearing erupted into chaos. The shadow demons, driven by Vincent's will, surged forward like a living tide of darkness. Sophie stood her ground, her amulet blazing with radiant light as she summoned barriers of vines to block their relentless advance. Beside her, Eli swung his Titanroot Hammer with earth-shaking force, each strike sending tremors rippling through the battlefield, shattering the ground beneath the oncoming demons.

Giuseppe moved with lethal precision, his blade crackling with lightning as he carved through the shadows, each slash leaving arcs of electricity crackling in the air. "Stay together!" he shouted, his voice sharp and commanding. "Focus on the demons! We'll deal with Vincent once they're down!"

To his left, Allegra twirled her trident, the weapon sent sharp, piercing strikes and sweeping waves that crashed through the ranks of shadow demons. With each thrust, torrents of water erupted, engulfing the creatures and dissolving them into wisps of darkness.

Nearby, Mei cracked her fire whip, the molten weapon slicing through the air in blazing arcs. Each flick of her wrist sent streaks of flame lashing through the demons, scorching them apart. She moved fluidly, dancing between attacks, using the whip's range to strike multiple enemies at once. "They just keep coming!" she growled, her eyes flashing with determination as she sent another wave of fire through the advancing horde.

Sophie glanced skyward, her heart pounding as she caught

sight of Chris still struggling in Vincent's grip, his form barely visible against the darkness above. "We have to help him!" she yelled, her voice laced with desperation.

Giuseppe spared a glance upward, his face dark with concern, but his focus remained on the battlefield. "We will," he said firmly, slicing through another demon with a flash of lightning. "But we can't reach him unless we deal with this first."

The shadow demons pressed forward, their hollow, glowing eyes gleaming as they lunged. Their claws slashed through the air, tearing through the warriors' defenses. Sophie's vines strained to hold them back, while Eli brought his hammer down with a mighty roar, splintering the earth beneath them.

Hiroshi, standing apart from the fray, watched the battle unfold with an unreadable expression. His staff glowed faintly in his grip, but he made no move to engage. Instead, he observed, waiting, calculating—his gaze fixed on Vincent high above.

The battlefield was a storm of power—water, fire, earth, and lightning colliding with pure darkness. The warriors fought with everything they had, their combined strength barely holding back the onslaught. The night was lit up with the clash of forces, a chaotic dance of light and shadow as the battle raged on.

Above the battlefield, Chris mustered all his strength, his hands clamping around Vincent's arm as he struggled to break free. Sparks of fire and lightning flickered around him, his soul essence flaring with raw, untamed energy.

"I'm not afraid of you," he spat, his voice hoarse but unyielding.

Vincent's grip tightened, his monstrous grin widening. "Good," he said, almost amused. "Fear is a weakness. I want to face someone strong."

From the swirling shadows around him, Vincent reached into the abyss and retrieved the thick, black liquid. It slithered between his fingers, writhing as if alive. It pulsed with an eerie glow, its fluid form shifting unnaturally.

Chris's eyes widened in alarm as Vincent raised the inky substance.

"Your power will be mine," Vincent murmured, his voice low and filled with malice.

Before Chris could react, Vincent slammed the writhing liquid against his chest. Instantly, it latched onto him, spreading like a living parasite. The cold, viscous substance crawled over his body, seeping into his skin, tightening around his limbs like shackles. Chris thrashed violently, trying to rip it off, but it moved faster than he could fight, coating his torso, snaking up his arms, slithering around his throat like a noose.

"No!" Chris roared, his voice raw with desperation. Flames flickered at his fingertips, sparks of lightning crackled in protest—but the liquid devoured them on contact, snuffing them out like dying embers.

Then came the pain.

A deafening hum filled the air as the black symbiote pulsed, anchoring itself deeper into him. Chris convulsed as the ethereal flame and his very soul essence was siphoned away. A searing, unbearable agony ripped through his core as the warmth that had defined him for so long was torn from his body, drawn into the writhing mass now bound to him. The golden glow of his fire flickered, then flowed out of him like a river of light, vanishing into the darkness.

"No! Stop!" he choked out, clawing at his chest, but the more he fought, the tighter the liquid constricted.

The last traces of his fire extinguished, and then, as if sensing its next prey, the symbiote turned to his lightning. The crackling yellow energy sputtered, flickering weakly, before it too was stolen away. The power that had once surged through his veins—the power he had fought so hard to control—was vanishing, siphoned into the black abyss tightening around him.

Chris's breath came in short, labored gasps. His body trembled, drained of its warmth, his limbs heavy as lead. The defiance in his eyes flickered, fear creeping into its place.

Vincent tilted his head, watching with an almost clinical fascination. "All that strength," he mused. "And now it belongs to me." His voice was smooth, almost mocking. "All that potential… wasted."

Chris slumped in his grip, his consciousness teetering on the edge.

From below, Sophie's scream tore through the battlefield. "Chris!"

She fought against the shadow demons with a fury she had never known, her amulet burning brighter with every pulse of power. Vines lashed out, striking down the dark tendrils that blocked her path, but no matter how hard she pushed, she couldn't break through. The creatures swarmed her, forcing her back as she watched helplessly, her heart hammering in her chest.

Chris was slipping away, and she couldn't reach him.

Vincent's laughter echoed through the night, cold and unfeeling. He gazed down at Chris's weakened form, his expression one of detached amusement.

"It's a shame, really," he mused, tilting his head. "You had so much potential. But power like this was never meant for someone like you."

Chris gritted his teeth, summoning every ounce of strength he had left. His body felt like lead, his limbs barely responding, but still, he forced himself to speak. "This… isn't over," he rasped, his voice faint but laced with defiance.

Vincent's eyes gleamed with cruel satisfaction as the symbiotic black liquid constricting Chris pulsed, binding itself deeper into his body.

"Oh, it is," he said, his tone smooth, almost pitying. "For you, at least."

With a flick of his wrist, Vincent let go.

Chris's body dropped like a stone, the wind tearing past him as he plummeted toward the earth.

"Chris!"

Sophie's scream ripped through the chaos, her voice raw with desperation. Her amulet flared brilliantly, her soul essence surging as she slashed through the dark tendrils around her, tearing a path forward. The shadow demons lunged at her, their hollow eyes glowing with hunger, but she didn't hesitate.

"Get out of my way!" she roared, lashing out with a whip of vines. The creatures recoiled as she charged ahead, her eyes locked on Chris's falling form.

Above, Chris struggled to keep his consciousness. The world spun violently around him, the stars and treetops blurring together. His strength was gone—drained, stolen—leaving only emptiness. His fingers twitched, but his limbs refused to move, and the sickening realization set in: he couldn't stop his fall.

Branches snapped as his body crashed through the treetops, the impact sending splinters and leaves flying in all directions. He hit the ground hard, the force knocking the breath from his lungs. And then—stillness.

Sophie burst through the trees moments later, dropping to her knees beside him.

"Chris!" she gasped, shaking him gently. "Come on, wake up. Please!"

There was no response. His body lay motionless, his chest rising and falling in shallow, unsteady breaths.

Her hands trembled as she pressed them against him, her soul essence flickering weakly as she tried to assess his injuries. But the battle had drained her, exhaustion clawing at her limbs.

She sucked in a sharp breath, forcing down the panic threatening to overtake her. The distant sounds of combat still raged in the background—swords clashing, fire crackling, the screams of warriors locked in battle. But at this moment, none of it mattered.

"I won't let this be the end," she whispered, determination flaring in her eyes

Vincent descended into the clearing with a heavy, ominous thud, the force of his landing sending cracks through the earth. His massive, shadowy wings folded behind him, their dark presence looming over the battlefield like a storm waiting to break. Around him, the swirling mass of shadow demons recoiled from their assault, their grotesque forms dissolving into black tendrils that slithered back toward him. The inky darkness coiled around his body, merging seamlessly into his form as he absorbed their essence.

The air grew deathly cold. A suffocating pressure weighed down on the exhausted warriors who stood scattered around the clearing, their breaths shallow, their bodies battered from the relentless battle.

This was no longer the Vincent they had once known.

The man who had once led Michael's squad of the Angel Corps, their trusted captain, was gone—twisted into something monstrous. His towering frame radiated an unearthly power, his once-human features sharpened into something more demonic, his glowing crimson eyes burning with an unnatural intensity. The vast, leathery wings at his back only added to his terrible new form, a grotesque fusion of man, angel, and something far darker.

Vincent surveyed the battlefield with a slow, predatory gaze, his lips curling into a smile. He exuded a twisted confidence, his mere presence oppressive, suffocating.

When he spoke, his voice rang through the clearing—smooth, assured, and laced with undeniable menace.

"I, Vincent, former captain of Michael's squad of the Angel Corps, have been granted a promotion." He spread his arms wide, the dark energy around him crackling like a living thing. "A transformation into something far greater than any of you could ever hope to comprehend."

Arrogance dripped from his every word as he flexed his clawed hand, tendrils of darkness writhing around his fingers.

"With the demonic power of Sargatanas, the soul essence of lightning and ice, and the ethereal flame itself, I have ascended beyond the limits of mortality. Beyond the limits of angels and demons alike." His smile widened, teeth gleaming in the dim light. "I have become the pinnacle of human evolution… and demonkind."

Vincent took a slow step forward, the ground cracking beneath his foot as if the earth itself recoiled from his presence. His voice was steady, unshaken, carrying the weight of absolute dominance.

"I offer you all a choice," he declared, his voice reverberating through the clearing like a death knell. "Surrender peacefully. Kneel before your new ruler of Earth."

A chilling silence followed.

No one moved. No one spoke.

The warriors stood frozen, their minds racing, their bodies tense as they struggled to comprehend what stood before them—and how, if at all, they could stop him.

25

Lightning Strikes Twice

"Chris!! Chris!!"

Sophie's voice echoed through the chaos, distant and distorted, barely piercing the haze clouding his mind. Chris blinked sluggishly, his head throbbing in sync with the erratic beat of his faltering heart. His vision blurred, a swirl of flickering lights and indistinct shapes shifting in and out of focus. The world around him felt unreal, like a dream unraveling at the edges, slipping beyond his grasp.

Something warm anchored him—Sophie's hand, her grip tight, grounding. But then, suddenly, it was gone. The warmth vanished, replaced by the chilling emptiness that followed. He barely registered the moment she let go, barely saw the desperate determination in her retreating form as she sprinted back into the fray. Her amulet pulsed weakly against the darkness, her movements frantic, unrelenting.

Chris tried to move, but his limbs remained useless, weighted down by exhaustion and something deeper—something missing. He forced his head to the side, pain lancing through his skull like a jagged blade.

Through his dazed vision, the battlefield came into focus.

The clearing was a fractured war zone, illuminated by Vincent's frost-laced aura and the eerie glow of the shadow demons swarming the warriors. The ground was cracked and scorched, littered with debris and the remnants of shattered trees.

Giuseppe moved like a tempest, his strikes sharp and calculated, his blade crackling with arcs of lightning as he clashed with Vincent's monstrous shadow constructs. Eli swung his Titanroot Hammer in devastating arcs, each blow sending shock waves rippling through the horde of demons, but the creatures reformed, undeterred. Sophie was everywhere at once, her vines lashing out, splitting through the darkness as she shielded her allies, her face hardened with resolve despite the exhaustion weighing her down.

Chris squeezed his eyes shut, reaching inward, searching for the fire and lightning that had once coursed through his veins. He reached for the familiar spark, for the roaring heat that had always answered his call.

But there was nothing.

No flame, no crackling surge of power.

Just a hollow emptiness where his strength used to be.

"I lost everything."

The thought echoed in Chris's mind, a whisper that grew into a deafening roar. A lump formed in his throat, and he clenched his jaw, forcing himself to stay composed. But the memories came unbidden, crashing over him like a tidal wave, relentless and cruel.

Visions of his original timeline tore through his mind, vivid and merciless.

He saw his father fall, his body crumpling lifelessly to the ground while Chris stood frozen, paralyzed by horror. He saw his mother's tear-streaked face, her cries of anguish ringing in his ears as their home was consumed by raging flames. And then—the fire. The fire he could no longer summon. It had devoured everything, reducing his world to nothing but ash and ghosts.

A crushing weight settled on his chest, a dread so suffocating it felt as if it would break him from the inside out. He was there again—trapped in the past, powerless, watching everything he loved slip through his fingers.

His breath hitched. A trembling hand pressed against his chest as his vision blurred.

"Why now?" The words barely left his lips, lost in the chaos surrounding him. His voice was weak, fragile. *"Why does it feel*

like I'm back there again?"

Tears pricked at the corners of his eyes, threatening to spill, mixing with the pain and despair flooding his body. He clenched his fists, his nails biting into his palms, grounding himself against the rising tide of hopelessness. But it wasn't enough. The battlefield, the present—none of it felt real anymore.

Somewhere in the distance, Sophie's voice called his name. Faint. Distant. A beacon he could barely register in the storm of his mind.

Chris forced his eyes open, staring up at the canopy of trees above. The moonlight filtering through the branches was pale and cold, indifferent to his suffering. It mocked him with its serenity, untouched by war, untouched by loss.

He felt small. Insignificant. Like the broken remnants of a person who had once believed he could change the world.

One by one, the warriors fell.

Their strength, their resolve—it was nothing against the monstrous power Vincent had become. He towered over them, his shadowy tendrils shifting like living nightmares, his frost-laden aura blanketing the battlefield in a suffocating chill. The clearing, once alive with the clash of soul essence and steel, was now a graveyard of broken resistance.

Giuseppe charged first, his lightning-infused blade crackling with raw energy. His strikes were precise, aimed at any weakness in Vincent's defenses, but the shadows swarmed him. Tendrils coiled around his limbs, slowing his movements like vines choking out the last breath of life. Vincent barely moved, the frost radiating from his form deflecting the blows with effortless ease. Then, with a flick of his wrist, a massive shadow construct slammed into Giuseppe, sending him crashing into the ground. His blade tumbled from his grip, sparking against the dirt. He gritted his teeth, trying to push himself up, but the weight of Vincent's darkness pinned him where he lay.

Eli swung his Titanroot Hammer, each strike sending tremors through the earth. The force shattered the shadows momentarily, breaking them apart in bursts of green energy. But it wasn't enough. The creatures reformed, their hollow eyes gleaming with relentless hunger as they surged toward him once more. He planted his feet, lifted his hammer again—but his strength was waning. His breaths came ragged, his limbs heavy with exhaustion. The tide of darkness engulfed him, forcing him to his knees.

Mei's fire whip snapped through the air, arcs of blazing embers slicing through the shadows. She moved with the grace of a dancer, each strike precise, her flames burning away the darkness. But Vincent's frost surged, snuffing out her fire before it could even reach him. The whip dimmed, its flames sputtering into embers. Mei's eyes widened in horror as a shadow tendril lashed out, striking her with brutal force. She was flung backward, slamming into the ground, her fire extinguished. She groaned, struggling to rise, but her body barely obeyed.

Sophie fought with everything she had left. Her amulet flared defiantly, summoning thick vines that lashed out at the darkness, forming barriers between her fallen allies and the advancing tide. She refused to yield, refused to let them fall without a fight. But Vincent was beyond her now. His frost aura swept through the battlefield, freezing the vines mid-motion, shattering them like brittle glass. A massive shadow construct struck her, sending her tumbling across the ground. She gasped for breath, forcing herself up, only to be knocked back down again. Her amulet flickered weakly, the light dimming.

Allegra stood her ground, the water of her trident shifting and pulsing like a living entity. She summoned waves of fluid force, her strikes sharp and calculated, sending cutting streams slicing through the dark. For a moment, she seemed to hold her own, weaving between attacks, her movements as fluid as the element she wielded. But then Vincent turned his gaze on her. With a cruel smirk, he sent a pulse of frost through the air, freezing the water mid-motion, turning her own weapon against her. The ice traveled up her trident, crawling up her arms, locking her movements. A shadow tendril lashed out, striking her square in the chest, sending her sprawling across the battlefield.

And then, there was silence.

Vincent stood at the center of it all—untouched, unbothered. Around him, the warriors who had once dared to defy him now lay scattered, weapons discarded, soul essence flickering like dying embers. His monstrous wings loomed, an omen of despair, his breath steaming in the frozen night air.

"You are all so *predictable,*" he sneered, his voice dripping with dark amusement. He lifted a clawed hand, and the shadows twisted at his command, forming a grotesque throne behind him. With a calculated ease, he lowered himself onto it, surveying the battlefield like a king overseeing his conquered lands.

Chris watched in horror, his body too weak to move, his heart pounding like a war drum against his ribs. His father, his friends—everyone he had fought for—defeated, crushed beneath Vincent's overwhelming power.

His fists clenched, nails digging into his palms as tears blurred his vision.

The fire and lightning that had once burned within him were gone. Stolen.

"I failed."

The words rang hollow in his mind, sinking deep into his chest like a weight he could never lift.

"I failed them all."

The clearing was silent, save for the crackle of Vincent's frost and the hum of his immense power.

And despair hung heavy in the air, suffocating what little hope remained.

Chris trembled as he fought to rise, his body battered, his breath ragged. The weight of his failure pressed down on him like an immovable force, crushing, suffocating. But somewhere deep within—beneath the exhaustion, the pain, the overwhelming despair—something primal stirred. Something that refused to let him stay down.

Vincent stood at the center of the battlefield, his monstrous form a monument to unchecked power. He gripped his blade— once a weapon of honor, now twisted, infused with shadow and laced with frost—and drove it into the earth with terrifying force. The ground trembled beneath him as waves of darkness pulsed outward, tendrils of shadow rippling across the clearing, corrupting everything they touched. The defeated warriors lay motionless around him, the weight of his presence alone enough to keep them subdued.

Vincent's glowing crimson eyes swept over the broken battle-field, his voice smooth, almost indifferent. "Before I kill each and every one of you," he mused, "I will offer you a choice. Kneel before me. Serve your new ruler, and I may let you live."

The words rang through the silence, heavy with finality.

Chris remained on his knees, his breath shallow, his muscles screaming in protest. Blood dripped from the corner of his mouth, his body wracked with exhaustion. But as Vincent's words sank in, something within him snapped. His fingers curled into the frozen earth, his nails digging deep. Slowly, inch by inch, he pushed himself up.

The pain was relentless. His legs shook beneath him, his vision blurred at the edges, but he forced himself to stand. His movements were sluggish, unsteady, but his resolve burned bright.

Across the battlefield, Vincent turned his gaze to him, cocking his head slightly, his lips twisting into an amused smirk. "You're not dead yet?" he mused, his voice dripping with mockery.

Chris exhaled sharply and spat blood onto the ground. His fists tightened at his sides, his body screaming for rest, for relief—but he ignored it. He met Vincent's gaze, his eyes filled not with fear, but defiance.

"I won't stop," he said, his voice raw but unwavering. "I'll never stop trying to defeat you."

Vincent chuckled, a slow, cold sound. "How noble," he said, his smirk widening. "But ultimately, pointless."

With a flick of his wrist, a tendril of pure shadow lashed out, moving like a whip through the air. Chris barely had time to react before it struck him with brutal force.

The impact sent him hurtling backward. He crashed into a tree with a sickening crack, pain detonating through his body like an explosion. The air was ripped from his lungs, and for a moment, he couldn't breathe.

Chris forced himself upright, his legs shaking beneath him, blood dripping from the corner of his mouth. Every breath burned, every muscle in his body screamed for relief, but he refused to give in. His vision blurred at the edges, his strength wavering, but he had to stand. For Sophie. For his father. For all of them.

But like clockwork, Vincent struck him down again.

The impact sent Chris crashing to the ground, his battered body groaning in protest. He barely had time to register the pain before a shadowy tendril lashed out, wrapping around him and slamming him into the earth.

Vincent towered over him, his presence suffocating, his voice dripping with mockery. "When will you give up?" he mused, tilting his head as if genuinely curious. "You're pathetic. Why keep trying when the outcome is so predictable?"

Chris coughed, the taste of iron thick in his mouth, but he still pushed himself up. His arms shook violently, but he refused to stay down.

Vincent's expression shifted, his amusement warping into something crueler. His smirk widened. "Oh, I know what will make you stop."

The shadows around him shifted, tendrils slithering across the battlefield like hungry vipers. Then, without warning, they coiled around Giuseppe.

Chris's heart nearly stopped.

His father was yanked into the air, Vincent's dark grip constricting around him like a vice. Giuseppe struggled, his lightning-infused blade crackling as he fought against the encroaching darkness, but the shadows only tightened.

"Your father's life," Vincent drawled, savoring every word, "is over."

Chris's breath hitched.

No.

Memories of his original timeline flooded his mind in a brutal wave. He saw it again—his father struck down, his mother's screams, the unbearable heat of the flames devouring their home. The helplessness, the agony—it crushed him, threatening to pull him under.

Not again.

His fingers dug into the dirt, his fists clenching with renewed determination. *I have to fix this. I have to stop him.*

"Vincent!" Chris roared, his voice raw with desperation. But his plea was drowned beneath Vincent's cold laughter.

Then, out of nowhere, thick vines shot through the air, striking Vincent like whips. The force yanked him off balance, his concentration momentarily broken.

Giuseppe fell, hitting the ground hard, but rolled to safety, gasping for breath.

Vincent spun, eyes blazing with fury. "Who dares—"

Sophie stood tall, her amulet pulsing with brilliant light, her hands outstretched as she summoned another wave of vines. The thick greenery lashed out, coiling around Vincent's limbs, pushing him back as she stepped protectively in front of Chris and Giuseppe.

"You petulant child," Vincent snarled, his voice slicing through the chaos like a blade. Shadows erupted from him in a cold, smothering wave, his aura freezing the vines mid-motion. They withered, snapping apart like brittle twigs as frost crawled along their lengths.

His crimson gaze locked onto Sophie, malice gleaming in his eyes.

"Your mother," he sneered, "was one of the greatest Soul Warriors to ever live. A true master of her craft." He took a slow step forward, his smirk widening.

"And you? You're nothing more than an average botanist playing hero."

Sophie's breath hitched, but she stood her ground, her vines twisting and growing rapidly around her, forming a living shield. She clenched her fists, her amulet pulsing with faint light.

"I'm not afraid of you," she said, her voice firm despite the slight tremor in her hands.

Vincent chuckled darkly. "Bravery is wasted on the weak."

With a flick of his wrist, shadowy tendrils shot forward, moving faster than Sophie could react. They coiled around her arms, her legs, tightening like chains. In an instant, they wrenched her off the ground and slammed her onto her knees before Chris.

Her amulet dimmed.

Her body trembled under the crushing force, her strength waning.

"No!" Chris roared, struggling violently against the shadows binding him. His muscles burned, but the restraints held fast, unyielding.

Vincent loomed over Sophie, his frosted blade materializing in his hand. He traced its edge with his fingers, the ice spreading from its core, radiating lethal intent.

"You'll make an excellent example," he mused, his voice cold and impassive. "Let your failure serve as a lesson to anyone foolish enough to defy me."

Chris's vision narrowed, his pulse pounding in his ears like a war drum.

Sophie's ragged breaths, the flicker of defiance in her eyes even as she faced death—everything else faded. His past and present blurred, colliding in a surge of emotion so powerful it felt as if something inside him was breaking open.

And then, in the midst of it all, she looked at him.

For the briefest moment, their eyes locked, and the battlefield fell away.

A flood of memories overtook him, vivid and unstoppable.

But they didn't stop at this timeline.

They pulled him back—further back—to a childhood long lost, to a life before everything was rewritten.

He saw her, younger, smaller, her dark curls bouncing as she darted across the gymnasium floor.

"Hi! I'm Sophie! Wanna play with us?"

She had approached him without hesitation, her grin wide, her voice full of warmth. He had been shy then, unsure of himself, hesitant to step forward. But something about her had drawn him in.

That was Sophie. She never waited for him to move—she pulled him forward, lifted him out of the silence he often found himself trapped in.

The memories unraveled faster. He saw her weaving through the hallways of his home, laughing as she tugged him by the wrist, insisting they play another game, another round of tag, another adventure of their own making.

He saw her at the dinner table, cheeks stuffed with bread, grinning as she joked with his father—his *father*—making Giuseppe laugh in a way Chris never could.

She wasn't just a friend back then.

She was family.

Chris's fists clenched so tightly his nails dug into his palms, his entire body trembling as his heart roared with newfound determination. He couldn't lose her. Not now. Not to *him*.

"I won't let this happen."

Gritting his teeth, he forced himself to move. His legs wobbled beneath him, his body weak, broken from Vincent's relentless onslaught. But he didn't care. He would stand, even if it killed him.

Sophie wasn't just a friend, wasn't just a comrade. She was his light in the darkest moments, the anchor that had kept him from slipping away. And as he looked at her now—her breath labored, her body beaten, but her defiant gaze never wavering—he *swore* he wouldn't fail her.

Not this time.

With a guttural growl, Chris pushed himself up, his legs screaming in protest, his fists trembling but steady. His vision blurred with pain, but he ignored it. He staggered forward, forcing his body to move, every step a battle against the crushing weight of exhaustion. He was almost there—just a little farther, just a little more—

And then the shadows struck.

Dark tendrils lashed out like serpents, wrapping around his limbs before he could react. In an instant, they coiled tight, constricting his arms and legs with a vice-like grip before yanking him off the ground.

Chris barely had time to cry out before they *slammed* him into the earth with bone-shattering force.

Pain exploded through his body, his vision flashing white. The impact left him gasping, struggling for breath, but the tendrils weren't done. Again and again, they whipped him into the ground, each strike sending fresh shock waves of agony through his battered frame.

By the time they lifted him again, his head lolled forward, blood dripping from his mouth, his limbs useless in their grip. The tendrils shifted, twisting his body upright, forcing him to hang suspended in front of Sophie.

She was still on her knees, bound and struggling, her face a mixture of pain and defiance.

Vincent towered over them both, his shadowy wings stretching wide, the sheer weight of his presence crushing the battlefield in oppressive darkness.

"You *both* have failed," Vincent declared, his voice cold and sharp as a blade.

Chris's breathing was ragged, his vision swimming. But when he locked eyes with Sophie, he still found her fighting. Her hands clenched against her restraints, her shoulders trembling, but she did not look away. She did not yield.

And neither would he.

Then, Vincent's voice rang out again.

"Hiroshi."

Chris's stomach dropped.

"Hand me his weapon."

A hush fell over the battlefield.

From the edge of the chaos, Hiroshi stepped forward. His movements were stiff, hesitant, but he did not disobey. In his hands, he held the Eclipse Blade.

Chris's breath hitched. *No. No, don't—*

Hiroshi's grip tightened on the hilt, his eyes flickering toward Chris for the briefest moment. A silent hesitation.

Then, finally, he stepped forward and placed the blade into Vincent's outstretched hand.

Chris felt something inside him *break.*

"NO!" he screamed, his voice raw with fury and anguish. He fought against the tendrils, his body twisting and thrashing with everything he had left. But they only tightened, digging into his flesh, cutting deep.

Vincent studied the blade with cruel amusement, running his clawed fingers along its edge. The weapon pulsed faintly, as if resisting, as if recognizing it was in the wrong hands.

"Such a powerful weapon," Vincent mused, tilting it slightly, admiring the craftsmanship. Then he scoffed, his expression twisting in disdain. *"And yet, in your hands, it was wasted."*

Chris's screams echoed through the clearing, wild and desperate. But before he could spit another curse, the tendrils snaked up his face, wrapping around his mouth, silencing him completely.

His muffled cries faded into nothing.

Vincent lifted the Eclipse Blade, his dark aura surging with terrifying power.

The sky above seemed to darken further, the air thick with cold, malevolent energy. The very earth beneath them seemed to hold its breath.

"This is the end," Vincent declared, his voice final.

Chris could do nothing but watch, powerless, as the blade—*his* blade—was turned against everything he held dear.

Time slowed.

The **Eclipse Blade** cut through the air, humming with sinister resonance, crackling with Vincent's unchecked power. The battlefield was bathed in its cold glow, its descent inevitable.

Chris thrashed against the tendrils constricting him, his muffled screams lost in the chaos. Sophie's wide, tear-filled eyes locked onto the blade, her body frozen in place as the moment stretched unbearably long.

She braced for the end.

Then—

"NO!"

A blur of motion. A streak of lightning.

Before anyone could react, Giuseppe threw himself between the blade and its intended victims.

The **Eclipse Blade** struck.

The dark steel sank into his chest, piercing through flesh and bone, its malevolent energy crackling as it consumed him from within. Giuseppe staggered, the force of the strike nearly driving him to the ground—but he *did not fall.* His body became the barrier, the final line of defense, shielding Sophie and Chris from Vincent's wrath.

Chris's world *shattered.*

"DAD!"

His scream ripped through the battlefield, raw and broken. The tendrils holding him faltered, then **shattered** completely as a surge of Giuseppe's power pulsed outward.

Giuseppe turned his head slightly, meeting his son's gaze with unwavering resolve. His face was pale, his breaths labored, but his eyes—his eyes *still burned* with the fire of a warrior.

"Chris…" he murmured, his voice weak but steady. Blood dripped from the corner of his mouth, staining his chin, but still, he managed a small, weary smile.

"I'm sorry."

The words struck Chris harder than any blade ever could.

"No, no, no—don't say that, not again—"

Giuseppe's body trembled, but his grip on the hilt of the blade **never wavered.**

"Tell your mother… and your sister… that I love them."

Chris choked on a sob, his whole body shaking. "Dad, please—"

Giuseppe's lips curved into the faintest of smiles.

"I love you, Chris."

Before Vincent could react, before anyone could stop him, Giuseppe *moved.*

His **hand clenched** around the hilt of the **Eclipse Blade**, still embedded in his chest. A deep, resonating hum filled the air as his soul essence surged. **Lightning crackled** across his body, wild and untamed, sparking through the veins of the weapon itself.

He met Vincent's gaze, his expression filled with something not even death could steal from him—**defiance.**

"This ends **NOW!**"

With an earth-shattering roar, Giuseppe **ripped the blade free from his own chest.**

A tidal wave of **pure lightning** exploded outward, the force so intense it turned the night into **day.** The sheer impact **obliterated** the shadows in its wake, tearing through Vincent and Hiroshi, hurling them backward with the force of a thunderstorm unleashed.

The battlefield trembled. The sky **cracked open** with the brilliance of the attack.

Then—silence.

Chris fell to his knees as the last of the tendrils dissolved into nothing. His entire body felt weightless, his breath caught in his throat as he **crawled** forward.

Giuseppe knelt on the ground, the remnants of his attack flickering and fading into the night like dying embers.

"Dad…" Chris gasped, his hands shaking as he reached for him.

Sophie scrambled beside him, her own hands trembling as she tried to steady Giuseppe, but his body was already failing him.

The once-vibrant man who had been an unstoppable force on the battlefield now looked at them with warmth, his strength fading, but his love unwavering.

He lifted a weak hand, placing it on Chris's shoulder. His

touch was light, but his words were heavy with meaning.

"**Protect each other,**" he whispered.

Chris felt his heart crack wide open.

"You're stronger together than you realize."

And with that, **Giuseppe's hand slipped away.**

Chris grasped his father's hand, his fingers trembling as he clung to the warmth that was already fading. Tears streamed freely down his face, his breath hitching between desperate sobs.

"Dad, no! You can't leave us! Please, stay with me!"

For a fleeting moment, Giuseppe's grip tightened—one last, faint squeeze. Then, his fingers slackened, his chest fell with a final breath, and his body went still.

Chris's anguished cry tore through the clearing, raw and unrelenting. It cut through the remnants of battle, silencing the warriors who remained. They stood frozen, their expressions stricken with disbelief, the weight of what they had just witnessed pressing down on them like a crushing tide.

Beside him, Sophie rested a trembling hand on his shoulder, silent tears slipping down her cheeks.

Then, laughter shattered the fragile stillness.

Low and cold at first, then growing, twisting with derision.

Vincent staggered to his feet, his body battered but far from broken. Shadows flickered around him, his power still dark and potent despite the force of Giuseppe's final attack. He rolled his shoulders, his crimson eyes gleaming with malice.

"How touching," he sneered. "A noble sacrifice... but ultimately futile."

Chris looked up, his grief twisting, hardening into something else. His hands curled into fists, his body trembling, but no longer from sorrow—from rage. The embers of his will reignited, but this was not the moment to strike. The wound was too fresh, his fury still raw and unfocused.

Not yet.

"Chris," Sophie said urgently, tugging at his arm. "We have to move. Now."

But Chris wasn't hearing her.

His breath came shallow, his chest constricting as he stared at his father's lifeless form. The image burned itself into his mind, overlapping with memories from a past he had desperately tried to change. The same moment, the same loss. No matter how hard he fought, no matter what choices he made—his father always died.

His hands trembled. His vision blurred. *Not again. Not this time.*

"Chris, please," Sophie urged, her voice thick with panic as Vincent took a slow step forward, his twisted grin widening. "We can't stay here! Move!"

Chris's head tilted slightly, his body stiff as he rose to his feet. Sophie instinctively took a step back.

Something in him had shifted.

The air around him felt heavier, darker. His presence— once desperate and weary—now radiated something cold and dangerous. It sent a chill through Sophie that had nothing to do with Vincent's frost.

Chris's eyes flickered toward the Eclipse Blade, lying beside his father's body.

His hand closed around its hilt.

Sparks flickered faintly from the weapon, the remnants of its stolen power responding to his touch.

"Chris…" Sophie whispered, her voice tight with fear. "What are you doing?"

He didn't answer.

His grip on the blade tightened as he turned, his gaze locking onto Vincent with an unrelenting fury that burned hotter than any fire he had ever summoned.

"You took him from me," Chris growled, his voice raw, his breath unsteady. He tightened his grip on the hilt, fury bleeding through every word he spoke.

"Again."

Vincent's smirk deepened, his wings unfurling slightly, watching him with amusement.

"Oh? So you've decided to stand again?" he mocked. "Haven't you learned by now? You're nothing without your powers. Without them, you're just a boy with a stick."

Chris exhaled sharply, his grip steady, his body rigid with fury.

"You don't get to talk about power," he spat. "Not when you steal it from others. Not when you—" His voice faltered for just a moment, the grief clawing at his throat before he forced it down. His jaw tightened.

"Not when you kill the people I care about."

Vincent chuckled darkly, his shadowy tendrils shifting and curling around him in anticipation.

"Careful, boy," he taunted. "You're walking a fine line between bravery and stupidity. But I must admit… I do enjoy watching you squirm."

"Chris, no!" Sophie pleaded, stepping forward, reaching for him.

But Chris lifted a hand—stopping her.

His voice was calm. Firm.

"Sophie. **Move**."

His tone left no room for argument.

Vincent's voice dripped with disdain.

"What could you possibly hope to accomplish, boy? Look at yourself—drained, weak, *powerless.* You're no match for me."

Chris took a step forward, the Eclipse Blade heavy in his grip. His body ached, exhaustion clawing at him, but none of it mattered. Not anymore.

Vincent chuckled, the sound slithering through the clearing like a cruel melody. He spread his arms wide, his wings casting jagged shadows across the battlefield.

"Then come, boy." His crimson eyes gleamed with malice. "Let me teach you the meaning of despair."

Chris tightened his grip around the hilt, his heart pounding like a war drum. Images flooded his mind—his father's final breath, his mother's tears, the flames that had swallowed his old timeline whole. Every loss, every failure, every moment he had stood helpless while the people he loved were taken from him.

This wasn't about revenge.

This was about breaking the cycle.

It was about ensuring that no one else suffered the way he had.

He took another step. Then another.

Sophie's voice rang out behind him, frantic, desperate.

"Chris! Don't do this! Please!"

But he didn't stop.

He didn't even look back.

His resolve was set.

This was his fight.

And no matter the cost—he would face Vincent.

26

Time Moving Slow

The clearing was a battlefield of chaos.

Frost blanketed the ground, shadows slithered like living

creatures, and Sophie's vines flickered weakly against the overwhelming darkness. At the center of it all stood Vincent—monstrous, unwavering, radiating power so dense it seemed to press against reality itself. Shadowy tendrils rippled outward from his form, moving with a will of their own, and in his grasp, his frost-laced blade gleamed under the moonlight, eager for more blood.

Chris stood firm. His chest heaved, his muscles burned, but he refused to give in. His father's lifeless body lay just feet away. Sophie was still in danger. And this monster—this *thing* that had stolen everything from him—stood before him, mocking everything he had left.

Vincent's voice sliced through the night, cutting deeper than any blade.

"You're wasting my time, boy," he said, his tone laced with amusement. "Do you think standing there, trembling, will make a difference? Face it—without your powers, you're nothing." He paused, his smirk widening. "Just like your father."

A dagger of white-hot rage plunged into Chris's chest.

A roar ripped from his throat as he lunged, swinging the Eclipse Blade with everything he had. There was no fire, no lightning—just raw, furious *will.* He swung again. And again. Each strike wild, reckless, fueled by grief and rage.

Vincent barely needed to move. He dodged effortlessly, a cruel smile tugging at his lips as he watched Chris burn himself out.

Then, with practiced ease, he parried the next strike and drove the hilt of his blade into Chris's ribs.

The impact stole the air from Chris's lungs. He staggered back, clutching his side, pain flaring through him like a fresh wound.

"Pathetic," Vincent sneered. "You're weak. That's why you'll lose."

Chris forced himself to stand, his grip tightening, the pain barely registering through the haze of his fury. He charged again. His blade clashed against Vincent's, the sound sharp, like shattering ice. He swung wildly, desperate, trying to break through.

Vincent didn't even flinch. He deflected each blow, his frost-coated blade meeting Chris's strikes with ease, until finally—

Shadows surged forward, wrapping around Chris's legs like chains.

Before he could react, they yanked him off his feet.

Chris hit the ground with a brutal thud, the Eclipse Blade flying from his grasp. His body throbbed, his breathing ragged, but before he could even move, Vincent was already towering over him, his presence suffocating.

"Do you see now?" he mused, tilting his head. "You're powerless. Broken." His voice dipped lower, cold and absolute.

"Just like your father."

Chris's breath came in short, shallow gasps. The words twisted inside him, wrapping around his heart like a vice. His gaze drifted to Giuseppe's motionless body, and something inside him cracked.

It's happening again.

Images from the past flooded his mind. His father—strong, proud, unshaken. And then—his father, lifeless, unmoving. The two images bled together, an unbroken cycle, a nightmare he couldn't escape.

No matter what he did. No matter how hard he tried. His father always died.

Chris's hands trembled. His vision blurred.

No. Not this time.

Somewhere in the depths of his mind, a voice—steady, familiar—called out to him.

"Chris."

His father's voice.

"Having emotions, even expressing them, is fine. We're human. Anger, fear, grief—these are natural, and they have their place. But letting them guide your actions? That's a formula for disaster. When you let emotions take the wheel, you make yourself vulnerable. And vulnerability like that will get you killed."

Chris clenched his fists.

His father wasn't here to pull him back this time.

But his words were.

He forced himself to breathe.

The chaos around him became distant, muffled, as if submerged beneath water. He focused on his heartbeat, on Sophie's voice somewhere in the distance, on the wisdom his father had spent years trying to teach him.

The blind, burning rage that had consumed him moments ago began to fade.

In its place, something sharper took root.

Something focused.

"Let go of the rage."

The words came from somewhere else now—soft, distant, almost melodic.

"Focus. Fire is your ally. Lightning is your ally. Time is your ally. Take it back."

Chris's eyes snapped open.

The world around him shifted.

The shadows seemed to slow. The tendrils that bound him wavered for the briefest moment. The air felt *different*—charged, heavier, still.

Vincent narrowed his eyes.

"What's this?" he muttered, watching as Chris began to rise to his feet.

Still breathing.

Still standing.

Chris ignored him.

His fingers reached out, closing around the Eclipse Blade's hilt.

The weight felt different now—not just heavy, but grounding. Familiar. A piece of himself he had nearly lost.

Vincent's frost aura flared as he steadied his stance, irritation flickering across his face.

"You're going to regret this," he growled, power surging around him once more.

Chris exhaled slowly, his grip firm, his mind clear.

He took a step forward, the blade steady in his grasp.

His lips curled into the faintest smirk.

"You talk too much."

Chris moved with precision, every step deliberate, his body weaving through Vincent's relentless attacks like a shadow in motion. The reckless, desperate swings from before were gone, replaced by sharp, measured strikes. Every dodge, sidestep, and counter forced Vincent to adjust, to react to an opponent who no longer fought with blind emotion but with calculated intent.

Vincent's frost-covered blade cut through the air, shadow tendrils lashing toward Chris like vipers. But Chris saw them coming. He ducked low, pivoted sharply, slipping through the narrowest gaps in Vincent's attacks. His blade found its mark again and again, carving into Vincent's form with swift, precise strikes. Sparks flew as steel clashed against frost and shadow, momentarily illuminating the battlefield.

Vincent's expression twisted with frustration. His attacks became more forceful, his movements more erratic.

"What is this?" he snarled, disbelief creeping into his voice. "You're nothing without your powers!"

Chris didn't respond. He remained focused, his blade a blur as it slashed across Vincent's chest, leaving a faint glowing scar of energy in its wake. Vincent stumbled back, eyes narrowing as he took in this new, composed version of his opponent.

Sophie watched from the sidelines, her heart hammering. The Chris in front of her was different—calm, controlled, unshaken. It wasn't just his skill with the blade that had changed; it was the way he carried himself. The reckless boy who fought with raw emotion had vanished. What remained was someone sharper, stronger, more dangerous.

A surge of determination coursed through her. Tightening her grip on her amulet, she scanned the battlefield, waiting for an opening.

Chris ducked under a wide arc of Vincent's blade and lunged, slicing deep into his side. The demon roared, staggering slightly.

Now.

Sophie's amulet flared to life as thick vines erupted from the ground. They struck Vincent hard, wrapping around his arms and legs like iron shackles, yanking him off balance.

"Now, Chris!" Sophie shouted, urgency lacing her voice.

Chris didn't hesitate. He surged forward, his blade flashing as he delivered a devastating slash across Vincent's torso. The force of the blow sent the demon reeling, his frost aura flickering, his form struggling to hold its shape.

Vincent let out a guttural growl, his eyes burning with fury. "You insolent pests!" His shadowy tendrils writhed violently, lashing out as he fought to regain control. But Chris and Sophie moved in perfect sync, their attacks relentless, their coordination seamless.

Every strike from Chris forced Vincent open for Sophie's vines to slam him back. Every lash of her vines created an opening for Chris to land another blow. They pressed Vincent harder and harder, forcing him into retreat.

For the first time, the tide of battle shifted.

Vincent's movements became erratic, his aura flickering, his tendrils slower to react.

Then, his frustration boiled over.

"I'VE HAD ENOUGH OF BOTH OF YOU!" he roared, the force of his voice shaking the battlefield.

With a violent thrust of his arms, a blast of frost exploded outward.

The wave of ice hit like a shock wave, hurling Chris and Sophie backward. They crashed onto the frozen ground, the cold biting into their skin like shards of glass.

Chris gasped, pain shooting through his body as he struggled to rise. His limbs were heavy, his body battered, but there was no time to recover.

Vincent strode toward them, his frost-coated blade dragging against the frozen earth, sending sparks into the air. His shadowy tendrils slithered and coiled around him, pulsing with malevolence.

"No mercy," Vincent said, his voice low, final. "No second chances."

Chris's breath came in short, labored gasps. His fingers tightened around the hilt of the Eclipse Blade, its edge dim, battered—a reflection of his own exhaustion. He looked up, his vision blurring, as Vincent loomed over him, his presence suffocating.

"You've fought well enough to amuse me," Vincent mused, his smirk returning. "But this ends now."

The shadows around him surged. Tendrils shot from the ground, moving like living serpents.

Before Chris could react, they slammed into him, pinning him to the ground. The impact knocked the air from his lungs, the crushing force leaving him breathless. He struggled against the restraints, but they only tightened, suffocating him in their grip.

"You're just like your father," he said, voice laced with mock sympathy.

Chris clenched his jaw, his whole body tense with fury.

Vincent leaned in closer, his smirk widening.

"Defiant to the end," he said softly.

He tilted his head.

"But ultimately powerless."

Chris clenched his jaw, every syllable of Vincent's words slicing deeper than the icy tendrils constricting his body. His chest heaved, each breath sharp and labored, his muscles screaming under the strain. The weight of his father's sacrifice pressed against him, merging with the sight of Sophie standing defiant beside him. He couldn't let it end like this.

Vincent raised his blade high, frost trailing from its edge, the air around them growing colder with each passing second. The temperature plummeted, the battlefield frozen in anticipation of the final strike.

But Chris didn't look away.

He refused to close his eyes.

His gaze locked onto Vincent's, and in that moment, the world began to fade—the battlefield, the pain, even the suffocating cold. A strange, unfamiliar calm settled over him, sharpening his focus like the edge of a honed blade.

Somewhere deep within, a voice whispered through the chaos. Soft, steady, serene.

"Feel it. Time bends for those who are ready to embrace it."

Chris inhaled, then exhaled. Slowly. Steadily. Each breath felt more deliberate, as if grounding him to something greater than himself. The frost encasing his limbs didn't seem as constricting. The shadowy tendrils that had pinned him in place loosened, their grip no longer absolute.

Then, the world slowed.

Vincent's blade, once a streak of death slicing through the air, now moved with agonizing lethargy, its arc unfolding like the slow swing of a pendulum. Chris could see it all—every crack along the ice-layered steel, every flicker of shadow essence pulsating through it. Time itself seemed to stretch, unraveling in front of him, allowing him to see the strike before it could land.

The voice returned, clearer now, resonating within him.

"You're ready. Let go of your fear. Trust in the flow of time."

A soft silver glow flickered around him, faint at first, like the first light of dawn breaking through the darkness. Then it grew, steady and rhythmic, pulsing from his core.

Chris let go.

The shadows that bound him disintegrated, crumbling into dust as his body felt weightless, unrestricted.

Vincent's narrowed eyes flickered with irritation. He noticed.

"What is this?" he growled, the first traces of unease creeping into his voice. "Still clinging to hope, are we?"

Chris rose to his feet, slow and unhurried, the silver aura around him shifting like flowing water. There was no urgency in his movements, no frantic struggle—only quiet certainty. He lifted the Eclipse Blade, its edge shimmering faintly as the energy coalesced around it, merging with him in a way that felt natural.

Vincent's blade came down, a wave of frost and darkness surging forward to consume him.

Chris stepped to the side.

Effortlessly.

The attack missed by a breath, passing harmlessly by as though Vincent had telegraphed his move *seconds* in advance.

The silver glow around Chris intensified. For the first time, Vincent's smirk wavered.

He saw it now.

Chris wasn't just moving faster.

He was *ahead*.

Vincent recoiled, his grip tightening on his weapon. "What… is this?" His voice, for the first time, trembled with frustration.

Chris didn't answer.

His fingers curled tighter around the hilt of his blade, his eyes steady, unwavering. The world around them blurred, its edges bending like ripples in water.

Then he took a step forward, his movements fluid, precise.

And for the first time, Vincent was too slow.

The battlefield fell into an eerie silence, the chaos of moments before now replaced by an uneasy stillness. Vincent stood rigid, his crimson eyes narrowing as he studied the silver aura pulsing around Chris. This wasn't fire, nor was it lightning—it was something else entirely, something unknown. And Vincent hated the unknown.

Scattered across the clearing, the warriors—Lilith, Mei, Hiroshi, Eli, Allegra, Sophie, and the others—lay battered and broken, their bodies writhing with pain. Their breaths were shallow, their limbs weak, but their eyes remained locked on the confrontation unfolding before them. In the center of it all, Chris stood unmoving, calm, his chest rising and falling in measured rhythm. The silver glow surrounding him pulsed like a steady heartbeat, radiating outward in soft, mesmerizing waves.

Vincent's fingers tightened around the hilt of his frost-covered blade. His grip was ironclad, but for the first time, there was something else beneath his rage—hesitation.

"What is this?" he muttered, voice barely more than a breath. But his moment of uncertainty didn't last. His face twisted with fury. "Enough of this!"

His roar split the air, his rage erupting in a storm of power.

Vincent launched forward, his shadowy tendrils exploding outward like a tidal wave, his blade gleaming with frost and malice. The ground beneath him cracked and splintered with the force of his charge. Frost and shadow fused into a lethal force, every strike a perfect blend of chaos and precision.

Chris remained still. Unshaken.

The voice that had guided him before returned, no longer distant, no longer faint. It was clear now—calm yet commanding, resonating deep within him.

"Time bends for those who listen. Feel it in your soul."

Chris inhaled, slow and steady. The silver glow around him brightened, flowing along his body like liquid light. And then— he understood.

He wasn't reacting to Vincent's attacks.

He was ahead of them.

Vincent's blade came down in a brutal arc, but Chris had already moved. A tendril shot toward his legs, but he twisted effortlessly, stepping just outside its reach. Another slash, another strike—each one more furious than the last—yet Chris danced between them, his movements impossibly smooth.

To the warriors watching, it was unreal. Vincent's attacks appeared sluggish, as if the very air resisted his movements. Every swing, every lunge—it was as though Chris had already seen it all before.

Vincent's frustration boiled over. His strikes turned wild, reckless, his form blurring as he unleashed a barrage of frost and shadow. The tendrils lashed out violently, seeking to ensnare Chris, but they found nothing but empty space. His blade flashed like lightning, cutting through the air with terrifying speed—yet Chris was faster.

Even through the haze of pain, the warriors watching saw the impossible unfold before them.

Sophie, still clutching her side as she struggled to sit up, whispered in awe, "Chris…"

Vincent, panting now, slowed his assault. His crimson eyes flickered with something rare—something foreign to him. Frustration, yes. But beneath that, buried deep, was the first spark of fear.

"How…?" he rasped, his voice laced with disbelief. "How are you doing this?"

Chris didn't answer. There was no need. He wasn't thinking anymore. He was moving, flowing with the rhythm of the moment, the pulse of time itself guiding his every step. For the first time in this battle, he wasn't reacting to Vincent.

He was controlling the fight.

The silver glow surrounding him flared, illuminating the battlefield as if dawn itself had broken. Vincent lunged again, his shadows surging forward like an unstoppable force, but

Chris barely seemed to notice. He pivoted smoothly, the tendrils brushing past him as another slash from the eclipse blade struck Vincent's body.

The voice within Chris returned, stronger than ever, steady as the flow of time itself.

"Time flows with you now. Trust it. Move as it moves."

Chris exhaled.

And this time, he moved first.

The world around Chris shifted, the battlefield stretching and warping as if submerged in a slow-moving current. Every sound—the crackling frost, the distant groans of the fallen, the wind rustling through the shattered trees—stretched into elongated echoes. Time itself bent at his command, and within this altered reality, Chris moved with a grace and precision he had never known.

Vincent staggered, blood seeping from the gash Chris had carved into his side. His frost armor cracked, his shadows recoiling, and for the first time, his expression twisted—not with control, but fury.

"I've had enough of this!" he roared.

With a snarl, he hurled his frost-covered blade aside. It clattered across the battlefield, forgotten. His body arched unnaturally—bones snapping, muscles tearing, wings stretching. But it didn't stop. He grew larger. Shadows surged around him as jagged obsidian scales spread down his limbs. Horns branched farther, curving like twisted antlers. His chest split open with molten light, and his wings—already massive— expanded until they blotted out the fractured sky.

Vincent had become something monstrous. A titan of chaos. More demon than man.

"You are nothing!" the beast bellowed, voice deep and broken.

"I stole this power. I surpassed every boundary—angel, man, soul. And you—!"

Chris didn't flinch.

His silver aura surged—not wild, but steady. His form shifted as the light climbed higher up his body. His presence deepened, elevated—not grotesque like Vincent, but transcendent. His transformation mirrored Vincent's, not in mass, but in magnitude.

Two forces—equal in power, opposite in nature—stood across from one another.

Vincent lunged, claws outstretched, wings tearing at the air.

Chris moved with purpose.

In one fluid motion, he sidestepped the charge and swung the Eclipse Blade. The strike was clean, precise—cutting deep through Vincent's twisted chest, right through the stolen power's core.

For a heartbeat, the world held still.

Then—

A torrent of the ethereal flame and lightning essence burst from the wound, spiraling into the sky in a blinding column of light. It curled downward, wrapping around Chris like a returning force—his stolen power drawn back to its rightful bearer. Light consumed him, but he stood unwavering, framed in radiant fire, whole again.

Vincent screamed.

His massive frame convulsed, shadows writhing wildly as more energy tore free. But he did not fall. His monstrous wings beat the air, barely holding him aloft. Smoke rose from the gash in his chest, his breath ragged, molten blood dripping into the cracked earth.

Chris watched in silence as the light faded. His silver aura glowed, the Eclipse Blade steady in his hand. Calm in victory. Unshaken.

Chris stood tall, bathed in light and fury, his body thrumming with reclaimed power.

Across from him, Vincent staggered, clutching his side, blood searing against shattered frost. His aura flickered violently, no longer stable—driven by panic, rage, and disbelief.

"This ends now!" Vincent roared, his voice tearing through the chaos like thunder.

From the void behind him, dozens of new shadow demons emerged, slithering and clawing their way into existence, their shrieks cutting through the night. They circled Chris like predators, their forms flickering between solid and smoke, hungry and waiting.

Chris's breath steadied.

The silver glow around him blazed brighter—flame burning hotter, lightning crackling sharper—as it surged against the creeping dark. Power coiled around him in an ethereal radiance, pure and unwavering, untouched by Vincent's chaos, uncorrupted by shadow.

Then—

Time stopped.

The battlefield fell silent.

The world stood still.

27

Thirty Years Ago

Chris exhaled deeply, surrendering himself fully to the flow of time. The chaos of the battlefield faded, replaced by an eerie stillness, as if the world itself held its breath. His silver aura pulsed rhythmically, syncing with his heartbeat, steady and deliberate.

"Time bends for those who listen."

The woman's voice whispered through his mind, a guiding force through the storm.

For the first time, Chris saw everything.

The gaps in Vincent's attacks. The openings in his defense. The fractures in his power.

His mind cleared. His purpose solidified.

"Let's finish this."

He surged forward.

A Temporal Echo remained behind—a perfect afterimage of himself mid-sprint, confusing Vincent and his demons as time resumed its flow.

Vincent snarled and attacked. He cleaved through the decoy with full force, sending a shockwave across the battlefield. His roar of triumph echoed—but it was hollow.

Chris was already behind him.

Before Vincent could react, Freeze Field activated.

Time shattered like glass.

Vincent froze mid-motion, his tendrils locked in place, his body suspended between seconds. His crimson eyes widened in shock, flickering with the first trace of fear as he struggled against the impossible force holding him still.

Chris didn't hesitate.

Summoning every ounce of his strength, he combined Time Distortion with the Ethereal Flame and the electric power of the Eclipse Blade.

The very air rippled as he struck. The blade sliced through Vincent's chest, cleaving deep, tearing through the demonic power he had hoarded for himself.

A wave of light erupted from the wound.

The battlefield trembled beneath the weight of unraveling power.

Vincent convulsed, his body seizing as the shadows that had once consumed him shuddered and writhed, their grip weakening. The stolen energy inside him, an unnatural fusion of stolen might, began to tear apart at the seams. The dark tendrils that had once bound him splintered, dissolving into nothingness as his form flickered between what he had become and what he once was.

The corruption was breaking.

Chris stood frozen in that moment, his breath heavy, his hands trembling from exhaustion. Then—his gaze fell to the ground near Vincent's fallen form.

A blade.

His father's blade.

A flood of memories rushed through him.

The sound of Giuseppe's voice, warm and steady. The weight of his father's hand on his shoulder after a long day of training. The quiet nights spent together, going over battle strategies. The laughter at the dinner table, the lessons, the wisdom.

"Whenever your back is against a wall," his father's voice echoed through his mind, *"or you come across a seemingly unsolvable problem—relax. Seek out the pattern, no matter how obscure. Everything's connected, so keep an open mind. Remember, you always have options. Trust in your knowledge. Trust in yourself."*

Chris bent down, gripping his father's blade with reverence. The cool steel felt familiar, comforting.

Memories pulsed through him, fueling him.

As he turned back to Vincent, his resolve was unshakable.

Time still held its breath as Chris moved.

He placed his father's blade alongside the Eclipse Blade. The two weapons hummed in unison, their energy merging, vibrating with the power reclaimed.

Then, with a fierce battle cry, Chris plunged the Eclipse Blade and his father's sword into Vincent's chest.

A cataclysmic surge of lightning erupted.

Everything fractured.

The battlefield blurred.

Light consumed everything.

And then—

Chris felt himself falling.

Not through space, not through time, but through something deeper.

A rush of air. A shift. A pull.

Then—silence.

Chris opened his eyes.

The battlefield was gone.

Instead, he stood in a dimly lit hallway, the soft glow of floating lanterns casting shifting patterns across the polished stone floor. The air carried the scent of aged parchment and faint traces of magic, woven into the very foundation of the school. Distant voices echoed from unseen classrooms, mingling with the rhythmic footsteps of students moving through the grand corridors.

He knew this place.

Eden Preparatory Academy.

Chris's breath caught as movement flickered in the distance.

A boy—young, full of life, his laughter light and unburdened— ran through the hall, his uniform slightly untucked, his energy boundless.

Chris's heart clenched.

He knew exactly who it was.

His father.

Chris watched the boy enter the classroom, his breath catching, his mind racing to make sense of what he was seeing.

"Is this my father's memory?" he muttered under his breath.

A voice behind him answered.

"No. It's mine."

Chris turned sharply, his body tensing. His hands instinctively reached for his weapon—but it wasn't there.

Vincent sat on the steps of a grand staircase behind him, no longer monstrous, no longer radiating the overwhelming power he had wielded moments ago. He looked human again. But more than that, he looked tired.

Chris took a cautious step back. "How are we here? When is here?"

Vincent exhaled, resting his arms on his knees. His gaze drifted toward the flickering lanterns that lined the corridor, watching them as if lost in thought.

"I remember this day," he murmured. "This was thirty years ago." He finally met Chris's stare, his voice quieter than usual. "As for how we got here… I think you have your power to thank for that."

Chris turned in awe, his eyes sweeping across the grand halls of Eden Preparatory Academy. His mind raced—how had his power brought him here? What had triggered this shift in time?

"You were hiding a third soul essence?" Vincent mused, watching Chris with intrigue. "Full of surprises, I see."

Chris barely heard him, still trying to make sense of what was happening. His power had taken him back thirty years into the past, but why? Before he could dwell on it, Vincent spoke again.

"This feels like Giuseppe's memory retrieval device."

Chris snapped his attention back to him. "You know about that?"

Vincent smirked slightly. "I helped him build it."

Chris blinked. That wasn't something he had expected to hear. Before he could press for more answers, movement in the hallway caught his eye.

A young boy—dressed in the same academy uniform as the others—ran full speed down the corridor, slipping through the classroom door just as the professor was about to close it.

Chris's eyes widened. "That was you?"

Vincent let out a rare laugh. "Spiritual Guidance 101," he said with a shake of his head. "I hated that class."

Chris stared at him, bewildered. This wasn't the Vincent he had come to know—the cold, calculating warrior who always seemed ten steps ahead of everyone else. The man standing before him now looked… relaxed. Amused, even.

For the first time, Chris saw a glimpse of the person Vincent had been before everything changed.

Chris turned away from the sight of young Vincent slipping into the classroom, his mind still struggling to reconcile the version of the man standing beside him with the carefree student he had just seen. The Vincent he knew was always unreadable, always five steps ahead, always calculating. But this Vincent, standing in a memory of his own past, felt different. More human.

He swallowed down the hesitation in his throat. There were too many things left unsaid between them, too many questions that had lingered for too long. If this was an opportunity to get answers, he wasn't going to waste it.

"Why do you hate my dad?" Chris asked, his voice quiet but

firm. He turned to Vincent, his gaze searching. "Why do you hate me?"

Vincent didn't flinch. He exhaled, rubbing a hand over his face as if Chris had asked him the most exhausting question in the world.

"I don't hate you," Vincent said simply. "And I don't hate Giuseppe, either."

Chris frowned. "Then why—"

"I just don't like not knowing," Vincent interrupted. His expression was unreadable again, but his tone was softer than usual, almost reflective. "Not understanding something means not being able to control it. And not being able to control something? That leads to loss."

Chris stared at him, the weight of those words settling between them. He thought about everything Vincent had done—the choices he had made, the risks he had taken. Had it all been to keep himself from feeling powerless? From repeating some kind of loss he never talked about?

"Then what about you?" Vincent asked, turning the conversation back on him. His eyes flickered with curiosity, but there was no malice behind them. "Why did you hide your power?"

Chris hesitated. He had spent so long avoiding that question, even from himself. His fingers twitched at his sides, and just as he opened his mouth to answer—

The world shifted.

The hallway blurred, stretching and twisting like a reflection in water, until the scene around them reformed.

They were inside the classroom now.

Rows of desks filled the room, students hunched over parchment and enchanted tablets as they scribbled down notes. The professor, an elderly man with a long, silver beard, stood at the front of the room, his back turned as he wrote something on the board with a flick of his glowing quill.

Chris barely had time to process the sudden shift before a pen sailed through the air.

It struck young Giuseppe squarely in the back of the head.

He jolted upright, stifling a laugh, while young Vincent, sitting beside him, smirked, trying to suppress his own amusement. The two had clearly been goofing off, whispering and snickering when they weren't supposed to.

Chris blinked, his gaze shifting toward the source of the thrown pen.

At a desk a few rows away, a girl sat with her arms crossed, an exasperated expression on her face. She flicked her dark curls over her shoulder, her sharp eyes narrowing at Giuseppe as if daring him to react.

Chris's breath caught in his throat.

It was his mother.

Young Vincent chuckled quietly at the sight, his amusement growing as Giuseppe shot the girl a sheepish look before reluctantly turning back toward the professor.

Chris felt his chest tighten. He had never seen his parents at this age, had never imagined them in this context—just students, just kids, laughing and teasing each other like none of the weight of the future existed yet.

He turned back to Vincent, who was watching the memory unfold with a distant look in his eyes.

"Giuseppe was my best friend." Vincent said. "Everyday we'd hang out, goof off in class, but we could afford too. We were both excelling in our studies, it seemed like we earned that right."

Then the alarm blared through the classroom, the air changed.

The idle hum of students whispering and the gentle scratching of quills against parchment disappeared, replaced by a sharp, deafening silence. The professor, mid-lecture, dropped his glowing quill. His normally composed expression twisted with urgency.

Chris stood frozen in place, watching as the past unfolded before him.

A single tear slipped down Vincent's cheek, barely visible in the dim classroom light.

"This was the day everything changed," Vincent murmured.

Students began moving swiftly, their training kicking in. No panic, no hesitation—just precision. Young Vincent and young Giuseppe exchanged a quick look, their usual playful smirks gone, replaced with something steely and serious. Without a word, they joined the line of students funneling out of the classroom.

The academy shook.

A deep, guttural roar tore through the walls, followed by an explosion that sent books and enchanted lamps tumbling from their shelves. Outside the windows, **the sky burned.**

Chris turned toward the glass, and his breath hitched. **They were under attack.**

The academy's towering spires, once proud and gleaming with arcane energy, were now wreathed in flames. Massive tears in the sky had opened, swirling with black voids of energy as countless demons poured through, their monstrous forms silhouetted against the infernal backdrop. Some flew, their skeletal wings cutting through the smoke-clogged air, while others scaled the academy's enchanted walls with razor-sharp claws.

Soul Warriors—professors, academy guardians, and elite

students—**were already fighting.**

From a distant tower, a **fire-wielding warrior** raised his staff, summoning a torrent of flame that coiled through the air like a living serpent before slamming into a horde of winged demons. The creatures screeched in agony as they were engulfed, their charred remains crumbling before they hit the ground.

Across the courtyard, a **lightning-wielding guardian** propelled himself forward with a single crackling step, his twin sabers glowing as he cut through a monstrous demon's armored hide. Electricity danced across his body, every movement a blur of speed and destruction.

Another warrior, wielding a **massive hammer infused with earth essence**, slammed it into the ground, sending seismic waves through the battlefield. Stone spikes erupted from beneath the invading creatures, impaling them before they could advance further into the academy's defenses.

In the sky, **archers using wind essence** launched arrows that split into multiple piercing gusts, cutting through the airborne demons with deadly precision.

Chris's stomach twisted as he watched. This wasn't a small attack.

This was **a full-scale invasion.**

The academy's defense towers activated, firing bursts of arcane energy at the incoming horde, but for every demon that fell, two more seemed to take its place. The sky darkened with their numbers, their guttural growls and unholy shrieks filling the air.

Through the chaos, the students ran—not to fight, but to **hide.**

Young Vincent, young Giuseppe, and a dozen others were

among them, **forced to take cover** while the warriors fought to keep the academy from falling.

Chris followed as they were ushered into a **bunker** beneath the main campus, a reinforced chamber protected by layers of enchanted barriers. The entrance slammed shut behind them, muffling the sounds of battle, but it couldn't silence the vibrations of each explosion shaking the academy's foundation.

Inside, students huddled together, some whispering prayers, others gripping their amulets or keepsakes for comfort. The air was thick with tension, the walls pressing in as they waited, uncertain if this was their sanctuary or their tomb.

Young Vincent and young Giuseppe stood near the entrance, staring at the sealed doors as if they could see through them.

"We should be out there," Young Vincent muttered.

"No," young Giuseppe said, his voice firm but not unkind. "Not yet."

Young Vincent exhaled sharply. "But what if—"

"They told us to stay here," Giuseppe cut in. He clenched his fists, his expression unreadable. "We're not strong enough."

A long silence followed.

Chris looked between them, his heart pounding. He had known something had changed Vincent back then. He had felt the weight of his bitterness, his need for control.

But now, standing in this moment, watching it happen in real time—

The bunker trembled violently as another explosion rattled the academy's foundation. Dust fell from the ceiling, and students huddled closer together, their whispers growing frantic.

Then came the sound.

A deep, guttural snarl.

It reverberated through the chamber, a low, unnatural growl that sent ice-cold fear creeping down Chris's spine. The students turned toward the sealed doors, their eyes wide with terror.

The metal groaned.

Something was outside.

Another tremor, then a deafening crash. The reinforced doors buckled inward, the thick enchanted steel warping like paper beneath an overwhelming force.

A single clawed hand tore through, curling around the edge of the warped barrier. The fingers were long, jagged, and wrong, dripping with an oozing black substance that sizzled where it touched the floor. The students screamed as the demon ripped the doors apart, tossing the broken steel to the side like discarded scraps.

The beast stepped through the threshold.

It was enormous, its hulking body covered in obsidian-black armor that pulsed with veins of glowing red energy. Its elongated jaw unhinged, revealing rows of jagged fangs dripping with acidic saliva. Its four burning eyes swept across the room, settling on the helpless students.

A horrible, wet snarl echoed through the chamber.

Panic erupted.

Some students scrambled backward, pressing against the walls, while others clutched their amulets in vain, their fledgling powers useless against such a monstrous force.

Young Vincent and young Giuseppe didn't move.

Neither did Mariah.

The three stood frozen, staring at death incarnate.

The demon lunged.

Before it could reach them, a blinding flash of energy tore

through the room.

A golden blade slashed through the demon's outstretched claws, severing its fingers before they could make contact. The creature howled, its voice an ear-splitting shriek that sent vibrations through the walls.

A moment later, the Soul Warriors arrived.

They came in a blur of motion—figures cloaked in light, wielding weapons pulsing with elemental energy. A warrior draped in lightning dashed forward, twin sabers humming as they cut through the demon's thick hide. Sparks erupted with each strike, the smell of burnt flesh filling the air.

Another warrior, her sword wreathed in flames, swung with devastating precision, the blade cleaving through the demon's side. Fire erupted from the wound, spreading across its body and forcing it back toward the broken doorway.

A third warrior, standing at the center of the formation, lifted a staff pulsing with pure light. He slammed the end against the ground, sending a wave of golden energy cascading through the room. The force repelled the demon, searing through its dark armor and forcing it into a staggering retreat.

The creature screeched, stumbling backward, its body now riddled with searing wounds. It thrashed violently, but the warriors didn't hesitate.

With one final, coordinated strike, they unleashed their power.

A surge of elemental energy—lightning, fire, and raw soul essence—collided with the demon, its body rupturing under the overwhelming force.

The creature exploded, its blackened remains disintegrating into nothingness.

Silence followed.

Chris let out a breath he hadn't realized he was holding.

Young Vincent's hands were shaking. Not out of fear—but out of something else. Frustration. Powerlessness.

Among the warriors, one of them turned toward Vincent. He was tall, his stance firm but relaxed, his dark hair streaked with faint silver. His blade, still humming with energy, rested at his side. He looked at young Vincent—not with pity, but with something else.

Encouragement.

The warrior gave him a slight nod, his eyes steady, as if silently telling him, *You're going to be fine. You just have to hold on.*

Chris felt Vincent tense beside him.

Present-day Vincent's jaw tightened, his usually impassive expression flickering with something far more complicated.

Chris turned to him, studying the way his hands curled into fists.

"You know him," Chris said, though it wasn't a question.

Vincent exhaled slowly before answering.

"Yeah," he murmured. "That's my older brother."

Young Vincent's breath was unsteady, his hands still shaking from the encounter. But when his eyes lifted, locking onto the battlefield beyond the shattered doorway, something in his face changed. The frustration, the helplessness—it solidified into determination.

Without a word, he ran.

"Vincent!" young Giuseppe hissed, eyes widening in panic.

But Vincent was already gone, tearing out of the bunker and into the chaos beyond.

Giuseppe cursed under his breath and took off after him. "You idiot, wait!"

Mariah reached out, as if to grab Giuseppe before he could

follow, but her fingers barely brushed his sleeve before he slipped past her.

"Noooo," she hissed under her breath, torn between running after them and following orders. She hovered at the entrance for a split second, but then, reluctantly, she stayed.

Chris and present-day Vincent followed, stepping through the memory as young Vincent and Giuseppe sprinted across the war-torn courtyard of Eden Preparatory Academy.

The battlefield was hell.

The once-pristine academy grounds were now a graveyard of shattered stone, collapsed towers, and bodies—both human and demon—strewn across the landscape. The air was thick with the scent of scorched magic, blood, and smoke. Explosions rocked the earth as elemental blasts clashed mid-air, warriors and demons locked in brutal combat.

Soul warriors fought with everything they had.

One guardian—his blade wreathed in golden flame—cut through a demon's throat, the creature's dying shriek piercing through the chaos.

Another warrior, her body glowing with a radiant shield of light, was overwhelmed by a pack of hell hounds, their jaws closing around her as her screams were drowned in the chaos.

A bolt of lightning speared through the sky, striking down a monstrous creature with massive horns, but the warrior who had cast it didn't see the shadow tendril creeping toward him from behind—until it was too late.

Young Vincent and Giuseppe dodged through the carnage, their boots slipping on the blood-slicked stone.

Giuseppe caught up, grabbing Vincent by the arm. "What the hell do you think you're doing!?"

Vincent yanked free, his expression fierce. "I'm going to help my brother!"

"You're going to get yourself killed!"

"I don't care!" Vincent snapped. "I'm not sitting in a damn bunker while everyone else fights for their lives!"

Chris felt his breath hitch as he watched the scene unfold. The intensity in young Vincent's voice, the desperation to do something, to be useful—he had never imagined Vincent like this before.

Beside him, present-day Vincent exhaled, shaking his head as he watched his younger self charge forward recklessly.

"Fool," Vincent muttered. "You weren't ready."

Chris turned to look at him. The expression on Vincent's face wasn't anger. It wasn't even regret.

It was understanding.

Chris realized that Vincent wasn't berating his past self. He was simply stating the truth.

And yet, young Vincent kept running.

Straight into the fire.

Young Vincent skidded to a halt near the body of a fallen Soul Warrior, his breath coming in ragged gasps. The warrior's weapon—an ornate long sword infused with crackling energy— lay abandoned in the dirt, its power still pulsing faintly. Without hesitation, Vincent snatched it up, his grip tightening around the hilt.

He turned to Giuseppe, eyes blazing. "We can fight!" he shouted over the chaos. "We have to fight!"

Giuseppe hesitated, torn between fear and instinct. His hands balled into fists at his sides. "Vincent, this isn't some sparring match! We're gonna die out here!"

Before Vincent could argue, a chilling howl tore through the battlefield.

A pack of demons, their grotesque bodies twisting unnaturally, lunged from the shadows, their jagged teeth gleaming as they closed in.

Vincent barely had time to react before a blazing arc of fire slashed through the air, incinerating the first wave of creatures.

His brother landed in front of them, his fire-blade still burning red-hot, its embers trailing through the smoke-filled sky. His dark hair was wild from battle, his armor scorched and dented, but his stance was firm, unwavering.

Vincent's stomach twisted.

"You absolute idiot," his brother snapped, his eyes flashing with fury. "What the hell are you doing out here!?"

Vincent tightened his grip on the stolen blade, but before he could respond, his brother shoved him backward.

"Stay behind me!" he barked.

More demons closed in, their grotesque forms weaving between the broken remains of the academy. Some slithered across the ground like living shadows, others stomped forward, their hulking bodies radiating malice. They were outnumbered, surrounded.

Then, the sky itself cracked open.

A massive portal—black as the void, searing at the edges with golden fire—tore through the heavens.

The battlefield froze. Even the demons hesitated, their grotesque heads snapping upward in eerie unison.

A deep, resonating presence filled the air, pressing down on the academy like an unstoppable force.

Chris, watching from the memory, felt his chest tighten as three figures descended through the swirling darkness.

Lucifer. Beelzebub. Astaroth.

Their mere presence sent a ripple through reality.

Lucifer drifted downward, his pristine robes untouched by the bloodshed, his golden eyes gleaming with unreadable intent. His aura alone could crush mountains.

Beelzebub followed, his many wings unfurling in slow, deliberate motions. He carried himself like a king among insects, his gaze sweeping over the battlefield with cold calculation.

Astaroth landed last, his skeletal frame shifting unnaturally, his jagged claws leaving scorch marks in the air itself.

Chris's breath caught in his throat.

This wasn't just an invasion.

This was a declaration.

And before young Giuseppe, Vincent, and his brother could react—the lower demons surged forward.

The three were overrun.

Vincent's brother fought like a storm unleashed, his fire-blade carving through the darkness with blinding precision. Every swing sent arcs of flames through the air, burning away the horde of demons closing in on them. His footwork was flawless, his stance unshakable as he became a wall between the young boys and the monsters that surrounded them.

But the enemy was relentless.

A massive, clawed demon lunged at Vincent, its serrated fangs inches from tearing into him—until Giuseppe tackled him to the ground.

Vincent barely had time to react before his brother stepped forward to shield them both.

The demons swarmed.

It happened too fast.

One moment, his brother stood defiant, unyielding. The next, the creatures dragged him down.

His fire blade clattered to the ground, its embers flickering out as claws, fangs, and shadowy limbs tore into him. He roared in defiance, still fighting even as they ripped him apart. Blood splattered across the cracked stone, his once-burning essence snuffed out in an instant.

Vincent screamed.

Giuseppe held him down, his own face twisted in horror as the creatures turned their hungry, glowing eyes toward them.

Chris, standing frozen in the memory, felt a sickening weight in his chest as young Vincent, the one who had run onto this battlefield believing he could help, could only watch in helpless terror as his brother was devoured in front of him.

The demons turned their sights on the two young boys.

A twisted chorus of snarls and growls filled the air as they closed in. Vincent struggled against Giuseppe's grip, his mind blank with rage, grief, and despair. This wasn't how it was supposed to happen. He was supposed to be strong enough.

The demons leapt—

Then, light erupted from the heavens.

A blinding, divine radiance split the sky, searing through the battlefield with an overwhelming force. The ground trembled, the very air vibrating as beams of pure, holy energy rained down like celestial fire.

Chris shielded his eyes from the brilliance, but through the blinding glow, he saw them.

The Seven Archangels.

They descended like meteors, each one burning with power so intense that the lower demons shriveled into dust just by being in their presence.

A single stroke from Uriel's flaming sword sent an entire wave of creatures screaming into oblivion.

Raguel's silver chain whip lashed through the air, wrapping

around a towering demon and crushing it into ash.

The battlefield, once overrun, was liberated in mere moments.

But the true battle had only begun.

Chris felt the ground shake as three titanic forces collided.

Michael, Gabriel, and Raphael charged.

Michael, the warrior of heaven, met Lucifer in a clash that sent shock waves through the academy ruins. Their blades clashed like thunder, raw celestial and infernal power colliding as they exchanged devastating blows.

Gabriel, wielding a spear of pure light, launched himself at Beelzebub, striking with divine speed. The winged demon retaliated with a storm of dark energy, their battle unfolding like a storm of clashing worlds.

Raphael, radiant and unyielding, squared off against Astaroth, the twisted fiend laughing as his dark magic clashed against the archangel's healing light.

The sky above Eden tore apart as angels and demons waged war.

And on the ground, in the blood-streaked dirt, Vincent and Giuseppe remained frozen.

One grieving his fallen brother.

The other desperately holding him back from making a mistake that would get him killed next.

The battlefield, once a storm of blood, fire, and celestial fury, began to fade.

The deafening roars of angels and demons clashing, the searing heat of magic tearing through the air, the raw grief carved into young Vincent's face—all of it dissolved like mist in the morning sun.

Chris barely had time to process what was happening before

everything around them vanished.

Then, silence.

Chris and Vincent stood alone in an endless white void.

It stretched in every direction, vast and featureless. There was no sky, no ground—just an infinite emptiness that swallowed sound, leaving nothing but the two of them.

Vincent stood motionless, his arms crossed, his expression unreadable.

Then he exhaled, shaking his head.

"Funny how the angels come after my brother is slaughtered," he said, his voice disturbingly calm.

Chris remained quiet.

What was there to say? He had watched it happen. Had seen his pain, his helplessness, his rage.

Vincent's gaze darkened, staring into the void as if the past was still playing before him.

"After that day, I vowed to myself that I would never feel powerless again," he said, his voice low but heavy with something unshakable. "Never do anything that reckless. And that I wouldn't rely on the 'grace' of the angels."

His fists clenched.

"I researched dark energy and shadow techniques. I sought out anything that could give me an edge. I would do whatever it took to bring my brother back. Nothing would stand in my way. Nothing would would stop me from getting—"

He trailed off.

Chris knew what he was about to say.

He watched Vincent's rage coil around him, a fire burning cold, not wild like Chris's own emotions, but deep, controlled— an obsession.

And in that moment, Chris saw himself in Vincent.

It hit him like a tidal wave.

Chris had spent so long running from his fear—from fire, from his own power, from the weight of everything he had lost. But fire was never what truly terrified him.

It was losing his father.

Just like Vincent had lost his brother.

And if he let that fear consume him… if he kept running, kept feeding the anger, kept chasing a path of no return…

He would become Vincent.

The realization rooted Chris in place, his breath shallow.

Vincent didn't look at him, didn't need to. He had already lived through this.

But Chris was still choosing.

28

Echoes of Resolve

As the last remnants of light faded, Chris opened his eyes and was back. He stood amidst the devastation of the battle, his body trembling but still upright. The silver glow around him flickered, dimming with every breath, the strain of his power weighing heavily on him. His gaze fell upon Vincent's defeated form, and for the first time, he didn't see a monster.

He saw a man broken by his past. A man consumed by loss.

Behind him, Sophie stirred. Her voice, soft yet filled with emotion, cut through the silence.

"Chris… you did it."

Chris turned toward her, the weight of everything settling over him like a crushing tide. The battlefield, once alive with chaos, was eerily still now. The only sounds left were the faint crackle of dissipating energy and the distant echoes of destruction. He took a deep breath—then his knees buckled.

The strain hit him all at once.

His silver aura flickered one last time before vanishing completely. The ethereal flame that had surrounded him surged upward, rising like a final beacon into the sky—and then dispersed, leaving Chris behind. The warmth, the power, the divine fire—it was gone.

He stood for a heartbeat longer, as if suspended in that silence. Then his knees gave out.

The power that had carried him through the battle had left him—drained, hollow. The Eclipse Blade slipped from his grip, embedding itself in the scorched earth beside him, its once-glowing edge now dull. His father's sword, the weapon he had wielded in the final strike, fell from his other hand with a dull thud.

The two blades lay beside him, silent witnesses to everything they had endured.

Chris barely noticed. He was too exhausted, too overwhelmed, his hands resting limply on his knees as he struggled to steady his breath.

A few feet away, Sophie staggered forward. Blood dripped from a deep gash on her arm, staining her tattered sleeve, but she didn't stop. Her steps were slow, unsteady, but relentless. She pressed a hand to her side, wincing as she moved, yet her focus never wavered.

She needed to reach him.

"Chris…" she called again, her voice carrying both relief and desperation.

She dropped to her knees beside him, her shaking hand finding his shoulder. He didn't flinch at the touch, but he didn't look up either. His breath came in ragged gasps, his head bowed, eyes locked on the ground.

"I'm fine," he muttered, though his trembling body and drained aura told a different story.

Sophie exhaled sharply, her grip on his shoulder tightening. "You're not fine." Her voice was firm despite the exhaustion weighing her down. "You pushed yourself too far."

Chris didn't respond. His eyes drifted to the two blades lying in the dirt beside him. Symbols of his struggle. Symbols of what he had lost.

The battlefield around them was littered with broken stone, shattered weapons, and the remnants of Vincent's power dissipating into the wind. Where there had once been destruction, now there was only silence.

Chris's gaze finally lifted—to Vincent.

The man who had once towered above them, monstrous with stolen power, now lay broken on the ground. The frost and shadows that had clung to him, twisting his form into something inhuman, were peeling away, dissolving like smoke. His grotesque features softened, and the eerie glow in his eyes faded, leaving behind only faint traces of the man he once was.

The others watched in silence.

Lilith. Eli. Mei. Allegra.

Their bodies were battered, barely able to hold themselves upright, their souls weighed down by exhaustion and uncertainty. They had fought with everything they had, and now, they stood in the aftermath, waiting for the battle's final echoes to fade.

Vincent's transformation ended in eerie stillness. The monstrous form he had wielded moments ago was gone, leaving behind a frail, broken man. His armor lay in shattered fragments around him, his frost-bitten skin pale and lifeless. He looked smaller now, like a shadow of the being who had once towered over them with stolen power.

But the energy he had released didn't fade.

Dark tendrils of mist rose from his collapsed form, swirling like smoke caught in an unseen current. The malevolent energy didn't dissipate—it spread, seeping into the earth, the sky, the very air. The forest trembled, its trees bending away from the unnatural force, as if recoiling from something they, too, feared.

Sophie's voice broke the silence, trembling with unease. "What… what's happening?"

Chris forced himself to look up, his breath uneven. His body screamed in protest, exhaustion pressing down on him, but he couldn't look away from the energy slithering into the world around them.

"The demon energy," he muttered. "It's not gone. It's… escaping."

A weak movement from Vincent's broken body caught his attention. His eyes fluttered open—no longer burning with malice, but heavy with pain and something dangerously close to desperation. His lips parted, as if to speak, as if to finally explain why.

But he never got the chance.

The shadows that had once obeyed him now moved of their own will, twisting unnaturally around his body. They pulsed, shuddered, then closed in.

"No!" Sophie shouted, stepping forward, desperation in her voice. "We need answers!"

Chris tried to move, to push past the exhaustion dragging him down, but the shadows moved too fast. The tendrils coiled tighter, suffocating, wrapping around Vincent's body until he was no longer visible beneath the black mist.

Then, in a single, violent pull—they swallowed him whole.

The darkness collapsed in on itself, shrinking into nothingness. The mist dissolved into the wind, its presence vanishing as if it had never been there at all.

Silence.

No sign of Vincent. No trace of where he had gone. Only the lingering stain of something unfinished.

The group stood frozen, the weight of what had just happened settling over them like a suffocating fog.

Mei let out a sharp breath, her fire whip hanging limply at her side. "What the hell was that?"

"He's gone," Eli said grimly, as he pressed his hammer into the ground. "But that energy… it's still here. I can feel it."

Chris barely heard them. His gaze remained locked on the spot where Vincent had been only moments ago. The battlefield, once a storm of power and destruction, felt eerily empty now. His body ached, but something inside him felt heavier than any wound.

His hands rested beside him, fingers brushing against the

weapons that had carried him through the fight. The Eclipse Blade. His father's sword. They still held weight, even resting on the ground.

Sophie knelt beside him, her voice softer now, but steady. "Chris... you stopped him."

Chris exhaled slowly, shaking his head.

"I didn't stop anything," he said, his voice hollow.

His eyes drifted toward the darkened sky, where traces of the ethereal flame still flickered like dying embers.

"Sargatanas's power... the energy Vincent stole... it's still out there."

Sophie rested her hand gently on Chris's shoulder, grounding him once more. He finally turned to face her. Despite her pale, bloodied face and the exhaustion etched into her features, she still managed to offer him a small, reassuring smile. It was the same quiet resolve that had inspired him time and time again.

He nodded slowly, his movements heavy with fatigue.

"I couldn't save him," Chris whispered, his voice breaking. "I couldn't save him again."

Sophie, ignoring her own pain, leaned closer. Without a word, she wrapped her arms around him, pulling him into a gentle embrace. She didn't try to comfort him with empty reassurances. She didn't say it was going to be okay. She just held him, letting the quiet speak for itself.

Moments later, Eli limped toward them, his battered frame barely upright. His armor was scorched, and his face was smeared with dirt and blood, but his blue eyes held steady as he approached. Without hesitation, he knelt beside Chris and placed a firm, reassuring hand on his shoulder.

The three of them stayed there, huddled together amidst the wreckage of the battlefield. There were no words, just the quiet solace of shared pain.

The two blades rested silently in the dirt, gleaming faintly in the fading light, silent witnesses to everything they had endured.

"We'll be okay," Chris said softly, his voice hoarse but steady. He wiped his eyes and looked at Sophie and Eli with a spark of hope, fragile but growing. "My dad made sure of that."

And for the first time in what felt like forever, Chris believed it.

The battlefield lay in ruins, bathed in the soft golden hues of the rising sun. Light filtered through the charred remains of trees, casting long shadows across the devastated clearing. The air was thick with the scent of scorched earth and fading energy, yet an eerie stillness had settled over the land, as if the world itself was holding its breath.

Mei approached cautiously, her fire whip still faintly glowing in the early light. Each step was careful, deliberate, as if afraid that even the slightest movement might disturb the fragile moment of peace. Stopping a few paces away, she studied the group—Chris, Sophie, and Eli, huddled together amidst the wreckage. Her expression was a mixture of sympathy and urgency.

"Chris… what was that?" she asked, her voice steady, but the weight of her concern was undeniable.

Before Chris could answer, the ground trembled.

A low, guttural rumble broke the silence, its sound unnatural and wrong. The earth split open a few feet away, and from the gash in reality, a shadowy abyss tore itself into existence.

Everyone's heads snapped toward the dark void. Weapons instinctively raised, bodies tensed, but before they could react, it struck.

Tendrils of darkness surged forward with unnatural speed, slithering across the battlefield like living things. They coiled around Lilith's unconscious form, their grip tight and absolute. Before anyone could move, before a single shout could be uttered, the shadows yanked her back into the abyss.

The void collapsed in on itself with a deafening finality. One moment, Lilith was there. The next, she was gone.

Silence.

The group remained frozen, shock and horror etched into their faces. The clearing returned to stillness, save for the faint rustling of leaves in the morning breeze, as if nothing had happened at all.

Mei's fiery gaze darted between Chris, Sophie, and Eli. Her voice, though low, carried an undeniable demand. "What just happened? What was that?"

Before anyone could answer, the sound of hurried footsteps reached their ears. Reinforcements arrived—Omari, Nyla, and their squads emerged from the treeline, their faces tense with confusion and alarm. The early sunlight highlighted the urgency in their eyes as they took in the destruction, the cracked ground, the remnants of Vincent's energy still lingering in the air, and the battle-worn warriors barely standing.

Omari's deep voice cut through the silence. "What in the world happened here?"

His sharp gaze swept over the scene—the devastation, the shattered bodies, the exhausted figures of Chris and the others, and Hiroshi, collapsed nearby, barely conscious.

Mei straightened, brushing dirt and ash from her torn uniform, her expression hardening as she took charge. "We'll explain everything," she said, her voice firm, carrying authority despite her exhaustion. Then her eyes shifted to Hiroshi, who lay still, his breath uneven, his face shadowed with guilt.

Mei's gaze remained locked on him. "But for now," she said, her tone dropping into something colder, sharper, "detain former Lieutenant Hiroshi."

Omari's brows furrowed, but he gave a firm nod and motioned to his team. Two warriors stepped forward, securing Hiroshi's wrists with restraints.

He didn't resist.

His gaze fell to the ground, his shoulders slumped beneath the weight of everything he had done.

The golden light of dawn painted the broken landscape in bittersweet hues, illuminating the battle's survivors and the scars left behind. Despite the warmth of the sun, the chill of uncertainty lingered.

Chris, Sophie, and Eli remained where they were, leaning on each other for support. None of them spoke. None of them moved.

Sophie was the first to break the silence, her voice barely above a whisper.

"What now?"

Her gaze shifted between Chris and Eli, looking for an answer none of them had.

The three of them remained close, their huddle a fragile island amidst the devastation. The quiet of the sunrise gave them no answers, only the faint promise of a new day—a day filled with uncertainty, but one they would face together.

When Chris awoke the next morning, exhaustion clung to him like an unshakable weight. Every inch of his body ached, but it was nothing compared to the heaviness in his chest. The memory of his father's sacrifice haunted his dreams, replaying over and over again. But the promise to honor his memory, to carry forward what he had left behind, kept Chris moving.

Today was not a day for battle. It was a day of remembrance.

The courtyard was quiet, the air still, save for the gentle rustling of leaves in the morning breeze. Warriors and captains alike had gathered, standing before a newly erected monument of gleaming marble. Its surface was pristine, reflecting the soft light of the sun, but the weight of the many names etched into its stone made it heavy beyond measure.

At the top, carved with unwavering permanence, was the name of Captain Giuseppe Cronetti.

Chris stood at the front of the gathering, Sophie and Eli by his side. Their faces were solemn, their grief tempered by determination. Behind them, Mariah stood holding little Genevieve close. The child clutched a bouquet of white lilies in her small hands, her wide eyes filled with sadness and confusion as she stared up at the monument.

To the side, the captains formed a silent line, their expressions grim. Mei and Maria stood with rigid postures, their grief masked beneath unwavering discipline. Omari and Nyla flanked them, their eyes dark with quiet reflection. Jeffrey, still recovering from the wounds Vincent had inflicted, leaned lightly on his staff, his head wrapped in bandages—a stark reminder of the battle they had barely survived.

No words were spoken, but none were needed.

This was a moment for the fallen.

A moment to mourn.

A moment to remember.

Scattered throughout the crowd were the surviving warriors—Allegra, Deepak, Luke, Yeji, Kim, Matthew, Faith, Edward, and others who had endured the impossible. Each bore the scars of battle, some visible, others buried deep within.

Their expressions carried a weight that words couldn't ease, a shared pain that would never truly fade.

Richard and Lyra were nowhere to be found.

There were no speeches, no grand declarations of victory. Only silence.

The names on the monument spoke for themselves, carved into the stone as eternal reminders of sacrifice. The gathered warriors stood as witnesses, their quiet presence a testament to the lives that had been lost.

One by one, they stepped forward, placing flowers at the base of the monument. Each offering was a silent promise, a gesture of remembrance that no soul would be forgotten.

When Chris's turn came, his heart clenched. He stepped forward, placing his palm against the cold marble. His fingers traced the letters of his father's name, the weight of loss pressing down on him like an anchor.

Behind him, Genevieve knelt carefully, her small hands trembling as she placed her lilies among the others. Mariah crouched beside her, wrapping a gentle arm around her shoulders. They lingered for a moment, the child's gaze locked on the names she couldn't yet understand, before they returned to the crowd.

The sun climbed higher, bathing the courtyard in warm light. But even with its glow, the chill of grief lingered. The warriors stood a little taller, their gazes a little sharper. The ceremony was over, but the battle wasn't.

The fight was far from over.

Later, in the war room of Eden Preparatory Academy, the truth hung heavy in the air.

Mei, Maria, Nyla, Omari, and Jeffrey sat around the circular table, their expressions grim but focused. The weight of the recent battle pressed down on them, exhaustion and determination warring in their eyes. Jeffrey leaned slightly against the table, a bandage wrapped around his head—a lingering reminder of his brutal encounter with Vincent.

Standing before them were Chris, Sophie, and Eli, their faces drawn but steady.

For a long moment, no one spoke.

Then Maria broke the silence, her voice measured but firm.

"We've paid our respects to the fallen. Now, we need answers."

She turned her gaze to Chris, expectant and unyielding.

"Start from the beginning."

Chris took a steady step forward, his gaze unwavering.

"During the fight with Vincent, something awakened in me— a third soul essence. Time manipulation."

The room grew tense. The weight of his words settled over the captains like a storm cloud. Mei leaned forward, arms crossed, her expression skeptical.

"Time manipulation?" she repeated, her voice edged with disbelief. "That's… unheard of."

Chris nodded, his fingers unconsciously tightening around the hilt of the Eclipse Blade.

"My father knew I had three soul essences—lightning, fire, and an unknown third. We now know the fire was actually the ethereal flame, and the third was time manipulation."

Silence hung heavy in the war room. The captains exchanged glances, trying to process what this revelation meant.

"I don't fully understand it yet," Chris admitted. "But it allowed me to slow down Vincent's attacks, predict his movements, and even freeze parts of the battlefield. At one point, I saw into the past—Vincent's past. But the power takes a toll. The strain almost killed me."

Omari frowned, arms resting on the table.

"And without it?"

Chris met his gaze without hesitation.

"I wouldn't be standing here."

The statement hit like a hammer. No one doubted its truth.

Sophie, standing beside him, spoke next.

"There's more. During the battle, the ethereal flame was released. That power has the ability to travel between realms, and now that it's loose, the barriers between them are weakening."

Nyla's expression darkened.

"Which means?"

"The line between realms is blurred now," Chris said.

Mei exhaled sharply.

"And that's not all, is it?"

Sophie shook her head.

"No. The demon energy that fueled Vincent didn't just vanish. It's still out there, scattered, free to take new form. And when Vincent fell… the shadows took him before we could get any answers."

A tense stillness followed. The implications were clear.

Nyla's voice was careful but firm.

"So, the ethereal flame has been unleashed, the realms are unstable, and Vincent is out there—possibly able to return even stronger?"

Sophie gave a grim nod.

"Exactly."

Before anyone could respond, the heavy door to the war room creaked open. All eyes turned as Kojo stepped inside. His movements were precise, every step deliberate, his gaze sharp and unreadable. The tension in the room was thick, but he carried himself with the same controlled confidence he always had.

Without hesitation, he gave a brief salute to the captains.

"Captain Giuseppe sent me on a recon mission during the battle at Celestia Academy." His voice was clipped and direct, his tone betraying none of his emotions. "I've returned with critical information."

Maria gestured for Kojo to continue, her expression unreadable but expectant.

"What did you find?"

Kojo stepped into the center of the room, placing a stack of papers and a data pad on the table. He took a breath, his voice steady as he began.

"Vincent wasn't just stealing soul essences—he was experimenting on them. His research details multiple attempts to merge different essences into a single host. His ultimate goal wasn't just power. He wanted to create a new kind of being—himself."

A heavy silence fell over the room.

Mei's expression darkened, her fists clenching at her sides.

"That explains how he was able to steal so many abilities during the fight."

Kojo nodded.

"But there's more. His family is missing. There's no trace of them. Either they were taken, or… they're gone."

Omari exhaled sharply, his jaw tightening.

"So he sacrificed his own family in pursuit of power."

Kojo's gaze didn't waver.

"That's a possibility. But the most significant discovery was this." He tapped the data pad, his voice sharp with emphasis. "Vincent used shadow demons to control soul warriors Richard and Lyra. I found them unconscious with no recollection of the battle. But his records—his own documentation—confirmed their subjugation. And worse, he used their soul essences to forge the appearance of the Archangels."

Maria stiffened, her eyes widening.

"What?"

Kojo continued without hesitation.

"His research and recordings provide undeniable evidence. Vincent created the illusion of the Archangel using a combination of light and sound manipulation. When Michael entrusted him with selecting new recruits, it was under the influence of those fabricated appearances. It was all an illusion."

Jeffrey leaned forward, his brow furrowed in disbelief.

"You're telling us he forged the Archangel Michael's appearance?"

"Yes," Kojo said bluntly.

"He manipulated our beliefs, our loyalty, using light and sound essence to make us think his actions were sanctioned by Heaven."

A wave of outrage rippled through the room. The captains exchanged tense glances, the enormity of Kojo's revelation settling over them like a lead weight.

Mei spoke first, her voice dangerously low.

"He played us. He used our faith, our trust—turned them into weapons against us."

Maria exhaled slowly, steadying herself.

"This explains everything. Vincent didn't just take control—he created a false authority, ensuring no one could challenge him. If we believed the Archangels were guiding him, there was nothing to question."

Omari's voice broke through the tension, a mix of anger and bitter realization.

"He didn't just manipulate us. He stole lives, twisted souls, and shattered trust. And now he's still out there, while the demon energy spreads unchecked."

Before anyone could respond, Maria lifted a hand, her expression tightening.

"There's another matter we must address: the missing sixty."

The weight in the room deepened immediately. Chris felt it knot tighter in his chest.

"What missing sixty?" Chris asked

"After the battle at Celestia Academy, we discovered 60 people were unaccounted for." Maria said.

Kojo stepped forward, clearing his throat. "I've been running soul signature scans across all known sectors." He tapped a few commands into a small projection pad. A map of Eden and the surrounding territories flickered to life above the table. "Nothing's turned up. Not a single confirmed reading."

Mei's brow furrowed. "Are you suggesting they're dead?"

"No," Kojo said quickly, his jaw tightening. "If they were dead, their soul essence would've dissipated. We would have picked up the remnants. But there's nothing. It's like they vanished into thin air."

A heavy silence gripped the room.

Then, from the edge of the room, a rough voice broke the stillness.

"I know where they are."

The room froze. Every gaze turned toward Hiroshi.

Still seated, his wrists bound, Hiroshi didn't lift his head. His voice was low but steady, his eyes locked on the floor.

"I froze," he said, the words scraping out of him. "When Vincent spiraled… I should've stopped him. I should've done *something*. But I stood there. And I did nothing."

Silence pressed down as Hiroshi slowly raised his eyes—

meeting Maria's without hesitation.

"Because of that failure, students and other soldiers were taken."

A flicker of unease passed across the room. Hiroshi pressed on, his voice gaining force.

"I know what Vincent did. That whole battle was just a big ploy. He used the chaos to take people. All to keep his pact with that demon. He didn't kill them—he hid them. Preserved them. That demon was going to use their soul essence for something far worse than we imagined."

Now he looked at everyone—not with pride, but with grim resolve.

"I don't expect forgiveness. I don't even expect you to trust me. But if there's still a chance to save them, I can lead you there."

Omari's voice cut in, sharp and urgent. "Where?"

Hiroshi drew a breath. "The Badlands," he said. "I know exactly where they are."

The room shifted instantly. Muscles tensed. Eyes darkened. Even the air felt heavier—as if the very mention of the place carried a curse.

And then, Chris froze.

A voice—quiet, uninvited—whispered into his mind like breath against his ear.

I'm Here.

His chest tightened. A shiver shot down his spine, sudden and cold. He shuddered, glancing around, but no one else reacted. Whatever it was, it was speaking only to him.

Nyla's voice broke the silence, grim and unshaken. "The Badlands are a death sentence," she said flatly. "We haven't returned in years—for good reason."

Jeffrey, his hand still bandaged from the battle with Vincent, tapped absently against the table. "And if we send our best now, who's left to defend Eden if another breach happens? How many more lives are we willing to risk?"

Mei folded her arms, her tone sharp. "We'd need full Council authorization before we even consider this. A mission that size into the Badlands could leave Eden wide open. If demons strike while we're stretched thin…"

She let the thought hang, unfinished but understood.

Chris's heart pounded. He could feel it rising in his throat. *We can't just leave them there.*

The captains continued debating—logistics, manpower, defenses—layer after layer of doubt. No decision was made. Only the fog of uncertainty remained.

Then Jeffrey interjected. "I don't believe a word this traitor says. He's trying to save himself. The Council will decide his fate."

"He's right." Nyla said. "No movements until the Council approves. Take Hiroshi back to his cell. This meeting is adjourned."

Chairs scraped back. The captains stood one by one, their faces hard, their next steps already forming in silence. The war room emptied slowly, like a wound being closed without healing.

Chris remained behind, his thoughts racing. The weight of what had been said—what hadn't—settled over him like a stone.

Today the war hadn't ended. But it had changed. And deep down, Chris knew: something had already begun.

Chris, Sophie, and Eli followed close behind, their steps slow and heavy as they processed everything that had been said. Though the wounds of battle were still fresh, and the uncertainties of the future loomed like storm clouds, one truth remained:

They had survived.

As they stepped out of the war room, the weight of it all seemed to settle over them like an unseen force. The battle. The losses. The revelations. It was too much to carry all at once. The trio stepped outside, bathed in the golden warmth of the sun as it lit up the city.

Sophie exhaled sharply, rubbing her temples. "It still doesn't feel real," she muttered. "We fought Vincent. We barely made it out alive. And now… we're supposed to just go back to normal? Like none of it happened?"

Chris rubbed his head, the exhaustion sinking deeper into his bones. "I don't think normal exists for us anymore."

Eli let out a low whistle, stuffing his hands into his pockets. "Yeah, no kidding. We survived a demon-powered Vincent, watched a guy literally steal soul essences, and now we're throwing around 'time manipulation' like it's just another Tuesday."

Sophie shook her head, a tired, almost disbelieving smile tugging at her lips. "When you say it like that, it sounds even crazier."

Eli grinned. "Gotta keep things in perspective. I mean, Chris, if you can mess with time now, can you, I don't know, jump us to the future? Preferably when this war's over and we're all retired on some quiet island somewhere?"

Chris let out a dry laugh, shaking his head. "If I ever figure out how to do that, you'll be the first person I test it on."

Eli smirked.

"Good, because I'm calling dibs on a beach house."

The comment earned a chuckle from Chris, breaking some

of the tension that clung to them.

But as their laughter faded, reality crept back in.

Sophie's expression sobered, her voice dropping.

"And what about the missing students?" she asked, her tone barely above a whisper.

"They're still out there. Somewhere. We just…left the room like it's someone else's problem."

"We're not leaving them," Chris said quietly.

His voice was steady, anchored by something harder than hope—**conviction**.

Eli glanced sideways at him, frowning.

"The captains won't authorize a rescue unless the Council gives the green light. And even then…"

He shook his head.

"They're scared. The Badlands nearly wiped out an entire squad last time."

Chris's gaze hardened, staring straight ahead.

"I have a lead."

Sophie's eyes widened.

The three of them walked on, their steps falling into rhythm once again. But this time, there was no laughter. Only the quiet, shared certainty that something bigger was already beginning— and this time, it would be their choice to fight.

Far above them, the hopeful skies of Eden Preparatory Academy stretched endless and blue. But for Chris, Sophie, and Eli… the road ahead was anything but clear.

Far away from friendship, from light, from anything resembling mercy, there was only the frozen desolation of Hell.

A frigid wind howled across a barren, shadowed expanse. Jagged mountains of obsidian loomed over endless frozen plains, their peaks cloaked in perpetual twilight. The air was razor-sharp, each breath like swallowing shards of glass. The ice-covered ground reflected an eerie, pale glow from an unseen light source—an illumination without warmth, casting everything in a spectral half-light. The atmosphere pressed down with an oppressive weight, thick with the whispers of lost souls, their mournful wails trapped within the frozen terrain.

High against the crumbling face of a blackened mountain, Vincent hung in chains.

Celestial runes pulsed with faint golden light, etched into the restraints binding him to the jagged rock. They burned into his flesh, searing away the remnants of the stolen power that had once made him untouchable. His arms were stretched wide, his legs barely brushing the icy ledge beneath him, forcing him to bear the relentless pull of the chains. Every moment was a test of endurance, every breath a battle against the agony consuming him.

The man who once stood as an unyielding force now appeared as a hollow shell. His once-imposing form was gaunt, his frostbitten skin marred by deep wounds where darkness leaked from his body like smoke dissolving into the cold. His crimson eyes, dim and hollow, flickered with the faintest embers of defiance—embers that weakened with each passing moment, smothered under the weight of endless torment.

Above him, a massive bird of flame circled, its wings crackling with divine fire. Each slow, deliberate beat of its wings sent embers scattering through the air, their glow swallowed by the darkness below. It let out a piercing cry, the sound reverberating through the mountain, shaking the very foundation of Vincent's prison.

Then, without warning, the creature struck.

Talons of blazing light tore through the air, slamming into

Vincent's chest with merciless force. The pain was instant, searing and all-consuming, burning deeper than any wound inflicted in battle. His body arched against the restraints, a strangled cry escaping his lips—one lost to the endless void of Hell's frozen wasteland.

Vincent's scream tore through the frozen wasteland, raw and agonized, as the flaming talons ripped into him once more. It wasn't just his body that burned—it was his very essence, unraveling with each savage strike. Shadowy remnants of the stolen power he had once wielded were wrenched from him in dark tendrils, spiraling into the abyss above as the fiery bird carried them away.

But the torment did not end with their departure. The wounds left behind did not heal as they would in Hell's cursed cycle of regeneration. No, these gashes remained raw, festering with divine punishment, only for his body to be restored moments later—forcing him to endure the agony again and again.

His breath was ragged, his voice hoarse. "You think this will… break me?" he rasped, each word a struggle. "I'll rise… I'll—"

The chains tightened, their celestial runes flaring in response to his defiance. The divine fire seared into his flesh, and his words died in his throat. His head slumped forward, strength waning, body trembling from the sheer weight of his suffering.

The icy winds howled, whipping against the jagged cliffs. Vincent hung motionless, suspended against the crumbling black mountain, the echoes of his own screams still vibrating in the frozen air. Then, through the endless fog and numbing cold, a new presence stirred.

A shadow moved beyond the darkness—a presence so vast, so utterly consuming, that it swallowed the dim light of Hell itself.

The ground beneath the mountain quaked as something enormous emerged from the abyss. Its form was cloaked in living darkness, a towering silhouette that eclipsed even the jagged peaks. Every step it took sent tremors through the frozen landscape, fractures splitting the ice beneath its colossal weight.

Vincent's eyelids fluttered, weak and bloodshot, his senses barely clinging to consciousness. And yet, something deeper than pain—something primal—forced him to acknowledge the overwhelming presence before him.

Not from the cold, not from the chains, but from fear.

A fear that only demons knew.

A fear that had a name.

The shadow loomed closer, blotting out what little light remained in the Hellscape. Though its form was shrouded in an abyss deeper than night itself, its eyes burned through the darkness—two molten embers, flickering with an ancient, all-consuming malice.

The voice that followed was not loud, yet it carried such weight that the very mountain shuddered under its power.

"You will rise?" it rumbled, the sheer force of its presence pressing against Vincent's already crushed spirit. "You cling to such delusions, even as you dangle here, broken and humiliated."

Vincent forced his head to lift, chains rattling as he weakly met the monstrous gaze. His throat felt raw, his voice barely a whisper. "Who… are you?"

But deep down, he already knew.

The shadow shifted, and within the void of its form, the faint outline of a grin stretched unnaturally wide. "I am the one whose power you dared to steal," the voice rasped, dark and venomous, each word slicing into Vincent like a blade. "The one whose essence you thought you could wield for your petty ambitions."

Vincent's breath hitched, his pulse thundering despite his exhaustion.

"I am Lucifer."

The name alone sent a bolt of ice through his core.

Lucifer's burning gaze narrowed as he loomed impossibly closer, his enormous form consuming the space between them. "You are here," he continued, voice dripping with contempt, "because of your arrogance. Your foolishness. You stole a power beyond your comprehension, believing you could claim dominion over what belongs to me."

The celestial chains tightened again, the divine runes searing into Vincent's flesh as if to brand him with his own failure. He gritted his teeth, but the pain was beyond mortal endurance.

Lucifer's grin did not fade. If anything, it deepened. "But you did one thing that intrigues me," he mused, his voice shifting from scorn to something resembling amusement. "One act that spares you from eternal oblivion."

Vincent's breathing hitched as Lucifer's presence pulsed with raw, unfiltered power.

"You opened a door," Lucifer continued. "Fragile, incomplete… but enough. The border between realms has weakened, and for that, you have earned my interest."

Vincent's dimmed eyes widened slightly. Despite the agony wracking his body, a flicker of something—hope?—began to rise. "Then… What do you want from me?" he croaked.

A deep, rolling laughter echoed through the Hellscape, reverberating across the frozen abyss. It was a sound of amusement, yes—but also of absolute control.

"You will serve me, Vincent."

The words hit like a death sentence.

"Until your soul burns out, you will be my pawn," Lucifer continued, his ember-like eyes burning brighter. "The power you stole was mine. Now your existence belongs to me."

Before Vincent could fully process the weight of those words, the air ignited once more.

The fiery bird descended from above, its massive wings setting the sky ablaze. It let out a piercing screech, its talons gleaming with divine fire as it dove toward him once more.

"You are mine now," Lucifer murmured, his grin stretching impossibly wide.

The flaming talons struck, and Vincent's screams echoed through the desolation—merging with the bird's piercing cry, rattling the very foundations of Hell itself.

Above it all, Lucifer watched, his molten gaze gleaming with satisfaction.

Back on Earth, Chris sat in his father's workshop, surrounded by the quiet hum of dormant machinery. The lab felt both alive and empty at the same time—holographic blueprints flickering on cluttered workbenches, disassembled devices resting in mid-repair, power cores pulsing faintly with energy. Shelves lined with crystalline circuits and precision tools stood untouched, relics of unfinished projects whose purpose only his father would have understood.

Without Giuseppe here, the space felt different. Hollow.

Chris exhaled slowly, his fingers tracing the edge of a half-finished device his father had been working on before everything changed. It was a simple thing—a modified core stabilizer, something Giuseppe had likely planned to integrate into a larger project. But now, it was just another reminder of what had been left behind.

Upstairs, the muffled sound of his mother's voice drifted down. "Chris! Dinner's ready."

He didn't answer.

A few moments passed before the sound of soft footsteps on the stairs reached his ears. Mariah appeared in the doorway, a dish towel still in her hand. She paused when she saw him—shoulders slumped, gaze distant, surrounded by the echoes of his father's brilliance.

Her heart clenched.

She stepped into the room quietly, walking up to him. "Chris," she said gently, placing a hand on his shoulder. He didn't flinch, but she could feel the weight of his grief pressing down on him. "I know how much this hurts."

Mariah pulled up a stool next to him, her voice warm, steady. "You never met your grandfather, but your father always talked about him. He used to say, 'I'm just like him,' and I remember thinking how proud he was of that—how connected they were."

A faint, wistful smile touched her lips. "But when your grandfather passed, something changed in him. He wasn't the same for a long time. Nothing seemed to make him smile, nothing could hold his attention for long."

Chris finally turned to look at her. His eyes searched hers, filled with sorrow, searching for something—comfort, understanding, anything that might ease the ache in his chest.

"You know what changed that?" Mariah asked.

Chris shook his head. "What?"

"It was you," she said softly, her voice breaking just a little. "When you were born, you taught him that love doesn't disappear. It stays. But there's always more love out there, Chris. Love that helps carry the pain. That's what keeps you going.

Grief…" She took a deep breath, her gaze filled with quiet wisdom. "Grief is just love with nowhere to go."

Chris swallowed hard, his throat tight.

Mariah brushed a strand of hair from his face, her touch light, motherly. "Your father loved you more than anything. That love doesn't fade, and neither does ours. Let it carry you." She pressed a kiss to his forehead before rising.

"Whenever you're ready, come upstairs. Dinner's getting cold."

She gave the room one last glance, her expression bittersweet, before she turned and walked back up the stairs.

Chris remained seated, staring at the workbench in front of him. His mother's words lingered, weaving through his thoughts, pressing against the grief that threatened to consume him.

Love doesn't disappear. It remains.

Chris sat there for a long time, the silence of the workshop wrapping around him like a heavy cloak. The faint hum of the machines, the scattered remnants of his father's work—all of it felt frozen in time, waiting for someone to bring it back to life. He wiped his eyes, glancing around once more, trying to absorb every detail. This space had been his father's sanctuary, a place of endless creation and problem-solving. Now, it was all that remained of him.

Taking a deep breath, Chris stood, his gaze catching on something in the corner of the room—a chessboard resting atop a small table, pieces frozen in the middle of a game. Curiosity tugged at him. He stepped closer, eyes scanning the familiar setup.

He sat down slowly, noting the position. White to move.

The last move played had been …Nf6. Chris instinctively

reached for the white queen.

"Let's see where this goes," he murmured.

With practiced calm, he played: **Qd2 h6, Ne6+ Bxe6, dxe6 Rad8, Qe3 Rxe6.**

His eyes narrowed as he followed the strategic thread. Black was strong, but not invincible. Still, something felt… orchestrated.

Red1 Red6, Rxd6 Rxd6, f3 Qd8, fxe4 Nxe4, Bxe4 Re6.

He leaned in, now fully invested. His fingers moved with quiet precision.

Qxc5 Rxe4, Qxb4 Qd4+, Kh2 Qxa1, Qb7+ Kf6, Qxa6+ Re6. He paused for a beat, then continued.

Qc8 Qe5+, Kg1 Qe1+, Kh2 Qe5+, Kg1 Qd4+, Kh2 Qd6+. A frown touched his face. He could sense the end coming.

Kg1 Re1+, Kf2 Qd2+, Kf3 Re3+, Kf4 Re4+, Kg3 Qf4# Checkmate.

The room fell still.

A quiet click echoed beneath the board.

Chris blinked. Slowly, the chessboard shuddered, then lifted slightly at the center. A false bottom unlocked itself, sliding back with a soft hiss to reveal a hidden compartment.

Inside it, gleaming faintly under the ambient light, lay a small silver disk—just like the others.

He exhaled slowly, lifting it out with care.

"Of course," he whispered. "It was never just a game."

Chris's heart pounded as he held it in his palm, staring at it for a long moment before moving to his father's old computer. His fingers trembled slightly as he slid the disk into the drive. The screen flickered to life, and a single file appeared.

He hesitated, his hand hovering over the mouse. Then, swallowing hard, he clicked.

The screen went black for a moment before a video began to play. Giuseppe's face appeared, worn but familiar, his eyes holding that same warm yet weary expression Chris had seen a thousand times before.

"Chris," his father's voice filled the room, steady and familiar. "If you're seeing this, it means things didn't go as I'd hoped." His tone carried an unmistakable sorrow. "I wanted to see this through with you—to fight by your side. But if you're watching this, then you already know the truth."

Chris leaned forward, gripping the edge of the desk, barely breathing as he listened.

"The battle you fought… it wasn't just about Vincent. Or the demons. It's bigger than that. There's something darker stirring beneath it all, something even I didn't fully understand." Giuseppe's gaze was firm but kind. "I don't know how this ends, but I do know this: you are stronger than you realize. Stronger than I ever was."

Chris's throat tightened.

"You will face challenges no one before you has. The world you've shaped, the power you hold—it may reject you at times. You might feel alone, but I need you to remember… you never are."

The screen flickered briefly as Giuseppe seemed to gather his thoughts. When he spoke again, his voice was softer.

"Don't let my absence weigh you down, son. Don't dwell on what we lost. Be grateful for what we had. And no matter how dark it gets, never stop fighting for what's right. There is always a way forward." His expression turned just a little lighter, his lips curving into a knowing smile. "Trust in yourself, Chris. You are the key to this world."

The screen faded to black, leaving Chris staring at his own

reflection in the monitor. The silence that followed was deafening.

For a long moment, he didn't move. Then, slowly, he turned his gaze to the weapons resting against the wall—his father's blade and the Eclipse Blade, side by side.

He stood, stepping forward, his fingers brushing over the hilt of Giuseppe's sword. The metal was cool to the touch, but it felt alive, almost humming with the weight of its past. A thousand memories surged forward—his father's laughter during training, the steady guidance in his words, the way he had always believed in Chris even when Chris had doubted himself.

He closed his eyes, exhaling deeply.

Chris opened his eyes, his grip tightening on the hilt. The weight of loss would always be there, lingering like a shadow, but it no longer suffocated him. Because his father was right— love never truly disappeared. It remained, carried forward in those left behind.

The future was uncertain. The battles were far from over. But for the first time in a long time, Chris felt ready.

A small, resolute smile formed on his lips.

Then, the air shifted.

A stillness settled over the workshop—not the quiet of grief, nor the lingering hum of the dormant machinery, but something deeper. Something vast. The temperature in the room didn't drop, but Chris felt a phantom chill crawl down his spine. The lights overhead flickered once, twice—then steadied.

And then, he heard it.

A voice—soft, knowing, and impossibly distant, yet intimately close. The same voice that had possessed Lilith in the garden. The same voice that had spoken to him in the testing pod. The same voice that had helped him focus his power during his battle with Vincent. The same voice he heard in the meeting with the squad captains.

"I'm Here"

Chris inhaled sharply, his body going rigid. His fingers tightened around the hilt of the blade, his pulse thudding in his ears. He turned, scanning the workshop, his breath shallow. But there was no one. No movement.

Yet the presence remained.

It wasn't an echo of the past. It wasn't his father, or Vincent, or some fractured memory whispering through his mind. This was real. Something—someone—was speaking to him, watching him, guiding him.

A presence older than anything he had faced.

Chris exhaled slowly, his heart steadying as he straightened his posture. The voice hadn't come to threaten him. It had come when he needed it most. When he had doubted himself. When he had stood on the edge of oblivion.

And now, it calls to him.

The weight of the moment settled into him. Whatever was coming next, whatever this voice meant—it wasn't over.

But Chris wasn't afraid.

He was ready.

www.ingramcontent.com/pod-product-compliance
Lightning Source LLC
Chambersburg PA
CBHW060808120726
47909CB00006B/1833